I0748576

THE VAMPIRE LARUS

CLASH OF CLANS

GREGORY MCEWAN

THE VAMPIRE LARUS: CLASH OF CLANS

THE IMMORTAL WAR SAGA
BOOK ONE

ISBN-13: 978-1-0696706-6-3

For Diavin M.

PART ONE

1

LARUS (1793)

I have stalked him for years, studying his every move, watching, waiting. Not just because I desire him, but because I am old—and alone. These nights of stalking will change his life—and end it. His family will never see him again.

Judge me if you must, call me selfish or cruel, but I must possess Larus. Yes, that is his name. I have watched him for so long, and I know that what I will give him is a gift. He is beautiful, this Larus Bleddyn. Strange to think I was once like him—young, naive. Not once has he sensed my presence. But soon, that will change.

I see myself in him, and I must rescue him from his miserable existence. The human embraces the night—he walks in the dark, his ritual. It is autumn. Most of the leaves have fallen from the trees, and with every step he takes, the crackling beneath his boots shatters the silence.

A moonless night swallows us whole. I follow Larus unseen, my thoughts tangled in the past. Would I change any of it? No. Perhaps. It does not matter now.

I do not know why my past haunts me so. Perhaps because my fate was never my own. I was not born free, nor was I a product of love. I believe my father loved my mother, but she despised him. Like her and so many others, I was chattel, nothing more than property to a man I was forced to call Master.

I am Micah.

I spent most of my childhood in the main house—it was all I knew. With its towering stone pillars and pristine white veranda, I once thought myself privileged to live there. But though Massa Duncan had given me life, I never dared to acknowledge the truth of it. Mama warned me never to say his name with mine, though everyone knew. But scared little boys forget. And fear is a poor shield against the whip.

Heaven knows I had the welts to prove it.

By fourteen, I had learned my lesson. I hated the man who owned me, yet I craved his love. How could I love a man who beat me for spilling wine or failing to shine his boots? A man who whipped me simply because he felt like it?

I was just a child when I was taken into the main house. I rarely saw my mother—only brief glances as she passed with the others on their way to the cotton fields. But she always smiled at me. Mama was Estlyn, a beautiful woman with long black plaits cascading over her shoulders. We spoke little—Massa Duncan hated that she loved me and hated him. But even in silence, I knew her love was mine.

One morning, after the carriage took the family to church, I met Mama beneath the Live Oak tree. She must have sensed the pride within me, seen it in my swagger.

"You is just like us." She took my hand, pressing it against hers. We sat together in the shade, her dark eyes watching me, piercing. "There ain't nothin' different 'bout you and me, boy." She looked toward the house. "'Specially in his big ol' blue eyes..."

I was nearly fifteen when Mama spoke those words. The next year, Massa Duncan sold her. I never saw her again.

That was long ago. Now, I have lived to see this world change in ways I never imagined. It is 1793. But I remember the summer of 1644 as if it were yesterday. I was twenty-one when my life ended—and began again. I did not want to die a slave, so I became something else. A creature of the night.

And now, Larus Bleddyn must choose. He does not know what he is, not yet. But he will.

Tonight, I will show him. Tonight, he will understand.
Or he will never wake from my bite.

I AM A VAMPIRE. I LOVE THE NIGHT.

To a mere human, my strength is unmatched. Yet among my kind, I am neither the strongest nor the fastest. But tonight, none of that matters. Tonight, my focus is Larus.

Though nearly a mile away, I see him clearly. I hear each brisk footfall, the urgency of his breath, the unsteady beat of his heart. Ahead, I see his destination upon a hill—the abandoned church. I have watched Larus since childhood and know this place to be his refuge, the only sanctuary where he believes he can find peace.

I watch as he ascends the steep path, and my thoughts drift to the Bleddyns of old—to their rise and their ruin, long before even I was born into this world. But Larus is young, unaware of his lineage or why his family fell from grace.

My kind are swift. By the time he reaches the summit, I am already there, waiting in the darkness.

From one of the four steeples, I gaze upon the lands below. Even now, with its gardens overgrown and wild, this place holds a quiet beauty. Just beyond the rear of the hill, a brook winds through the trees, its waters whispering against the stones. I do not blame the boy for seeking solace here.

The great door groans open, its rusted hinges crying out in protest. Larus steps inside.

I do not move. I simply wait.

2

CREATURE

As he had done countless times before, Larus pushed against the heavy oak door, closing his eyes as the rusty hinges groaned through the empty church. He took a deep breath, smiling as he crossed the narthex and made his way down the nave toward the altar.

As always, he left the door ajar, letting the autumn wind sweep through his sanctuary. No one else came here; this place was his alone.

The old church, perched on the flat crest of the hill, was magnificent despite its decay. Larus paused before the altar—a ritual he had performed each night—and smiled again. Here, he felt at peace. More than that, he felt alive. He tilted his head back, gazing up in awe at the arched vault of stone.

"I'm here again," he murmured, though he was certain he was alone. His breath curled into the cold air before vanishing. He rubbed his hands together for warmth, then, out of habit, bit his lower lip until he tasted blood.

Fear had been his constant companion, woven into the fabric of his life. This place had always been his escape, a refuge from the inescapable truth. But tonight, even here, he could not outrun it. Time was running out.

In less than a fortnight, he would turn twenty—a milestone not to be celebrated, but feared. He was the firstborn of four, yet he would never inherit his family's legacy. His twin sister would live; he would not. His father, a powerful patrician, had tried and failed to sire another son, leaving him only with daughters.

His mother had begged him to have faith, to believe in miracles. But his father was not a man of faith. To him, Larus was a pariah.

While his mother clung to hope, his father demanded acceptance.

Save for the altar, several stone benches along the aisle, and the towering high altar, the ancient church was empty. The sanctuary had stood abandoned for as long as Larus could remember, yet most of the stained-glass windows remained miraculously intact. He knew little of its history, only that it had been part of his family's lands for generations.

Standing at the chancel, he glanced upward at the shadowed galleries before shifting his gaze toward the darkened archways on either side of him. Beyond them, staircases led up to the balconies and steeples.

Had the God his devout mother prayed to still lingered within these walls? The thought unsettled him. It angered him. His mother's voice resounded in his mind, sending his already weakened heart into a frantic flutter. Fear seized him. He pressed a hand to his chest and took deep, steadying breaths.

"Tell me why!" His voice broke as it echoed through the emptiness, a desperate cry swallowed by cold stone. "Why must it be me? Why am I the one who has to die?"

A flutter of wings. The soft coo of doves high in the vault.

Larus stilled, breath shallow, gaze searching the rafters. The birds settled quickly. Then, a voice—deep and smooth—emerged from the silence.

"Death is not the end, Larus Bleddyn."

Larus startled violently, stumbling back from the chancel. His heart pounded against his ribs, and he collapsed to his knees, certain his time had come. A final punishment. A cruel trick of fate.

He tried to speak, but his voice failed him. Terror stole his breath.

"No, Larus Bleddyn," the voice continued, calm and patient. "I am not the devil, nor am I the God your mother serves."

The sound seemed to come from everywhere at once. Larus scrambled backward, eyes darting around the nave, expecting something—someone—to emerge from the shadows.

"I am no spirit," the voice assured. "I will not harm you."

Larus swallowed hard. His voice was hoarse, barely more than a whisper. "Who...what are you?"

A pause. Then:

"I am Micah."

"Micah?"

"It is my name, young one." A soft laugh. "No, boy, I do not mock you."

Larus clenched his fists. "I'm no boy! Show yourself!"

The vault erupted with motion as dozens of doves burst from the rafters, wings slashing through the air as they funnelled through a shattered window. A sudden wind whipped around him, and within a heartbeat, something was upon him.

A strong hand seized his wrist. Then, the ground was gone.

The world blurred. The nave fell away beneath him. Within seconds, he was high above it all, weightless, suspended in the vaulted ceiling. A few lingering doves scattered into the night.

Larus couldn't move. His feet dangled over nothingness. But before him—so close he could see the flicker of candlelight reflected in his eyes—stood a man.

No. Not a man. Something else.

The creature held him effortlessly, his face chiseled, his skin pale brown. His hazel eyes burned with unnatural intensity.

Larus had never seen a negro like this—like a statue, beautiful and deathless. And he moved too fast, too strong. No human could be this way.

With impossible ease, the being leapt through the air, carrying Larus into one of the towers. The wind howled through the steeple as they landed upon solid stone. Larus stumbled, legs shaking beneath him. He looked around frantically, searching for an escape.

A laugh—soft, knowing.

"I was once a man," the creature said, his voice laced with something like amusement. "As much a man as you are now."

Larus staggered back, but the only thing behind him was the precipice—a sheer drop into darkness.

"I would catch you before you hit the rocks below." Micah's expression softened, something ancient and sorrowful settling over his face. "If I wished you harm, I would have done so years ago."

Larus swallowed hard. "What...what are you?" His voice barely carried over the wind.

Micah smiled, slow and deliberate. Then, he bared his teeth.

Sharp. White. Fanged.

"I am a vampire."

Larus shook his head violently. "Fables—"

"Yet here I stand," Micah said simply. He extended a hand. "Take it."

Larus hesitated. Then, cautiously, he reached out—only to recoil the instant their skin met.

"You're ice cold!"

Micah nodded. "I am dead, yet I live."

Larus wiped his palm on his thigh, mind spinning. "This is a dream...a nightmare."

Micah turned to the edge of the steeple, gazing down into the abyss. "My kind have lived among men for ages. Our existence is a secret. It must remain that way." He looked back at Larus sharply, his expression unreadable.

"Which means I am afraid I must kill you."

Larus froze.

Micah smiled—not cruelly, but with something like regret. And yet... there was a strange warmth in that expression, something that unsettled Larus more than the fangs.

Larus exhaled shakily.

"I am already dead."

THE VAMPIRE WAS DRESSED AS A GENTLEMAN. HIS DARK CLOTHING, FINELY tailored, contrasted against the pale glow of his skin. On his right hand, he wore a gold ring, its band embossed with an intricate family crest—a symbol of power and heritage that had endured through the centuries, marking him as one of the ancient bloodlines.

Larus stood in silence, unable to tear his gaze from Micah. The vampire was tall, lean, and looked no older than twenty-five. His skin gleamed against the night, yet he was a negro. How could a negro be a gentleman?

"It is our strength and long life that define my kind, not the colour of our skin," Micah said smoothly, as if plucking the question straight from Larus's mind. He lifted his hands, turning them in the moonlight, as though seeing them anew. "Over the ages, we grow stronger. Power, knowledge, the essence of what we are—it is all carried in the blood."

A cool wind swept across the steeple. Larus inhaled deeply, savouring the crisp air. He had always loved the way the wind moved through the church on the hill. Below, Bleddyn Manor lay quiet, its candlelit windows glowing like distant stars. His family slept peacefully, unaware of the thing that stood beside him.

Without looking at Micah, Larus stepped to the edge of the tower and peered down at the rocky ridge below.

"What do you want from me?"

"It is your desire that interests me, Larus Bleddyn."

A cold touch brushed the back of his neck. Larus stiffened. Micah was beside him now, closer than before.

"Your visits with the learned doctors and skilled apothecaries have been fruitless, have they not?"

Larus turned sharply. "How do you know that?"

He studied the vampire's profile—high cheekbones, a strong jaw, full lips. Even in the darkness, his features were striking. Larus's pulse quickened. He stepped away.

Micah smiled. "I offer you immortality."

Larus let out a sharp, breathless laugh. The very idea repulsed him—yet there was something enticing about it. He could not speak. Could not think. His mind reeled, suddenly flooded with thoughts of a future beyond his twenty-second birthday.

He had always known his fate. The family affliction took them all before thirty. A failing heart, an inevitable end. He had lived in fear of dying mid-meal, mid-walk, mid-sleep. And now this creature—this vampire—offered him an escape.

Micah's voice cut through his thoughts.

"Our laws are absolute. In a coven—"

"A coven?"

Micah's smile deepened. "Yes. A family of vampires is called a coven." He steepled his fingers before his chest. "It is forbidden to enter one's home without invitation, so we are here." He gestured to the open night around them. "If you choose to become my child, it shall be my duty to teach you how to survive. How to remain unseen."

His hazel eyes glowed faintly in the dark. "The night shall be yours, but you will never walk beneath the sun again."

Larus swallowed. "And my family?"

"No, Larus. You will never see them again."

Micah turned, gazing into the distance. "You may do as I have done. Watch them from afar. But you may not like what you see." His voice lowered. "It is a terrible thing to watch those you love wither and die while you linger on."

Larus hesitated. "Long life? You look no older than I am."

For the first time since their meeting, he smiled—a strange, fleeting thing. The absurdity of the situation weighed upon him, yet he found himself speaking as though it were real.

"My grandfather told stories of vampires when I was young," Larus said. "But I doubt he believed them."

Micah's expression darkened. "Creature." The word came like an accusation. "I do not like that word." His eyes flickered shut, and his lips parted, as if tasting something bitter. "The destroyers of my kind call us creatures..."

Larus opened his mouth to apologize, but Micah cut him off.

"Apology accepted."

The sky above them had begun to shift. The deep black of night was softening, taking on the first hints of dawn.

Larus exhaled. "There is so much I need to know."

"You have but one decision to make." Micah stroked his goatee, his tone measured. "You must choose. Remain as you are and perish... or accept my offer and have a chance to live."

"A chance?"

"Yes, Larus. We may be immortal, but we can die."

Larus hesitated. "How old are you?"

Micah's smile was almost wistful. "I was made a vampire at twenty-one. My life was in the hands of others until then." He lifted his chin slightly. "I am 165 years old."

Larus inhaled sharply. "Unbelievable."

"I am young," Micah admitted. "Had I remained as I was, I would have been long dead."

He turned away, leaning against the stone wall, his voice quieter now. "My maker was eight hundred years old when he was... destroyed."

Larus hesitated. "How did—"

"We must not speak of him."

Micah turned abruptly. Larus recoiled, startled. A dark, thick fluid streamed from the corners of the vampire's eyes—tears, but not human tears. Blood.

Micah did not wipe them away. He only lifted his gaze eastward. "Daylight will soon be upon us. I must leave you."

Larus barely had time to react before Micah seized him again, and the world blurred.

Within a breath, Larus stood alone in the church once more. The silence was suffocating.

Then, the vampire's voice echoed through the empty sanctuary.

"I shall give you time to decide, Larus Bleddyn. Choose wisely. For your family's sake, say nothing of my existence."

And then—nothing.

Micah was gone.

Larus stood frozen, listening to the silence, to the whisper of the wind through the broken windows.

The choice was his.

But was it ever truly a choice at all?

3

RIGHTFUL HEIR

Larus was still in shock and struggling to decide what to do. He was afraid to think, for he had no clue if the vampire was close and reading his thoughts. As he walked homeward along the dirt road, bordered by leafless oaks, the wind bit sharply at his skin. It was nearly the end of September, and the chilly breeze carried with it the promise of a harsh winter. He had lingered in the church after the vampire left, still in disbelief. But he had seen the creature, looked into Micah's eyes, and touched his cold hand. What was there not to believe?

Looking toward the east, Larus saw the first signs of dawn and suddenly realized he had been out all night. He breathed a sigh of relief, recalling what Micah had said. Vampires did not like the sun. He walked on, the rooftops of his family's estate finally coming into view above the trees. Micah had left him to decide, but the vampire had not mentioned when he would return.

As he arrived home, Larus quietly slipped through the main gate, opting for the back door to avoid passing his father's study. He could smell the aroma of bread baking, the familiar scent of Tilley's cooking filling the air as he neared the kitchen. Larus stuck his head through the door and smiled, seeing the older woman, her greying hair neatly pinned in a bun as she busied herself. He found it remarkable that after all these years,

Tilley's life seemed to revolve solely around preparing meals for his family. She was like family to him, and Larus loved her dearly.

"Psst!"

"Young master, that's no way for a gentleman to address a lady!" Her voice was light, full of mirth, as she turned, dusting her hands with flour. She smiled at him, then whispered, "Master Bleddyn is angry—he's been wondering where you've been all night."

"Oh, Tilley, I just went for a walk," Larus said with a shrug.

"Well, your father thinks you've been out with a young lady," she teased, wagging a finger at him. "Now, Larus, you know the last thing your father needs is a blemish on his good name."

Larus winced inwardly, thinking the only blemish to his father's good name was his existence, but he leaned in and gently kissed Tilley's cheek. "Come on, Tilley, you're the only lady in my life," he joked.

The older woman fluttered her eyelashes and grinned. "Well, it's a good thing you're not going for any young ladies at the moment. Not with your birthday coming up."

Tilley's eyes turned sad, her brow furrowing. She turned away for a moment, lifting the hem of her apron to dab at her eyes. "Oh, my dear boy..." She paused, then, with a quiver in her voice, embraced him. "You're a good lad...a good, good lad."

"It's alright, Tilley..." Larus murmured, his voice soft. He hated seeing her upset.

After a long moment, Tilley dried her eyes and glanced toward the door. "Your father's in his study. He wasn't expecting you to come in through the back. And your sister—she told him you were out. That dreadful girl."

Larus's lips curled into a smile, but it was bittersweet. "Don't worry, Tilley. I can handle Max." He wiped the last of the tear from her cheek with his thumb.

Tilley winced. "I can't abide that dreadful name."

Larus chuckled. "You've known her long enough to know how much she hates it." He sighed. "Max is my twin, and she's a handful, but you know I love her."

Tilley's eyes widened. "She wishes she had been born a boy."

Larus nodded. He knew it was true. Max was beautiful, but she had no desire to be married off to some gentleman. Their father indulged her, letting her do as she pleased. "I doubt I'll be around in five years," Larus said softly, glancing at the door. "Besides, Father has already groomed Max to manage his affairs."

Tilley shook her head, her face full of concern. "This isn't right, Larus. You're a man grown now. You should have married."

Larus smiled sadly. "Father's ashamed of me. He's afraid his grandchildren will inherit my affliction—this heart condition, this curse. It's why he's already arranging marriages for my sisters." He paused, his thoughts turning to the future. "Isabelle and Catherine, they'll live on long after me. But Max..." He sighed again. "She'll probably never marry."

Tilley sighed deeply. "It isn't fair, Larus. Max is always in your father's ear, telling him what to do. No parent should pick favourites."

Larus smiled gently, but there was no joy in it. "Father loves us all, Tilley, in his own way." His voice faltered, and he doubted the sincerity of his own words.

"Maxine is his favourite," Tilley insisted, her voice laced with concern.

Larus chuckled again. "You know how she hates you calling her that."

"It's her Christian name." Tilley's voice softened as she returned to her work, kneading dough with a quiet, rhythmic motion. She looked up at Larus, her green eyes kind. "Best you go up to your room and get some rest. At least sleep before the sun rises."

Larus smiled at her, pecking her cheek once more. Grabbing a freshly baked roll from the tray, he dashed for the stairs.

WITH THE WARM, SAVOURY LOAF BETWEEN HIS TEETH, LARUS QUICKLY stripped naked, leaving his clothes scattered carelessly on the floor. He climbed into bed and bit into the small loaf of bread, chewing eagerly. He was famished. The crackling sound of the fire across the room caught his attention, its flames still dancing. Someone had kept the fire burning through the night.

The door to the anteroom creaked open, and Max entered. She wore a velvet housecoat, one more suited for a gentleman than a lady. Unlike Isabelle and Catherine, Max had always scorned the expectation that women should dress in silks and laces to please men. The irony, however, was that of his three sisters, Max was by far the most beautiful.

"Finally decided to come home, have you?" Max said, taking a seat in the chair at the end of his bed. "Father's furious, you know?"

"And how did he know I was gone, hmm?" Larus winked, though the tension in his voice betrayed his jest.

"The last thing Father wants is for you to be found dead out in the woods," Max replied, her voice almost flat. She was nearly as tall as Larus, and this physical presence made her an intimidating figure for any man hoping to court her.

Larus scowled, feeling the familiar rage stirring. "So, he accepts that my heart will fail within the next year or two... but can't accept that being sick is not a curse." His anger bubbled over, a deep frustration with his father that had been building for years. "I must die at home, quietly buried in the family crypt, and no one will know I'm gone." With a sharp motion, Larus tossed the remaining piece of the loaf into the fire. "Tell me, Max, am I even worthy of being buried with our ancestors? Or will Father throw me into some nameless grave in the woods?"

Max shifted in her seat, her expression softening slightly. "You must understand him, Larus," she said, her voice quieter now, but firm. Like their father, she crossed her legs and gripped the padded arms of the chair. "You know how difficult it has been for him."

"I'm the one dying, Max."

There was a long silence before Max turned away from him, her gaze fixed on the fire. Finally, she spoke. "Father and I have decided... I'm to be married the day before our birthday."

Larus sat up, startled. "Married? To whom?"

"The son of Percival Hearne," she replied, her voice lacking any real emotion.

Larus blinked in surprise, his mind racing. "It's a good match," he said, though the words felt hollow. Bartholomew Hearne was handsome, wealthy, and well-regarded—far more than any of the other suitors Max had entertained. Still, there was something missing in her eyes that made him wonder why she had agreed to this union.

"You're truly Father's daughter, made from the same stock." Larus couldn't help but grin, though there was little humour in it. "Max, you should have been born a boy."

Max sat in silence, her gaze locked on the flames.

"Will you be moving to the Hearne estate?" Larus asked, his curiosity piqued despite the growing bitterness in his chest.

Max whipped her head toward him, her eyes suddenly blazing with fury. "Never! The Hearnes are fools; Bartholomew is a fool. I chose him for his money."

Larus nodded. "Father's idea, I see."

"Don't be silly," Max shot back, her voice still sharp. "I chose to have the wedding the day before our birthday because you never celebrate it." She glared at him, a look of resentment in her eyes. "Besides, all our lives, I've been deprived of a happy birthday. All because we shared our mother's womb at the same time." Her words were cold, without remorse, and Larus could feel the sting of them settle deep in his chest.

Max rose abruptly from the chair and walked toward the door. "Get some sleep," she called over her shoulder. "Father wants the entire family to have lunch with him today."

Larus's heart felt heavy once more, a burden he had carried for as long as he could remember. In that moment, he realized that Tilley, more than anyone else in the household, had always offered him the possibility of happiness. All his life, he had lived with the expectation of death looming over him, with a father who could barely look him in the eye, a mother who saw herself as a failure for not producing more sons, and three sisters who seemed to live in entirely different worlds.

Larus slid beneath the covers and let the warmth of the fire seep into his bones. Thoughts of Micah, the vampire, crept into his mind. For the first time since meeting him, Larus wondered what it would be like to live a thousand lives. The idea of immortality, of escaping the confines of his fragile existence, was strangely alluring. He closed his eyes, and as sleep took him, the burning desire for something more than this life—a life so full of suffocating expectations—washed over him like a wave.

FAMILY LUNCHES WERE A RARITY IN THE BLEDDYN HOUSEHOLD, AND LARUS descended the stairs with a sense of reluctance. Max had already informed him of her impending wedding, making him wonder what business their father needed to discuss. Pausing outside the dining hall door, he took a deep breath. He had dressed in a manner that satisfied his father's expectations. A long, hot bath had been necessary—one he felt he desperately needed after the unsettling encounter with the vampire. Micah still lingered in his mind.

As he entered the dining hall, Larus felt a wave of embarrassment. He was the last to arrive, and the servants stood on either side of the grand oak table, waiting to serve the aromatic lunch that filled the air. Taking a seat next to Max, who sat at their father's right, Larus glanced across the table at his younger sisters. They offered him only brief nods and faint smiles, their eyes clouded with unease under their father's scrutiny. Tardiness had always been one of the many things he loathed. Larus knew the rules well—no one could speak until the head of the family initiated the conversation.

His father's gaze shifted from his gold pocket watch to Larus, and a slow, calculated rise of his right brow told Larus that his punctuality, or lack thereof, had not gone unnoticed.

At the far end of the table, opposite their father, sat Larus's mother. At fifty, she still carried an air of grace, her grey eyes pleading silently for peace, though they were often clouded with sorrow when the father and son argued.

Breaking the silence, his father cleared his throat, a prelude to one of his usual, one-sided discussions. "I trust you got enough rest after your long night's work." The attempt at sarcasm fell flat, but the stern expression remained. "I hear you were out until dawn."

Larus shot a glance at Max, who met his gaze with a bold, unwavering stare.

"Father, I do nothing but walk on our lands. I don't see how that's a problem."

"It's the defiance I abhor!"

"I go out to clear my head... all things considered." His words hung heavy in the air, and he felt his pulse quicken as the familiar rage started to rise. He could no longer ignore the truth that gnawed at him, no longer pretend to be content in this suffocating life. "Could you sleep well, knowing your days are numbered?" Larus turned his gaze across the table. "Could any of you?"

His mother's eyes welled with tears. "Larus, please!"

"I can't live like this, Mother! I refuse to pretend anymore." His heart thudded violently, and his breath came in shallow bursts. The physicians had warned him countless times about the danger of anger—his condition could deteriorate with just a single burst of emotion.

Ignoring the distress in his voice, his father slammed a fist onto the table, the sound sharp and final. "I've made arrangements. You will spend several months at a medical facility. You'll leave at the end of October, before the harsh winter sets in."

Larus could only laugh, bitter and hollow. "You're sending me away?"

"My decision is final!"

"I won't go!" Larus realized, only then, that he had risen from his chair. His gaze locked with his father's, unwavering. There was nothing more to say. He turned on his heel and walked toward the door.

"You dare walk away from me, boy?"

Larus kept walking. Not even the desperate plea from his mother could make him look back. As he left the dining hall, he slammed the door shut behind him, the sound echoing through the house like a final declaration of defiance.

It had taken nearly an hour for Larus to calm his racing heart and unsettled mind. Seated at his desk in the anteroom to his bedchamber, he cupped his aching head in his hands. His hair was disheveled, his coat discarded on the floor, and his eyes were red from the strain of his emotions. In all his life, he had never dared to stand up to his father's authority, and he knew there would be consequences for this rebellion.

Looking out the window, Larus noticed the sun had receded behind thick clouds, and the gloom outside mirrored the weight of his own thoughts. His mind wandered to the loneliness of the old church, a sanctuary he longed for, and he walked to the window, where he could just see the steeples above the treetops. Although they appeared close, Larus knew the reality—it would take over an hour to reach the church. His thoughts shifted to Micah, the vampire, whose presence had become as inseparable from the church as the church itself. Even though the thought of the creature had once terrified him, Larus now found some strange comfort in it. The vampire, in a way, had become a strange pillar of hope, as much as the church had once been.

Lost in his thoughts of Micah and the unsettling offer he had made, Larus didn't notice the approach of his sister. He gasped, startled, as a hand touched his arm. "Isabelle!"

His youngest sister wasn't alone. Tilley stood a few steps behind, holding a tray. "I didn't hear you come in," Larus murmured, trying to shake off his lingering thoughts.

"You poor boy," Tilley clucked, shaking her head in disapproval. "You must be famished. Now eat." She set the tray down before him with a gentle smile.

"I'm sorry I didn't speak up for you, big brother." Isabelle's voice was quiet, her eyes clouded with concern. "But I fear Father will marry me off to some old fat tyrant." She grasped his hand, squeezing it tightly. "You mustn't try Father's temper, Larus... he's vexed... terribly vexed."

Larus smiled, though it was tinged with bitterness. "And when is our father ever happy?" He kissed Isabelle's forehead, the warmth of her touch offering a small comfort amidst the storm in his chest.

As Tilley lifted the lid from the tray, Larus began to eat. The old woman watched him with an almost maternal pride, content to see him enjoy the meal.

"Your father gave strict orders to bring no food to you," Tilley said, her voice laced with defiance. "But I would not have it. Told him it was inhumane." She cast a glance at Isabelle. "Right, child?"

Isabelle nodded with a smile, though it was brief. "You know Tilley is the only person Father ever allows to have the last word." She paced the room restlessly. "Well, she takes her liberties when she can."

Tilley's gaze flickered toward the door, then back to Isabelle. Her voice softened. "Little one..." She placed a gentle hand on Isabelle's arm, then turned back to Larus. "You'd best tell him now."

Larus frowned, sensing something was wrong. "Tell me what?" He looked at Isabelle, noticing the tear stains on her cheeks, the way her eyes were clouded with distress.

"Father mustn't know I've told you, Larus." Isabelle's voice broke as she rushed toward him and threw herself against his chest. Her sobs were muffled in his coat, and Larus held her tightly, trying to calm her.

Tilley could barely get the words out. "Well, my boy..." Her voice trembled with sorrow. "Isabelle found a letter. You see..." She wiped her eyes, then continued, "Your father has made arrangements with the doctor he's sending you to—"

"He's already decided to donate your body for research," Isabelle finished, her voice thick with sadness. "That's why he's sending you away, Larus."

The revelation hit him like a cold wave. Larus stared at Isabelle, speechless, his hands trembling as he held her at arm's length. The truth was clear, and in that moment, Larus knew what he had to do.

4

ORIGINS

It was the night before his sister's wedding. Larus had kept to himself ever since learning of his father's plans, avoiding the head of their house at all costs. He had not seen or spoken to his father since the day he stormed out of the dining hall. Isabelle and Tilley remained unchanged, but his mother, Catherine, and Max kept their distance, as though walking on eggshells around him. Larus dared not mention what Isabelle and Tilley had confided in him, and as far as he was concerned, there was no reason to confront his father—nothing could change what had already been decided.

Larus had no intention of attending his sister's wedding. He was determined not to. The entire manor was alive with preparations. Servants were everywhere, making the estate beautiful for the celebration. Tilley bustled about, managing cooks and maids for the wedding feast, while visitors moved in a flurry of excitement. But Larus remained holed up in his rooms, only venturing to the kitchen for food. On occasion, Tilley would send up a tray of his favourite meals, but he had little appetite for them. The nights had grown colder, and Larus dressed warmly, though his physical discomfort was nothing compared to the restlessness that plagued his thoughts.

Each night since his encounter with Micah, he had visited the church, but the vampire had not returned. Larus worried that something had happened to him, that Micah had met some cruel fate. This fear kept him awake at night. For the first time in his life, he didn't want to die—not when there was still so much left unanswered, not when his father had so callously planned to turn his body over to science. The thought of his father, who had never shown an ounce of concern for his condition, now eagerly surrendering his son's body for dissection and research was a bitter pill to swallow.

Larus had spoken with Isabelle in detail about the letter she had found, and she explained that their father believed it would benefit modern medicine to understand the ailment that had plagued Larus's heart. But to Larus, it felt like nothing more than a final betrayal.

He had packed a small bag with supplies—food, a few other essentials—everything he thought he would need for his journey to the church. Earlier that evening, Larus had instructed the stableman to ready his horse for a night ride. The long walk to the church became unbearable at times, and he needed to reach it as quickly as possible. Larus couldn't quite explain it, but there was a growing urgency inside him, a longing to see the vampire again. The fear he had once felt upon meeting Micah had transformed into something else—something darker, yet strangely comforting. He had to know what Micah wanted, and why he had come into Larus's life when he did.

THE STALLION GALLOPED HARD TOWARD THE CHURCH, AND DESPITE THE biting cold, Larus relished the swift ride. He hoped he would see Micah again, for it had been two weeks since their first encounter. He had pushed Raven, his black stallion, hard, and now he felt a pang of guilt for overworking the beast. Larus tugged at the reins, slowing the horse to a steady trot, and reached down to gently pat Raven's thick neck. The stallion was a powerful creature, as beautiful as he was strong, and Larus loved him deeply. He had named Raven the day the horse was born, watching from a distance as the foal took its first breath. Larus had begged his father to let him keep the thoroughbred, a plea that was granted only when his mother intervened. It was the one time Larus could recall his mother speaking up on his behalf, convincing his father to allow him the gift. It was the only act of kindness he had ever received from the man.

He led Raven to a nearby brook, watching as the horse drank from the clear water. The black coat shone under the moonlight, and Larus remembered why he had named the stallion Raven—its coat was as dark as the bird's wings.

After untethering his sack of supplies, Larus left Raven at the bottom of the hill and began the climb to the church. As he walked up the steep road, his heart raced in anticipation, the hope that Micah would be there pushing him forward. The church loomed ahead, cold and silent, just as it had been when Larus left the night before. Despite its grandeur, the church felt lonely, and Larus couldn't shake the chill that crept into his bones.

He removed candles from the sack and placed them on the floor beneath the altar, lighting them one by one. The soft glow of the flames warmed the air and brought some comfort, and Larus sat down before the flickering light, preparing to warm his hands. But just as he settled into the quiet, a voice echoed through the vast sanctuary.

"Am I to be flattered, Larus?" Micah's voice seemed to come from every corner of the room, sending a thrill through Larus's chest. "Must we dine together this night?"

Larus turned, startled, his eyes darting around the church. His excitement bloomed into a frantic rush as he searched for Micah's presence. Then, as if appearing from thin air, the vampire stood only inches from him, so close that Larus could see the flawless skin of his face, his features almost otherworldly. The scent of the vampire filled the air, a mix of something sweet and unfamiliar.

The sight of Micah sent a strange feeling through Larus—something not quite fear, but a deep yearning. The vampire grinned, his fangs glinting in the candlelight. "Ah, you have decided."

Larus stumbled back, momentarily losing his balance and nearly stepping into the flames. "How is it you can do this?" He blurted, a mix of awe and confusion in his voice. "How do you... appear like that?"

"It is a common gift among my kind," Micah replied, his voice low and smooth. He wore a black silken shirt beneath a coat made of the finest wool, and Larus, for the first time, wondered where the vampire called home. What kind of life did Micah lead?

"There are so many things I would like to know," Larus said, his voice quieter now, filled with curiosity. "Where do vampires live?"

Micah's lips curved into a smile, though there was a coldness in his eyes. "We rule the night and need the days to rest... we hide." His gaze remained locked on Larus's. "My dwelling is secret and must remain so, even to you... until you become my child."

Larus's heart sank. Disappointment flickered through him, and he turned away. Micah's secrecy frustrated him; he longed for answers, yet the vampire remained enigmatic.

"Secrets are the cornerstone of our survival," Micah continued, his voice softening slightly. "Many of my kind have died because of betrayal. As powerful as we are, we are vulnerable during the day, in our weakened state. Exposure to the sun is fatal to us." Micah sighed, as though remembering some painful memory. "I have lived through it, Larus. I have seen my brethren destroyed by those who hunt us."

Larus frowned, shaking his head. "But how do I know your kind exists? I have never seen proof."

"The hunters, like us, have been around for ages," Micah answered, his voice darkening. "Few of their kind are immortal, but they do not fear us. Like ours, the hunter society is also secret."

Larus thought for a moment, trying to process the information. "So, I could die at the hands of a vampire hunter?"

"Not if you know how to survive, young one," Micah said with a sly smile.

Larus nodded, taking in the vampire's words. The conversation shifted then, and Larus spent nearly an hour explaining the events at home over the last fortnight. Micah listened intently, occasionally offering a smile or a quiet nod of approval. When Larus finished, he knew what he needed to ask. The one question that had been consuming him for days. "How is it done? How do I become a vampire?"

Micah's piercing gaze locked onto Larus's. His expression became serious, and for the first time, Larus saw a flicker of something ancient in his eyes. "You must die."

Larus stood motionless, stunned into silence. The candle flames flickered in Micah's dark eyes, and Larus struggled to push aside the thought of his own demise. Yet no matter how he tried, the idea clung to him like a shadow. He swallowed hard, his voice barely above a whisper.

"How?"

"There is only one way." Micah's voice was calm, unwavering. "My legacy, my power—it is in my blood."

Larus felt his stomach tighten. He had lived with the fear of dying for as long as he could remember, had spent years preparing himself for the inevitable. But the thought of dying so that he might live forever left him numb.

"How can this be right?" he asked, more to himself than to Micah.

Micah tilted his head slightly. "How can it be wrong? There is no right or wrong, Larus. What matters is that the choice exists."

Larus's gaze drifted around the church, his mother's voice echoing in his mind. God is always watching.

Micah smiled faintly. "Yes, this place is consecrated ground... yet here we stand." There was something like frustration in his expression, but it was fleeting.

Larus hesitated before speaking again. "How did you become a vampire?"

Micah's smile returned, though this one was softer, edged with something that might have been nostalgia. "That, young one, is a long tale." He turned and walked toward the massive church doors. "Walk with me."

Larus followed him out into the night. They made their way down the hill, the air crisp and sharp in Larus's lungs. As they passed Raven, Micah placed an arm around his shoulder, a casual yet possessive gesture.

"My maker was Emilio," the vampire said.

Ahead of them, the cemetery loomed, enclosed by a high iron fence. The rusty hinges of the black gate groaned as it swung open beneath Micah's touch.

Larus frowned slightly. "Eight hundred years... how can anyone live so long?"

Micah stepped forward into the graveyard, his voice carrying over the cold air. "Emilio knew how to survive. He taught me everything I know." He glanced back and beckoned Larus forward. "Come."

Larus hesitated. He had never ventured into the cemetery, despite all the years he had come to the church. It was abandoned, long forgotten, and now, as he stepped past the gate, he felt the weight of silence pressing down on him. He fell behind as he paused to glance at the tombstones—so many graves, more than he had ever seen in one place.

Micah continued speaking, his voice steady. "Emilio saved me when I would have died. He could have drained me dry, left me to rot in the earth... but he didn't."

Larus quickened his steps, catching up.

"My father owned many slaves," Micah said, his voice even, though there was an undercurrent of something darker beneath it. "Though I was of his blood, it made no difference. My people were his property. Their lives belonged to him. My life belonged to him."

They were nearing a mausoleum at the centre of the cemetery.

"Mama hated him," Micah continued. "Despised what he was... but she did not have the heart to hate the seed he planted within her, though the times he took her were never by her will. But she was his chattel."

The words hung in the air between them as they reached the mausoleum. Without effort, Micah pressed his hand against the heavy stone slab and slid it aside as though it were no heavier than parchment.

Larus stared. "What is this place?"

Micah turned back to him, smiling. "You shall see."

He stepped inside, and Larus hesitated only a moment before following. The space was larger than he expected, the air thick with the scent of age and dust. The only object within the octagonal chamber was a massive stone sarcophagus, its presence commanding and heavy.

Micah lit a torch, its flickering light casting long shadows against the walls. Then, with ease, he pressed his hands against the sarcophagus and pushed.

Larus watched, breath caught in his throat, as the stone slid aside, revealing an opening in the ground—stone steps vanishing into darkness.

LARUS STOOD AT THE FOOT OF THE STONE STEPS, ASTONISHED. "A catacomb!"

Micah smiled, nodding in confirmation.

The underground crypt was not what Larus expected. There were no bodies, no skeletal remains, for the recesses lay empty. Yet the space was far from barren. Exquisite furnishings adorned the chambers, thick tapestries hung from the walls, and the painted ceilings rivalled those of any patrician home. It was eerie yet beautiful.

"Is this your home?" Larus asked, his voice hushed.

"One of them," Micah replied. "A place of refuge. I have many." He gestured toward the arched doorways ahead. "But this place is unique—a real treasure. Emilio brought me here long ago."

"Who could have built something like this?"

Micah glanced toward a black velvet couch and ran a hand over its surface. "The builders are long dead."

Larus hesitated before sitting beside him, realizing with some surprise that he no longer felt fear.

After a pause, he asked, "Who was he? The vampire who... made Emilio?"

Micah's sharp nails trailed lightly over the velvet. "Makers are secretive," he murmured. Then, meeting Larus's gaze, he said, "Guard your secrets well, and you guard your life."

Micah leaned back, settling into the couch. "Emilio rarely spoke of his maker, but he is one of the oldest and most powerful of our kind." His tone became measured, almost formal. "As for you, it will be my responsibility to protect you, for you will be my child—my pupil. No one must know what you are. A vampire must never take his own life, nor should he kill his own kind." He paused, letting the words sink in. "That does not mean it has never happened."

Larus swallowed hard.

"There is one thing you must know," Micah continued. "The elders—ancient and powerful vampires—rule our secret world. They alone hold dominion over us. If you are ever summoned before them, it will be for one of two reasons: they admire you... or they mean to destroy you."

Larus exhaled slowly. "Did Emilio do something wrong?"

Micah's grin returned, sharp as a blade. "This night is about you, dear one." He leaned forward, resting an elbow on his knee. "You have accepted my offer, but first, I must tell you how I was made. Like you, I was at the mercy of my maker. Emilio turned me because he wished to save my life. When he found me, I was near death."

Larus listened, enraptured. He sank deeper into the couch, watching the way Micah's lips moved as he spoke, amazed that this tale was nearly two centuries old.

"I have told you before," Micah went on. "I was born a slave. My mother's master—my father—owned me as he did her. Massa Duncan, they called him." A wry smile flickered across his face. "He had a daughter—his white daughter—who was my sister. But I was never his family, never his child.

"Mama used to say I had his eyes, though his were blue as a clear summer sky. But resemblance meant nothing." Micah's voice took on a distant quality. "She lived in the slave quarters. I lived in his house. As I grew older, Mama and I found stolen moments together, but when Massa Duncan learned of this, he sold her."

The sadness in Micah's hazel eyes was unmistakable.

"I never saw her again." He exhaled, running a hand over his bald head. "Emilio once taught me that memories—human and vampire alike—are preserved not only in the mind but in the blood. And yet, when I was made, when I searched... she was gone. I could find no trace of her."

He shook his head. "But no. First, I must tell you about Emilio. I must tell you how I became what I am."

Larus remained silent, his attention rapt.

"After Mama was sold, I was alone, Larus. And I hate loneliness. Most vampires do." Micah sighed, his posture shifting as he relaxed his hands in his lap. "For five years, I lived in that house, wondering where she was. And then, three slaves approached me with a plan to escape. I trusted them because one of them was Mama's friend.

"Runaway slaves would rather die than be recaptured. And for me, Massa Duncan's bastard son, punishment would have been worse than death." Micah smiled faintly. "So we planned. We waited. And then, one night, we ran."

Larus leaned in slightly, engrossed.

"There were four of us. Three strong men... and one even stronger woman. Her name was Beauty."

Larus raised an eyebrow. "Beauty?"

Micah chuckled. "Not for her looks. She could break a man in half. The others used to say the only way to prove she was a woman was to lift her skirt and check."

Larus laughed, covering his mouth.

Micah grinned. "She took more lashes than any of us, yet never made a sound. That day, she defied Massa Duncan. When he raised his whip, she just stood there and smiled. I was young, but I'll never forget that moment."

His expression darkened slightly. "She was the only one who protested when they took Mama away. And when she came to me with plans to run, I didn't hesitate."

Micah's voice grew quieter. "For a time, it seemed we had made it. We crossed the swamp, made it deep into the woods. But then, at sunrise... we heard the hounds."

Larus stiffened.

"We ran. But the dogs were faster." Micah's eyes seemed to darken with memory. "Beauty and I were ahead. The others... they didn't make it. I turned back and saw them dragged into the grass."

Larus swallowed, his chest tightening.

"When I couldn't run anymore, I fell. The slavers caught us. The last thing I saw before I hit the ground was Beauty, still fighting, bloodied and weary... but standing."

Micah exhaled slowly. "Massa Duncan gave strict orders—his men were to bring me back alive. That was both a blessing... and a curse."

Larus shifted forward. "And then?"

"They circled me. Six of them. I realized then that my father's orders didn't include bringing me back unharmed." Micah's voice turned distant. "The first lash knocked me to my knees. The whips tore into me, over and over, until I blacked out."

When he continued, his voice was colder.

"When I woke, my hands were bound. I was chained to a willow tree. My body was broken, bloodied. The sun had set. And the men... were still there."

Larus tensed.

"One of them approached," Micah said. His lip curled slightly. "There was a look in his eyes I didn't understand. Not at first."

Larus felt a prickle of dread.

"Then I saw him untie his pants."

The room felt smaller, heavier.

"The others laughed." Micah's voice was barely above a whisper. "I forgot my pain. I only saw him. I only saw what he meant to do.

"I tried to fight, but I was weak. He forced my face into the dirt."

Larus's breath caught in his throat.

Micah's hazel eyes glowed faintly in the dim light.

"But then, everything changed."

LARUS HAD LOST ALL TRACK OF TIME BENEATH THE CEMETERY. HE SAT transfixed on the couch, his mouth slightly ajar. The sting of Micah's wounds, the terror of being shackled to a tree, the horror of what nearly happened—it all played vividly in his mind. The thought of such a violation sent a shiver through him. He wanted to speak, to say something, but fear of interrupting kept him silent.

Micah pressed his lips together, his eyes briefly closing as if reliving the moment. "When I thought all hope was gone, when I believed I was doomed to spend my days beneath my father's boot, my salvation came."

Larus watched him intently.

"I could feel the brute's weight pressing against my back," Micah continued, his voice quieter now, almost distant. "I knew what was about to happen. I would experience what my mother must have felt when she bore me. The dogs were still barking when everything changed. Before the act could even begin, the man was ripped away, his throat torn open before he hit the ground." Micah exhaled sharply. "The wound was terrible. Swollen as my eyes were, I forced myself to look. I saw nothing—no one. The others didn't either. Then, one by one, they died."

Larus leaned in.

"I still remember how it felt—watching my tormentors fall like wheat to a scythe. The last two were left alive, trembling in disbelief." Micah's hazel eyes flickered in the torchlight. "And then I saw him."

Larus held his breath.

"He was tall, taller than any man I'd ever seen. I thought, for a moment, that God himself had come down to rescue me. But no—he was no saviour. He was a vampire." Micah paused, a shadow of a smile touching his lips. "He was Emilio."

The name hung between them.

"That night, beneath the weeping willow, Emilio piled the bodies by the river and turned to me. My flesh was torn, my body weak, but he saw something in me. He gave me a choice." Micah's gaze locked onto Larus. "The two men left alive watched in terror as Emilio, clad in black, moved like a phantom. With one hand, he lifted one of them off the ground. I saw the fangs before I understood. He drained the man's life away in mere moments."

Larus swallowed.

"I was just a boy—a slave with my master's blood in my veins. And yet, in that moment, I saw only one future. Emilio used my own shackles to bind the last man, and then… he made me."

Larus's voice was barely above a whisper. "How?"

Micah smiled, slow and knowing. "You shall soon find out, young one."

5

MAKER

They walked into the night together, the cold pressing in around them. Larus glanced back at the mausoleum, a strange unease settling in his chest. Why here? Why out in the open, beneath the cold night sky? He hadn't asked Micah, sensing the vampire already knew his thoughts.

The cemetery was silent, save for the brittle crunch of dry leaves beneath their feet. Larus tilted his head toward the sky. The full moon hung above them, casting a pale glow over the tombstones, their names and epitaphs etched centuries ago. How many had lain here, forgotten? How many would remain when he was centuries old himself?

By the time the last of the headstones were lost to darkness, the woods had swallowed them whole. Micah turned to face him. His expression was unreadable, his hazel eyes catching the moonlight.

"As of this night, you will never again walk beneath the sun, nor taste the food of mortals," Micah murmured. "You will never grow old. But there is much you must learn as a newborn." He placed a hand on Larus's shoulder, his touch unnaturally cool. "You will be my child."

Larus swallowed. "Micah, how will—"

A gasp caught in his throat. The chill of Micah's lips brushed his neck, a whisper of something both foreign and familiar. Then came the slow, deliberate caress of his tongue against Larus's skin. A shudder ran through him. The anticipation. The silence. The waiting.

And then, the bite.

Fangs pierced deep, sharper than he imagined. Pain flared hot, laced with an aching pull as his blood left him. His limbs weakened, his body turning to glass, fragile beneath the hands of something infinitely stronger. Darkness curled at the edges of his vision, and still, Micah drank.

Larus trembled. This was the end. This was the beginning.

Larus opened his eyes slowly, his body leaden with weakness, his mind clouded with confusion. He lay upon a bed of crisp, dry leaves, their edges crackling beneath him as he shifted. A wave of horror rolled through his thoughts. His muscles ached, spasmed uncontrollably. His legs—useless. His skin burned as though set aflame from the inside.

A violent nausea seized him. He heaved, choking, then vomited onto the earth. His body convulsed. Rolling onto his back, he gasped for breath, his vision swimming. Against the backdrop of the night sky, a figure loomed above him, smiling.

Micah.

Perched atop a massive tombstone, the vampire regarded him with calm amusement. "It is not too late to change your mind, young one."

Larus groaned, gripping at the damp earth beneath him. He wanted the pain to end. The unnatural thoughts invading his mind. The searing sensitivity to the moon's glow.

Micah's voice was patient, almost kind. "I can take you to your father's manor. Lay you in your bed, if you invite me in. There, you will die. Your family will assume your heart has finally succumbed to its affliction."

Micah spoke so slowly, as if time were his to command. Larus felt a surge of rage—raw, irrational, but consuming.

"What's happening to me?" His voice came out hoarse, barely a whisper. Then, a strange, humiliating pressure struck his gut. His body betrayed him in every possible way.

Micah watched him with eerie stillness. "Your death comes."

Larus's head swam. His thoughts unraveled into fevered hallucinations. He saw his father standing over him, towering, faceless. He saw his family withering with age, their faces creased with time while he—unchanged—sat beside their deathbeds, laughing. His stallion, Raven, galloped into the distance, its dark mane flowing like a shadow.

And then—coldness. Comforting, inescapable. He was not in his old church seeking solace. He was in Micah's arms.

Micah was inside his head.

Larus trembled. He could surrender. He could let go, slip into death and leave behind the fragile, failing life he had known. Or—

His lips parted. His voice came weak, but certain.

"I want to live."

His eyelids felt too heavy to lift, but he knew Micah was near. He felt the vampire's presence, an icy whisper against his fevered skin. Then, something thick and bitter dripped onto his lips, coating his tongue.

"Drink, young one," Micah murmured. His voice was distant now, like a fading dream. "Die... live forever."

And Larus lapped at the cold blood.

6

A POWERFUL UNION

Max sat at her dressing table, scowling at her reflection. She couldn't decide which was worse—the suffocating cinch of her corset or the way the powder on her face made her look ghostly. Behind her, the servant girl Catherine had chosen fussed over the silk gown, smoothing and adjusting every fold as if perfection could be willed into existence.

Unlike her younger sisters, Max had never equated beauty with pain. She studied their reflections in the mirror, reading them as easily as a book. Isabelle's smile was warm, brimming with genuine pride. Catherine's, however, was thinner, tighter. Max knew her sister's love was real, but so was her discontent. Catherine had never been satisfied, always longing for more—more wealth, more status, more of whatever their father's fortune could not buy. And tonight, behind the excitement in her eyes, Max saw something else. Jealousy.

"You look beautiful, Max." Isabelle's hands rested lightly on her shoulders. "Bartholomew Hearne will be speechless when Father walks you down the aisle."

Catherine sighed. "I still don't understand why Father insisted on an evening wedding. Everyone knows summer weddings are better, when the sun is shining."

"A wedding is a formality, Cate, not a spectacle," Max replied. "At least, not for me."

Catherine scoffed, twisting a loose curl of Max's hair. "What good is a wedding if not to show everyone what Father has accomplished? Marrying you to Bartholomew Hearne is a triumph. He's the richest, most eligible bachelor in the city."

Ever the romantic, Isabelle clasped her hands together. "But do you love him, Max? Does he love you?"

Max exhaled sharply, her patience thinning. "Isabelle, I've met him once." She turned from the mirror. "And when he kissed my hand, I wanted to cut it off."

Catherine gasped, clutching her chest as if Max had uttered blasphemy. "Good heavens! Bartholomew Hearne is the most handsome man I have ever seen. Every woman in this city will be enraged that you—of all people—are marrying the son of Percival Hearne."

Max rose, her corset biting into her ribs. Clad in only her undergarments, she crossed to the window, wincing with each step. The evening air pressed cool against the glass. "Marriages are seldom about love," she said, gazing out over the grounds. "The most powerful unions are those forged by powerful families. Father and I both knew this. It is better to have the Hearnes as allies, not rivals."

"I shall only marry for love," Isabelle said softly.

Max turned, facing her sisters. They stood side by side, their expressions nearly identical—like she was speaking a foreign language.

"Have you two learned nothing from all that Father has taught us?"

Catherine folded her arms. "If you won't love him, why marry him?"

Max's lips curved into a knowing smile. "Because I'm the only one strong enough—woman enough—to manage Bartholomew Hearne."

She motioned toward Isabelle. "You would submit to him completely, and he would never respect you. Father knows a gentler husband would suit you best." Isabelle lowered her gaze. Max turned to Catherine. "And you? He would keep you busy with gowns and jewels until you were as powerless and accommodating as Mother—too comfortable to ever challenge him."

Neither of them argued.

Max already knew the truth. She was the best choice for Bartholomew Hearne.

The three sisters left the servant to finish preparing the wedding gown and moved to the anteroom, where a light lunch awaited them. Outside, the afternoon sun peeked through shifting clouds, casting fleeting patterns of light across the parquet floor. The ceremony was still hours away, followed by a long night of feasting and dancing. Max had planned a grand social affair.

Seated across from her on the burgundy velvet couch, Catherine nibbled at cucumber sandwiches while Isabelle indulged in a perfect cheese soufflé.

"You must try this, Max." Isabelle tapped the rim of her bowl with her spoon. "It's divine."

"I have no stomach for it," Max said.

Catherine smirked. "And what of Bartholomew Hearne's kisses?"

Isabelle giggled behind her hand, but Max only gazed at them, a flicker of pity crossing her face.

She was relieved when Isabelle changed the subject. "It's your birthday tomorrow," she said, then hesitated. "And our brother's as well. Will you not try to mend this rift between him and Father?"

Max turned her head slightly, staring past her sisters, as if the answer lay somewhere beyond the window. "Larus and I are too different," she said. "He is more like you, Isabelle—sweet and perfect. And he's as stubborn as you, Catherine. Though we share a womb, we are like day and night."

"Let him be, Max." Isabelle pushed her soufflé aside.

"Little Isabelle, always rushing to our brother's aid."

"I would do the same for you." Isabelle's brows lifted. "And for you, Catherine." Her voice softened. "It must be a terrible thing, celebrating a birthday knowing your days are numbered."

Catherine scowled, tossing her sandwich onto the tray. "Now you've ruined my appetite. Why must we speak of such sad things on our sister's wedding day?"

"He is our brother," Isabelle said, her voice unsteady.

Max leaned back, lacing her fingers together. "Where is our dear brother, anyway?"

"His rooms are empty," Isabelle said. "He was gone last night when Tilley brought up his tray, and he hasn't returned. It isn't like Larus to stay out this long."

"I doubt he'll attend the wedding," Max said, though there was no pleasure in the thought.

Catherine picked up another sandwich, hesitated before taking a bite. "Maybe it's for the best. Imagine the scene if he and Father quarrelled."

The sudden clatter of hooves against cobblestones cut through their conversation. Catherine sprang to the window. "They've arrived—the Hearnes!"

Max hesitated, then joined her sisters just in time to see the tall, broad-shouldered figure of Percival Hearne step down from the carriage. He carried himself with quiet authority, his head held high. Unlike their own father, he doted upon his wife, smiling as he extended his arm to help her down. But when the next figure stepped from the carriage, Percival's demeanour changed. His smile vanished, his posture stiffened. Max knew that look—disapproval, perhaps resentment.

So, she thought. The rift between father and son is not unlike our own.

Bartholomew Hearne emerged, tall as his father, carrying himself with the same air of confidence. He scanned his surroundings, assessing them like a man who saw himself above it all.

Max would admit—though only to herself—that her betrothed was a handsome man. But beauty was a trivial thing.

"Is he not perfect?" Catherine bit her lip, eyes gleaming with something too close to lust.

As if sensing their presence, Bartholomew's gaze flicked upward. His eyes locked onto theirs. With a startled giggle, Catherine and Isabelle ducked out of sight, but Max remained still. Their eyes met, neither willing to be the first to look away.

It was a test.

A game.

A battle of wills.

Max let the moment stretch, watching for the first flicker of weakness. When she grew tired of the standoff, she did not look away—she merely lifted her hand, fingers grazing the corset that pressed against her ribs, the fabric pushing her full breasts high.

Bartholomew's eyes dipped, just for a fraction of a second.

Max smiled.

Triumphant, she turned away from the window.

7

NEWBORN

Death had become his life.

Larus blinked awake, and instantly, his new eyes adjusted to the blackness within the crypt. The silence pressed against him, thick and stifling, as if the very air carried the weight of the dead. He wasn't breathing. His chest did not rise, nor did his heart beat. He reached up, fingers trembling, pressing against the place where his pulse had once been. Nothing.

A choked sound crawled up his throat.

The cold stone walls of the hidden mausoleum surrounded him, and he lay inside a sarcophagus, entombed yet very much awake. He flung his hands against the stone lid, panicked, and before he could even process what he was doing, the heavy slab groaned and slid aside. Strength surged through him—unnatural, inhuman. He sat up, gasping, but there was no breath, no relief.

Micah was waiting. Silent. Watching.

Larus recoiled from the sight of him. The pale-faced man was his maker now. His saviour. His murderer.

"What have you done to me?" Larus whispered. His voice did not tremble as he expected it to. It was too smooth, too steady, as if it no longer belonged to him.

Micah tilted his head, studying him. "You already know."

Larus pressed his hands over his face. He felt the shape of himself, but it was wrong. His skin was too smooth, too cool, like marble warmed only by the remnants of his former life.

"This is madness," he rasped. "This is—"

A scent hit him then. Copper and salt. A sharp hunger twisted inside his gut so suddenly that he doubled over, pressing his hand against his stomach.

Micah's smile was patient, knowing. "You are starving."

Larus clenched his jaw. "No." He forced himself upright, gripping the edges of the stone coffin. "I will not drink. I will not become—"

"You already are." Micah took a step closer, his presence calm, unshaken. "Fighting it will only make it worse."

Larus shook his head. "I will not feed."

Micah sighed, but there was no true disappointment in it. "Very well. Let us see how long your resolve lasts." He turned, moving toward the steps that led up into the crypt. "Come."

Larus did not want to follow, but his body betrayed him. The craving inside him was unbearable, gnawing at the edges of his sanity. His hands shook at his sides, fingers twitching with a restless, animalistic need.

He swallowed hard, hoping for moisture in his mouth, but none came. He was parched in a way he had never known before.

Still, he followed.

THE FOREST WAS ALIVE WITH SOUNDS—THE RUSTLING OF UNSEEN creatures, the whisper of wind through the bare trees. But Larus heard more than he ever had before. He heard the heartbeat of the earth, the scurry of life hidden beneath the frozen ground. And he heard them—humans.

Distant. Laughing. Unaware.

His throat burned. He swayed on his feet, fists clenched. The scent of warm, pulsing blood sent daggers of hunger through him.

He lurched backward.

"No," he gasped. "I cannot."

Micah watched him carefully. "You must."

Larus gritted his teeth, nostrils flaring. "I refuse to be a monster."

Micah sighed again. "You are a newborn. I will not let you lose control." He turned his head slightly. "There is another way."

A new scent filled the air. Old. Frail. Dying.

Larus turned, drawn despite himself. A man lay slumped against a tree, barely breathing, his body already surrendering to time. Micah stepped forward, crouching beside him, and when the man's watery eyes flickered open, he did not flinch. He did not fight. He only smiled, as if he had been waiting.

Micah whispered something—too low for Larus to hear, or perhaps he simply did not wish to hear it. The old man nodded.

Micah turned to Larus.

"You will drink."

Larus trembled. "He's dying—"

"Yes. He is already leaving this world. You will only ease his passing."

The scent of blood was intoxicating. His hunger clawed at him, demanding. He clenched his fists, but his body moved of its own accord. His fangs ached, throbbing, desperate for release.

"No," he whispered again, but this time, it was weaker.

The old man's smile did not falter. He reached out, his frail fingers trembling as they closed over Larus's wrist. His pulse was barely there, a flickering candle in a storm.

"It's all right, son," the man whispered. "Let me go."

Larus could not stop himself. He could not deny the hunger any longer. With a final, shuddering breath of resistance, he lowered his mouth to the old man's throat.

Warmth flooded him. It was unlike anything he had ever tasted—rich, sweet, powerful. The rush of it sent his mind reeling, his body trembling as strength poured into him. The man exhaled one final breath, and Larus could feel his life slipping away.

He jerked back, horrified, blood dripping from his lips.

Micah was there in an instant, gripping his shoulder, steadying him. "It is done."

Larus wiped at his mouth, shame burning in his chest. "I—"

"Do not mourn him," Micah said. "He made his choice."

Larus swallowed hard. The hunger had eased, but it was not gone. It would never be gone.

He was damned now.

Forever.

THE FRIGID NIGHT HAD LITTLE EFFECT ON LARUS. AS A NEWBORN, HIS BODY no longer recognized the cold. He and Micah had raced deep into the forest in what seemed like seconds. When Larus paused and turned back, he could still see the church steeples rising above the leafless canopy.

"We've come so far..." he murmured.

Micah chuckled in the dark. "Yes, Larus. But now you must feed. To do this, you must put all your senses to the test." He gestured toward the sloping terrain ahead. "Listen."

Larus closed his eyes. He could hear the smallest of movements—the scurrying of rodents beneath the brittle leaves, the beating wings of an owl before its distant hoot. Then, Micah's voice threaded through his mind.

"Concentrate, young one."

Larus focused, drowning out the insignificant sounds, searching for what he truly needed. And then he heard it—the slow, steady rhythm of a heartbeat. Strong. Calm. A resting creature. His hunger surged.

In a blur, he moved toward the sound, and in that instant, his prey sensed him. Its heart pounded in alarm. Its instinct to flee took over. Larus spotted the stag—a magnificent beast with towering antlers. He lunged—but too directly, too recklessly. The deer lowered its head, and in an instant, its antlers drove into Larus's abdomen, throwing him back.

Pain flared, but it faded almost as quickly as it came. The deer made a desperate attempt to flee, but before it could, Micah struck, bringing it to the ground.

"Quickly!" The command rang in Larus's mind.

Without hesitation, the two fed together.

When they had taken their fill, they left the carcass behind and walked deeper into the forest. Larus looked down at his torn, bloodied clothes, surprised to find no wound.

Micah smirked. "Does a lion face its prey head-on?"

Larus scowled at himself. "I was careless."

"You are young. You will learn." Micah gestured toward Larus's unmarred skin. "And do not worry—immortals heal. Feeding accelerates the process."

Larus wiped his mouth with the back of his hand, his hunger still gnawing. "We can survive on animal blood?"

"We survive on blood." Micah corrected. "But hunger will not kill us—it only weakens us. If we are out of reach from slayers, we can sleep for decades, even centuries. Blood alone will wake us."

Larus frowned. "But how do vampires hunt if they grow too weak?"

With an effortless leap, Micah sprang into the branches of a massive tree, perching on a thick limb. He looked down at Larus. "In a coven, we wake each other from slumber." He turned his gaze eastward. "But I am young—not yet two hundred years old. Over time, after living many lives and watching so many die, even immortality grows tiresome."

Larus tilted his head. "You said your maker, Emilio, never took his sleep after he turned you. Why?"

Micah's expression darkened. "Because I was young. But Emilio was ancient. He had grown weary of starting new lives."

Larus hesitated before asking, "New lives?"

Micah exhaled. "Vampires fall in love with mortals, Larus. And the most terrible thing is watching them leave this world."

Larus scoffed. "Then why love a human at all? Why not turn them?"

Micah smiled, but there was sorrow in it. "Because, young one, we crave the one thing we can never be. Mortals burn bright and fast—but they live."

Larus absorbed this, though he did not yet understand it.

"Are we... a coven?"

Micah met his eyes. "Yes, dear Larus. You are now of my coven."

Pride swelled in Larus's chest. He belonged to something again.

Micah leapt from the tree, landing lightly on his feet. "Now come. You must feed again. It is no easy task for a newborn to mingle with the living."

Larus nodded. He would drink his fill. He would learn control. He would return to the world he had once belonged to.

Even if he no longer belonged there.

8

THE WEDDING FEAST

Any human standing among the countless tombstones would see the ancient mausoleum as a crumbling monument to the dead, a place where only dust and silence remained. But Larus knew the truth—there was life beneath the stone. Not the warm, fleeting kind he once knew, but a different existence altogether. A haven for the living dead.

Micah had given him free rein to explore the labyrinthine catacombs beneath the cemetery, save for one chamber—sealed with red wax, untouched, undisturbed. A warning, unspoken yet absolute. It was two levels below the cemetery grounds, far from the flickering torchlight that lined the more familiar corridors. Though Micah had shown him the door, he had offered no explanation, only a firm command: Do not enter.

Larus had not questioned it. Not yet.

Now, dressed for the night's festivities, he stood at the base of the hill, his gaze fixed on the towering church in the distance. His sister's wedding. A moment of joy, of family, of warmth—and he, a creature of the night, would step among them as if nothing had changed.

The sharp neigh of his stallion pulled him from his thoughts.

He turned, heart clenching at the sight of Raven, the proud beast he had raised since he was a boy. The stallion had always responded to his voice, his touch. Now, he barely tolerated his presence.

Larus took a hesitant step forward. "Raven..."

The horse shied away, ears pinned back. The rejection stung more than it should have.

"Give him time," Micah said, stepping from the thicket, his presence as silent as the night itself.

Larus exhaled, watching Raven's breath cloud in the cold air. "I should take him back to my father's stables. He belongs there, not here."

Micah studied the horse for a moment before approaching. Unlike Larus, he moved with confidence, and to the young vampire's surprise, Raven did not flinch. The stallion stood still as Micah ran a hand along his forehead, fingers brushing against the smooth black coat. Then, with a quiet pat, he untethered the reins.

Larus watched, bewildered, as Raven did not hesitate. The stallion turned and galloped away, his dark form disappearing down the dirt road.

"It is as if he never knew me," Larus murmured.

Micah smiled faintly. "Sensitive creatures, horses. They know what you are, even if you do not." He waved a hand, dismissing the thought before turning his attention back to the night ahead. "Now, remember what I have taught you. Give nothing away. If you feel the hunger, you must leave at once."

Larus clenched his fists. "Why let me go at all if you think I might lose control?"

Micah's gaze was steady, unreadable. "Because you must learn." A pause. "And because I shall be watching."

Larus searched his maker's face, hoping to catch some hint of what he was thinking, but he found nothing. Instead, only a void—a mind sealed against him.

His lips parted in realization.

Micah nodded slightly. "It is a gift, knowing how to peer into one's thoughts." He tilted his head. "But it is equally important to guard your own."

The distant sound of hooves drew Larus's attention. He turned to see a carriage approaching, its lantern swaying as it rolled down the uneven road. The coachman's face was expressionless as he brought the horses to a stop. With a practiced, almost unnatural motion, he reached back and pulled open the door.

Larus hesitated. Something about the man unsettled him. His presence was...wrong. Larus strained to listen, to reach into his mind, but found only silence.

Turning to Micah, he was met with the slightest shake of his maker's head. Do not ask.

Suppressing the unease curling in his stomach, Larus stepped into the carriage. The door shut behind him, the horses lurched forward, and the night swallowed them whole.

Micah remained behind. Watching. Waiting.

GETTING TO HIS ROOMS UNSEEN WAS EASY—TOO EASY. HIS FOOTSTEPS MADE no sound; his movements were a whisper in the darkness. Even Tilley, bustling about in the kitchens, failed to sense his passing. Before, she would have caught him sneaking in and scolded him with a knowing smile. Now, he was a ghost in his own home.

Larus spent some time in his chamber, steadying himself before stepping into the world of the living once more. The clothes he wore—fine, dark fabrics befitting the son of a noble house—felt foreign against his skin, as though they belonged to someone else entirely.

Slowly, he reminded himself as he left his room. Move slowly. Every step, every turn of his head had to be deliberate. If he moved as he felt compelled to, he would seem unnatural. His body, brimming with a newborn's unnatural power, yearned to move at inhuman speed. Instead, he placed one foot before the other with careful restraint, descending the circular staircase toward the grand ballroom.

The moment he stepped onto the landing, the world below crashed into him.

A sea of bodies, their warmth radiating in waves, their laughter rising and falling in time with the lilting waltz played by the orchestra. But beyond the music, beyond the voices, was the pulsing of life—hundreds of heartbeats, each one calling to him like a siren's song.

Larus staggered, clutching the wooden railing.

The sheer weight of it—the rush of thoughts that were not his own, the shifting tempos of every beating heart—pressed against his mind like a tide threatening to drag him under. Without looking, he could feel them all. The young, whose blood was vibrant and strong. The old, whose pulses faltered like candle flames in a breeze. The sick, their bodies weak but their blood still calling to him. The healthy, full of life, full of warmth—

A sharp pain splintered in his hand. The railing cracked beneath his grip.

The world blurred. Hunger, raw and insatiable, consumed him. A terrible image flashed in his mind—his body springing over the railing, fangs bared, arms outstretched to seize the first warm throat he could find. To drink. To devour.

A voice cut through the haze.

"Larus!"

The sound hit him like a hammer, and he gasped, realizing he had already reached the ballroom floor. Isabelle—his youngest sister—rushed toward him, her face glowing with relief.

Before he could react, she threw herself into his arms.

Larus stiffened, breath catching as her warmth enveloped him. The heat of her body, the scent of her skin, the rhythmic pulse just beneath—

He was drowning.

Isabelle pulled back slightly, taking his hands in hers. "I have been worried sick, big brother! Where have you—" She stopped abruptly, squeezing his hands tighter. "Heavens! You are cold as ice, Larus."

Larus looked down into her bright, trusting eyes. Her mind was open to him, and he saw it all—the fear, the longing, the unwavering love she held for him. *She thinks I am ill*, he realized.

Summoning every ounce of control, he forced a smile. "It is the chill air outside," he lied. "I was out in the stables with Raven."

Isabelle's expression softened. "Yes... We have all been worried, Larus.

When Raven rode in alone, we thought—" Her voice faltered. "We thought..."

She clung to him again, burying her face against his chest.

Larus squeezed his eyes shut. She was too close. He could hear the rush of her blood, feel the warmth of it coursing just beneath the surface. The urge to lean down, to taste, to drink—

He tore himself away, laughing nervously. "I cannot imagine Father would fret over me, Isabelle."

She frowned. "Do put this rift between you and Father aside, Larus." Taking his hand, she tugged him forward, deeper into the crowd.

Larus let himself be led, his body tense but outwardly composed. The ballroom unfolded before him—a swirling mass of silken gowns, polished boots gliding across the marble floor, candlelight flickering in gilded chandeliers. The orchestra played on, their music weaving through the mingling scents of perfume, sweat, and roasted meats.

None of it tempted him. Not the rich foods, not the revelry. Only blood.

They reached their sister Catherine and their mother.

Catherine studied him with her sharp gaze before pressing a light kiss to his cheek. "Late as always, aren't you, brother?" She turned to their mother with a knowing smirk. "See, Mother? I told you he would come—late as always."

Larus turned his attention to his mother. He bowed his head slightly before pressing a kiss to her gloved hand.

Something flickered in her expression.

Lifting her hand, she touched her cheek where he had kissed her—as if to wipe it away.

"You are as frigid as a block of ice, Larus."

The words sent a jolt of fear through him.

She waved a hand dismissively, as though it were nothing. "You must find your father—let him know you are here. He would never forgive your absence, especially tonight." She reached up, her touch suddenly gentle, brushing his cheek. "You look pale, dear. You should see Tilley for a cup of her herb tea."

Larus forced a chuckle. "I am fine, Mother. I have been a bit... tired."

But as he spoke, he caught Catherine's gaze lingering on him again.

She knows something is different.

"There's something about you, brother," she said slowly. "Something in your eyes."

His heart—if it still beat—would have stopped.

Looking away, he turned to his mother. "Perhaps you are right, Mother. I should see Tilley."

"Nonsense!" Catherine took his arm, linking it with hers before he could protest. "You must meet our new brother-in-law." She shot a glance at Isabelle. "Come along!"

Larus had no choice but to follow as Catherine pulled him across the ballroom, weaving through the crowd. His anxiety increased.

Every step took him closer to Max and her husband, Bartholomew Hearne.

Every step took him deeper into the lion's den.

LARUS STOOD FROZEN, HIS BODY LOCKED IN PLACE AS IF TURNED TO STONE.

Bartholomew Hearne was an imposing man—tall, broad-shouldered, with dark eyes set beneath thick black brows. His hair was as dark as Raven's mane, and in him, Larus saw the reflection of his father, Percival Hearne, save for the older man's streaks of silver. But it was not Bartholomew's physical presence that unnerved Larus.

It was the silence.

Larus could hear the thoughts of everyone in the room—the fleeting worries, the concealed jealousy, the whispers of longing and regret. But when he looked into Bartholomew's eyes, he found... nothing. A void. A wall. It was the same with Percival Hearne, the same with Lady Hearne.

He stood unmoving between his sisters, staring at the man he was meant to greet, before he finally forced himself to come to his senses.

Taking his twin sister's hand, he brought it to his lips in a light kiss before pulling her into an embrace. "You look beautiful as ever," he murmured.

Max opened her mouth to speak, but Larus cut her off before the words formed. "I was out for a walk, and then I stopped in the stables..."

"You know our brother loves the outdoors, Max," Isabelle said, stepping in smoothly. "Especially when it's cold."

Larus gave her a small, grateful glance, but before he could respond, he felt a familiar presence.

His father.

Larus turned his head slightly, locking eyes with him across the ballroom. Lord Bleddyn stood tall beside Percival Hearne, his expression unreadable, though the tension in his stance betrayed his true feelings. Larus knew that look well—the tightness around the mouth, the steel in his gaze. The last time they had spoken, there had been only contempt, disappointment, rage.

Larus braced himself for the same.

But when he reached into his father's thoughts, what he found shook him.

Yes, there was anger—resentment, even. A storm of emotion simmered beneath the surface, a fury his father had carried for years. But underneath it, buried deep, was something else.

Relief.

His father was relieved to see him.

Larus exhaled slowly. He bowed, just slightly, in greeting. "Father."

He felt no need to extend his hand, for he feared the unnatural chill of his skin would give him away. He glanced again at the Hearnes and resisted the urge to step back. The impenetrability of their minds made his skin prickle. It was unnatural. What were they?

Before he could dwell on it, a sound carried over the hum of conversation—laughter. A small gathering of men stood not far from his father, engaged in what seemed to be a lively discussion. Larus barely spared them a glance. Physicians, by the looks of them. He could smell the sharp scent of ink and parchment, the faint traces of herbal tinctures on their clothes.

Then his father cleared his throat.

The laughter faded. Conversations stilled.

The head of the Bleddyn household had commanded the room's attention with a single sound.

His father turned to him, his expression unreadable, before offering one of his rare smiles.

"Larus," he said, his voice even, controlled. "Allow me to introduce a good friend of mine."

A strange sense of unease slithered up Larus's spine.

His father stepped aside, beckoning the men forward. He moved closer to Larus, speaking in a voice so low only he could hear.

"Remember where you are."

Then he turned back to the group, gesturing toward one man in particular.

"Gentlemen, meet my son."

Larus barely registered the rest of his father's words, for the moment the man stepped forward, the world lurched.

No.

The ballroom melted away. The music, the perfume, the murmuring of voices—all of it faded into a distant hum.

There, standing before him, was Micah.

His maker.

Larus felt his body go rigid, his words stolen from him. He was drowning in the memory—the press of cold lips on his throat, the sharp sting of fangs sinking into flesh, the moment when warmth became ice. He had expected to see Micah at his sister's wedding, and yet here he was, standing in the glow of candlelight, dressed in a fine coat, the very image of a learned man.

His father spoke again, oblivious to the horror coursing through Larus's veins.

"This is Doctor Duncan," he said. "The good man we spoke of—Doctor Micah Duncan."

Larus felt himself gasp.

Micah's hazel eyes gleamed with amusement. If there was any recognition in them, he did not show it. Instead, he tilted his head slightly, as if appraising him for the first time.

Then he smiled.

Larus would have preferred a dagger to the chest.

There was no escape. No choice but to play the part.

With an effort that nearly cost him his composure, Larus lifted his right hand and extended it toward the man who had stolen his soul.

Micah clasped it firmly, his touch cool but not unnatural. He squeezed slightly, an unspoken message passing between them.

"Ah, young Master Bleddyn," Micah said smoothly. He took a step back, as if to get a better look at him. "It is a pleasure."

Larus swallowed the bile rising in his throat.

Micah turned to his father and smiled. "I would speak with your son in private, if I may."

Larus's father nodded.

Micah's fingers curled around his shoulder, a gesture that to anyone else seemed perfectly natural. To Larus, it was a shackle.

"Shall we?" Micah murmured.

Larus glanced at his father, half-expecting—hoping—for some sign of protest. But no. His father was watching him closely, his eyes unreadable.

He knew Larus would not dare cause a scene.

Larus swallowed hard, casting one last glance at his sisters before allowing Micah to guide him away from the warmth of the living.

THEY WERE HARDLY OUT OF EARSHOT BEFORE LARUS TURNED ON MICAH, HIS voice low and trembling with fury. "What is this?" His breath came in sharp, unnecessary bursts—a habit of life that no longer served him. His body demanded air, but not for survival. The hunger burned deeper than his lungs, deeper than reason. "You never said you knew my father."

Micah did not answer. He moved forward, unconcerned, leading them away from the glow of the house. The cold night wind swept over Larus, but it was nothing to him. He did not shiver. He did not feel. That, more than anything, frightened him.

"You have deceived me," Larus snarled. His voice was quieter now, dangerous. He walked faster, moving past clusters of coachmen, but every heartbeat—a stuttering rhythm of life—snapped at his control like a whip. The scent of them filled his nostrils, a thousand layered notes of flesh and salt and rushing blood. He clenched his jaw so hard it ached.

Then Micah seized him by the throat.

Larus gasped, his fingers flying to Micah's wrist. He should have struggled, but what good was it? Micah lifted him with inhuman ease, pinning him to the rough bark of an oak tree. The force of it would have crushed a mortal's windpipe.

"You act like a spoiled child." Micah's voice was calm, but his grip was steel. This was not a threat. This was a lesson. Slowly, he loosened his hold, allowing Larus to drop to his feet. Larus remained still, barely resisting the urge to rub his throat—there was no pain, not really. There was no breath to lose. That, too, was gone.

He swallowed, hating the way his body responded—not with fear, but with something like submission. Micah had made him. Micah had power over him.

"How long have you and my father known each other?" Larus rasped.

Micah exhaled sharply, as if disappointed. "Be sensible. Think." He tapped his temple. "Like you, I appear no older than twenty-five. I could not have revealed myself to your father until recently. If I had done so years before, what would he think? Why does a man never age while the world withers around him?" He shook his head. "Patience is a vampire's greatest virtue, Larus."

Larus clenched his fists. He thought of his father. Of the anger he had seen in his mind. Of the relief.

"You must trust me, young one." Micah's voice softened. "I must protect you."

Larus did not answer. He felt something foreign and awful clawing at his chest. His father had planned to send him away. Had seen him as a disgrace. But Micah... Micah would have come for him anyway.

"You are a doctor?" Larus whispered.

"I am." Micah's lips twitched into something that was almost a smile. "When you live many lives, you can be anything you desire."

Larus turned his face away, feeling sick. He had wanted to be something. Had dreamed of adventure, of discovery, of proving to his father that he was not some wasted thing. But this? This was not what he had imagined.

Micah stepped closer. "Your father expects you to leave with me this night."

Larus's head snapped up, red-tinged tears burning at his eyes. "No."

"He believes you are ill," Micah continued, undeterred. "I have promised him I shall help you."

Larus shook his head. No. No, he would not be taken like this. Like a wayward son sent off for correction. "I won't go."

Micah sighed, almost pitying. "Larus, you must control your emotions. If you cannot, I will not be able to protect you."

Something in his tone made Larus pause. "Protect me from what?"

Micah hesitated. "There are other matters we must discuss after we leave this place." His voice was careful now, measured. "It involves your sister's husband."

Larus felt a strange, hollow dread settle in his chest. "Bartholomew Hearne?"

"Yes." Micah's hazel eyes darkened. "We must be careful."

"I could not read their minds," Larus murmured.

Micah nodded. "I was able to break the mind of Lady Hearne, but only because she dotes upon her son. Even she is strong. They are all strong, the Hearnes."

"Percival Hearne is one of the wealthiest men in the country." Larus frowned. "His family's wealth goes back generations."

"Yes, yes," Micah said impatiently. "But that is not all." He looked toward the house, toward the glittering ballroom. "The Hearnes are hunters, Larus."

Larus stiffened.

Micah's voice was quiet. "Vampire hunters."

9

GOODBYE

Larus wiped away the blood tears before rejoining the festivities, but deep inside, his emotions churned. His mind was in chaos—not just from the weight of his sister's wedding guests' thoughts pressing in on him, but from the truth Micah had revealed. Percival and Bartholomew Hearne were hunters. Vampire hunters.

And tonight, Larus would leave behind everything he had ever known.

Micah had told him exactly what needed to be done. His father expected him to agree, and so he would. The rest, Micah had assured him, would work itself out.

The two vampires passed through the gilded halls of the Bleddyn estate, weaving through clusters of finely dressed guests. Larus hardly noticed them. His stomach twisted as they neared Maxwell Bleddyn's study—his father's haven. He had never been welcome there as a boy, and even now, something in his blood recoiled at the thought of entering.

But when he stepped inside, he faltered.

The entire family was gathered.

For a brief moment, Larus staggered back, caught off guard. Had he walked into a trap? A firm but reassuring touch on his shoulder steadied him—Micah. Silent. Watchful.

The room was still. The fire in the massive hearth crackled, its warmth reaching toward them, but Larus felt nothing.

His three sisters sat together on a backless couch, their gazes unreadable. Near his father's desk stood his mother, Igraine Bleddyn, ever composed, her fingers resting lightly on the carved arm of his father's chair. And there—closer to the fire—sat Tilley, the woman who had raised him with more love than his own mother ever had. She looked nervous.

His father, Maxwell Bleddyn, did not sit. He stood, both palms pressed firmly against the polished surface of his desk, staring into Larus's eyes as if issuing a challenge.

Larus hesitated. For the first time since his turning, he did not reach into their minds. He did not want to know what they were thinking. He welcomed the silence.

Micah stepped forward, effortlessly assuming command of the room. "Maxwell. Lady Igraine." His voice was warm, practiced, as if addressing old friends. He moved toward the fireplace, his tall frame casting shifting shadows across the bookshelves. The light caught his skin—dusky brown, but paler than it should have been.

Then, to Larus's quiet astonishment, Micah turned his attention to Tilley. He smiled, and something in his expression softened. "Ah, Tilley, the famous cook Larus spoke of. How nice to meet you again."

Tilley stiffened as Micah reached for her hand, but he did not grip it with the unnatural chill of their kind. He had warmed himself by the fire first.

Micah pressed a kiss to her knuckles. "You are as beautiful as ever."

Larus saw it then—the subtle way Micah had controlled the moment, drawing attention away from himself, putting the humans at ease. Manipulation, elegantly done.

His maker crossed the room, approaching Larus's sisters with the same effortless grace. His gaze landed first on Max, the boldest of them. He took her hand, lingering just long enough to test her reaction.

"Maxine..." A pause, deliberate. Then, with a quiet, knowing smile—"No, Max... beautiful Max."

Larus tensed. Micah was reading their thoughts. And Max—proud, sharp-witted Max—smiled up at him. It was genuine.

"Thank you, Doctor Duncan." Her voice was confident, unflinching. "You are too kind."

Larus barely suppressed a scowl. He did not like how she looked at Micah.

Catherine, the second-eldest, was less patient. She pushed forward, nudging her sister aside with practiced ease. The tight bodice of her gown accentuated the curve of her breasts, and she positioned herself with the precision of a woman who knew her effect.

Micah took her hand, and instead of merely kissing it, he lifted her arm, turning her in a graceful twirl. Catherine laughed, breathless.

"A lovely gown for a lovely lady," Micah murmured.

Catherine preened under the attention.

Larus caught movement from the corner of his eye—Isabelle, the youngest, rolling her eyes. But when Micah turned to her, she did not push forward or smile coyly. Instead, she studied him.

She curtsied, slow and deliberate, her sharp eyes searching his face.

Micah took her hand. Unlike with the others, he did not kiss it immediately. He held it there, the moment stretching.

Then, he spoke a single word.

"Isabelle."

Larus did not understand what passed between them, but his sister's lips parted slightly, and something in her posture eased.

She was satisfied.

Larus exhaled, barely realizing he had been holding his breath, another nervous habit he'd practiced long before his rebirth. Micah had taken control of the entire room. Of his father. His mother. His sisters. Even Tilley.

And Larus wasn't sure if he should be impressed—or terrified.

A POLITE BUT POSSESSIVE CLEARING OF HIS THROAT ENDED THE SILENCE, breaking the strange tension between Isabelle and Micah. Even then, Larus saw how his sister's gaze lingered on his maker, searching for something unspoken.

Micah turned away first. He faced Maxwell Bleddyn, his voice smooth and assured. "Maxwell, your son and I have discussed it." He flicked a glance toward Larus. "And he has decided to make the journey to the capital. I shall do all I can for him. We leave tonight."

Larus watched the flicker of relief in his father's expression—brief but unmistakable. The realization struck like a blade to the ribs. He was now immortal, yet his absence brought his father comfort.

Catherine, Isabelle, and Tilley had begun to weep, believing they would never see him again. Max, as always, caged her emotions behind an unreadable mask.

"Igraine and I will speak with our son alone," his father said.

Larus embraced his sisters, their tears dampening his coat, and then Tilley, who clung to him as if she could anchor him to the life he was leaving behind. Micah followed them out, closing the door softly behind him.

Larus barely noticed the study around him. The fire crackled, throwing long shadows over the polished oak desk, the heavy bookshelves, the oil paintings of long-dead ancestors. He had hardly moved from the same spot since stepping inside. The space that had once made him feel like an intruder now felt like a confessional.

His mother spoke first. "Larus, you must know... we have always wanted what is best for you." Her voice was steady, but she glanced at his father, seeking silent agreement.

Larus dropped his gaze to the thick woollen rug beneath his feet. He heard the shift of silk, the soft scuff of shoes. His mother was small, delicate in frame, yet when she reached for him, he tensed. Was he still cold? Had the fire warmed him enough?

Then, suddenly, she threw herself against him.

"Oh, my dear boy... my son." She wept openly, her sobs breaking against his chest. "My only son!"

Larus stiffened, caught between shock and an overwhelming, inescapable grief. His mother had never shown such emotion—not once in all his life. And now, as she clung to him, trembling, he felt her pain. He felt his own.

His body shook, and he willed himself not to shed the damning blood tears that threatened to rise. He shut his eyes, gripping her tightly, memorizing this moment before it was lost forever.

"I love you so much, my boy," she whispered.

A deep rumble forced Larus's eyes open. His father.

Maxwell Bleddyn had drawn closer, his presence commanding as always, yet his face... his face was not stern. There was no anger there, only something raw and unfamiliar.

"Igraine, my love," his father murmured, placing a steadying hand on her shoulder. "You mustn't—"

"I cannot help it, Maxwell." She turned to him, tilting her chin up, her grief giving her a boldness Larus had never seen before. "We did a terrible thing, Maxwell... a terrible thing."

His father stiffened.

"And now you must fix it," she demanded, pressing a gloved hand against his chest. "Fix it, Maxwell! Or I shall die an unhappy woman!"

She turned back to Larus, cupped his face briefly, and kissed his cheek. Then, without another word, she swept from the room, her absence a vacuum that pulled at something deep inside him.

The door clicked shut.

Larus turned to his father.

The firelight flickered in the glossy sheen of Maxwell Bleddyn's eyes. The proud and unshakable Maxwell Bleddyn. Speechless.

Larus had never seen his father like this. Yet the weight of the moment pressed on him, and he knew—his father had much to say.

"You are my son," Maxwell said, his voice quieter than Larus had ever heard it. "My only son. And..." A single tear escaped, tracing down the sharp plane of his cheek. "I know you believe I never loved you, Larus—"

"Father, I—"

"I am speaking."

The sharp lift of his father's brow stilled Larus immediately. The familiar tic—the same raised brow that had always accompanied scoldings, disappointments, frustrations. Yet this time, Maxwell exhaled shakily and dragged his fingers through his beard, as if he himself was afraid of what he was about to say.

"I was afraid to show that love," he admitted. "Unwilling to become attached to the one thing I loved more than anything else in this world... my only son."

Larus inhaled sharply.

Maxwell's voice grew hoarse, ragged. "Do you know what it is to live every day knowing you will lose your child? To accept that my son and heir—my only son—would die long before I did? It was impossible, Larus."

And then, for the first time in his life, Larus saw his father weep.

Tears that had never been shed for childhood wounds or harsh words. Tears that Larus had believed his father incapable of.

Maxwell Bleddyn sobbed.

Larus's throat closed. How does one comfort a man he has feared all his life?

The fear was still there, but it had changed. It was no longer the fear of an unyielding, untouchable man—it was the fear of something fragile. Something breakable.

Larus hesitated, then took a step forward. Another.

And then, with quiet reluctance, he wrapped his arms around his father.

Maxwell's body convulsed as he clung to him. "You are my son, and I love you, Larus." His arms, strong as they had always been, squeezed Larus against him. "Your mother begged me to treat you as I did your sisters, to let you live a happy life. But I was afraid, my boy. Ashamed. And I hope you can forgive me."

Larus swallowed the ache in his throat. "I do, Father. I always loved you, always admired you." He did not mention the hurt, the loneliness. Some wounds did not need to be reopened.

He cleared his throat. "Micah... Doctor Duncan says there are treatments—ways to help me live longer."

His father straightened slightly. "Larus, I should have told you long ago. Explained everything." A sigh. "But you have always fought me on everything."

A trace of amusement flickered through Larus, but it was brief.

Maxwell turned, wiping his tears away as he walked back to his desk. Larus discreetly took out a handkerchief and dabbed the corners of his own eyes.

Clearing his throat, Maxwell sat and motioned for Larus to take the wingback chair near him. His tone turned businesslike, as if regaining control was the only way to cope.

"I have spoken with the doctor, Larus," he said. "And I don't want us to argue over it." He steepled his fingers. "Should anything happen—"

"Father, Doctor Duncan explained everything." Larus cut in, sparing him from having to say it aloud. "I have agreed to it all. Even to what will become of my remains if I die."

Maxwell inhaled deeply, exhaling slow. Again, that flicker of pain.

Larus had been blind to it before. But now, he saw it for what it was.

"I wish we had spoken sooner," Maxwell murmured.

Larus nodded. "I will write often, Father. And I will visit."

His father smiled then—a real smile.

And Larus, despite everything, smiled back.

For the first time, he saw it clearly. It had not been hatred that had shaped his father's coldness.

It had been fear.

And now, more than anything, Larus wanted to tell his father the truth. To tell him what he had become.

But it was not time. Not yet.

LARUS COULD HEAR THE MUSIC FROM THE BALLROOM BELOW—LAUGHTER, dancing, the swell of strings and flutes. The wedding celebration continued, oblivious to the quiet farewell taking place in his chambers.

His mother, his three sisters, and Tilley remained with him. His trunks were already loaded into the carriage, though he doubted he would ever truly need anything in his new life. A vampire had few earthly needs. But the memories—those, he wished to keep.

From Max, he had begged for her gold bracelet, the one she never removed. Isabelle had given him a silver locket she had worn as a child. Catherine, reluctant to part with her precious trinkets, instead snipped a lock of her hair, tying it with a silk ribbon.

Tilley had only smiled. "I have love to give," she had said simply.

Larus had wanted nothing more.

Then his mother left the room. When she returned, it was with something unexpected. In her hands, she carried a small, folded parchment.

"Your father may not forgive me for this," she admitted, casting a brief glance at Max, who frowned at the sight of it. "But I feel you should have it."

Larus took the letter hesitantly, running his fingers over the familiar wax seal—the crest of Bleddyn.

"Your father wrote this the day I told him I was with child," she said.

Max scowled. "You needn't run to him about this, Max," their mother warned. "I shall tell him myself."

Larus turned the letter over in his palm, weighing its significance. What had his father written all those years ago? He would not open it now. Not yet.

Downstairs, the wedding feast continued, chandeliers casting golden light across the hall. The scent of candlewax, wine, and roasted meat lingered in the air. Laughter rang from the ballroom, but Larus felt none of its warmth.

His goodbyes had been said in the privacy of his rooms. Now, as he descended the grand staircase, the weight of what he was leaving behind settled heavily upon him.

Would he ever walk these halls again?

At the entrance, his father was waiting. Before prying eyes, Maxwell Bleddyn did not embrace him. Instead, he extended his hand. Larus clasped it, the grip firm and deliberate. But when his father met his gaze, there was something else—something unspoken, yet deeply felt.

A smile. A true one.

"This is my last hope," his father said, so softly that only Larus could hear. "I did this only to save you."

Larus hesitated, looking past him to where Micah waited by the carriage. He wanted to tell him. Wanted to ease the pain in his father's eyes and say, I will live.

But how could he ever explain that he was already dead?

He had promised himself he would not look back.

Yet, as he climbed into the carriage, a sudden wave of unease swept over him.

From the shadows beyond the lamplight, three figures stood watching. The Hearne family.

Bartholomew Hearne's gaze did not waver. His eyes were fixed upon Larus and Micah, dark with knowing.

It was as though he saw them. Knew them for what they were.

A cold dread settled in Larus's bones.

He knows.

10

A NEW HOME

The journey to the capital was long, and though sunrise was still hours away, Larus dreaded its arrival.

Much had been discussed in the confines of the carriage—chief among them, the revelation that Micah was the founder of a prominent medical facility. It was, according to him, vital to their survival.

As they passed through the city, Larus gazed out the window in quiet awe. Though the night softened its edges, his vampire sight revealed every detail—the towering spires, the grand townhouses, the gleaming shopfronts. It stirred something in him, a distant memory tugging at the edges of his mind.

"Father must have brought the family here," he murmured. "I was just a boy... yes, very young."

Micah chuckled. "The little prince of the Bleddyn family."

Larus turned sharply. "What do you know of my life?"

Micah placed a hand on his knee, and Larus tensed at the sudden contact. "You may find some memories difficult to reach now," Micah said. "Your mind is open—unguarded." His smile was sly. "Among our kind, that is dangerous. I must teach you to shield yourself before you meet others."

"There are others?"

Micah's gaze darkened. "We are everywhere, Larus. Even here, in this city."

Larus felt a thrill of excitement, but his maker lifted a cautionary finger. "Do not let curiosity make you careless. Vampires can be treacherous beings. We are of many houses, many covens, and they do not always thrive in peace."

Larus hesitated. "You speak from experience."

"I was of Emilio's coven," Micah said, his voice turning cold. "After his destruction, there was nothing to hold the younger vampires together. Some fled. Some were hunted. Many died." His grip on Larus's knee tightened, betraying his anger.

Larus hesitated before asking, "And the catacombs? The old church?"

Micah's expression shifted. He leaned back, smiling faintly. "You ask this now, young one?"

Larus frowned, puzzled by his reaction.

"I am the only living vampire who knows what lies beneath your family's land," Micah said.

Larus thought of the hidden chamber two levels beneath the cemetery—the sealed door. What was beyond it?

"But about those lands..." Micah's tone became sharp. "I am bound to secrecy."

Larus opened his mouth to press further—

"Ah, we have arrived!" Micah declared, just as the carriage came to an abrupt halt.

The coachman leapt down to open the tall black gates. As they passed through, Larus leaned out to take in the estate beyond. The castle loomed ahead, its silhouette outlined against the deep blue of the night. To the west, gardens stretched into darkness; to the east, a towering hedge wall marked the entrance to a labyrinth.

"A maze," Micah murmured, watching Larus's reaction.

Larus could not hide his awe. Micah was powerful.

The carriage rolled to a stop in the courtyard. As the double doors of the castle swung open, a tall, lean man stepped into view.

"Mr. Duncan," he greeted with a slight bow. "Welcome home, sir."

"As always, Giles," Micah replied smoothly. "Your timing is impeccable."

The servant straightened his striped waistcoat, his sharp features betraying only the faintest trace of amusement. "I saw the carriage lamps from my window, sir."

His gaze flickered toward Larus, assessing him with cool precision. And though he said nothing, Larus could feel that the man knew.

His unease must have shown, for Micah placed a hand on his back. "Giles, this is Larus," he said. "He is family. He has come home."

At that, Giles bowed. Without another word, he led them inside.

THE FOYER WAS ALIVE WITH CANDLELIGHT, THE SCENT OF FRESH FLOWERS drifting through the air. Velvet benches lined the walls, and ancient portraits watched from above. A grand chandelier cast golden illumination across the polished marble floors.

Micah led the way down a long corridor. Giles disappeared somewhere within the vast mansion.

"This place..." Larus whispered, taking it all in. "How is it that you live like this?"

Micah's smirk was slow. "You mean, why don't I live underground?"

Larus hesitated. "The catacombs—"

"Were fitting... once." Micah closed the doors behind them and sank onto one of the twin couches. He gestured for Larus to sit opposite. "For one who lived as a slave, they were all I had."

Larus stilled.

Micah leaned back, eyes flickering to the ceiling. "Emilio was the master of this house. After his destruction, I quickly learned that a long life was not the only legacy he left me." He exhaled, almost wistful. "If only Mama could see me now."

Something in his voice had changed.

"I searched for her," he admitted. "For years. I wasted decades chasing rumours, traveling from city to city. But I never found her. I never knew if she was dead, or simply… beyond my reach."

Larus's throat tightened. "Micah, I—"

"My maker convinced me to let go," Micah cut in, voice quieter now. "He said she was gone. And I believed him."

A silence settled between them.

Eventually, Larus rose from the couch, his attention drawn to something on the far wall. A massive canvas. He hadn't noticed it before, yet now, he couldn't look away.

A woman stood at the centre of the painting.

Her skin was dark as polished mahogany, glowing beneath a sunlit sky. She stood tall, unyielding, strength exuding from every inch of her. Her black plaits cascaded beyond her shoulders, one resting against her forehead. She wore a torn red skirt that brushed against the long blades of grass at her feet. An indigo blouse clung to her, accentuating the proud lift of her shoulders. She did not smile—yet there was joy in her. A force that seemed to radiate from the very canvas.

Larus swallowed. "Your mother."

Micah said nothing.

"She is… beautiful."

"It is how I remember her."

Larus stepped closer. "You captured her essence." His voice was hushed. "I feel she is here with us now."

Micah gave a faint, sad smile.

"I didn't know you were an artist."

"I have many gifts, young one."

Micah joined him before the painting, draping an arm over his shoulder. For a long moment, they stood in silence.

Finally, Micah turned him gently toward the door.

"I come here when I am at my weakest," he said. Then, softer, "But now, we must leave Mama in peace."

He guided Larus forward.

"Come," he said. "Let me show you your new home."

11

BARTHOLOMEW HEARNE

The wedding was over.

By tradition, Bartholomew had taken his new wife under his protection, but nothing about this marriage had unfolded as he had imagined.

Maxine had not allowed him to touch her—not in the way a husband was meant to touch a wife. They had shared a bed after the wedding feast, but that was all.

Now, Bartholomew lay beneath the covers, watching as Maxine paced at the foot of their bed. Her long hair cascaded down her back, dark silk over pale skin, and the dressing gown she wore clung to her curves. The vision of her stirred something primal within him, an overwhelming desire that quickly turned to frustration.

No, not frustration. Anger.

Maxine—Max, as she insisted he call her—had spent the night taunting him. He had caught the glint in her eye, the slight tilt of her chin, the way she let the candlelight dance over the bare skin of her throat and wrists. Yet, despite it all, she had withheld the one thing a wife was supposed to give.

What good was a wife who refused her womanly duties?

Bartholomew clenched his jaw, his hands curling into fists beneath the sheets. He did not understand why his father had been so adamant about this match. And worse still, why had Maxwell Bleddyn demanded that his daughter remain in his household?

What hold does he have over my father?

His father-in-law had insisted on this marriage. Bartholomew had thought it would bring him power, yet here he was, stripped of control before the union had even begun.

It was still early. The night had been long, and he was tired of watching Max flaunt her shapely figure before him, pretending he was not there, as if he were some lesser man.

Max turned, her eyes bright with calculation. "We must speak with our fathers," she said, as if she had not just spent the night in his bed untouched. "Together, we could build a shipping empire—expand our reach, import luxury goods."

Her gaze flicked over him, but she did not see him.

Bartholomew exhaled sharply. Business. Always business.

A woman should know little of such things. That was his domain.

"Come to bed, wife." His voice was low, coaxing. "We have all morning to make our plans." He pushed the sheets aside, revealing himself, his body already stirring at the sight of her. A slow smile spread across his face as he saw her reaction.

Max's breath hitched. She stood motionless at the foot of the bed, her gaze locked onto the hardness between his legs.

Now, he thought, *let us see how long you can resist.*

But something changed.

Max hugged herself, her body trembling—not with want, but with rage. Her brows drew together, her lips curling, not in desire, but disgust.

"You are a horrible man," she spat.

Then she turned and stalked out of the room, leaving him alone with the remnants of his anger and something far worse—humiliation.

"THIS IS NOT THE PLACE TO BE THE MORNING AFTER YOUR WEDDING NIGHT, Bart."

Bartholomew's father sat near the fire, still dressed in his housecoat, a cup of dark tea cradled in his hands. He barely spared his son a glance before turning his gaze back to the flames. "The morning after your mother and I were married, we didn't leave our chambers until suppertime." His voice carried a smug satisfaction, thick with pride.

Bartholomew said nothing. He had spent an hour lying in bed, scowling at the ceiling after Max had left him. She never returned.

Now, seething, he had sought out his father, only to be met with indifference. The older Hearne waved a dismissive hand. "I say, these chambers are hardly fit for people of our standing." His eyes flicked around the room, his expression souring. "Bleddyn has surely let his family fall from grace. His ancestors must be turning in their graves." He shook his head and turned back toward the fire.

"Your mother has gone for morning tea with Bleddyn's wife—the poor thing." He took a slow sip of tea, then finally looked at his son, as though only just noticing him. "God knows what I would have done if I learned you would drop dead by your twenty-second birthday. But we are of good stock, us Hearnes."

Bartholomew exhaled sharply, fists clenched at his sides. "Father, have you not heard a word I've said?"

The words had barely left his mouth when he realized his mistake. He had raised his voice.

His father stilled.

Slowly, he set his tea down and turned to face him.

Bartholomew swallowed hard, heart hammering. "Forgive me, Father, it's just that—"

"I see you have failed." His father's voice was low, venomous. He rose from the chair, closing the distance between them in measured, deliberate steps. "You let this little girl strip away whatever manhood you had left."

They were of equal height. Inches apart, Bartholomew forced himself to stand still as his father's breath, thick with tea and age, warmed his face.

"You are my only son," his father murmured. "I have no spare. If I did, I suspect he would manage this little wench better than you."

Spittle landed on Bartholomew's cheek. He flinched.

His father scoffed. "Have you forgotten who we are?" He grasped Bartholomew's shoulder, his fingers digging in with bruising strength. "We are hunters. Our very name carries that meaning. Hearne. We take what we want."

Bartholomew hesitated.

"She speaks only of business, Father."

His father's grip tightened. "Then break her."

Bartholomew tensed.

"You must strip away whatever power she thinks she has." His father's lips curled into a knowing smile. "Women are like horses, boy. Break their spirit, and you have their loyalty and obedience forever."

He turned away, back toward the fire, as though the conversation was already over.

"You need my help with this, boy?"

Bartholomew hesitated, then forced himself to say the words.

"Yes, Father."

His father did not turn.

"You will do as I tell you."

12

A SPIRIT BROKEN

The Bleddyn home had settled back into its usual rhythm. Nearly two weeks had passed since the wedding, and despite the biting cold of the Sunday morning, Max had no interest in attending church with her family. Instead, she pulled her fur cloak tightly around her shoulders and wandered into the woods, seeking solace among the bare trees.

She could still see the main house through the skeletal branches, its chimney smoke curling into the sky. The sight should have comforted her, but instead, it only reminded her of the guests who had long overstayed their welcome. Why haven't they left? Bartholomew's parents should have returned to their own home days ago, yet Percival Hearne lingered, as if waiting for something.

Max exhaled sharply, her breath misting in the cold air. She had needed this walk—to clear her head, to put distance between herself and the house where she felt more like a prisoner than a bride. That morning, she had met with her father, seeking guidance, only to leave seething with rage.

He sided with Bartholomew.

She had always trusted her father's wisdom, relied on him as her confidant. A part of her had even considered going to her mother instead, but something told her that would have been even worse. Surely her father would understand. But when she had spoken of Bartholomew's demands, of her disgust at the expectation placed upon her, he had simply told her to give in.

Max had stormed from the house, furious. My body is my own. No one should decide who touches it but me.

Her grip tightened around a fallen branch, and without thinking, she swung it hard against the nearest tree. Once. Twice. Three times. The sharp cracks echoed through the silent woods before she let the branch drop uselessly into the frozen leaves.

She clenched her jaw. Even he has betrayed me.

For the first time in her life, she saw herself for what she truly was—a pawn in her father's grandest, most successful business transaction.

"Why is it my duty to lie there and be ravished?" The words came unbidden, her voice sharp in the empty forest.

No answer came. Only the wind, rustling through the brittle branches.

By the time she returned to the manor, the servants were already deep in their work. Tilley was still at church, and Max climbed the stairs, hearing the muffled voices of Bartholomew and his father locked in one of their endless debates in the library. She ignored them.

In her room, she let the fur cloak slip from her shoulders and crumple onto the floor. She sat heavily on the bed, exhaustion creeping over her, and after a moment, she lay back against the pillows, eyes slipping shut.

She tried—tried—to see things differently.

Her sisters would have envied her position. They had giggled at the very mention of Bartholomew's name, swooned over his strong jaw and his piercing eyes. Should she be grateful? Should she surrender to him and play the role she was expected to?

The thought made her stomach twist.

Max had never known a man's touch, had never wanted to. The idea of Bartholomew—towering over her, pressing her into the mattress—sent a bolt of fear through her. And yet...

A traitorous warmth stirred in her belly.

She frowned, eyes still closed.

It was wrong to feel even a flicker of desire, yet it crept into her, unbidden, unwelcome.

The moment sickened her.

And yet, as sleep pulled her under, that warmth refused to fade.

SHE HAD BEEN DREAMING.

Max remained still, eyes closed, clinging to the lingering warmth of slumber. A part of her longed to return to that world, to the phantom touch that had set her aflame. A faint smile ghosted across her lips as she willed the dream to stay, holding onto the fragments before they faded into waking.

In that dream, she had been free.

Her hair had tumbled loose over her shoulders, her hands cupping the fullness of her breasts as she moved atop Bartholomew. He lay beneath her, his head pressed into the pillows, tossing from side to side. His breath came in ragged gasps. She had him under her spell—she was in control. He had begged her, pleaded for release, but she had held him there, teetering on the edge of that intoxicating crescendo.

A shiver ran through her.

And then—something changed.

A whisper of awareness prickled at the back of her mind. The air in the room felt different, charged in a way that did not belong to sleep. A presence. She was not alone.

Max's breath hitched.

Her eyes fluttered open.

Max's breath caught in her throat. Percival stood closest to her bed, his imposing frame blocking the room's only exit. He had promised his son things would go his way, and now he intended to see it through. The girl was shuffling back against the pillows, her dark blue gown bunched around her legs, her chest rising and falling too quickly.

Good, Percival thought. Let her be afraid.

Bartholomew stood behind him, rigid, unmoving. Percival scowled. He had raised his son to be a hunter, not a coward. He turned slightly, his voice low and commanding.

"Get on with it, boy."

But Bartholomew hesitated. His father's words, once law, now scraped against something raw inside him. He had wanted Max to submit, to obey—but this? This was not how it was supposed to be. She was supposed to give in willingly. She was supposed to want him.

Max's gaze flicked between father and son, her fear shifting into something else—disgust, defiance.

Bartholomew swallowed hard, a cold sweat gathering at his nape. This was wrong.

"Father, I—"

Percival turned on him sharply. "You hesitate?" His voice was quiet but deadly. "You let a girl rule you?"

Bartholomew's hands clenched at his sides. He had spent his life seeking his father's approval, believing strength meant control. But standing here now, watching the terror in Max's eyes, something inside him cracked.

She was not his to take.

And suddenly, for the first time, Bartholomew wondered if his father was a man he should follow at all.

Bartholomew had seen his father's nakedness in the baths when he was younger, but now, watching him disrobe, a wave of terror washed over him like never before. He stood frozen at the foot of the bed, unable to tear his gaze away from Max.

He saw the fear in her eyes, and for the first time, he realized the gravity of what his father had pushed him into. Max didn't scream. She slapped his father's face and pounded at his chest, but it was useless. His father was too strong, and with one hand, he held her down. She fought with every ounce of her will, but she was no match for his power.

Max groaned, her resistance crumbling, and finally, she lay still. Tears pooled in her eyes, and she didn't blink or turn her head. Her gaze stayed locked on Bartholomew. In that moment, he knew: she hated him.

The minutes stretched on like hours. Bartholomew felt a sickening weight settle in his chest as his father finished what he had begun. His father's body relaxed, and with a final motion, he rolled off of Max, leaving her limp and broken.

"Now, boy, be a man and take what's yours," his father growled, locking eyes with Bartholomew. There was no choice.

Bartholomew's feet felt like lead as he walked toward the bed. His heart pounded, and his hands trembled. He saw the fists clenched in helpless rage, the slow rise and fall of her chest.

As he lowered himself to her, Max turned her face away and shut her eyes, trying to retreat into herself.

Bartholomew couldn't do it. He couldn't look at her. His body hovered above hers, but the hatred and the disgust that twisted in his gut kept him frozen. He heard his father getting dressed in the background, the sound of the door creaking shut, and then silence.

Bartholomew was alone with his wife. Still lying on top of her, his body shaking with emotion, he felt the tears begin to fall. Silent, uncontrollable sobs racked his chest as he realized the depth of the betrayal. The weight of what they had done—what he had allowed to happen—was unbearable. And in that moment, he understood the extent of the pain, not just for Max, but for himself.

13

A NEW COVEN

Snow blanketed the city in early December, its abundance softening the harsh lines of the cobbled streets. Larus barely noticed the cold. He had grown up in the countryside and was accustomed to unforgiving winters. Over the months, he had come to know his coachman, Ashkan, though drawing conversation from him was a rarity. Micah found this amusing.

"I believe Ashkan likes you, young one," Micah said as their carriage moved slowly through the gates of White Castle, descending the hill toward the city road. "He rarely takes to visitors or friends."

Larus bit his lip. "I cannot read his thoughts."

Micah laughed. "That is no surprise. Ashkan has been with me since he was a boy. He has been my willing donor for nearly thirty years." He reclined against the padded seat, eyes distant as he spoke. "I found him wandering the docks of a Persian port. The boy had no one. I was about to embark on a long journey by sea and needed a helper. A vampire's voyage is no simple thing, you see—trapped in a crate with the cargo by day, forced to hunt among the crew and passengers by night. Too many deaths, and suspicion arises."

He turned slightly, meeting Larus's gaze. "I told Ashkan what I was, and without fear, he agreed to come with me. I believe he saw it as salvation." Micah's lips curved slightly. "He saved many lives aboard that vessel—passengers, crew...even the vermin skittering below deck. I drank from him sparingly, enough to sustain me for a night, sometimes two. And in return, he lived like a prince, with his own cabin and all the food he could eat."

Larus frowned. "He must be close to forty now."

"You wonder why I have not turned him." Micah draped an arm over Larus's shoulder, an unexpectedly familiar gesture that stirred something unfamiliar in him. "He made a vow the day I found him—to serve as a donor. I know he longs for more."

"Will you turn him?"

Micah's expression remained unreadable. "I do all things for a purpose."

Larus could only imagine the torment of yearning for immortality and being denied. But he said no more. The carriage wheels crunched over the frozen road, and the two vampires sat in silence.

Larus turned his gaze to the window, watching the delicate white flakes spiral downward. The sight stirred a different longing within him. Memories crept into his mind—his family, his father's embrace. He had read the letter his father had written long before his birth, words that had imprinted themselves onto his soul. From the moment he existed, his father had loved him. Yet love had not been enough.

Max had been showered with their father's devotion while Larus had been cast aside. Every plan, every promise meant for him had gone to his twin instead. He did not hate them for it—he could not—but the ache of what might have been gnawed at him.

Larus longed to see them again.

MUCH OF THE CITY LAY IN SLUMBER. MIDNIGHT APPROACHED, AND THE streets were nearly silent—save for the distant creak of wagon wheels and the occasional murmur of labourers clearing the snow.

Shortly after Ashkan had delivered them to Micah's medical building, the two vampires had left the sick and dying behind, stepping into the frigid night. Snow fell in a slow, soundless drift, clinging to their coats as they walked. They passed several men working tirelessly to clear the streets, and Larus felt the hunger stir within him. The scent of their blood, thick and warm beneath their layers of wool, made his throat tighten. The instinct to hunt was primal, insistent.

Micah had warned him of this.

"You must never give in to impulse," his maker had said. "Every corpse found drained of blood invites suspicion."

So instead, they fed on those who were already slipping away—the sick, the dying. Those who, as Micah reasoned, would not be missed.

Larus studied his maker as they walked, admiring the wisdom in his restraint. "What becomes of the bodies after we feed?" he asked.

A faint smile touched Micah's lips. A fine dusting of snow had gathered on his black hat and shoulders. "The wealthy have options. Those who donate their bodies to medical research must enter a binding contract." He stepped lightly over a frozen puddle. "With the poor, we need only their word, their promise."

Larus quickened his steps to keep pace. "But why not save them?" he asked. "Surely some—"

"And where would I keep hundreds of newly turned vampires?" Micah interrupted. "You are the exception, Larus. Most newborns are difficult to control." He glanced at him. "I have seen my own maker destroy fledglings within days of turning them—because they threatened to expose our existence. Wayward, disobedient children can bring ruin to a coven."

Micah fell silent for a moment before continuing. "I once knew a vampire who lost everything because he spared a newborn he could not control. Stelio Ballas was very dear to me, but the council took his head for his mistake." He exhaled, the faintest trace of breath visible in the icy air. "There are large covens in this city, but I choose to keep my distance."

He stopped and placed a firm hand on Larus's shoulder. "And then there's the fact that they know I am Emilio's child."

Larus held his gaze. "What was Emilio to you? And to them?"

Micah's expression darkened. "Emilio was the father of us all. He was powerful. Every vampire wanted to belong to his coven. Most feared him." His voice grew quieter, as if lost in the weight of old memories.

Larus wanted to press him for more, but he knew better.

Micah shook off the reverie. "Emilio feared one thing above all else—that a newborn's recklessness could doom us all. If I had left you to roam freely after your turning, how many would have died? How many would have disappeared in the night?" He met Larus's eyes. "I have seen fledglings return to their homes and slaughter their own kin because they could not control their thirst."

Larus hesitated. "You don't like to kill."

"I kill when I must." Micah's tone was even. "I do not starve, thanks to those poor souls." He motioned toward the medical building—their source of food. "Not all of them have to die. I save those I can. I am a doctor." His steps slowed. "But if I know a patient will not live through the night... why should I let their blood go to waste? Once death claims them, their blood is useless to us."

He turned, offering Larus his arm. "Come, young one. Goodwife Barnes will meet her maker tonight. We must feed."

Larus followed, still unsettled by the act, yet unable to deny its practicality. In securing access to human blood, Micah had ensured they would never go hungry.

GOODWIFE BARNES LAY IN BED, HER BREATH SHALLOW, SWEAT BEADING ON her brow. "Doctor..." she whispered, voice brittle as old parchment. "... Think it's time."

Her eyes fluttered closed for a moment. Each breath came slower, more laboured.

Larus glanced across the bed at his maker. Micah held his gaze and gave a single nod—silent, expectant. The meaning was clear.

Take her.

Larus hesitated.

"Do it now, young one," Micah murmured. His voice was low, insistent. "Take her over the river of life."

Still, Larus wavered.

"She has given her permission," Micah reminded him. "Ease her pain."

The truth of it beat like a dying drum in Larus's ears. He could hear the woman's heart struggling, each slow, weakening pulse a signal of the inevitable. Death was coming for her. He was merely hastening its arrival.

Slowly, he leaned in.

The old woman gasped as his fangs pierced the thin, papery skin of her neck. A final shudder passed through her body—then she relaxed.

"Thank you," she whispered.

Larus stilled. He had not expected gratitude.

The warmth of her blood filled his mouth, rich and fleeting. And as he drank, a strange contentment settled over him.

14

HUNGER

Life as a vampire was comfortable enough, yet loneliness crept in like an unwelcome shadow. The silence, at times, was unbearable.

Micah had given Larus everything—immortality, shelter, and knowledge—but nothing could prepare him for the weight of solitude.

He woke that night to an empty castle. Micah was gone. So was Ashkan, along with the black carriage. Larus assumed they had gone to the medical building.

A blizzard raged outside, but Larus was restless. He decided to walk. He could reach his maker in moments, but he preferred to take his time, to savour the snowy night.

By the time he reached the towering black gates, his boots were caked in frost. With a single leap, he cleared the iron bars and landed gracefully on the other side. The ease of it brought a smile to his face.

He set off toward the city.

The castle sat alone in a remote quarter, where human presence was rare, but south of it lay a quiet town, its streets lined with grand homes for the wealthy and humble dwellings for the poor. Larus chose to pass through, admiring the scenery.

Then he smelled it—warm breath in the cold air, laced with ale.

He heard it—footsteps crunching through fresh snow, a steady heartbeat pulsing through the dark.

The man appeared moments later, walking toward him, oblivious. He was young, perhaps thirty, wrapped in a thin coat. Rough hands. A simple labourer.

He whistled to himself, at ease in his drunkenness.

Larus should have walked away.

But something new stirred inside him. A hunger unlike anything he had known.

The human finally noticed him, a dark silhouette lingering ahead. The whistling stopped. He faltered, confused.

Larus's fangs slid into place.

The man took a step back.

It was already too late.

Larus moved in a blur, lifting his prey off the ground, sinking his teeth deep into warm, yielding flesh. Hot blood flooded his mouth. The man convulsed, then slackened in his grip.

Larus knelt, lowering him into the snow, still drinking, drinking, drinking.

The body beneath him grew limp. He barely stopped in time.

Then—

A gasp.

Larus looked up.

A second man stood at the end of the alley, frozen in horror.

"No," Larus breathed.

His hands were still bloodied. His fangs still bared. The corpse at his feet lay wide-eyed in the snow.

The witness stumbled back, then fell before scrambling onto hands and knees. In an instant, he was up and running.

Larus didn't chase him. He couldn't move.

"What have I done?"

But the moment of stillness passed. He had no choice now. He leapt onto the rooftops, tracking the man's pounding heart and ragged breaths. The rooftops blurred beneath his feet. Then he dropped, landing soundlessly before the terrified human.

The man skidded to a halt.

"Please... leave me be!"

Larus hesitated. He wiped the blood from his mouth with a trembling hand.

"I... mean you no harm—"

"You killed him. You... you sucked—"

A blur of black behind him.

A sickening crack.

The man crumpled.

Larus staggered back. Micah loomed above the fresh corpse, his expression grim.

"Return to the castle."

"Micah—something came over me. I—I'm sorry. I couldn't—"

"Leave." Micah didn't look at him. His voice was ice. "Go now before I destroy you."

Larus fled.

15

A NEW HEIR

Percival Hearne sat behind his desk, pipe in hand, watching the door with measured patience.

He had not seen Bartholomew since leaving the Bleddyn estate. The boy had been avoiding him. But today, father and son would finally stand face to face.

The door creaked open.

Bartholomew stepped inside, his eyes dark with rage.

Percival smiled.

"There he is! My son! My boy!"

Bartholomew stood motionless, his hands clenched at his sides. Was that hatred in his eyes?

Percival leaned back, exhaling a stream of smoke. "I doubt you've come to tell me your beautiful wife is madly in love with you." His gaze flicked toward the chair by his desk. The moment Bartholomew moved to it, Percival knew—he still had a hold on him.

"And I doubt she's breathed a word to her family about what happened that Sunday."

Bartholomew sat stiffly, his silence louder than any outburst. For the first time, Percival felt something unexpected—disappointment. He had failed the boy somehow. He had not done enough to make him a man.

"If you hate me for putting that girl in her place, I care not," Percival said, thumping the desk with his fist.

Bartholomew finally spoke.

"She hates me, Father."

Percival scoffed. "This match had nothing to do with love."

Bartholomew's voice was quiet but firm. "Max... she's different."

"We broke her." Percival exhaled, satisfied. "You would have let that woman wield power over you, just as she does her father. But you are a Hearne. We come from a line of strong men, boy. You know our history. I have told you of Chasen Hearne and his son, my great-grandfather, Cyrus Hearne."

Bartholomew hesitated, then said, "Max is with child, Father." His jaw tightened. "And every time I look at her, I... I cannot help but think—"

"Which one of us fathered it."

Bartholomew stiffened.

Percival grinned. "What does it matter? The child is a Hearne."

He tapped the pipe against the edge of the desk, watching his son closely. "There is much we need to discuss, you and I. It concerns the Bleddyns and their ancestry."

Bartholomew's brow furrowed. "Max's family? Father, I don't understand."

Percival leaned in, his voice low and deliberate. "Maxwell Bleddyn inherited those lands and wealth without knowing the truth of his past."

He held his son's gaze.

"What I tell you now must never leave this room."

BARTHOLOMEW'S FATHER HAD RISEN FROM HIS DESK AND WAS PACING THE floor.

A thousand questions burned on Bartholomew's tongue, but he remained silent, watching his father's frown deepen. The older Hearne's demeanour commanded stillness, echoing the words drilled into him as a boy—*Now, boy, you will listen!*

He exhaled slowly, fingers laced across his lap, his right foot tapping against the floor.

Percival noticed. His sharp glance was enough. Bartholomew stopped.

At last, his father spoke.

“Do you know the true meaning of our great name?”

Bartholomew hesitated. This was a lesson he had learned long ago. “Yes, Father. Our name—Hearne—means hunter.”

Percival paused before him, shoulders squared, hands buried deep in his pockets. “From this day forward, Bartholomew, I urge you to take that meaning literally, my boy.”

He moved back toward his desk.

“For centuries, those who bore our name were feared. We were hunters. But times change.” His voice grew more animated. “History, however, repeats itself.”

Bartholomew frowned but held his tongue.

“And what of your wife’s name?” Percival asked.

Bartholomew shrugged.

“What do you know of Bleddyn, Bartholomew?”

He grimaced slightly, tilting his head. “Father, I’ve never stopped to—”

“Names define us.” Percival’s voice was sharp. “And they carry knowledge.”

He plucked an aged parchment from his desk and handed it to his son.

Bartholomew’s eyes skimmed the page. “It says… the name Bleddyn means *wolf hero*.”

“Indeed.” Percival snatched the parchment back before he could read further.

Returning to his desk, Percival’s voice dropped to a measured tone. “Centuries ago, long before my great-grandfather’s time, there was a family of immortals.”

Bartholomew barely suppressed a smirk.

Percival’s eyes flashed. “This is serious business, boy! You would do well to listen.”

Bartholomew straightened. “Forgive me, Father, I—”

"A fool you are." Percival's voice was cutting. "Hold your tongue and listen."

Bartholomew felt the familiar weight of his father's authority pressing down on him, stripping away his confidence.

"This family—these immortals—possessed a rare gift. Two gifts. Not only did some among them live eternally, but they could transform, Bartholomew."

Percival leaned forward, lowering his voice to a whisper.

"Some among them became beasts—wolves. Hence their noble name: Bleddyn. Wolf hero."

He let the words settle before continuing. "They were this. And are still. But the Bleddyns of this age are blind to their past. Maxwell Bleddyn is a fool, and he does not realize the thing in his blood—the truth behind his only son's affliction."

Bartholomew stiffened. "The boy... Larus?"

Percival nodded. "You may be older than the young Bleddyn boy, Bartholomew." His voice grew deliberate. "But he will not live long. It is his twin sister—your wife—who carries the legacy of the wolf."

Bartholomew's breath caught. "Max's baby... my..." He faltered, unable to finish.

Visions of his father's body atop his wife consumed him.

Percival's smile was cold.

"We shall never truly know, shall we?" His voice was almost amused. "Which of us fathered that child."

Bartholomew felt sick.

"But rest assured, it will be a son," Percival continued. "A Hearne. And he will have the legacy of the wolf."

Bartholomew swallowed hard.

Now, at last, he understood.

This had never been about business. Never about securing alliances.

His father had married him to Max Bleddyn for this.

For the bloodline.

16

THE SOIRÉE

It was the end of December, and winter seemed endless.

By day, Larus and Micah slept in stone sarcophagi deep beneath the castle, entombed beneath slabs so heavy that not even Ashkan and Giles together could shift them. The locks sealed them both from within and without, and Larus often marvelled at the craftsmanship. How had such mechanisms been created?

The castle's underground chambers were vast, with enough sarcophagi to house an entire coven. Yet, only two of them lived there.

Just after sunset, hunger stirred him from his rest. He emerged alone. Micah was already gone.

Larus left the cellars and stepped out into the cold. The castle's hedge maze stretched before him, its passages thick with snow. The once-vibrant hedges had lost their rich green hues, but to Larus, the maze remained beautiful. In time, he knew, the castle and the maze would crumble into history, yet he would endure.

Giles and Ashkan were busy preparing for guests, and Larus wondered what it would be like to see the halls of his new home filled with visitors. Micah had given him rooms in the northern wing, not far from his own, yet Larus found himself drawn to the crypt's dark embrace over the comfort of his chambers.

The moon was full, casting silver light across the maze. He walked its familiar paths, much as he had once roamed the abandoned church on his father's lands. Here, too, he found a strange kind of peace.

But peace could not silence the ache of longing.

He thought of his family—the life he had left behind. Micah had handled all communication on his behalf, but it was not enough. He wanted to see them. Yet, deep down, he knew the truth: Micah was his only family now. His father. His friend. His confidant.

It had taken days to regain his maker's trust after that night—the night.

Larus clenched his jaw, shame creeping over him like frost. He had lost control. Taken a life.

Micah had been furious, but Larus had obeyed in the end. He had returned to the castle while his maker disposed of the dead. Since then, he had grown to hate the presence of humans. Their scent. Their heat. Their fragility. And now, with guests arriving tonight, he dreaded the thought of being among them.

Would he be able to restrain himself?

The thought gnawed at him. He barely noticed the faint music drifting from the castle. His mind, a minefield of regrets and hunger, had wandered again—a dangerous habit, as Micah often warned.

But Larus was a dreamer.

In his mind's eye, he imagined a perfect world—one where he did not have to hide, where vampires and humans coexisted without fear. But Micah had dismissed such fantasies as foolish.

"If humans knew what we were, they would choose eternity over death. And in time, they would overrun the world. Their extinction would follow."

Larus sighed, forcing himself back to the present.

Then—something changed.

The music in the castle faded as he became aware of another sound. A whisper of movement in the hedge. The faint crunch of packed snow beneath boots.

He was no longer alone.

Larus stilled, listening. There was no heartbeat.

His eyes snapped open.

A figure stood at the edge of the hedge—watching. A vampire.

And the mischief in their gaze sent a thrill down his spine.

THE TWO VAMPIRES STOOD MOTIONLESS, LOCKED IN EACH OTHER'S GAZE.

Larus was terrified.

Micah had warned him—it is forbidden for vampires to kill their own—but he could not tell whether this creature was friend or foe.

The stranger's eyes were a piercing green, his dark hair neatly cut at the shoulders, straight and scented with oil. He smelled exquisite. Why had Larus not sensed him before? Beneath the moon's glow, the vampire's pale skin gleamed like polished marble. He wore a white lace shirt under a velvet coat of deep burgundy.

The vampire flexed his fingers. Larus stiffened at the sight of his long, claw-like nails.

He knew his own strength—newborns were powerful, dangerous. And yet, instinct told him that this one, lean and poised, could easily destroy him. The stranger's face was striking, not just handsome but otherworldly, an androgynous beauty that blurred the line between the masculine and the ethereal.

Then the vampire moved. A single step, slow and fluid, like silk unraveling. Larus took an involuntary step back.

The stranger's lips parted, and his voice, impossibly deep, slid through the cold air.

"So, this is Micah's precious newborn."

He extended a hand.

"Greetings, Larus. I'm Sebastian." A slow, knowing smile curved his lips. "Welcome to White Castle. Yes, that is the name of your home."

Larus faltered. When Giles had mentioned preparing for guests, he had assumed they would be human. Now, standing before another vampire, he realized how little he knew of Micah's world.

He hesitated, meeting Sebastian's gaze, drawn in despite himself. Was it fear that stole his voice? Or was it something else—the sheer wonder of seeing another like himself?

What does one say to another vampire?

Sebastian's smirk deepened.

"'Hello' would be an amazing start, mon chéri."

Larus startled. *He can read my thoughts?*

"Yes, chéri," Sebastian murmured, his tone playful. "And no, I am not French. But I have lived all over the world... lived many lives."

Larus swallowed, scrambling for composure.

"Uh... hello, Sebastian."

He took the vampire's hand, gripping it firmly. "I am Larus." And then immediately regretted it—of course Sebastian knew who he was.

"Well, you know what I mean," Larus muttered, feeling foolish.

Sebastian chuckled.

Then, with a deliberate slowness, he lifted Larus's hand to his lips and pressed a kiss to his skin.

"Ah... the rumours among our kind are true, then. Micah's new pet is beautiful indeed."

Larus stiffened. "Pet?"

Sebastian laughed, a rich, velvety sound. "Believe me, chéri, you are exactly that—Micah's pet. Or, if you prefer..." His green eyes glinted with mischief. "His precious treasure."

Larus frowned.

Sebastian winked. "Come, chéri. The others await."

And then, with a single, effortless leap, he vanished over the hedge.

Larus hesitated only a moment before following.

LARUS ENTERED THE CASTLE SEVERAL PACES BEHIND SEBASTIAN, FEELING LIKE a guest trailing behind his host.

The moment he stepped into the vast ballroom, he was struck by the music—rich, melodious, and intoxicating. But it was not the music alone that captured him. Nearly thirty vampires filled the room.

Excitement surged through him like an electric current.

Vampires waltzed across the floor in seamless synchrony, moving with an effortless grace that made them appear weightless. Others lounged together on ornate sofas, locked in hushed conversations, while small cliques gathered near the grand fireplace, their laughter blending into the music.

And then, there was the blood.

Gallons of it.

Crimson liquid swirled in delicate crystal glasses, sipped leisurely by those reclining in pleasure. Larus had never seen so many vampires in one place. He stood motionless near the entrance, watching them in awe.

A hand touched the small of his back.

He turned—Micah stood beside him.

"These are friends, Larus," Micah said gently. "None shall harm you. I trust them all."

Larus barely heard him, his gaze darting from one vampire to another. Who are they? He wanted to know them all at once.

"They are like you," Micah answered, as if reading his thoughts.

"No, I mean... how? Where?"

"I have told you many times," Micah replied patiently. "Vampires live in secret. We are everywhere. Discretion is paramount—our very survival depends on it."

Larus barely processed his words. He could only stare at the scene before him, his voice barely above a whisper.

"They're... so happy."

Micah chuckled. "Come, Larus. You must meet Geraldine."

Larus felt the shift in the air before he saw her.

Geraldine moved through the crowd like a queen among courtiers. Her gown of red silk clung to her body, the sleeves so tight they looked painted onto her deep brown skin. Though she was not old—perhaps thirty-five in appearance—her hair was a striking silver, long and flowing.

Larus's gaze was drawn to the intricate henna patterns on her hands, winding across her fingers and palms like delicate lace. The small red bindi between her brows caught the firelight, sparkling as brilliantly as her hazel eyes.

She reached Micah first, embracing him with a kiss to each cheek.

Then, she turned to Larus.

In that instant, he felt the full weight of her presence. It was as if she had forgotten Micah entirely, offering Larus her complete attention.

"Dear Larus."

She smiled—a smile meant only for him.

Larus barely remembered to breathe.

She was nearly as tall as he was, and as she took his hands, he felt warmth where there should have been none.

Her gaze never wavered.

But her words were for Micah.

"Why have you kept him from us this long, Micah?" Her hazel eyes gleamed with mischief. "Are you afraid our dear brother Sebastian will steal your prize?"

Larus glanced at Micah, puzzled.

Micah nodded. "We were both made by Emilio. Brothers, indeed."

Geraldine chuckled, her gaze flickering between them. "And yet, one is Cain... and the other, Abel."

A presence stirred nearby.

Sebastian appeared, emerging from the crowd like a shadow slipping into the light. But he was not alone.

"Darling," he purred, pressing a kiss to Geraldine's cheek, "when will you cease slandering my good name?"

She turned her face away, denying him even the courtesy of a returned greeting.

"Which name, brother? Cain or Sebastian?"

Sebastian smirked. "Ever so clever, dear Geraldine."

He flicked his wrist in a theatrical gesture, drawing attention to the figure beside him.

"Look who I found sulking in a corner."

Larus's gaze lifted.

The vampire before him met his stare with a calm, knowing expression. He was tall and lean, his long black braid reaching his waist. His dark pupils reflected the flickering light from the fireplace behind them.

Sebastian stepped closer to Larus, his voice a teasing whisper.

"Mon chéri, this is Haruki."

Larus barely heard him, his attention snagged on the twin swords resting at the vampire's waist—one long, one short.

Sebastian chuckled. "I know what you're thinking, chéri. Why would a vampire need swords?" He flashed his fangs. "Well, I'll leave that for Haruki to explain."

Haruki inclined his head in greeting, bowing first to Micah, then Geraldine. His black shirt bore the image of a crimson dragon embroidered across the sleeves, its tail coiling around his wrist.

Then, his gaze settled on Larus.

"It is good to meet you."

With both hands resting lightly on the hilts of his swords, Haruki bowed again.

"For two decades, I have longed to meet you."

Larus stiffened.

His gaze darted to Micah. Two decades? His mind spun with questions, but one thought cut through the noise.

Sebastian's words.

Micah's new pet.

Anger stirred in his chest.

Micah had told him nothing.

Sebastian sighed theatrically. With a smirk, he took Geraldine's hand, his other resting lightly on Haruki's shoulder.

"Oh, dear me," he murmured.

Then, louder—his voice laced with amusement.

"Our dear brother has yet to enlighten his charge of his true nature."

He laughed, the sound carrying above the music.

And Larus, standing at the centre of it all, found himself lost in a maze of mystery.

Micah abruptly ended the conversation by raising his hand, then led Larus and the others to his favourite place in the castle. Giles arrived moments later, carrying five glasses filled to the brim with thick, crimson blood.

Larus sat between Micah and Geraldine on a velvet couch, while Sebastian and Haruki lounged opposite them. Sebastian sipped from his glass, licking the blood from his lips before glancing up at the massive painting on the wall.

"Ah, there she is... the beautiful Estlyn."

Larus turned to the canvas, seeing it with new eyes. Estlyn. Micah had never spoken his mother's name before.

Geraldine sighed, clearly irritated by Sebastian's distraction. She turned her gaze to Micah. "You haven't told him?"

Micah exhaled slowly, as if weighing his next words. "I wonder if he is ready." His hand rested on Larus's shoulder, fingers tightening slightly. The silence stretched, excruciating.

Sebastian scoffed. "Now seems like a good time."

Haruki, who had been sitting with his eyes closed, finally opened them. "He must know."

Micah nodded and rose to his feet, pacing before them before stopping at the painting. Facing the canvas, he seemed at ease.

"Larus, I have never lied to you," he said at last. "But I have... withheld certain truths. I did so to protect you." He gestured toward the others. "What I tell you now is known only to those in this room. Geraldine, Haruki, and Sebastian were with Emilio long before he made me. We are the last of Emilio's children—all that remains of his coven."

Larus shook his head, confused. "But... what does this have to do with me? Emilio turned you over a century ago—long before I was even born."

Micah's gaze remained on the painting. "Larus, why do you think I watched you? Followed you your entire life?" His voice was steady, but Larus heard the weight behind it. "Do you believe I simply found you by chance?"

Larus's stomach tightened. "I—"

Micah didn't wait for an answer. "Long before Emilio died, he made me swear I would wait for you."

Larus stiffened. "But you said Emilio died a century ago. That would have been long before my father—"

"Yes." Micah finally turned, his dark eyes locking onto Larus's. "And yet Emilio knew you would come. He foresaw it. And so I waited."

A sharp silence followed.

Sebastian leaned back against the couch, smiling faintly. "And now, mon chéri, here you are."

Micah crossed the room, clasping Sebastian and Haruki's shoulders before placing a kiss on Geraldine's cheek. "Geraldine, Haruki, Sebastian—I owe you all an apology. You are my closest friends, my family, and I love you all." He hesitated. "But Emilio swore me to secrecy. There is more you do not know. There is more I must now tell."

The other three vampires exchanged glances, clearly intrigued. But Larus barely noticed. His mind reeled.

For the first time, he wasn't sure if he was merely a part of Micah's world—or its centre.

Sebastian exhaled through his nose, shaking his head. "I would expect nothing less from Emilio." His voice was dry, but there was something else beneath it. "We all knew he loved you best."

"Emilio loved us all," Geraldine said softly, tracing the henna patterns on her hands.

Haruki studied Micah. "Then tell us, brother. What are these secrets you swore to keep?"

Sebastian's smile returned, sharp as a knife. "Yes, do tell."

Larus turned to Micah, breath unsteady. He needed to know.

Why was he at the centre of secrets and oaths made over a century ago?

FOUR PAIRS OF EYES FIXED UPON MICAH AS HE OPENED HIS MOUTH TO SPEAK.

"Emilio has left me in a predicament." His voice was quiet, burdened. "Where do I begin?"

Beyond the closed door, music played, festive and bright. Laughter rang through the castle halls, a sharp contrast to the heavy silence in the room. Micah paced, circling the two couches where the others sat. Geraldine, legs crossed, studied him with a frown; Haruki, calm as ever, waited in silence.

Micah exhaled. "Your father, Larus, appears to be oblivious to the true nature of your family and its history." He stopped pacing just long enough to point at him. "After you were born, your father chose to keep his brother a secret—as well as the affliction that has plagued the eldest son of the Bleddyn family for centuries. Contrary to what he told you, your father was neither the only child of Clayborne Bleddyn nor the eldest."

Larus stared. "But he always told me—"

"Maxwell Bleddyn was the second son," Micah continued, "and unlike your uncle, he did not suffer from a weakened heart."

Micah moved to the trolley Giles had left, lifting his glass. He took a slow drink before looking at Larus again.

"My father never told me he had a brother," Larus murmured. "He's always struggled with my illness."

"Yes, Larus." Micah set his glass down. "Because after Merrick Bleddyn's death, your father never spoke of him again. But what he never told you is that they were twins."

Larus's breath caught.

Micah's face was unreadable. "And as you are, Larus, the firstborn carried a gift."

Larus hugged himself. "A curse."

"No, chéri." Sebastian shifted from his couch, sitting beside Larus. "Not a curse. Nestled in your blood is a power most precious."

Larus shook his head. "Micah, I don't understand."

Micah dragged a hand over his face. "The answer lies in your name. Bleddyn. It carries the legacy of your family. It means 'wolf hero.'"

Larus stiffened. "Wolves?"

"Not wolves," Sebastian murmured. "Lycanthropes."

Larus grimaced. "Ly—?"

"They can shift," Haruki explained. "Change their form at will—from human to something... more."

"But over time," Geraldine added, "those born with the gift—usually the firstborn—couldn't sustain it. The change typically occurred around their twenty-fifth year—even earlier. Many never lived long enough to experience it."

Larus ran his fingers through his hair, his pulse quickening. "How is that possible? How could something like that exist?"

Sebastian rose smoothly from the couch. "We exist, chéri. Vampires. Why would you doubt the existence of your own family's legacy?"

Larus squeezed his eyes shut. His world had unraveled, piece by piece, and now all that remained was this—vampires and beasts and his own unquenchable thirst for blood.

"How are they connected?" he whispered. "Vampires and... shapeshifters?"

Sebastian's laughter echoed in the room. "They are not. Vampires and lycanthropes are mortal enemies. One kills the other."

"And yet," Geraldine murmured, "another enemy hunts us both."

Larus looked to Micah, searching for answers. "Why didn't you tell me before? Why offer me this life?"

Micah's gaze darkened. "Because I did as I swore, Larus. I saved your life." He turned, eyes settling on his mother's portrait. "Emilio's maker was like you."

Silence fell.

Micah's voice was distant, as if he spoke to the woman in the painting rather than the vampires in the room. "Cecil Bleddyn was the first to suffer your affliction. And like you, he was saved."

Sebastian's head snapped up. "Saved?" His voice cracked with disbelief.

Micah nodded. "This night, I break my vow. I am free." A small smile played at his lips. "Emilio commanded that I keep this knowledge hidden for as long as possible. But the time has come."

He turned to them all, his expression unreadable.

"By his twenty-fifth year, Cecil had not yet transformed, but he struggled with the affliction. He spent much of his youth bedridden. His father, fearing the inevitable, stayed at his bedside, waiting for him to die. But Cecil lived on—past his thirtieth year."

Larus's fingers curled into fists.

Micah continued. "Death seemed inevitable, until Cecil's father decided to act. A servant spoke of a healer—a soothsayer. Desperate, the old man placed his son in a carriage and sent him with his most trusted servant, Rubina. They never arrived."

Micah's expression darkened.

"The wreckage was found at the bottom of a precipice. The coachman, the servants... even Rubina. All dead." His voice lowered. "Cecil was never found."

Larus barely breathed.

Micah sighed. "This is as Emilio told it to me. These are his words."

Sebastian's lips curled into a smirk. "And what other secrets did our maker leave you with?" He leaned forward. "I know Cecil and Emilio were mated. And I know how Emilio met his end."

Micah's jaw tightened.

"His father died believing his son perished that night," he continued. "The family legacy passed to Cecil's uncle—a man blessed with many sons. And as there were no other heirs, Cecil's mother spent the rest of her days in a convent."

Geraldine shuddered. "Horrific. That poor woman."

Micah pressed on. "But Cecil was not killed that night. The vampire who attacked the carriage spared him. Her name was Telsiea."

Haruki's brows lifted. "And what became of this Telsiea?"

Micah shook his head. "I don't know. Only that she made Cecil immortal."

Larus's throat felt tight. "And then?"

Micah exhaled. "Telsiea and Cecil loved each other. But those were different times. Telsiea had fled from her own kind, for she had killed her maker. She was strong, but poor. Eventually, she convinced Cecil to return to his ancestral home—thirty years after the accident—to reclaim his birthright."

"But by then," Sebastian murmured, "his family had flourished."

Micah nodded. "By then, the gift within the Bleddyn bloodline had awakened. There were shapeshifters among them. And so the war between vampires and lycanthropes began."

Larus was captivated. The idea that his own bloodline had once waged war against the very creatures he now called kin…

But one question burned in his mind.

"How did Cecil die?"

Micah hesitated. Then, at last, he spoke.

"He didn't."

The silence was deafening.

Micah held their gaze, his expression unreadable.

"Cecil Bleddyn lives."

17

A WOMAN CHANGED

She had named him Silas, for the night before his birth, the full moon had illuminated the woods, and Max had felt an irresistible pull toward it. Forest dweller—her son's name meant just that. Now, seated by the window with her baby in her arms, nothing could tear her gaze away from him. From the moment she had woken that morning, Silas had become the centre of her world. She hadn't expected it, but little Silas Hearne had become the apple of her eye. The summer days stretched long, and with each new day, Max found herself looking forward to the next. The sweet songs of the birds outside filled the air, but none of their melodies could match the sound of Silas's cries.

She knew the signs well now—her son was hungry. She didn't need to look away from him as she undid her blouse and revealed her breast. Silas, with eyes as grey as moonlight, eagerly suckled, his small hands wrapped around her, as if he understood how much she needed him, too. When he finished, she cradled him against her chest, humming an old lullaby from her childhood.

The door opened, and Max's heart lightened as her parents and two sisters entered, their faces bright with joy. Tilley followed, holding a tray stacked with Max's favourite foods.

"A new mother mustn't neglect her cravings," Tilley teased as she set the tray down. "It's easy to forget to eat, Maxine." She took Silas from her arms and cradled him as she settled across the room with him. Catherine and Isabelle hurried to join her, eager to play with their nephew. Max's mother beamed, sitting across from Tilley, gazing at her first grandchild.

Max's father took a seat beside her, pride in his eyes. For the first time that morning, Max was allowed a moment away from her son, and she turned to look out the window with her father. Silence fell between them until he spoke, his voice thick with emotion.

"He's a fine boy, Max. A healthy boy."

Max's heart swelled with love. "I love him so much," she whispered, meeting her father's gaze. Then, a sudden, unexpected thought gripped her, and the words spilled out before she could stop them. "How... how could you not love him as I love Silas?"

Her father's eyes filled with sorrow, and Max instantly regretted the question.

"I loved Larus ever since you and he were born," he said quietly. "Your mother placed him in my arms, and I know I loved my son." He paused, as if choosing his next words carefully. "Max, there are things I have not mentioned."

Max felt a pang in her chest. Her father's pain was evident, and she didn't want to burden him further.

"You must see him, Father. Send a messenger to Doctor Duncan," she urged, hoping to change the subject.

"I have written to Larus some time ago," her father said, his tone distant. "He wrote back with news of some improvement. But it was his wish to stay away."

"Surely, Father, he will want to see his nephew," Max insisted.

"Yes, yes, I think he would like that." Her father gave her hands a gentle squeeze before turning to look at Silas, a soft smile tugging at his lips. "I see how much you love him, Max. I was afraid to show that love to Larus. I was ashamed."

Max froze, her throat tightening as memories of that dreadful day flooded her mind. The image of Percival Hearne, his monstrous actions, flashed before her eyes. She hadn't spoken of it to anyone, not even her father, the man she had always shared everything with. But that day,

Percival had taken something from her, something Max could never get back.

Her hands trembled slightly, but she held them still, refusing to let the past ruin this moment.

"Father, we needn't speak of this," she whispered, her voice tight. "Silas is strong and healthy."

Her father met her gaze, as though searching her face for any sign of what had truly happened. Max couldn't bear it.

Flashes of Percival's brutality. Of Bartholomew's weakness. Those men had forced themselves upon her, but it was not hatred Max felt for them. It was pity. Her husband, though begging for forgiveness, had no place in her heart. She could never forgive him.

But Silas was different. Silas was her strength. She loved him more than her own life.

Her father squeezed her hand again, breaking the silence. Max smiled, but it was fragile. "I'm so happy, Father," she said, as her heart swelled with love for the boy who had somehow healed her heart.

"Our little Silas." Her father's smile deepened as he looked at his grandson across the room.

Max felt a momentary flicker of hesitation before her father raised an eyebrow, glancing at her. "How did you choose my grandson's name?"

Max hesitated, unsure how to explain. She couldn't say that Silas had chosen his name long before he was born. That in the quiet of her mind, his voice had whispered through her thoughts, guiding her. The name had come with a sense of certainty, as though it had been preordained.

She smiled softly, unwilling to reveal the truth. "I just felt it was right," she said, keeping the mystery between them. How could she explain that her son had shown her the distant trees and that his name had sent tremors through her body? How could she admit that she had no choice in the matter?

Her father, oblivious to the strange connection between mother and son, smiled back at her. "Silas is a good name," he said, a contented sigh escaping his lips. Max could only nod, her heart heavy with the secrets she could never share.

PART TWO

18

UNCLE LARUS

It was near the end of July, arguably the warmest time of the year. However, being a vampire, Larus found no discomfort in the heat; he was never cold in the frigid months, nor did the summer's sweltering heat trouble him. The carriage, large enough to fit ten passengers, carried only five vampires along the lonely road toward the Bleddyn lands. They had left White Castle just after sunset, knowing the journey would be long. They needed to arrive long before sunrise.

Nearly a year had passed since Larus had left his family for the castle. As the team of stallions galloped through the night, heading toward the home he had missed so much, he wondered what it would be like to see them again. But worry weighed on him, for it would be impossible to stay at the Bleddyn manor during his visit. Micah had arranged rooms at an inn, though it was hardly ideal for a vampire during the day. The five of them would only be safe in the catacombs.

Larus sat next to Micah, his thoughts distant. Across from them sat Sebastian, Geraldine, and Haruki. Since the night of Micah's soirée, much had changed. Larus spoke little on the journey. He was sure that both Micah and Sebastian, with their mind-reading abilities, could hear his thoughts. Though Larus had this gift as well, it was still crude and underdeveloped. Micah had urged him to hone it, but Larus struggled. He could not abide the violation of reading others' minds, and because of it, his skill remained rudimentary.

Haruki appeared to be meditating, his eyes closed, while Geraldine sat between him and Sebastian, her hands delicately folded in her lap, exchanging knowing glances with Micah. Sebastian, seated by the open window, stared out into the night, acknowledging the presence of the others only through random thoughts that made little sense. His occasional glances and challenging stares at Micah, however, were enough to cause an undercurrent of tension. The two vampires had not forgotten the bitter argument that nearly broke out the night they discovered Cecil Bleddyn still lived.

Larus couldn't keep his mind quiet, and his thoughts kept circling back to the revelation of Cecil's existence. It was impossible to shield his thoughts from Micah and Sebastian, and every time he thought about the conflict between them, Sebastian would glance over, a reminder of his presence. Larus couldn't escape the flamboyant vampire's probing gaze.

After over an hour of listening to the constant sounds of the carriage—the squeaks of the bearings, the pounding hooves of the horses, the creaky leather seats—Geraldine broke the silence. "We must discuss what course to take."

Sebastian shrugged without speaking.

Haruki, usually calm, was uncharacteristically animated. "Think of the benefits. Consider the knowledge Cecil must possess!" His enthusiasm was a stark contrast to his usual demeanour. "Cecil was Emilio's maker. We would not be here tonight without him."

"We've all heard what Micah has said." Geraldine's voice was sharp, measured. "To awaken Cecil would be reckless. We don't know what he is capable of, and if the elders find out—" She paused, glancing at Larus. "Emilio was nearly 800 years old. We know nothing of Cecil's abilities. Should the elders discover his existence, it could mean our destruction. Emilio should have known what revealing this secret would cause. He shouldn't have trusted only you, Micah."

Haruki shifted in his seat, his tone heavy. "Why didn't Emilio tell us everything? Why only mention the history of the Bleddyn clan and leave out that Cecil Bleddyn still lived?"

Micah leaned forward, his face heavy with sorrow as he met their gazes. "You all ask questions I've already answered. Emilio and Cecil were mates—bound by love. The elders knew this, yet they commanded Emilio to destroy the one he loved. Now, tell me, what would any of you have done in his place?" He pointed to each of them, one by one.

Sebastian's eyes narrowed. "Did he not love Telsiea, his maker?"

Micah glared at Sebastian. "A vampire's love knows no bounds, Sebastian."

Sebastian's gaze shifted to Larus, and the younger vampire felt a chill run through him. He quickly looked away, staring out the window to avoid Sebastian's eyes.

"You told us that Cecil had been hunted, tried for the crimes he committed with his maker," Sebastian continued, his voice laced with bitterness. "The elders are fools. Why didn't they destroy him themselves? You mentioned Benoît and Babette—vampires who were supposed to aid in Cecil's destruction. Why did they risk their lives for Emilio?"

"I don't know," Micah said, his voice quiet. "I never met Babette and Benoît. Emilio never told me what became of them. But my maker did mention one other vampire condemned to death—Odelia. Emilio spoke little of her."

Sebastian shook his head in disbelief. "This Odelia is dead, but Cecil lived. What of Babette and Benoît? Did Emilio say where to find them?"

A sardonic laugh escaped Sebastian's lips. It wasn't joyful—more a sharp expression of frustration. "Do you realize this secret might still lead to our doom?"

Micah's eyes softened as he ran a hand over his face. "I'm beginning to think you're right, Sebastian. We have to assume Babette and Benoît are still alive."

"What must we do?" Haruki asked.

"For now, nothing," Micah said firmly, his voice resolute. "They may not know us."

"But they believe they're the only ones who know where Cecil sleeps," Geraldine interjected, her voice tinged with urgency.

"If they live," Haruki said, "we must find them."

Larus felt a surge of curiosity. He wanted to learn more about this strange new world of vampires, creatures older than himself. "But how?" he asked, his voice quiet, yet eager.

"They will be much older," Sebastian replied, his eyes narrowing. "Stronger."

Larus gazed out the window as the conversation continued. The carriage sped down the narrow road, the darkness of the night deepening as they climbed higher into the hills. His vampire eyes allowed him to see clearly in the dark, and he relished the view, feeling a sense of calm wash over him. After all the tension, it seemed his new family was finally beginning to find common ground. Even Sebastian, despite his provocations, was calm for now.

A faint smile tugged at Larus's lips as the discussion went on.

Larus was the last to enter the level below the living quarters of the catacombs. He paused at the foot of the stairs, looking upward, still struck by the comfort and elegance of his second home. The catacombs were vast, capable of housing hundreds of vampires, yet Micah had made it clear that only those carefully selected would become part of his coven. For Larus, there was no greater bond than the one he shared with his maker. At times, he found himself pining for Micah as an infant would for its mother, desperate for the connection they shared.

He turned his gaze to the others. They were all he had now. A coven of five—small, but bound by something far greater. They were his family.

The others had gathered before the sealed chamber, where Cecil, his kin, was said to lie in centuries-long slumber. Sebastian was insistent that they break the seal to confirm Cecil's existence. His eyes locked with Larus's as he spoke. "Let us break the seal and look upon his face." His voice was firm, but his gaze softened as he added, "Trust me, chéri. I've seen such things."

Sebastian's hand gripped Micah's shoulder, urging their leader to side with him. "Blood alone can revive him, Micah. Let us open this thing. Let us make certain he's within!"

"We cannot be certain," Geraldine cautioned, her tone sharp. "We don't know what lies within. There could be traps."

Haruki, who had been watching the exchange in silence, slowly stepped forward, placing his hand upon the stone. The red wax seal was thick, its edges worn from age. "Geraldine, you think there may be... traps?"

"These vampires were ancient, Haruki," Geraldine replied, her voice steady but laced with concern. "We cannot underestimate them, especially if they intended to keep Cecil's existence a secret."

Micah's voice cut through the tension. "Let us be cautious." He turned away from the sealed door, his expression unreadable. "And, as you said, Sebastian, let us assume Benoît and Babette still live. If they do, we must find them." He paused before continuing, his gaze lingering on the chamber. "If we find them, we must be careful."

Sebastian, leaning against the stone wall, raised an eyebrow. "And then what?" he asked, his voice cool but heavy with impatience. "Do we open this chamber or leave it as it is? Or perhaps we should wake Cecil. After all, only he can give us the answers we seek."

Micah spun around, the sudden movement catching everyone off guard. "You think I lie to you?" His voice was sharp, and there was a deep frustration behind his words. "I have spoken the truth. Waking Cecil does not guarantee he'll give us the answers we need. Even you, Sebastian, should know this."

Sebastian closed his eyes, leaning deeper into the stone, his body language suggesting indifference, though his mind clearly raced. He was silent for several moments before speaking again, his voice low. "We could end him," he said with a cold finality. "Do what the elders commanded and simply destroy the old vampire, Cecil."

Geraldine's shock was evident. She reached for Sebastian's hand, her fingers trembling as she took hold of it. "Would you have the death of an innocent vampire on our hands, Sebastian? We cannot act as executioners." Her voice faltered, but there was a quiet strength beneath it. "Remember Emilio's teachings."

Sebastian's laughter came without humour, a bitter sound that echoed in the chamber. "Emilio thought only of himself, it seems." His gaze swept over the group, daring them to see the truth as he did. "If our maker truly cared for us, he would never have left us in this predicament."

Micah's patience snapped. "Let us leave this alone for now!" He motioned toward the sealed stone door, frustration in his voice. "We must think before we act." Without another word, he turned and began to ascend the stone steps, his footsteps deliberate and heavy with the weight of the decisions ahead. "Let knowledge guide us. And if it leads us to Cecil's destruction, so it shall be."

Larus's heart twisted at the thought of Cecil's destruction. He felt an unexpected surge of pity for a vampire he had never met. Cecil was his kin, his family, and though they shared no direct bond, Larus couldn't bear the thought of condemning him without understanding.

He followed Micah upward, the weight of his emotions pressing heavily on his chest. He wanted to speak out, to plead for Cecil's life, but the words stuck in his throat. They shared the same blood, the same curse, and perhaps even the same suffering. Cecil's story mirrored his own, and in that moment, Larus felt an undeniable connection to the ancient vampire.

Not yet knowing the full truth of Cecil's existence, Larus's heart ached for him. They were kin, bound by a shared struggle, and Larus could not shake the feeling that their fates were intertwined.

IT WAS WELL PAST MIDNIGHT WHEN THE MAKER AND NEWBORN WALKED through the cemetery, alone. The air was heavy, thick with the warmth of a late summer night. As they moved in silence, Larus attuned himself to the myriad sounds that filled the air—sounds beyond human hearing. He heard the terrified screech of a rodent as it was lifted from the ground by an owl's talons, the hiss of a snake somewhere in the distance, and the splash of water as a toad leapt from a lily into the nearby pond.

Larus matched Micah's slow, measured pace as they wandered among the winding paths and gravestones. Earlier that evening, just after sunset, the five vampires had briefly visited the town's inn. It was an appearance made out of necessity; should others come calling, Micah, known for his profession as a doctor, would be there to receive them. Micah had planned to spend several days at the inn, but that would be alone.

It was not uncommon for vampires to interact with humans during the daylight hours, when the sun shone brightly and no questions were asked. Larus had seen their rooms at the inn and noted how Micah had chosen wisely. The windows, carefully cloaked, faced away from the sun, allowing them to remain undisturbed. Sebastian and the others had left early in the evening, cloaked by the darkness, to hunt. And now, as the two walked the cemetery grounds, Larus and Micah were finally discussing the one thing they had avoided since their return from the capital.

Micah's nails scraped across the surface of a gravestone as he circled it, and after leaning against the black marble inscribed with the words of the dead, he turned to Larus with a grim smile. "You must visit your family."

The words cut through the stillness, and Larus felt a jolt in his chest. Micah's tone was calm, but it commanded Larus's full attention.

"Your father worries for you," Micah continued, his voice soft but firm. "Do you not miss your sisters, Larus?"

Larus hesitated, a cloud of doubt lingering in his thoughts. "I fear they will know... they will see that I am different."

"They know you are coming," Micah replied, his eyes steady. "I sent a messenger with a letter to your father this night."

Larus's brow furrowed. "Will they come to the inn?"

"Your father's pride won't allow that. You must go to him," Micah said, his voice matter-of-fact.

Larus smiled faintly, marvelling at his maker's wisdom. "That's Father, all right. Always expecting everyone to come crawling back."

Micah's expression softened. "He has a good heart."

Larus grinned, unable to hide his amusement. "So you keep reminding me. But you're right... I was a fool to doubt how much he cares."

"You are lucky, Larus," Micah said, rubbing his palms together thoughtfully. "More than you know. I was never my father's son. I was chattel. Mere property. If I had died—whether by his hand or some act of

God—it would have meant nothing to him. Your father concealed his love to hide his pain. You must remember this."

Larus stood still, considering his maker's words. His family was not perfect, but he had never doubted their love, not like Micah had. It struck him again just how different their lives had been.

Micah pushed himself off the gravestone and turned to walk down the path again. "There is more we must discuss before you see those you love. You must remember to breathe."

"Breathe?" Larus asked, confused.

"I've told you this before, young one. Some humans are observant, especially those who suspect our existence. They may never encounter a single vampire in their entire lives, but they can still believe we exist." Micah paused, his tone serious now. "Emilio once spoke of our enemies—those who would see us destroyed. I haven't encountered them, but they exist. Some humans hunt and kill our kind."

Larus's eyes narrowed. "Why?"

"They fear us. They want to protect the human race." Micah's grip tightened on Larus's shoulder, pulling him into his gaze. "Can you blame them, Larus? Can you condemn them for doing all they can to preserve themselves?"

Larus stood frozen, feeling the weight of his maker's words. There was something in the air between them, something shifting, though he couldn't quite grasp it. It reminded him of the night they'd left the capital, that strange, inexplicable connection between them. He remembered the way Micah had spoken then: *A vampire's love knows no bounds.*

Larus felt the familiar rush of heat rising in him, a quickening that had nothing to do with the physical world. If he had a heartbeat, he knew it would be pounding in his chest. His thoughts became a tangled mess, a mixture of desire and confusion.

Micah's gaze softened, his expression faltering for a moment, but then he looked away, breaking the spell. "We must not do this," he muttered, and before Larus could speak, Micah was already walking ahead, leaving him behind in the darkness.

Larus followed slowly, embarrassed, the night's tension thick between them. "When must I visit my father?"

"Two nights hence," Micah replied without looking back. "Sunday evening. There will be a feast for the newest member of your family—the christening of your young nephew, Silas Hearne." Micah's smile returned, but it was tinged with something unreadable. "I'm afraid, Larus, that you'll find your family changed. They are awash with joy."

"Have you been to see my family, Micah?"

"I have seen them," Micah said, his smile lingering with a touch of mystery. "But they have not seen me."

Micah's tone shifted then, a familiar darkness returning as he turned his gaze toward the night sky. "Come. It's time to hunt. The night is still young. Let's find a human or two deserving of death this night..."

19

BLOOD MEMORIES

They moved quickly, covering miles before they could make what Micah called guiltless kills. Larus had learned that his maker did not believe in taking a life indiscriminately; Micah chose his victims with great care. That night, after scanning the minds of many, Micah had found one deserving human—a man who had murdered an innocent family. Tossing the empty corpse over a precipice, Micah muttered, "Killing him set those poor souls free."

The two made their way into the old church across from the cemetery. Larus moved with solemn reverence; this place was dear to him. He had first met Micah here, and though he had been turned in the cemetery just beyond the lane, the church felt like his true birthplace. They stood in silence for several moments, Larus gazing out into the darkness. Finally, he spoke. "I remember looking out from the steeple."

In a single leap, Larus reached the spot. Moments later, Micah joined him on the high brick ledge.

"You are at peace here," Micah observed, his voice low.

Larus nodded, still staring into the night. He could see so far, but not far enough. His vampire eyes strained against the limits of the dark. "Why am I connected to Cecil?" he asked, his voice quiet. "Why did Emilio want you to turn me?"

Micah's smile deepened. "Emilio did not." He turned to face Larus. "He commanded me to turn the first Bleddyn with your affliction when the opportunity arose."

Larus furrowed his brow. "Were there no others?"

"There were few," Micah replied, pacing along the edge of the steeple. "Cecil's uncle had thirty years to grow his pack. He had many sons, and through him, their numbers swelled, offering protection. There was something in that bloodline—something his father lacked. The Lycanthropes prospered for a time because of it."

Larus looked down, considering. "How did you know I—"

"Knowledge, Larus. Information." Micah's voice was calm, but there was a weight behind his words. "Emilio gave me all I needed to know."

Larus's mind raced. "Why not keep a journal?"

"I will not die from a fall, young one," Micah said with a shrug. "But we must never record the details of our lives. It would serve as proof of our existence. The elders have ancient scrolls, but they guard them carefully."

Larus looked confused. "Then how can we trust mere words?"

Micah's lips curled into a wry smile. "Not just words, dear one. The truth is in our memories." He placed a hand on Larus's shoulder. "All our knowledge is stored in our blood. It is both a gift and a curse. Every intention, every deed is open to any vampire who tastes our blood."

Larus's eyes widened as the implications settled in. "No secrets?"

"None," Micah affirmed. "Our memories live on in our blood. And the only protection we have, Larus, is to willingly abstain from knowing. Knowledge can be dangerous in our world. It can be the path to our doom."

Larus absorbed this, feeling the weight of his maker's words. He struggled to make sense of it all. "So, if we find Babette and her brother Benoît, we could... taste their knowledge?"

Micah nodded but his tone turned cautionary. "It works on humans, but I warn you, Larus—if you drink their blood, you will most likely have to kill them."

Larus stared at his maker, still not fully understanding. "I don't—why is it that when I feed—" He faltered, but Micah's laughter interrupted him.

"It's a skill. A vampire must have the desire to see blood memories."

"Blood memories?" Larus whispered, confused.

"Yes." Micah's voice was firm. "That is what we call them." He took a step closer, eyes narrowing with intent. "Focus, Larus. Taste my blood. Take what you wish to know."

Without another word, Micah bit into his own lip, the dark blood flowing immediately. "Quickly now, before I heal," he urged. Larus hesitated, still caught in the intensity of the moment. His maker leaned forward, closing the distance between them, and their lips touched. The coldness of Micah's blood filled Larus's mouth. He struggled to ignore the rush of desire, but it was impossible to focus entirely. The sensations of Micah's tongue, the smoothness of his lips—it was intoxicating.

Larus closed his eyes and forced himself to focus, pushing his overwhelming passions aside. Suddenly, a storm of visions hit him. The flood was rapid, disorienting. He fought to regain control, but it was like trying to stop a torrent. Finally, he focused on the memory he wanted: Emilio.

It was as though he were seeing through his maker's eyes—Emilio's dark, sharp features, his long hair, his heavy accent. Visions poured in faster, each one more vivid than the last. Micah's mother appeared in one —her likeness captured in a canvas in White Castle. Another memory followed: whips cracking, the cries of the tortured. Beauty's brutal death. The piercing blue eyes of Massa Duncan, the sound of hounds barking in the distance. The images were overwhelming.

Then, among it all, he heard Emilio's voice. Larus pulled away from the kiss, his mind still reeling.

"Emilio," Larus gasped, eyes wide with shock. "You loved him."

Micah smiled, a warmth spreading across his face. "Yes, Larus. Emilio feared being alone, and though nothing came of my feelings, he must have known of my desire for him. But that is the past. Emilio could not destroy Cecil—not because he loved him, but because Cecil was unique."

Larus blinked, still trying to make sense of it all. "Emilio said you would know... when to wake him."

Micah's eyes darkened. "You saw what I saw, Larus. You know what I know."

The confusion lingered. "What became of the shapeshifters, the lycanthropes?"

"Sebastian is much older than I am," Micah replied. "He and Haruki know more about the shapeshifters than I do."

Larus stared out into the night, trying to process the flood of information. "You've fought them... you and Sebastian."

Micah smiled but shrugged. "Sebastian means well. When Emilio brought me to White Castle, the coven accepted me, but Sebastian refused. To him, I was a threat. And I was lost, Larus. In my world, no one but Mama wanted me. My father saw me as nothing but his slave; the others saw me as an enigma. But Emilio—Emilio saw me long before I knew myself."

"Do you trust him?" Larus asked.

"I would give my life to save Sebastian's if I had to." Micah's gaze pierced Larus, sharp as ever. "You admire him."

Larus looked away, but Micah's voice was soft, almost reassuring. "You must not fear what you feel. Deep down, Sebastian has a good heart."

Larus met his maker's gaze, knowing there was nothing he could say to deny it. He embraced Micah, the warmth of the moment grounding him.

"No vampire," Larus murmured, "has a beating heart..."

Micah chuckled. "No. But Sebastian cares for you."

Larus felt the weight of the words and said nothing more. There was truth in them, whether he was ready to accept it or not.

20

SILAS

They arrived after sunset, and Larus walked into Bleddyn Manor sick with apprehension. His steps faltered for just a moment at the threshold before he moved forward with Micah, Sebastian, and Geraldine at his side.

The servant greeted him with a bow before leading them toward the great hall. Most of his family was already there, but Larus did not see his sister Max or her child. His parents stood near Percival Hearne and his wife, their backs to him as they admired the massive family tapestry.

The quiet hum of conversation shattered with Isabelle's shrill cry of delight.

"Larus!" She ran to him, flinging herself into his arms. "I thought you would never return to us."

He kissed the crown of her head, careful to avoid direct contact with her skin. "It is good to see you, sister."

Isabelle pulled back to study him. "You look well, Larus... but so pale."

Before he could respond, Sebastian stepped forward, extending a gloved hand. He took Isabelle's fingers lightly, brushing them with his lips.

"You are as beautiful as your brother boasts, Isabelle."

Isabelle stiffened. She had not noticed him before, but now, looking into his dark, piercing eyes, her smile wavered.

"You must forgive your dear brother's manners, my dear. I am Sebastian."

She hesitated, looking between him and Larus.

"Sebastian is my colleague," Micah said smoothly.

Isabelle turned, and her face brightened. "Doctor Duncan!"

Micah smiled at the familiarity before gesturing toward their final companion. "May I introduce my dear friend, Geraldine."

Larus watched as his sister's gaze swept over Geraldine. At first, Isabelle smiled, but her expression shifted as she took in the contrast—the youthful face framed by silver hair, the delicate lace gown paired with the intricate henna on her hands.

Before she could question it, Catherine approached, drawing Isabelle's attention away.

"Larus." Catherine's embrace was brief, her movements practiced. She turned swiftly, the swish of her gown deliberate as she faced his companions.

Extending a delicate hand, she smiled at Sebastian. "I am Catherine."

Sebastian took her hand, his lips curling into a knowing smile. "Charmed, Catherine."

She barely glanced at Micah before stepping past him, her focus settling on Geraldine. It was clear she was drawn to her attire—the understated elegance of the lace and the henna that mirrored its pattern. She murmured a greeting but said nothing more.

Larus took in the room, his sharpened senses picking up every hushed conversation, every heartbeat. His eyes landed on his parents. They stood beneath the tapestry, watching him in silence. His father's expression was unreadable, his mother's gaze carefully averted.

Micah stepped closer, voice low in his ear.

"Larus, you must go to your father. Remember his pride—he will not come to you."

Larus's jaw tightened. "And I suppose he has convinced my mother to ignore her only son?" A simmering anger stirred, an old resentment threatening to resurface.

Micah placed a steadying hand on his shoulder. "Listen to me. Go."

Larus exhaled sharply, then nodded.

LARUS GREETED PERCIVAL HEARNE AND HIS WIFE BEFORE EMBRACING HIS mother and shaking his father's hand. Only after his mother had guided their guests toward yet another family heirloom did he finally exchange words with his father.

"Hello, Father."

A slight nod. Then, to Larus's surprise, a smile.

He's changed, Larus thought.

"You look well," his father said. "It appears Duncan's skills are as good as many say."

Larus felt the urge to smile but did not. *If only you knew, Father. If only you knew what your doctor was—and what I have become.*

"It is best not to get our hopes up," Larus said carefully.

Micah had warned him: one day, he might need to appear to die for his family's sake. The thought of it left a hollow ache in his chest.

His father's expression darkened. "So, you intend to rob me of what hope I have left."

Before Larus could respond, Percival Hearne's deep voice rumbled through the hall.

"So, your boy has come home, Maxwell."

Larus turned as the massive man approached, his piercing eyes fixed on him. Hearne's grip was iron-like as he clamped a hand on Larus's shoulder, shaking him vigorously. There was something in his tone—taunting, needling.

Larus met the man's gaze, searching for a reason for his unease. He attempted to probe Hearne's mind... but found nothing.

"Your sister and my son," Hearne continued, studying Larus with unsettling amusement, "have given us a fine grandson, haven't they, Maxwell?"

The pointed remark didn't go unnoticed. It was clear the man meant to remind Larus of his "illness." That same edge laced his voice.

Then his attention shifted toward the door. "Ah! Here is the fine lad now!"

Larus and his father turned as Max entered, cradling the child in her arms. Bartholomew followed several steps behind.

The appearance of little Silas drew the entire room's attention. Max sat, focused on her child, while her husband lingered nearby—but Larus noted with quiet interest that Bartholomew never touched his wife. If Max noticed, she gave no indication that she cared.

The great hall filled with murmurs of adoration for the child. Larus moved closer, placing a brief kiss on his sister's cheek.

"Brother." Max smiled, but her gaze returned to Silas.

Bartholomew offered Larus a curt nod, nothing more. Again, Larus attempted to read his brother-in-law's thoughts. Again, he got nothing.

Finally, his gaze fell upon the child.

Larus gasped.

The boy was exquisite. The most beautiful child he had ever seen. But more than that—something about him struck Larus with a strange, unsettling awe.

Max and her son seemed locked in their own world, mother and child staring at one another in perfect stillness.

"It is good to see you, Max. Your son is beautiful."

Max looked at him briefly before cradling Silas closer to her body.

"Such a lovely child," Geraldine murmured.

The family gathered around, drawn toward the couch as the child gazed up at his admirers. And that was when Larus saw it—the silver glint of Silas's pupils.

His eyes.

The colour of a full moon.

Larus stiffened, his gaze darting toward Micah, then Geraldine and Sebastian. They had seen it too. They knew what the child was.

He sat beside Max, who barely acknowledged his presence.

Silas's silver eyes locked onto his, the infant's steely gaze unrelenting, willing him to look away. Larus reached for his nephew's tiny hand. The child let out a sharp squeal.

Max shielded him instantly. "He does not like strangers," she said.

"Nonsense, Larus," Isabelle interjected. "Silas takes well to everyone..." Her gaze flickered toward her brother. "Well, except our dear Larus."

With a teasing smile, she nudged him aside and plucked the child from Max's arms. The moment Silas was in her grasp, his wailing stopped.

"There, little Silas," she cooed, dabbing his tears away. "That was just Uncle Larus." She turned to her brother with a grin. "Naughty uncle!"

Laughter rippled through the hall.

But Larus's mind remained fixed on the child's silver eyes—and the weight of what it meant.

PERCIVAL PACED AT A DISTANCE FROM THE GATHERED ADMIRERS OF HIS grandson, his steps slow and measured. He stood before the grand Bleddyn tapestry, his gaze shifting from its woven history to the man who called himself the head of this house.

Maxwell Bleddyn.

Percival studied him, then the tapestry, and found Maxwell lacking. A weak man. Unworthy of the name he bore.

The tapestry was a masterpiece, a vision of the Bleddyn lands as they had been before—before their clan of shapeshifters had grown soft. Percival's eyes traced the familiar scene: the church steeples on the hill, the sprawling forests, the figures of the once-great Bleddyns. At the centre stood the alpha, a silver-furred cloak draped over his broad shoulders. To his right, his sons. To his left, his wife and daughters. And upon a ridge near the church, a lone wolf, its head lifted in a silent howl beneath the full moon.

Percival let his fingers graze the woven threads. If only that fool Maxwell knew the true history of his bloodline.

He was lost in that world of the past when Bartholomew joined him.

"Father."

Percival did not respond at once. He had always believed a man should only speak when he had something worth saying. Finally, without turning, he murmured, "I feel out of touch."

He glanced over his shoulder at the gathered crowd.

"We have lost touch with who we are, Bartholomew. Our ancestors hunted these beasts—both the wolves and the vampires. We were the balance between them. And now? Now we are nothing." His voice darkened. "And I wonder... have we—have I—unleashed an abomination upon this world?"

He gestured to the tapestry.

"That world, Bartholomew, is long gone. And perhaps it should have stayed that way."

Bartholomew hesitated. His father's words held weight, but his mind was elsewhere.

"Father... have you noticed anything strange about Max's brother?"

Percival's eyes narrowed.

"Speak plainly, boy."

Bartholomew lowered his voice. "You once told me that shapeshifters can sense a vampire's presence." His words slowed. "And that vampires can scent the wolves."

Percival's brow furrowed. "Only after maturity. After their first transformation."

Bartholomew swallowed. "Then does that mean that my—our—"

Percival silenced him with a single sharp glare.

"Do you think this is the place for that conversation?"

Bartholomew cast a glance toward the others, lowering his head. "No, Father. But... Larus. The way Silas cried when he touched him."

A flicker of something crossed Percival's face.

"Hold your tongue. Now is not the time."

How could he have been so blind? His grip tightened behind his back. He turned to his son, studying him for a long moment.

Bartholomew had noticed. He had been right to.

And yet, Percival found no pride in it—only the bitter taste of failure.

Four vampires stood among them.

His stomach twisted at the realization. He had lost his way. His family had lost their way. *Once, we were hunters.* Once, they had ensured that neither species ruled the other.

His hand fell to Bartholomew's shoulder, fingers pressing firmly.

"I know now," Percival murmured, more to himself than to his son. "We have done the right thing."

His gaze drifted across the hall, toward the child at the heart of it all.

"Silas was born for a purpose."

THE DOOR TO MAX'S ROOMS CLICKED SHUT AFTER TILLEY LEFT. LARUS stared at the tray of food the old woman had brought for him—only she had noticed he had eaten nothing all evening. The roasted chicken and fresh bread, once a comfort, now repulsed him. The scent was cloying, thick with nostalgia, a reminder of a life that no longer belonged to him. He turned away, swallowing down the hunger that gnawed at him—not for food, but for something darker.

It was late. The guests had departed, leaving Bleddyn Manor in silence. Larus sat on the couch in his sister's chambers, watching as Max stood by the window, her gaze lost in the forest beyond.

"It's beautiful out there," she murmured. "Better during the day, of course."

Larus nodded, unwilling to admit how much he loved the night now. She had changed—no longer the spirited girl he had known but a woman tethered to something fragile. Her child was safely abed, yet she looked... lost. She spoke of the forest, of the world outside, yet it was clear she hardly lived in it.

"I am proud of you, Max," he said at last. "It's strange seeing you like this... a mother. Who would have thought you'd take to it so well?" He meant it, but his words barely seemed to reach her. She hugged herself, her expression unreadable.

"Do you think he's alright?" she asked, her voice small. "Silas and I are hardly ever apart."

Larus stiffened. He knew why she was asking. The child had been sent away to the adjoining room earlier after wailing at his touch. Twice now, Silas had shrieked in his presence, as though his very existence unsettled the boy. And worse, Percival and Bartholomew Hearne had taken notice. Their abrupt departure had sent a ripple of unease through the gathering, their eyes sharp with silent accusations.

Larus let the moment stretch before he spoke again. "Max... are things alright with you and your husband?"

She flinched. It was barely perceptible, but he saw it. She folded her arms tighter around herself, looking away. That small, instinctive gesture unraveled something in him.

A sick feeling twisted in his gut. He had promised himself he would never pry, never invade her thoughts, but— God help me, I have to know.

He reached into her mind. And what he saw sickened him.

Pain. Fear. Shadows clinging to her like a second skin. The bruises were not on her flesh but in her soul. Not from her husband—no, it was Percival Hearne she feared. The weight of his presence, his control. Bartholomew was little better. And yet, she would never speak of it. He saw that, too. She would endure it for her son, for the life she had built.

Larus clenched his jaw, his hands curling into fists. "What did he do to you, Max?" His voice was low, barely controlled. "Tell me."

She didn't. She wouldn't. But she didn't have to.

Larus closed his eyes for a moment, forcing his rage into something sharp, something cold. He leaned forward and kissed the crown of her head, just as he had when they were children. If she would not say the words, then he would not force her.

But as he left the room, one thought burned in his mind, searing through his restraint like fire through parchment.

They will pay.

And I will take pleasure in drinking their blood.

He shut the door behind him.

21

BAND OF HUNTERS

The midday sun blazed overhead, leaving the cemetery grounds cracked and parched. Graves lay forgotten beneath a tangle of long grass, weeds, and creeping shrubs. Below, five vampires moved deeper into the catacombs—so far that Larus wondered if the passages had an end. They remained hidden, bound by daylight's restraint, none of them having taken their daily sleep since the revelation of Silas.

Larus cast a glance around, studying yet another unfamiliar passage. This place stretched endlessly, a labyrinth of stone and shadow. "It is so old... How was it ever built?" His voice echoed off the walls.

Unlike the chambers above, these older tunnels were musty and thick with cobwebs. Crypts lined the walls, their inscriptions long faded, their bones dry and undisturbed. The scurrying of rats reached Larus's ears, tiny feet rustling in the darkness. A single torch flickered, unnecessary but present, its dim light casting long, jagged shadows.

Sebastian, brushing cobwebs from his black shirt, smirked. "The answer, chéri, lies within the tapestry."

Larus turned to him, frowning.

"The tapestry," Sebastian continued, "is a map of the Bleddyn lands, as they were centuries ago."

Larus blinked. As a child, he had played beneath that tapestry countless times—never once considering it held secrets.

"The old manor has long since crumbled," Geraldine added, "but the church still stands. And these catacombs remain as strong as ever."

Haruki, his long black braid now pinned into a precise bun, scratched his clean-shaven chin in thought. "This place… the graveyard…" He stepped closer, draping an arm over Larus's shoulder. His dark eyes gleamed with curiosity. "Most of your ancestors rest here. And now, we have access to your oldest living kin—a vampire."

Haruki had always insisted an awakening would provide the answers they sought. He wished to see Cecil, to speak with him. But Micah had been adamant. It was not yet time.

Sebastian, seated casually on the dusty steps beside Micah, stretched his long legs. "We must focus on what we learned two nights past."

Micah inclined his head. "Sebastian is right." Larus caught the slight quirk of Sebastian's lips at hearing his name from Micah's mouth. "We cannot assume they are ignorant of our existence. What we now know is certain—there are hunters among us."

Geraldine's voice was calm but firm. "But it is forbidden for a hunter to mate with a shapeshifter. The ancient covenant demands neutrality."

Larus, still adjusting to the politics of his kind, felt his confusion deepen. "Covenant?"

Sebastian sighed, closing his eyes for a moment before opening them again with an indulgent smile. "Ah, mon chéri, to be so young… so innocent… so pure."

Rising from the steps, he paced slowly around Larus, his voice taking on the cadence of a storyteller.

"Lycanthropes and vampires have been at war for ages—natural enemies. It is in our very blood to see the other destroyed. And for centuries, we fought over the one thing we both craved most: humans. Their blood. Their lifeblood."

Sebastian's fingers grazed Larus's shoulder, trailing lazily down his arm until their fingers briefly touched. A shiver ran through Larus, unbidden.

"Yes, chéri, we could survive on beasts… rats, even." Sebastian's lips curved into a smirk. "But human blood is sweeter."

He resumed pacing. "The hunters' purpose was never just to slay our kind. They were mediators—charged with maintaining balance. If the lycanthropes destroyed all vampires, they would eventually turn on themselves. And humans?" He gave a one-shouldered shrug. "Wiped out in the crossfire."

"The elders forged a pact," he continued. "Territories were established, terms agreed upon. Only the hunters could roam freely. But they were never—never—to align with either species."

Larus frowned. "But... vampires cannot have children."

"No," Sebastian agreed, his voice quieter now. "But they can love." His gaze turned knowing. "And what do you think happens when a hunter loves a vampire?"

Larus's stomach clenched. The thought of his sister and what she had endured sent a flare of rage through him.

He exhaled sharply. "Bartholomew loves Max," he said, voice tight.

Sebastian nodded. "You shall have your vengeance, chéri. But killing a hunter is no easy feat."

Geraldine's voice was gentle. "Do not underestimate them, dear one."

"They are strong," Haruki added. "Some... immortal. Though rare, a few possess longevity similar to our own."

Sebastian's smile returned, dark and knowing. "But unlike us, they do not heal instantly. Wound them deeply, and they will bleed out. Of course..." He tilted his head. "A cleaner way is to sever the head. Then burn the remains."

Larus barely heard him. His mind was spinning. The covenant. The hunters. Silas.

Then Sebastian's voice cut through his thoughts like a blade.

"I was a fool."

The shift in his tone made them all turn. Sebastian looked... furious.

Micah narrowed his eyes. "Losing your touch?"

"Never, mon frère." But his gaze was fixed on Larus now, his expression dark with realization.

"The child," Sebastian said, "is immortal."

A stunned silence filled the catacombs.

Sebastian's fingers curled into a fist. "Percival Hearne knew what he was doing. He orchestrated this." His voice was edged with rage. "He wagered that one of them—either himself or his son—carried the gift of immortality. He gambled on nature. And when Bartholomew proved lacking, Percival took matters into his own hands."

Sebastian's lips curled in disgust. "He ravished your sister, chéri. And now, he has what he wanted—the perfect heir."

Larus's chest tightened. He could barely breathe.

"The instincts and strength of a hunter," Sebastian continued, "combined with the blood of the wolf. That is what Silas is."

Micah exhaled slowly, his expression unreadable. "We must wake Cecil."

Larus swallowed hard. "Now?"

Micah nodded. "Silas is still a child. He will not mature for years. But we cannot afford to be unprepared."

Haruki's voice was grim. "We must also find Babette and Benoît."

Larus could barely comprehend it all. His nephew—the child whose cries of fear still echoed in his mind—was something… unthinkable.

A hunter and a wolf combined.

And they had no idea what that meant for them all.

It had been a week since his return to the capital, and although White Castle was his new home, Larus felt empty inside. He had become something magnificent as an immortal, yet part of him ached for the life he left behind. He and the others had left the catacombs, not knowing when they would return or when he would see his family again. It had been decided that Cecil would remain in his long sleep, with Micah personally ensuring his safety.

The moon was full. Larus and Sebastian ran fast and far from White Castle to a distant town where they could feed. Their coven was small, and although Micah's centre for the sick provided some blood, it was never enough to sustain five ravenous vampires. Larus, a newborn, struggled with cravings that sometimes became unbearable. That night, while Micah dined on the blood of Ashkan, and Geraldine eased a dying patient into the next world, Larus and Sebastian had to hunt.

They stopped outside the entrance of a tavern. The Black Cauldron Inn. It was an old two-story building, weathered but alive with drunken voices spilling into the night.

Sebastian studied the wooden sign above the door. "Don't worry, chéri, we will not go hungry tonight."

Larus closed his eyes. The air was thick with the scent of sweat, ale, and old wood, but what consumed him was the noise inside—so many thoughts, so many minds overlapping. All innocent.

"No, chéri," Sebastian murmured. "Not all." His lips curled as his gaze flicked toward the upper level of the tavern. "There are nine humans asleep above. Their dreams are... delicious." He closed his eyes for a moment, exhaling softly. "Ah, passion. Ecstasy. Fear. A wonderful mix."

Larus frowned. "I only see flashes. A rush of images—I can't always tell who they belong to." Even as he spoke, the chaotic flood of thoughts battered his mind. Death. Desire. Guilt. Sorrow. He barely knew how to separate one voice from another.

"Patience, chéri. By the time you are one hundred, it will be second nature." Sebastian's grin was all mischief. "The sleepers are of no use to us. But those below? There is potential." His eyes gleamed as he turned to Larus. "Tonight, we dine well."

He took Larus's hand and squeezed it. The touch sent a shiver through him. Larus closed his eyes, confusion stirring within him.

"Let it flow, chéri..." Sebastian's voice was a whisper of silk. "Move through their thoughts. Listen to their voices. They are all different. Find the one who deserves death."

For two hours, they waited, watching from the roof, listening as the night unfolded beneath them. Then, a man stepped out of the tavern—a large, broad-shouldered brute, staggering slightly from drink.

Larus knew. Him.

He had seen into this man's mind. This one deserves to die.

"Go after him, chéri," Sebastian murmured. "And do try not to make a mess this time."

Larus tensed. He knew what Sebastian had seen—his memory of that first kill, the one where he had lost control. He said nothing, slipping into the shadows, moving with speed and silence as he followed his prey.

The man left the main road, cutting through the forest—his usual shortcut home. He was alone. Vulnerable.

Larus moved ahead, waiting in the darkness. When the human finally emerged, his steps uneven but his posture firm, Larus stepped forward, letting the moonlight catch his face.

The man stopped. His pulse jumped. "Who's there?" His voice was rough, impatient.

Larus remained silent.

The human squinted into the dark, inhaling sharply as he caught sight of him. Then, a smirk. "Well, lookie here. A pretty lad."

Larus took a step forward. "I am Larus."

The man's smirk faded. His body shifted, shoulders squaring, fists curling. "Bugger that! What's your business with me, boy?"

Larus moved. In a blink, he had the man's throat in his grip, lifting him effortlessly, shoving him hard against the trunk of a tree. The human gasped, thrashing. Fear poured from him in waves.

Larus bared his fangs. "I am your death."

He struck. His teeth sank into flesh, warm blood spilling over his tongue. It burned through him, filling him with fire. And then—

A vision.

A woman. A man. A name.

Babette.

Larus wrenched himself back, his breath ragged, blood dripping from his lips. He stared into those green eyes—eyes that now saw him as nothing more than a monster.

"The woman, Babette," Larus demanded. "And her brother. Who are they to you?"

The man coughed, his body sagging. "Why the hell... do you think I know Babette?" His words slurred. The venom was taking hold.

Larus hesitated. The blood did not lie. But what does this mean?

This man should have died. Instead, Larus lifted a hand and struck him hard across the temple. The body crumpled to the ground. Unconscious.

Not dead.

Larus stood there, staring down at him, the hunger still gnawing at his core.

But something stronger held him back.

HE HEARD SEBASTIAN'S FOOTSTEPS BEFORE THE VAMPIRE EVEN SPOKE.

"Well, chéri, you have made a mess of things again." Sebastian's voice was laced with amusement, but beneath it, something else lingered—curiosity, perhaps. "What have you done, child?"

Larus didn't turn. He was still in shock, his gaze locked on the unconscious man, eyes fixated on the bloody wound at his throat.

Sebastian exhaled softly. "Ah, a discovery, chéri... and a fruitful one."

Larus whirled on him, rage flaring hot in his chest. "Why do you do it?" His voice was raw, demanding. "Why the hell do you invade my mind without my permission? Why do you torment me so?" He faltered, guilt striking the moment the words left his mouth. His anger wavered. When he spoke again, his voice had softened. "Why is everything a joke to you, Sebastian?"

Sebastian's smirk faltered. He gave a small nod, lips pressing into a grimace—almost as if shamed. "Forgive me, chéri."

But the moment passed quickly. His eyes flicked to the man on the ground, darkening with something far more serious. Larus had never seen him like this.

"You've bitten him."

The human stirred, groaning as his head lolled side to side. His body shuddered, the venom sinking deeper into his veins.

"He will die, Larus," Sebastian murmured.

"But... he—"

"He has seen the vampires we seek." Sebastian stepped closer, gesturing toward the writhing human. "You must decide, chéri. I saw only fragments of what you found in his blood. You must finish what you started."

Larus shook his head. "You finish it."

Sebastian's expression hardened. "Your venom rushes through his veins," he said. "You have a choice." His voice was calm, almost coaxing. "Either way, chéri, you must have his blood."

"Either way?"

"If he dies now, he takes everything he knows of the two vampires we seek with him. You cannot drink from him once he's dead." Sebastian's hand closed firmly around Larus's shoulder, steadying him. "You are a vampire, chéri. Embrace what you are. Search through his blood memories... or turn him."

Larus took a step back. "Sebastian... I don't—"

"Our coven is small," Sebastian pressed. "And this one—he will be formidable if you turn him now. We cannot allow him to take what he knows to the grave."

Confusion clawed at Larus's mind. He had no clue how to make a vampire. No idea how to take this life and shape it into something new.

"You do it," he said, his voice barely above a whisper.

Sebastian moved the instant the words left Larus's lips. He fell upon the human's throat, drinking deep. The venom subdued the man quickly, his struggles weakening, body slackening as the last remnants of his mortal life faded away. When Sebastian was done, he tore open his own wrist, pressing it firmly to the human's lips.

"Yes, drink, my friend," he whispered, voice almost tender. "Drink and be reborn."

The human's lips parted, instinct taking over. He swallowed.

Sebastian waited another moment before pulling his wrist away. "Come," he said. "We must return him to the castle. He must sleep." He glanced at Larus, eyes gleaming with something knowing. "Micah will want to hear what this one knows of Babette and Benoît. I have seen their faces."

Larus nodded slowly. He had seen them too.

Babette.

Beautiful. Enigmatic. A name written in blood.

And now, everything was about to change.

Four vampires sat in silence within the castle's dimly lit chamber. Micah paced, his footsteps soft against the stone floor, yet each one carried the weight of his anger. No one spoke. His fury had been palpable ever since he learned that Sebastian had turned a human without his consent.

Above them, beneath the flickering glow of candlelight, Estlyn's watchful gaze bore down upon them. The negress stood bold as ever, trapped in her world of oil and canvas. Larus studied the painting, wondering what the woman in the portrait might have thought of this gathering, of Micah's anger, of the silent tension that bound them all. More than that, he wondered why his maker had been so enraged by Sebastian's decision.

The new vampire had already fed—Giles had given him blood—and after long hours alone with Micah, he had been allowed to rest. The sun loomed beyond the shuttered windows, its presence unwelcome. They had yet to take their sleep.

Finally, Micah turned to Larus.

"You could have taken his memories and let him die."

His words were cold. Calculated. Then, he faced Sebastian. Their eyes locked, the tension between them like a blade drawn too tight.

"I did what I thought was best," Sebastian said, his voice smooth but unwavering.

Micah laughed, though there was nothing amused about it. "Oh, I am certain you did exactly that, brother." He spat the word like it disgusted him.

Larus glanced at Geraldine, who shook her head. Haruki grimaced but said nothing. Geraldine raised a hand—a silent command for Larus to hold his tongue.

Sebastian rose to his feet, standing tall before Micah. "I was the one!" His voice broke through the heavy air. "Me! I was the oldest of Emilio's children."

Micah's fury darkened his eyes. "Emilio left me in charge!" His voice was thunder. "I was the one who stood by him. And where were you, Sebastian? Off chasing love, stirring trouble—always creating problems that only Emilio could fix!"

Sebastian's lip curled, his fangs flashing. "And you—" He took a step closer. "It was because of you that our coven was lost!"

Geraldine shot to her feet. "Sebastian!"

"Why mustn't I say it, Geraldine?" Blood welled in Sebastian's eyes. "Why should we not speak the truth? It was because of him that Emilio died!"

Larus barely had time to react before Micah's hand struck Sebastian's face with brutal force. The blow sent him tumbling, his body crashing hard against the stone wall.

Sebastian sprang forward, and the two collided in a frenzy of fists and fury. The fight was quick, but vicious. Micah stopped defending himself first, allowing several punishing blows to land before Sebastian finally relented. Both vampires slumped against the floor, breathless despite their undead nature.

"You must accept it, Micah." Sebastian's voice was ragged. "We are equals now. We rule this coven together."

He turned sharply and strode from the room, the door slamming behind him with an echoing boom.

Micah sat there, back against the wall, his face unreadable.

"Leave me," he said.

Larus moved to follow Geraldine and Haruki toward the door, but before he could step through, Micah spoke again.

"Not you, Larus."

Larus hesitated.

"You stay."

Larus did not know what to do. Should he comfort his maker? Apologize? Guilt coiled in his chest, suffocating. If only he had done what Micah had taught him—searched Yaro's blood memories and let him die. Yaro. The name of their newest coven member. If he had ended the man's life, none of this would have happened.

Micah's voice pulled him from his thoughts.

"Mama always said everything happens for a reason. But I doubt she believed she was born to be a slave." He winced as he pushed himself upright. "Still, for most things, she would say there was a purpose."

Larus rushed to his side. "Are you hurt, Micah?"

His maker gave a pained smile. "As you know, vampires possess a high threshold for pain. We are strong. Sebastian is strong. And if he truly wanted to kill me… he could have."

Larus frowned. "Then why fight at all?"

A shadow passed through Micah's hazel eyes. "Because the moment Sebastian turned Yaro, he challenged my place as elder of this coven." He moved to one of the couches and sat gingerly. "My body will heal. My pride, however…" He exhaled. "That may not."

Larus hesitated, then joined him on the couch. "What do you mean?"

Micah leaned forward, steepling his fingers. "A coven must have an elder. Emilio was ours because he made us all. Vampires who join a coven —those who were turned outside of it—must be subject to its leader and are forbidden from siring their own progeny." His gaze sharpened. "A newborn is bound to their maker for a long time, Larus. Sometimes centuries before they create a house of their own. Yaro will be bound to Sebastian, not to me."

Larus's eyes dropped to the floor. "But… Sebastian must have known that."

Micah's smile was mirthless. "Oh, he knew." He leaned back, his voice distant. "Emilio made him long before my mother brought me into this world. I was Emilio's favourite. But before I existed, it was Sebastian he loved best." He exhaled, shaking his head. "Sebastian got away with breaking every rule. Emilio let him. Because that's who he is, Larus. A bringer of mischief and confusion."

Larus clenched his fists. Sebastian knew exactly what he was doing.

"And Yaro?" he asked. "What will become of him?"

"Yaro is one of us now. We cannot abandon him. But it means our coven has two masters—Sebastian and I are now equals."

Larus stiffened. Sebastian had tricked him. He had no doubt the flamboyant vampire could have pulled the memories from Yaro's blood himself. Instead, he had pushed Larus into an impossible choice, forcing him down a path that had forever changed their coven.

"You must not hate him, Larus." Micah's voice was calm, but firm. "Sebastian will only ever be himself. He is our brother. And he is your elder."

Larus bit his tongue.

Micah studied him a moment before continuing. "I have spoken with Yaro and confirmed what you and Sebastian saw in his blood memories." He sat back, folding his arms. "Yaro is Slavic, descended from the old pagans. He was raised in Paris until his family crossed the sea."

Paris. Larus had only heard of the city as a child—stories of its beauty, its grandeur. But in recent years, all he had heard were whispers of death and war.

"After his parents died, Yaro returned to France to settle their affairs," Micah went on. "That was nearly a decade ago. He met Babette and Benoît when they purchased his family's estate."

Larus straightened. "They bought the entire estate?"

Micah nodded. "That means they are not merely passing through. They are settled. Which means we can find them."

"Then... it will be easy?"

Micah's expression darkened. "I hope so, young one. But we must tread carefully. I suspect they are not alone. We may be walking into a den of dangerous vampires."

We. The word struck Larus harder than he expected.

"You mean—"

"Yes, Larus. We leave for Paris in three days." Micah clapped a firm hand on his shoulder as he rose. "Geraldine and Haruki will remain here with Yaro. You will travel with Sebastian and me."

A thrill of excitement surged through Larus—but it was chased quickly by fear. He had never crossed the sea. The thought of being trapped on a ship for days made his stomach knot.

Micah's voice interrupted his thoughts one last time. "Until we depart, you will train with Sebastian. You must learn to shield your mind."

Larus swallowed hard.

Sebastian.

22

PARIS (1794)

The journey to Paris would last several more weeks, though Larus was grateful for the strong winds. Nearly four weeks at sea, and the thought of another night trapped in the bowels of the ship made his skin crawl. He, Micah, and Sebastian were at their most vulnerable during the day, their safety entrusted to Ashkan.

Larus often walked the deck at night, listening to the ship's creaks and groans, the whispering of the waves against the hull. He respected the Persian for his vigilance, for standing guard while they rested. And yet, he pitied him, too.

Ashkan longed to be like them.

Larus had seen it in his eyes, heard it in his voice. But Micah had yet to grant him the one thing he desired above all else. Still, Larus understood why. The coven depended on Ashkan, trusted him implicitly. A human could walk in the sun, move unnoticed among mortals, secure them safe passage when they slumbered. If Ashkan became one of them, he would be powerful—but he would also be bound by the same limitations.

Larus exhaled, gazing out over the vast black ocean from the ship's stern. It was August, yet the wind carried a bitter chill. The moon rode high above, silver light spilling across the restless water. He had mastered the art of shielding his mind—had learned to sift through the thoughts of others, deciphering them like a weaver untangling threads. Below deck, he heard the captain's heavy pacing. At the bow, two crewmen whispered in hushed voices. And from their footsteps alone, Larus could tell them apart.

Paris was less than three weeks away.

He could hardly wait to set foot on land again. The ship unsettled him, its confinement suffocating. He looked as far as his vampire eyes allowed—nothing but endless water in all directions. The hunger was always there, gnawing at his insides. It was impossible to feed well aboard the ship, leaving him to make do with rodents and livestock—swine, horses. It was enough to keep him sated, but never enough to quell the need.

He sensed them before he saw them.

Micah and Sebastian moved as soundless as shadows, but Larus had learned to feel their presence.

"Your skill improves, chéri." Sebastian's voice curled around him like smoke.

Larus turned to them with a grin.

"Sebastian speaks true, young one." Micah nodded, his hazel eyes keen. "You grow stronger."

Larus glanced past them. "Where is Ashkan?"

"Our loyal friend rests," Sebastian said. "He is human, chéri, and these long days of vigilance take their toll."

Larus hesitated. "Micah... why not make him one of us?" He could not imagine the torment of a life spent guarding vampires while denied their power.

Micah's expression was unreadable. "Ashkan's time will come."

It was clear he would say no more on the matter.

Instead, his gaze drifted toward the horizon. "France is in turmoil," he murmured. "It has been only a year since they executed Louis XVI."

Sebastian's lips curled in something between amusement and disdain. "They have had their revolution, chéri... but we must not become entangled in their Reign of Terror."

Micah's voice was firm. "We find Babette and Benoît. Then we leave Paris."

Nothing more. Nothing less.

Larus nodded, but the unease in his chest remained.

THEY STAYED AT A RURAL ESTATE WHERE THEY COULD HUNT FREELY BY NIGHT and rest in safety by day. Again, the three vampires took their sleep with confidence, knowing Ashkan would give his life to protect them.

Larus roamed the countryside after sunset, captivated by Paris. If only he could see it beneath the light of day—walk by the brooks, wander through the vales, feel the sun kiss his face. But such a dream was lost to him forever.

That night, he perched atop the steep roof of their château, surveying the land. It astounded him that Micah's wealth extended even here, beyond the sea. The sprawling estate stretched into the darkness, an empire built in silence. Above, the sky was an abyss without moonlight.

He did not stir when Sebastian joined him on the thatched roof.

"How can Micah own all this?" Larus asked, his voice quiet.

Sebastian reclined beside him, draping an arm over his bent knee. "Wealth can last for ages, chéri." His voice was laced with amusement. "It is sometimes vital for our survival. We live many lives. Humans die. We remain."

Larus glanced at him. "How do vampires acquire such wealth?"

"Micah inherited our maker's estates. It was Emilio who gave him this legacy." Sebastian's fingers idly played with the golden embroidery on his sleeve. "You see, chéri, Emilio was born to a noble family. He understood that our kind must always have refuge." He squeezed Larus's shoulder, his grip firm but warm. "But enough talk of fortunes. The night is young, and Micah has a surprise for you. Let us feed."

They returned to the château within an hour. As Micah had warned, Paris was in turmoil, and it was all too easy to find prey. Larus fed well, but after over a week in the city, he had yet to experience anything truly exciting.

They found Micah alone in the château's small library, surrounded by books.

Sebastian sighed dramatically as they entered. "I will never understand your obsession with books, Micah." He gestured at the shelves, turning to Larus with a smirk. "He has always been like this, chéri. Even in the first years after Emilio made him, Micah would spend days buried in scrolls and tomes, ignoring all else."

Micah slid a book back into its slot and turned to face them. His gaze settled on Larus. "I have made inquiries."

Larus straightened. Since their arrival, Micah had left the estate each night, always returning in the last hours before dawn—always alone. Never once had he permitted Larus to accompany him. As for Sebastian, he came and went as he pleased.

"I have met with an old acquaintance," Micah continued. "Someone I trust. Yaro's information has proven useful. The vampires Babette and Benoît are here in Paris—and they are hosting a ball."

Sebastian hummed, trailing his nails across the leather spines of books as he walked along the shelves. "Selected humans will be in attendance, chéri." His voice was laced with mischief. "Wealthy ones. Some will be turned. Others will die. This ball is to welcome the newborns."

Micah nodded. "Monique has secured us an invitation."

Larus sat at the edge of the couch, pulse quickened by anticipation. A gathering of hundreds of vampires? He could hardly believe it.

Micah's tone turned grave. "But we must be careful. Our hosts can never know why we have come to Paris." His hazel eyes darkened. "And they must never discover that we are the children of Emilio."

LARUS MET THE VAMPIRE MONIQUE INSIDE THEIR CARRIAGE. HE HAD ENJOYED the ride into the city, taking in the sights as Ashkan guided them along the cobbled streets. They were all dressed for the occasion—even Ashkan, who had donned a fine black silk Coachman's top hat. His hair and beard had been meticulously groomed with scented oil.

Larus's gaze remained fixed on the quaint city house steps, waiting for Micah's mysterious friend to appear. His maker stepped out of the carriage, leaving the door ajar. Across from Larus, Sebastian reclined lazily, his ever-troublesome smile playing at his lips.

"Ah, mon chéri," Sebastian mused. "If I were still human, I would weep at the sight of you—our young chéri coming of age."

Larus barely suppressed his grin, but a question lingered in his mind. "This Monique... can she be trusted?"

Sebastian exhaled in amusement. "Micah and I are not the same, chéri, but, unfortunately, I must confess—I trust him." He leaned slightly toward the open door. "Ah... chéri, the lady comes."

Larus turned his head just in time to see an elegant figure descending the steps. She moved with effortless grace, the embroidered blue silk of her gown catching the dim glow of the city lanterns. Monique's dark skin shimmered in the moonlight, her shaved head accentuating the striking contours of her high cheekbones. Larus caught his breath. She was beautiful.

Her narrow hips swayed as she approached Micah, exuding an air of confidence that made her petite stature seem trivial. Micah bent low, pressing a kiss to her lips.

"My dear Monique," he murmured. "The most beautiful vampire this night."

Monique's voice, light and almost childlike, carried a hint of teasing. "Micah, mon amour, you flatter me."

Her gaze shifted toward the carriage, sweeping over Sebastian before settling on Larus. She dragged a gloved hand across Micah's chest as she stepped past him. Then, with a subtle arch of her brow, she turned slightly, addressing Micah without looking at him.

"So... this is your newborn?" Her tone was almost one of dismay. "Micah, have you not taught him the charms of a gentleman?"

Larus, startled, stumbled as he stood within the confined space of the carriage. He extended his hand hastily to assist her inside.

"I—I am sorry," he stammered.

Monique stepped in smoothly and, with a playful shove, guided Larus back into his seat before settling close beside him. She smelled of jasmine, and the sheen of oil on her scalp gleamed in the dim carriage light. Larus could tell she was an ancient one, possibly older than Micah, though she could not have been more than thirty when she was turned.

"A pleasure to meet you, Larus." Her voice was warm, but her dark eyes held a knowing gleam as they shifted to Sebastian. "And you, Sebastian—I had heard you had come."

Sebastian grinned, taking her hand and pressing a kiss to it.

Micah boarded, and with that, the carriage rolled forward, bound for Babette's ball. Larus remained still, keenly listening as the others spoke of the night's coming events.

"I did as you asked, Micah." Monique's voice was smooth, confident. "I spoke your name to Babette, and I saw no sign that she or Benoît recognized it." A small, knowing smile played on her lips as she turned to Sebastian. "Babette is a clever one." She raised a single finger. "But Benoît... not so much. At least, not without her."

Sebastian frowned. "What nonsense is this? How can he be clever with her and a fool without her?"

Monique tilted her head, her smile mischievous. "They are inseparable... most of the time."

Micah let out a soft chuckle. "Again, Monique, you leave things unexplained."

She ignored him. "Many say the two were enchanted at birth."

Sebastian scoffed. "Witchery? Mon Dieu, surely you jest."

Monique's smile did not waver. "I do not. Babette and Benoît are old—some say over a thousand years."

The sound of Ashkan's whip cracked against the night, the horses' hooves echoing against the stone road as Monique continued.

"Their mother, the witch, met a monk on the road during his long pilgrimage. Weary from his travels, the holy man accepted shelter in her meagre dwelling one stormy night. And there, beneath the howling winds, she seduced him. She was a négresse like myself, and he, a dark Moor."

Larus leaned forward, entranced.

"The monk, tormented by his sin, returned to his monastery and confessed all. He never left again. But the witch, knowing she carried his child, took comfort in the knowledge that she would never again be alone."

Larus hesitated. "They are witches?"

Monique lifted a delicate shoulder. "I doubt it." Her gloved finger rose again. "But the brother and sister... they are different. And yet, they are alike. They are twins, after all."

Sebastian's patience wore thin. "Enough riddles, woman. Speak plainly."

Monique's dark eyes gleamed with amusement. "Babette's right eye is brown. Her left, green as an emerald. Benoît is the same—but mirrored. A green right eye, a brown left." She let the weight of her words settle before continuing. "With their distinct looks, they are known by all. All of Paris—all of our kind—knows of Babette and Benoît Lenoir."

Her finger lifted once more, silencing Sebastian before he could interrupt.

"It is well known," she continued, "that Benoît and Babette are lovers."

Larus inhaled sharply. Micah and Sebastian exchanged a glance. Monique only smiled, enjoying the sudden shift in attention.

Finally, after a pause, she leaned in slightly. "But there is one secret between them."

Sebastian's grin returned, slow and wicked. "And what might that be?"

Monique tilted her head coyly. "Babette loves another."

Larus could feel the shift in the air. Even Micah sat up a little straighter.

Monique's voice dropped to a hushed whisper. "Benoît must never know. Babette keeps her lover hidden—not out of fear, but for the safety of the one she adores."

Sebastian leaned closer, his voice laced with curiosity. "And who is this human? This man?"

Monique's lips curled. "No man..." She let the words linger before revealing the truth. "A woman. Babette's lover is none other than Helene Rozelle."

Sebastian burst into laughter, holding his stomach. "The heiress?"

"The very one."

The carriage rocked gently as the city streets stretched before them. Monique let a moment of silence hang before speaking again.

"You know me, Sebastian. And you, Micah. I am known among all vampires that matter—even those within the great council." Her voice lowered. "And Babette is well thought of among them. Over the centuries, she and her brother have aided the council's cause."

Larus watched as Sebastian and Micah shared another glance.

"I have sung at their gatherings," Monique continued. "I have listened to their confidants. And I have learned things." She smirked. "These friends guard their minds well from Benoît, for they know of Helene."

Micah's brow furrowed. "Why has she not turned the heiress?"

Monique's gaze grew distant. "Babette loves her immortality." A pause. "And she hates it." She sighed. "She envies Helene's mortality. It torments her. Helene begs Babette to turn her—it is the only thing they quarrel about."

Larus thought of Ashkan and wondered if Micah and his devoted servant had such quarrels.

Suddenly, the distant sounds of music and laughter drifted through the air.

"We are nearly there," Monique said. She looked at each of them in turn. "Remember. Let me bring Babette to you. She detests flattery and cannot abide those who seek her attention. Greet her—then depart."

She smiled knowingly.

"Do this, and I guarantee—Babette will want more of you."

THE CARRIAGE ROLLED INTO A VAST COURTYARD, ILLUMINATED BY HUNDREDS of lamps. Larus leaned out the window, his eyes wide with awe. The grounds were exquisite: fountains cascaded into sparkling pools, sculpted hedges glowed with hidden lamps, and tiny illuminated boats drifted across the water. "Babette," Monique said with a knowing smile, "is famous for hosting the most extravagant balls." She lightly brushed Larus's cheek with her gloved hand.

Larus could hardly believe his eyes. His first step out of the carriage was a moment of wonder, and he stood there, speechless, as his gaze swept over the grounds. Vampires and humans alike roamed the gardens, their laughter and chatter blending with the distant music.

"There are hundreds more inside," Monique said, linking her arm with Micah's as they made their way up the grand stairs.

Micah looked over his shoulder, his voice firm but calm. "Remember your lessons, young one. Ashkan, leave now as I instructed."

Sebastian's presence at Larus's side was a comforting weight. The older vampire took his arm with a reassuring grip. "You worry too much, chéri." His voice was soft, but Larus could hear the confidence in it. "Look around you."

Larus followed Sebastian's gaze. Vampires, pairs of them, were entwined in intimate embrace—some male, some female—each seemingly at ease in their own world. In the distance, a tall vampire led a woman off toward the shadowed edges of the courtyard. Sebastian moved ahead, his stride purposeful. Larus, still adjusting to the chaos of the event, kept close.

Inside the grand ballroom, the music swelled, a blend of strings and voices that filled the towering space. Vampires danced, twirling gracefully across the floor, their movements as fluid as the sound surrounding them. Larus's heart raced with excitement, the sensory overload intoxicating. Sebastian guided him through the crowd, his hand at Larus's back, as they joined the dance.

In the middle of the ballroom, Larus spotted his maker. Micah stood with Monique at his side, but it was the presence of two figures behind them that made Larus's breath catch in his throat. Babette. And her twin brother, Benoît. Their eyes locked on Micah, sharp and unblinking.

Sebastian saw it too, his expression unreadable. "Come, chéri," he whispered. "Let's take a walk, shall we? There's no need to linger here."

Larus barely registered his words. His mind spun with a whirlwind of thoughts, and the moment Babette's gaze shifted toward him, his heart skipped. He tried, desperately, to shield his thoughts from her, but her eyes—those mismatched, piercing eyes—were unyielding.

Sebastian shook him, his voice low and urgent. "Shield your thoughts, Larus." He gave a small, but forceful nudge, and Larus finally snapped out of his reverie. Babette had already seen too much.

Micah's voice cut through the tension. "Come, join us," he beckoned.

Larus, feeling as though he was moving through a dream, stepped forward. Babette extended her hand to him, her lips curling into a smile.

"You surprise me, Micah. Oui?" Her eyes swept over him, measuring, probing, before flicking back to Sebastian. "You have a fondness for beauty, don't you?"

Larus couldn't move, his legs stiff. Babette's presence was overwhelming. She was radiant, her dark skin almost glowing under the chandelier's light. Her fan fluttered as she lightly tapped it against her fingers, a rhythmic sound that somehow made the air around them feel heavier.

Micah responded before Larus could find his voice. "Larus is young, still in his first year," he said, his tone light, as if brushing aside the tension. "I thought to leave him behind, but I feared I'd return to find far too many dead humans on my hands."

Babette's eyes, however, remained fixed on Larus, sharp and unblinking. She studied him for a long moment, her gaze searching, before turning her attention back to her brother.

Without warning, Benoît spoke his thoughts aloud, his voice cold and distant. "Come," he said, his tone commanding. "We speak in private."

Babette's skirt swished as she moved, and Larus, Sebastian, and Micah followed her with their eyes, caught in a silent awe. Benoît, ever the shadow, trailed behind his sister, his presence as unsettling as hers.

23

BABETTE

Babette knew this vampire was no fool. She had tried once—and failed—to break Micah's defences. He was young, but he was strong. She had searched the minds of the others, even Monique's, and though she sensed no deception from the singing vampire, Babette couldn't help but wonder why the three strangers guarded their thoughts so fiercely. But she was patient. She would bide her time, entertain them, and as she made them feel welcome, she would find a way to interrogate the newborn.

Babette could feel the bond between the three vampires. Micah and Sebastian cared for the petit one, and that would be their weakness. She would break him, and then all would be revealed.

Alone in her drawing room, Babette reclined comfortably on a plush couch, watching Larus as he admired the paintings hanging on the walls. "Louis XVI," she said with pride. "It's priceless, oui? I took it from the palace after his execution."

Larus's eyes gleamed with interest. She noted the way he studied the portrait, absorbing the history it represented. Babette's gaze softened for a moment, remembering her own life as a human, the struggles and turmoil she had endured before becoming a vampire.

"It's... beautiful," Larus said, his voice quiet.

Babette's eyes narrowed, intrigued by the newborn's vulnerability. There was something lonely in his gaze, a sadness she found oddly familiar. She felt a fleeting moment of pity for him.

Then Larus smiled, and the sudden warmth in his expression caught her off guard. "I think I would have done the same... uh, I mean, taking the painting."

Babette swished her fan open and laughed softly, but she noticed the wariness in the eyes of the other two vampires. They were afraid—afraid their newborn's defences might falter. Babette rose from the couch, her anger simmering beneath the surface. These three had come into her home thinking her a fool.

As she crossed the room toward the newborn, she admired her priceless possession again, then dragged the tip of her fan along Larus's shoulder. She locked eyes with his maker. The silence spoke volumes. They had come here for a reason.

Micah's realization came too late. "Larus!" he called, rushing forward, but Benoît was faster. Her twin was upon Micah before he could reach the newborn, pinning him to the ground with unnatural strength.

Sebastian, the sly one, attempted to reach Larus, but Babette was confident Benoît could handle him. She had underestimated them both.

In a flash, Sebastian was upon her. He moved with blinding speed, but Babette was ready. As she pressed Larus against the wall, ready to sink her fangs into his neck, Sebastian struck. The newborn broke free. Babette hissed in fury as Sebastian grabbed her, pulling her away.

"Go to Micah!" Sebastian commanded, his voice low but urgent.

Larus, shaken but not resisting, sprang to his maker's side. Babette struggled in Sebastian's grasp, her fangs bared as she pounded at his face. He was strong, stronger than she had anticipated. She needed just a drop of his blood, to read the truth buried in his memories.

She lunged for him, but before she could sink her fangs into Sebastian, he leapt upward, dragging her with him. Her body slammed against the coffered ceiling, and in that split second, he bit down on her neck.

They crashed to the floor in a tangled heap, the impact reverberating through the room.

Babette's mind raced as she heard Micah's deep voice.

"Stop!"

She turned to see Benoît subdued—not by two vampires, but by three. Her heart sank. Monique had betrayed her.

Benoît, enraged, struggled beneath Monique's weight, but it was no use. The newborn held his arms, while Micah loomed over him, ready to strike.

"*Sister, help me!*" Benoît's voice echoed in her mind, raw with desperation.

Micah locked eyes with Babette. "We came in peace, Babette. We seek information." He gestured to Sebastian. "Release him, or I'll tear Benoît's head from his body."

Babette's defiance cracked, but only for a moment. Her gaze flicked to her brother, who continued to plead silently.

"Let him go," Micah said. "The beautiful heiress will suffer the same fate if you don't."

The mention of Helene Rozelle stung, deepening the wound Babette had tried to keep buried. She could no longer hold on to her pride. Fear surged within her, and she finally relented.

Babette watched in silence as Micah sank his fangs into Benoît's neck. Her brother's blood memories poured into him, and she could do nothing but watch.

"I'll kill all of you!" she hissed, her voice full of venom.

Sebastian's laugh cut through her fury. "Over the long years," he taunted, "your memories have fermented your blood, ma petite dame."

"You'll never leave Paris alive!" Babette spat, but deep inside, she feared for her brother's life and for Helene.

Sebastian's voice, smooth and insidious, whispered in her ear. "Your lovely heiress, Helene Rozelle, will die if we don't leave now."

Babette shot Monique a scathing glance. How could these strangers know of her love for Helene? How could they have known that Benoît must never learn the truth?

"Leave!" Babette conceded, but her mind burned with promises of vengeance. She would make them pay for what they had done.

THEY ESCAPED THE FESTIVITIES ON FOOT, SLIPPING THROUGH THE DENSE forest and into the hills. Larus had tested his speed countless times, but this was different. Like Micah, Sebastian, and Monique, he ran now to save his life. Micah had ordered them to avoid the city streets of Paris, and their only goal was to reach their country estate, where Ashkan was keeping the heiress, Helene Rozelle, safe.

Larus kept pace with Monique, while Sebastian and Micah led the way. The female vampire had torn the skirt from her elegant gown, her movements fluid and swift. The trees blurred past them, their branches reaching out like dark fingers in the night. Though danger loomed, Larus couldn't help but smile—he was still in awe of his newfound strength, the power pulsing through his veins.

He watched in awe as Sebastian scaled a massive tree with ease, his movements quick as lightning. Within moments, he reached the top and surveyed the land behind them. Larus and Monique raced beneath him, but they all heard his voice carried through the air. "We must hurry," Sebastian called. "Five vampires are after us." He shot past them like a streak of light. "Hurry, chéri, we cannot lose you this night!"

When they reached the country estate, Ashkan was waiting by the door, his expression unreadable. "Micah," he said with a slight bow, "I have done as you commanded. The lady is secure."

"Thank you, Ashkan," Micah replied, his tone a mixture of relief and urgency. "But five vampires are on their way... right now." He offered a small, grateful smile as Ashkan's hand instinctively went to the hilt of his sword.

"I'm afraid this is one fight you cannot join, my friend," Micah continued, his voice low. "And I cannot lose you. I've watched you grow into the man you are, Ashkan. Go now, and remember—protect your mind. Babette must not find you."

Ashkan nodded without a word and left them.

Larus watched the exchange, feeling the quiet but undeniable bond between Ashkan and Micah. He realized now what it must have been like for Micah to find such a young boy, one he had raised and molded into the man he had become. Ashkan might have seemed older to the untrained eye, but Larus could see it now—the father-son connection between them, built over time.

Before Larus could dwell on the thought, Micah called his name. “Larus! Go with Ashkan. Babette will be upon us soon.”

“No, Micah, I can fight!” Larus protested, glancing at Sebastian for support. “There are five of them… and only three of you.”

“Give him a chance, Micah,” Sebastian said, his voice calm. “Let your newborn prove his worth.”

Micah’s expression darkened. “I will not allow—”

“What would Emilio have done, Micah?” Sebastian cut in. “Did our maker not allow us to fight for what we believed in? Did he not watch over us as we stood by him?”

Micah’s features tightened as the weight of their shared past settled over him. His bow of his head was a silent admission, and for a moment, Larus couldn’t tell whether the look on his maker’s face was one of sorrow or rage. “He did, Sebastian. But he died because of me… it is as you said.”

“Now is not the time for this, Micah.” Sebastian’s voice was firm as he turned his gaze toward the forest. “They’re coming. We must meet them in the woods.”

Larus didn’t hesitate. He followed his maker and Sebastian into the trees, Monique close by his side. The air grew colder as they dashed through the forest, the tension thickening with each step. They would fight. And Larus was ready to prove he was worthy of the trust they had placed in him.

Two packs of vampires faced each other. Larus stood with his back to Micah’s, his gaze darting to Sebastian, who stood beside Monique. He planted his feet apart, steeling himself against the terror clawing at his insides. He was a newborn vampire, and his existence as an immortal hung by a thread. Micah had laid out his plan before they entered the forest, but doubt gnawed at Larus—how could they possibly defeat five strong vampires? He had felt Babette's strength firsthand when she restrained him, and now she stood before them, a predator ready to strike.

Babette and Benoît stood together, their mismatched eyes fixed on their enemies. Behind them, three older vampires formed a line—a tall woman with red hair pulled back from her face, a grey-haired male who must have been turned in his forties, and a third vampire, younger in appearance but undoubtedly ancient. The latter hissed, barely containing his lust for battle, flicking his dreadlocks over his shoulders. He looked like a warrior, poised on the edge of violence.

Micah leaned toward Larus, whispering his intent. "The young one," he murmured, "is like you... perhaps fifty years a vampire. You are stronger. Subdue him, but do not kill him."

Larus set his sights on the younger vampire. A heartbeat later, Babette led the charge.

All fear vanished the moment Larus's opponent struck. The force sent him crashing into a tree trunk, knocking the breath from his lungs. He tried to rise, but his adversary was on him in an instant, driving a fist into his face and sending him tumbling through the undergrowth. But this time, Larus twisted midair, flipping gracefully before landing on both feet. Instinct took over. When his opponent lunged again, Larus met him with a brutal strike, launching the vampire backward. He crashed into a massive boulder and crumpled to the ground.

Larus stole a glance at the others. Sebastian grappled with the older male vampire, their bodies locked in a vicious struggle. Monique fought the red-haired woman, who shrieked in her grasp, her hair wild and tangled. And Micah—he alone faced the twins.

Larus turned back just as Benoît lunged. He barely had time to react before the force of the attack sent him crashing into the other newborn. They tumbled together, slamming into trees, grappling for control. But Larus had already bested one opponent, and now he fought harder, fuelled by the need to protect his maker. He overpowered the younger vampire at last and wrenched himself free.

Then he saw Micah.

Benoît had him in a crushing grip, forcing him to his knees. Babette stood over them, her arms coiled around Micah's throat like a serpent.

"I warn you," Babette snarled, "I will kill all of you!"

Larus's stomach twisted. He looked to Sebastian, who had subdued his opponent, forcing the vampire's face into the dirt. It didn't matter. They had lost. Babette would kill Micah, and there was nothing they could do to stop her.

Then, someone else saved them all.

"Release him!"

The voice cut through the chaos like a blade.

Ashkan.

Larus turned to see him standing at the edge of the clearing, holding a woman in front of him—a blade pressed to her throat. The firelight from the estate flickered behind them, illuminating her dark hair, her delicate features. Helene Rozelle.

Larus saw the agony in Babette's face. And in that moment, he understood.

"You will release us, Babette," Micah said softly, "or I shall have Ashkan kill the one thing you hold dear... your only love... your heartbeat."

Benoît stiffened, his mismatched eyes widening. "What?" He turned to his sister, his voice thick with disbelief. "Sister, you... love her?" He pointed toward Helene, his lips curling in fury.

The truth shattered him.

With a roar, Benoît lunged—straight for Helene.

Babette moved before she could think, launching herself after him. Ashkan stepped back, dragging Helene with him, but it didn't matter. Benoît didn't see anything, didn't hear anything. His rage consumed him. He wanted her dead.

Helene's shrill scream pierced the night.

And then Babette struck.

With a single, brutal motion, she tore her brother's head from his body.

Silence fell.

The battle forgotten, Babette dropped to her knees, her hands trembling as she clutched her brother's lifeless body. A sob raked through her, raw and broken. Blood-tears streaked her face.

Micah knelt beside her, gripping her shoulders, pulling her away. Just moments ago, they had been mortal enemies, but now, he held her as she wept.

He lifted his gaze to Babette's remaining companions. "Get her inside."

They obeyed without question.

Micah turned then, his eyes falling on Benoît's body. His severed head lay inches away, his expression frozen in fury.

At last, he spoke. "Larus, wait here until I return."

And so the newborn vampire was left alone, standing over the corpse of the fallen.

24

CECIL BLEDDYN

Larus stared down at the headless corpse, alone at the edge of the forest, enveloped by sorrow. Benoît's open eyes were frozen in shock, his lifeblood soaking into the earth. The newborn vampire wondered if he, too, would one day meet such an end.

He heard Micah's footsteps but didn't turn. He couldn't move. Micah stopped beside him, holding a blazing torch. The firelight flickered over Benoît's lifeless face. A vampire who had lived for ages, now reduced to nothing.

"It was our fault," Larus murmured, voice raw. "He died because of us."

Micah exhaled slowly. "Vampires are immortal," he said, "but I wonder if we truly are." He crouched and placed Benoît's severed head on his chest. "I wanted you to see this, Larus. How we die. When I set him ablaze, there will be nothing left. A millennium erased. What a waste."

"Why did she kill him?"

Micah gazed at the body for a moment before answering. "I doubt she meant to. Benoît would have killed Helene. Babette knew that, and she made her choice. It's never easy—to choose between the people you love."

He touched the flame to the corpse. Fire roared to life, devouring Benoît's remains in an instant. Larus stumbled back, watching in astonishment as the body turned to ash.

A cold dread coiled in his chest. "What of his bones?"

"We are the living dead, Larus. Benoît lived for centuries—his body had long since defied nature. When we die, nothing remains. But if a vampire takes the long sleep, their body withers to skin and bone, lingering until revived by blood."

Larus swallowed hard. "Micah, there's so much I don't understand. So much I need to know."

"There will be time, young one." Micah's face was striking in the firelight, his eyes reflecting the flames. "You can't learn everything in a day."

Larus pointed to the scorched ground. "And if I get my head torn off?"

"Then you will no longer exist."

They stood in silence, the scent of burning flesh fading into the night. Then, with sudden force, Micah drove the torch into the ground, extinguishing it.

"Babette asked me to do this," he admitted. "She couldn't bear to." His voice turned distant. "It is not an easy thing to watch someone you love die, Larus. I saw Emilio die, and I am still haunted by it."

Larus hesitated. "Sebastian... what he said—that Emilio died because of you. Micah, what happened?"

Micah was silent for a long moment. Then, at last, he spoke.

"I was young and arrogant. And yes, there were moments when, like Sebastian, I disobeyed my maker." His voice was heavy, laced with regret. "Emilio favoured me, and it caused a rift between Sebastian and me. There was a vampire named Gang, Sebastian's rival, and they waged a private war for years. Gang's leader, Marquez, tolerated it—until Sebastian destroyed him. Marquez called for Sebastian's death in return."

Larus listened, transfixed.

"A meeting was called. Emilio and Sebastian went, but I was forbidden to follow. I went anyway." Micah's jaw tightened. "I learned Marquez had no intention of sparing them. It was a trap. I was ready to fight, but we were three, and they were five. Seeing me, Emilio tried to negotiate. He proposed a duel—leader against leader—to spare our coven."

Micah's expression darkened. "Emilio was winning. But I was young. Reckless. I thought—if I intervened, if I helped him strike the killing blow, we would win. I was wrong." His voice broke. "Because I stepped in,

Emilio was distracted. He tried to protect me. And in that moment, Marquez killed him."

A sharp ache twisted in Larus's chest. "What happened to Marquez?"

"Sebastian found his revenge," Micah said, "but it cost us everything. Marquez slaughtered nearly our entire coven. The few of us who survived spent years in hiding. But in the end, Sebastian destroyed him." He let out a bitter breath. "I will never underestimate him again, Larus. Sebastian can accomplish anything he sets his mind to. He will kill what he hates—and protect what he loves."

Micah smiled faintly and cupped Larus's cheek. "Always let him love you, young one."

Larus trembled. All his human life, he had feared death. Now, in a world of immortality, mind reading, and blood memories, he realized that fear had not left him.

"Your blood memories," he said slowly. "I tasted your blood, but I didn't see all of this."

"Blood memories are truths," Micah explained. "They come in flashes—unfiltered, uncontrollable. The longer you drink, the clearer they become. Remember, Larus, Sebastian took Babette's blood memories by biting. Had he drained her for longer, he would have seen everything."

Larus swallowed. "And Babette's memories... they revealed something about Cecil, didn't they?"

Micah's gaze turned sharp. "Come." He placed a hand on Larus's shoulder. "There will be no need for blood memories tonight. Babette will tell us herself."

SUNRISE WAS STILL HOURS AWAY, AND THE FULL MOON HUNG HIGH, BATHING the night in silver light. Larus stood by the window, gazing at the small sitting room. Babette's face was streaked with blood tears, her sorrow palpable. The three vampires stayed close to her, silent in her grief.

By the door, Ashkan stood watchful as ever. Not far from Babette, Sebastian and Micah lingered, their presence heavy with unspoken words. Monique sat atop a desk, watching them all.

Larus turned back to the window. The moon's glow soothed him in a way he could not explain.

Finally, Babette spoke, her voice raw. "You come to my maison—my home." Her eyes darkened as they moved across the room, landing on Helene. "And you endanger the ones I love." She swallowed, then whispered, "I killed my brother."

Her gaze snapped to Micah, her next words venomous. "Why did you come to Paris?"

Micah met her glare without flinching. "We seek information," he said. "We must know about Cecil."

Babette stilled. "Cecil?" She repeated the name as if testing it on her tongue. Then she looked between Micah and Sebastian, suspicion flickering in her mismatched eyes. "How you know of Cecil?"

Sebastian took a step closer. "I have seen your blood memories." His voice was steady. "Who was this other vampire condemned to death? Odelia?"

Babette's expression tightened. "You knew of Cecil before you came." She exhaled sharply. "Odelia was the true leader of our coven, long ago. She died by Nathan's command." She paused. "Odelia is Nathan's mother."

She studied Micah and Sebastian for a moment, then her gaze drifted to Larus. Something shifted in her expression—something almost like recognition.

"You."

Larus stiffened as Babette leaned forward, her sorrow momentarily forgotten. Her eyes gleamed with strange curiosity.

"I know you... and yet, I do not."

Before he could react, she was suddenly before him, crossing the room in a heartbeat. Larus flinched, but Micah and Sebastian were just as fast, moving instinctively to shield him.

Babette laughed. "Don't worry, sillies," she said, waving them off. "I will not harm your pet."

She reached out and lifted Larus's chin with delicate fingers.

"Oui, oui... I see you now." Her gaze flickered toward the window. "Petit loup... young wolf."

Larus recoiled. "No," he said. "I'm no wolf."

Babette only laughed again. "Oui," she insisted. "You are like him. Like Cecil."

Larus met her gaze, still captivated by the contrast of her eyes.

"You know where he sleeps," Babette murmured with a knowing smile. Then, waving a single finger before his face, she whispered, "But do not wake him... not yet."

Larus's pulse quickened. "The elders," he said. "Why did they want him killed?"

Babette's smile faded. "Because Cecil could kill them... all of them."

"They feared him," Micah said.

"But you saved him," Larus pressed. "You helped Emilio. Why?"

Babette turned to Micah and Sebastian. "You have my blood memories. Why not tell him what he is?"

Larus shifted, looking at his maker—but it was Babette who answered.

"You are special, petit one."

Larus frowned. "That doesn't mean anything."

Babette's expression darkened, a shadow of sorrow flickering across her face. She took Larus's hand in hers, her touch cool.

"Cecil was... difficult," she said softly. "Cecil was nice... but not good."

Micah and Sebastian exchanged glances.

"Babette," Micah said, "your blood memories showed Sebastian much about Cecil. We came here to discover why you and Emilio disobeyed the council."

Babette's voice broke as she snapped, "You could have asked me!" Her grief sharpened into anger. "Now Benoît is gone forever... because of you all."

Larus's frustration bubbled over. "Someone—anyone!" He turned to the room, desperate. "Tell me what Cecil is—what I am!"

Babette's features softened. She cupped his face in both hands, her nails brushing his skin.

"Oui, petit loup. You must know."

Monique edged closer, intrigued.

"The nature of the wolf still lives in your blood," Babette murmured.

"It is no affliction. The ones who died before were not strong. Perhaps Cecil would have survived as a man, but he became vampire instead. And that made him powerful."

Larus's breath hitched. "But... how?"

Babette's eyes flickered toward the moon. "When a vampire is made, their body heals. Their heart is restored. And sometimes, petit loup, that means... change."

Her gaze returned to him.

"Cecil turned."

She lifted a hand and pointed out the window.

"Cecil is both vampire and loup. He is still lycanthrope—still wolf. And very strong."

Larus felt his stomach twist. "That's impossible."

"No, it is not," Babette said simply. "And one day, petit loup, you will turn as well."

"Turn?" The word caught in his throat.

"Oui," Babette whispered. "Like Cecil... you will change."

Her eyes glowed with something unreadable.

"You will walk in the sun."

Larus turned to Micah and Sebastian, but their expressions mirrored his own shock.

They had remained in Paris for nearly a month. Now, as the ship cut through dark waters, Larus lay awake in his cabin, staring into the blackness. The vessel swayed with the rhythm of the storm, rain hammering the deck above.

Unlike before, there was no need to hide in the cargo hold. Thanks to Helene Rozelle—the shipping heiress—they had secured their own vessel. Their journey across the sea had been protected by Ashkan's ever-watchful presence, but now, as they sailed homeward, they moved freely beneath the moonlight.

Larus had left for Paris with Sebastian, Micah, and Ashkan, seeking answers about Cecil, the sleeping vampire. But no answers had prepared him for the truth Babette had revealed.

Rising from the bed, Larus crossed the small space and pushed aside the black screen covering the porthole. The storm raged, grey waves crashing against the hull, the wind howling through the night. He had not fed in days, but blood—swine's or otherwise—was the least of his concerns.

The cabin door creaked open. He didn't turn. He knew who it was.

Babette stepped beside him, gazing out at the turbulent sea.

"I was afraid of storms," she said softly, pressing a hand against the glass. "Long before I was vampire."

Larus turned, studying the sorrow in her mismatched eyes. "Be happy, petit loup..."

"How can I be happy, Babette? Was Cecil ever happy?"

The weight of what he would become pressed against him like an unseen force.

"Oh... mon petit loup, you mustn't fret."

"I don't know what I am anymore."

"You exist." Babette turned toward him, motioning slightly toward the door. "And they love you."

"I am supposed to be a vampire, Babette. But I am something else."

Images of a monstrous, fur-covered creature clawed through his mind.

Babette reached up, cupping his face between her hands. "You will be strong, petit loup... You are vampire, but when you change, you become something else."

She stepped away, crossing to the far side of the cabin.

"They worry, little wolf. Micah and the other one." A sly smile touched her lips. "Come back to us, petit loup."

She looked over her shoulder. "I left Paris to help you. Cecil can be difficult. He kills what he does not know. If you wake him, he will kill all of you."

Larus had been relieved when Babette insisted on returning with them. And though she had refused to make Helene a vampire, the beautiful heiress would not be left behind.

Monique was aboard as well, having pleaded with Micah to accept her into his coven.

The ship rocked, and Larus felt the weight of his fate pressing in on all sides.

The storm had only just begun.

25

YOUNG LYCANTHROPE

She was a proud and devoted mother. Silas, her young son, was thriving. Max sat in the garden, smiling as he ran to and fro, darting behind hedges and climbing small trees with the ease of a creature born for it. No one in the family dared comment on his wild nature—Max would not allow it. She despised punishing him, for Silas was her entire world. Everyone in the manor adored him, save for a few servants he tormented daily.

At nearly four years old, Silas thought and acted like an adult. Max saw so much of herself in him—his strength, his will, his cunning. He scaled tree trunks as if he had claws, and he loved the night. More than once, Max had woken to find him standing by the window, bathed in moonlight, staring at the sky as if it spoke to him. She never let him out of her sight. Bartholomew, who had long since moved to a separate bedroom, called it coddling. But Max reminded him, coldly, that he had no claim to the boy—he could hardly be sure he was the father. That knowledge gave her power, and she wielded it mercilessly.

She had taught Silas the importance of secrets, and to her astonishment, he understood. She would never forget the way his silver-grey eyes darkened with comprehension the night she warned him never to speak of his ability. He could touch her mind, send his thoughts into her head as easily as breathing. He had done so even before birth—his presence had whispered inside her womb. But he could not read her thoughts, only share his own. This was their bond, and no one, not even Bartholomew, was to know.

She had not heard his footsteps approach, but if Silas had been beside her, he would have known long before. His ears were sharper than any child's ought to be—another thing she could not explain.

"Our son thrives," Bartholomew said.

Max did not turn to look at him. Since that dreadful Sunday, since the violation she could never forget, she had not met his eyes nor allowed him to touch her. He stood too close now, and she stiffened, but before she could speak, Silas emerged from the tall shrubs like a shadow slipping free from the dark.

Small as he was, he moved with the confidence of a hunter. He stood at the far end of the garden, his piercing gaze locking onto Bartholomew. The man faltered, his words drying in his throat.

"Truly, my son is..."

Max saw the hesitation. Silas had unsettled him. She smiled.

Silas darted forward and threw himself into her arms. "Mother!"

She smothered him with kisses, revelling in his bright laughter. Then he turned, peering up at Bartholomew with scrutiny far beyond his years. "Hello, Father."

Max lifted her gaze, just for a moment, and satisfaction bloomed in her chest. She saw it in Bartholomew's eyes—the jealousy, the fear.

"Run along, Silas," she murmured, setting him down. "Enjoy the sun while it lasts. Winter will be upon us soon, my love."

The boy nodded and sprinted away.

"Yes, husband," she said, her voice like silk laced with poison. "My son thrives."

Bartholomew hesitated. "Max... what my father did—"

"What you did." Her voice was ice. She did not look at him. "Were you not there when he forced himself on me? Did you not join him?"

"There were reasons, Max. Reasons I cannot explain."

"I do not care for your reasons." Her fingers curled around the fabric of her gown. "The very sight of you disgusts me."

She heard his breath catch. Then his footsteps retreated, slow and uncertain.

She did not turn to watch him go. Her arms ached to hold her son again, but even the warmth of Silas could not drive away the shadow of how he was conceived.

CATHERINE HAD NEVER KNOWN SUCH PAIN. HER HAIR CLUNG TO HER DAMP forehead in wild tangles, but she didn't care. She gripped Tilley's hand, unaware of the bruising strength in her fingers. A midwife dabbed sweat from her brow, but the world around her was slipping away, drowned beneath the agony.

Voices swirled in the room—one urging her to push, another soothing her, telling her she was doing well. The third voice blurred into the background. Her mind could hold only one thought: Morgan.

She had married him a year ago, content enough, though she sometimes felt she had settled. Morgan was nothing like Max's husband. He was handsome, but not tall—barely taller than she was. And now, because of him, her body was being torn apart.

A fresh wave of pain struck, sharp and all-consuming. Catherine threw her head back against the pillow and screamed, "I hate you, Morgan Frye!"

"Careful, child!" Tilley scolded, squeezing her hand.

The other midwife pressed her legs apart, and in that moment, Catherine hated everything—marriage, childbearing, even the life she had chosen.

"You mustn't say such things," Tilley chided, glancing toward the shut door. "You know Morgan is a good man. He loves you."

Tilley was right. Morgan did love her. But at that moment, Catherine hated him. He had ruined her perfect figure, and worse—he had put this atrocity inside her.

"Oh, Tilley," she sobbed. "Let them get it out... please, get it out of me!"

"You must breathe, dear," the midwife said firmly. "Push! Push! That's it—nearly there. Just a little more, girl!"

Catherine gave one final, desperate push, pouring every ounce of strength into it. Then—suddenly—the pressure was gone. The pain dulled.

A sharp slap, then a cry—soft at first, then rising into a piercing wail.

It was the sweetest sound she had ever heard.

As they placed the blood-streaked child in her arms, Catherine's hatred, her pain, her exhaustion—everything vanished in an instant. She looked down at the tiny, wrinkled face, and love filled her so swiftly, so completely, that it brought fresh tears to her eyes.

She cradled her baby girl and wept.

Catherine awoke to the distant cries of her child.

Blinking away sleep, she stirred beneath the covers, her body still aching from the birth two days prior. Hannah's cradle was only steps away, tucked beside an old wooden trunk Catherine had owned since childhood. But as her eyes adjusted to the dim light, her breath caught in her throat.

Silas sat atop the trunk, gazing down into the cradle.

For a moment, she froze, her heart hammering. The three-year-old's silver-grey eyes gleamed in the dimness, unreadable, unnervingly intense. What is he thinking? Her stomach twisted. Silas was unpredictable. At any moment, he could—

He turned his head toward her and grinned. "Aunty!"

Catherine let out a shaky breath, forcing a smile. She adored Silas—to an extent—but she also knew her sister did little to curb his wild nature. In Max's eyes, Silas could do no wrong.

"Oh, Silas... little Silas," she coaxed softly. "Come to Aunty."

The boy tilted his head, studying her in that unnerving way of his.

Then he simply turned back to Hannah, who was still wailing. Catherine remained frozen, unsure whether to move toward the cradle or stay put. Just as her pulse quickened, relief flooded her as Max entered the room.

"There you are, Silas."

At once, all worry vanished from Max's face. She swept the boy into her arms, and Silas buried his face against her neck, clinging to her as he always did. Catherine exhaled, watching her sister's eyes flick to the cradle.

"She is a beauty, Catherine." Max's smile was warm, genuine.

Silas clapped his tiny hands together, and Hannah's cries grew louder.

"You're frightening your cousin," Max chided gently.

Catherine finally slid from the bed and lifted Hannah into her arms, pressing a kiss to her damp forehead. "Hush now, my love," she murmured. When she glanced up, she found Silas still watching her daughter, unblinking.

"He stirred us from our sleep," Catherine said lightly, trying to settle the unease in her chest.

Max stepped closer, hesitating, then reached out and brushed her fingers along Hannah's arm. A brief silence settled between them.

Then, without a word, Silas reached out too.

His small hand barely grazed Hannah's cheek—a featherlight touch, startling in its tenderness.

Both women gasped.

Hannah stilled at once, her cries fading into quiet breaths. Silas smiled.

Strangely enough, so did Hannah.

IT WAS HIS FOURTH BIRTHDAY, AND HE WAS SURROUNDED BY EVERYONE HE loved.

Well, some more than others.

The grownups towered above him, all smiles and gifts, their voices blending together in a hum of chatter. Silas sat alone at the table, staring at his birthday cake. Four candles flickered atop the frosting, their glow steady, waiting.

Tilley stood nearby. She was always kind to him, always smiling, always true.

Across the room, his two grandfathers stood side by side, arguing over which of them he resembled most. Silas scowled and turned his gaze back to the cake. Grownups talk too much.

He felt his mother behind him—hovering, as always. His father stood near Grandfather Hearne, speaking in a voice too low to hear.

The doors opened, and Aunt Isabelle swept in, her presence as bright as her voice. She bent down and ruffled his hair, unaware of how much he hated it. Grownups were always touching his curls.

"Happy Birthday, Silas!" she said, stooping lower to kiss his cheek.

She was pretty, with big eyes, but Silas still pulled away, wiping his cheek with the palm of his hand.

Laughter rippled through the room.

Silas didn't care.

He cocked his head, moments before the doors opened again. She was coming.

Uncle Morgan entered first, but Silas barely noticed him. His gaze locked on Hannah, nestled in Aunt Catherine's arms.

His cousin. His tiny, perfect cousin.

Silas's lips curled into a smile. Hannah made him happy.

Aunt Catherine carried her closer, her own smile warm. "Happy birthday, Silas," she said, leaning down. She tilted Hannah toward him, offering her cheek.

Silas kissed it.

Catherine straightened, glancing at the others. "Such a gentleman, my young nephew. Sometimes, little man, I swear you're much older than your four years."

"And it's unbelievable," Max added, stepping forward, "how much Hannah has grown. Six months old today."

Silas didn't respond.

His gaze remained fixed on Hannah, the only one in the room who truly mattered.

26

REVELATIONS

The festivities had ended, and her little man had gladly accompanied Tilley to the kitchens. For the first time that day, Max was alone.

She sat in the library, sinking into the silence, enjoying the brief respite. But it would not last—Silas would soon be at her side again. She smiled at the thought. He was growing so fast, already a little man in his own right. Strong, confident. Some would call him petulant, but Silas was simply a boy.

A boy she would protect with her life.

The door creaked open.

"We must speak."

Max stiffened. She hadn't heard his approach, but she knew that voice.

Slowly, she rose from the couch, but she forced herself to remain composed, refusing to let him see her fear.

Four years.

She had not spoken a word to Percival Hearne in four years. Not since the day he stole everything from her.

Blood pounded in her ears. Her pulse quickened, fury rising like bile in her throat. She locked eyes with him—the man who could be Silas's father—and let him see the hatred burning in her gaze.

He was calm. Too calm.

Max drew in a slow breath, summoning the woman she used to be—the one who had been strong before her marriage, before her suffering.

"We have nothing to say to each other." Her voice was low but shaking with barely contained rage. "I do not want you in my presence. Leave. Now."

Percival didn't move.

He merely pivoted slightly, slipping his hands into his pockets. His stance was relaxed, yet unyielding, and Max knew he had no intention of obeying her.

Memories clawed at her—the weight of him, the pain, the helplessness. She shoved them down.

"You will come to Hearne Manor tomorrow," Percival said, as if they were discussing the weather. "With Bartholomew and Silas."

Max's fingers curled into fists.

"You needn't fear me, Maxine."

Her fury ignited.

"I told you never to call me that." Her voice was ice, but he did not flinch.

Instead, he studied her, his expression unreadable. Then, in an almost unnatural shift, his features softened.

"Look, Max. I have never been one to apologize for my choices. Every decision I have made has had a purpose. That day..." He tilted his head. "When my son and I walked into your rooms, I had a purpose."

"Pure lust," she spat. "You are an animal."

Percival's lips curled into something resembling a smirk.

"Animal? Yes." His silver-grey eyes gleamed, the same colour as Silas's. "But not I, child."

Max's breath caught.

"The animal," he continued, "is within the little boy you adore."

Silence stretched between them.

Max's chin dipped, her mouth slightly open. He had spoken the words with certainty, not cruelty—but they sliced through her all the same.

He knew something.

She had spent four years guarding Silas's secret, shielding him, warning him never to reveal his ability. Yet somehow, Percival had seen what she fought to hide.

"There is much you need to know about your son," he said. "And I have the answers you seek."

Max wanted to deny him. To throw him from the room, to let her rage consume her.

But she said nothing.

Because deep down, she knew he was right.

Percival turned for the door, his footsteps measured, unhurried.

"Tomorrow. At noon."

Then he was gone.

EARLY THAT MORNING, BEFORE STEPPING INTO THE CARRIAGE WITH HER SON, Max had insisted Bartholomew remain at Bleddyn Manor. She waited until the last possible moment, knowing exactly how to get what she wanted.

She had told him she needed to face his father alone—that she could not have her husband present after what they had done to her. As expected, Bartholomew had protested, but she knew how to quiet him. He was a private man, and he would not risk a quarrel where the servants might overhear.

Now, as the carriage rattled down the road, she stared ahead, her grip tightening around Silas's small hand.

Again, she found herself hoping—praying—that Percival Hearne was Silas's father. He was strong. Bartholomew, for all his outward power, was weak.

They were not alone. Silas's governess sat stiffly beside them, though her presence was hardly necessary. Silas could hardly stand the mousey woman.

The carriage passed through the gates of Hearne Manor, and Max kept her eyes fixed on the dark stone structure ahead.

"Do not be afraid, Mother," her son said.

She turned, startled by the quiet certainty in his voice. Then she forced a smile, glancing at the governess. "I am not afraid, my love. We are simply visiting Grandfather Hearne."

I feel your fear, Mother.

The words echoed in her head. Silas had not spoken them aloud, yet she heard them as clearly as if he had.

Max's breath hitched.

Her son was only four years old, but his tone carried a weight, an intellect, far beyond his years. She closed her eyes, shutting him out, refusing to acknowledge what had been happening since his conception.

How could he do this? How could he reach inside her mind?

She had never spoken to him about it, never given him a reason to believe such a thing was possible. And yet... somehow, he felt her emotions.

The carriage slowed, then stopped.

Max inhaled sharply. The door swung open, and there stood Percival Hearne.

He descended the stone steps, arms open in greeting, a practiced warmth in his expression.

Max hesitated, then placed a hand on Silas's back, urging him forward. "You must go to him, Silas... go to your grandfather."

A wide smile spread across her son's face.

Percival scooped him into his arms effortlessly, his silver-grey eyes meeting hers over the boy's shoulder.

"How is my best grandson?"

Max stiffened. The words taunted her, though he spoke them lightly.

Without another word, Percival turned and strode toward the stables. He expected her to follow.

And she did.

Inside, the scent of hay and horses filled the air, and Max's pulse slowed. She had always found the stables peaceful.

Then, Percival gestured toward a stall, and Max gasped.

A colt stood before them, its coat a striking silvery grey—the same shade as Silas's eyes. The creature was breathtaking, its legs still slightly gangly, but it would grow into a magnificent stallion.

Max turned to her son.

Silas's small hands gripped the stall door, his face awash with awe. His eyes shone, and for a moment, Max saw something she had never seen before.

Tears.

Her son's eyes glistened with unshed tears.

Max swallowed hard, realization striking her.

Percival was winning him.

And worse—his plan was working.

She exhaled, watching as her father-in-law rubbed his hands together, pleased. Then, without turning to her, he spoke.

"Now, we have time to discuss business."

Max's stomach clenched, but she nodded.

She had come for answers.

And she would get them.

IT HAD TAKEN PERCIVAL HEARNE OVER TWO HOURS TO RECOUNT WHAT HE called the forgotten past of Max's family.

Everything—her lineage, the true meaning of her name, the legacy of the Hearnes—was laid bare before her. She had listened, questioning the absurdity of his claims, yet deep inside, she could not deny that much of it made sense.

Now, as she sat across from him in his dimly lit study, her gaze drifted to the Hearne family crest mounted on the wall. Two archers, bows drawn. Hunters.

Their only interruption had been the quiet arrival of refreshments, which Max barely touched. Silas had not come to find her, no doubt still enthralled by his beautiful colt.

"I admire your strength, Max." Percival's voice broke the silence.

She looked up.

"I was not interrupted once," he mused, studying her carefully. "You listened. You asked questions only after I had told you everything." He leaned back in his chair, fingers steepled. "And you were wise to leave my son behind." His thick brows furrowed, betraying disappointment. "I am not surprised he listened to you... not at all shocked that he allowed himself to be cowed by a—"

"By a woman," Max cut in, her voice calm but firm. "A mere girl."

Percival did not look away.

Max's fingers curled against the armrest. "Bartholomew's affliction is not cowardice," she said. "It is guilt that plagues him."

She saw no remorse in Percival's eyes.

"He cannot look at my son without wondering if the child he puts to bed each night—the child he adores—is his son or his brother."

Percival's expression remained impassive. "I did not call you here to apologize for what I felt was the right decision," he said, his voice steady. "Have you not heard a word I've said?"

"Oh, I have." Max's eyes burned into his. "You have told me of beasts and vampires—wolves and blood-drinkers." She exhaled sharply. "You claim my family are... lycanthropes. What does that history—this past—have to do with the fact that you raped me?"

"Because I knew what would come of it."

The certainty in his voice sent a chill through her.

"I knew Silas would be the result of my transgression," he said.

Max saw it in his eyes—this man had accepted what he had done, even convinced himself it was necessary.

"My family has been hunters for ages... thousands of years. And I tell you this, Max—" He pointed a finger across the desk. "As with your family, not all will carry the strain of the hunter's blood. I was unfortunate to have only one child. I could not let my family's legacy end." His fist pounded the desk. "Bartholomew is spineless—a shame to my lineage. Times have changed. There are things I never shared with my son—things I feel I must tell you."

"You sought to preserve this legacy," Max said coldly. "So you struck a deal with my father—an offer he could not refuse."

Percival's lip curled. "I gave Maxwell what he wanted. The best husband for his best child."

A bitter laugh escaped him as he threw his arms up. "I had no way of knowing if Bartholomew possessed the hunter's blood. So I did what I had to do. And I was right."

His eyes gleamed. "Silas is a wolf, Max."

She inhaled sharply.

"Have you looked into his eyes?" he pressed.

Max hesitated. Then, slowly, she nodded.

Percival sat back, satisfied. "Your father lost touch with his past... but he is no fool. I suspect Maxwell knows more than he lets on."

Her brows furrowed. "What do you mean?"

A chuckle rumbled in her father-in-law's chest.

"Have you truly not pieced it together?" He leaned forward. "Maxwell's brother suffered the same affliction as your brother."

A breath caught in her throat.

"Yes, my dear daughter-in-law. Your father has lied to you all."

Max swallowed hard. "How do you know this?"

"Because I am a hunter. We keep records." His tone was laced with a grim pride. "We intervene between the species. We protect human lives and maintain the balance."

Max's mind raced.

"You said my father knew what I am. What do you mean?"

Percival's smile widened.

"You are Larus's twin, child."

She froze.

"In your blood is locked all that your brother was to be." His voice lowered, deliberate. "You carry the life of the wolves within you. Though... few female lycanthropes exist in our records." He studied her closely. "It seems, my dear, that your duty in life was to pass the gift to your son. To Silas."

A tremor ran through her.

Max inhaled sharply. "And what of my brother? What of Larus?"

A strange look flickered in Percival's eyes. "Ah... you are clever, Max. Attentive."

A slow smirk crossed his face. "If only my son had your keen mind."

Then, a shadow of disappointment darkened his expression. "The poor boy," he muttered. "A disgrace."

Max clenched her jaw. "You said my brother had an affliction."

Percival exhaled through his nose. "Yes... Larus." His voice dropped to a whisper.

Then, at last, he said it.

"Larus, the vampire."

Max let out a stunned laugh.

But Percival only stared at her.

"Think, girl, before deeming me a foolish old man," he warned. "For I can assure you—I am not."

Max's laughter died on her lips.

"Think back to the night of your wedding," he said, almost absently, his gaze dropping to his desk.

A cold prickle ran up her spine.

"Perhaps I was a fool that night," he mused. "I should have noticed it then. How pale he was. How nervous the boy seemed. And that doctor—"

"Doctor Duncan."

Max barely whispered the name.

Memories bled into her mind.

Larus.

Standing before her. So cold. So pale.

Her heart pounded. "But you said nothing."

Percival spread his hands. "And what would I have said? Vampires are vicious. Strong. If their survival had demanded it, they could have slaughtered everyone in that room."

His voice lowered. "No one must ever know what you know. You will not speak of this to your family."

Max's throat tightened. "And my brother? Where is he?"

Percival's lips pressed into a thin line.

"I doubt you shall ever see him again," he said. "I suspect the good doctor may soon send news of his death."

Max's pulse roared in her ears.

"But we have Silas now," Percival murmured. His gaze sharpened. "He is the key to making our families one."

She swallowed hard.

"You said it was forbidden for hunters to mate with lycanthropes," she challenged. "And yet, you broke that covenant."

A dark grin tugged at his lips.

"For too long, the vampires have dominated, while the wolves and hunters have dwindled."

Then, his voice softened.

"Silas is special."

A flicker of something almost human passed through Percival's eyes.

"Your brother and his maker may know what Silas is," he admitted. "And if they do... my grandson is in danger."

His next words chilled Max to her core.

"We must work together, Max. To protect him."

Slowly, reluctantly, Max nodded.

For her son—her Silas—she would do anything.

27

A HUSBAND'S PRIDE

The tension in Bartholomew's chest only deepened as he listened to Max's words. She had found a newfound sense of clarity and resolve in her interactions with his father, and it unsettled him. She had never been so firm, so unwavering, especially when it came to Silas. Bartholomew's thoughts twisted in circles—his father's manipulations, the secrets, and the unspeakable truth of Silas's true nature. Max had accepted this new reality, and it gnawed at him. The boy he had raised was not entirely his. Not by blood, and not by the strange, unknown fate his father had designed. He had been made, manipulated, and Bartholomew couldn't shake the thought that he had been betrayed in ways he still couldn't fully understand.

Max was right about one thing: Silas was his blood. But that didn't make him feel any better. That didn't erase the fact that Silas was a threat. A child, yes, but one with powers and destinies far beyond what Bartholomew could have ever imagined for his own heir. The thought of his own son—this twisted, fractured relationship with his father, the constant sense of inadequacy he felt standing next to Percival, made him feel hollow. But to think of Silas as an immortal child, bound by this strange inheritance, as some potential threat to the Hearne legacy, was an unbearable truth.

Max's words about protecting Silas rang in his ears. She was right, of course. They had to protect him. But the deeper truth behind her words—the unspoken understanding that Silas was part of a world Bartholomew could never fully belong to—struck him like a heavy weight. She was no longer simply his wife, standing beside him; Max had transformed into someone who would do anything for Silas, even if it meant defying him.

Bartholomew's gaze wandered, his thoughts returning to the pale face of his brother, Larus. He had become more than just a sibling in his mind. He was a reminder of the bitter truth that lay beneath the surface of their family. The vampires, their strength, their immortality, it all threatened to unravel everything Bartholomew had held onto—his inheritance, his place in the world. Now, there was Silas, caught between the blood of a hunter and the curse of lycanthropy, but with the potential to surpass them all.

Max's eyes were locked on his, unwavering. "Your father has said this before," she said softly, breaking through his spiralling thoughts. "He believes Silas is the key to bridging the divide between our families. To end the long conflict between the hunters, lycanthropes, and vampires. If we protect him, we can ensure that he grows into something powerful."

Bartholomew clenched his fists, his own fear creeping in. "But if Silas grows into his full power," he said, voice thick with dread, "what does that mean for me? For my place in all this? I fear that Silas will become the hunter my father always wanted, but with a different destiny in mind."

Max stared at him, and for the first time, Bartholomew saw the weight of her decision in her eyes. She was caught between two worlds—one where her loyalty to Silas and the future of their son mattered most, and another where the past, the history of their bloodlines, threatened to consume everything.

"If Silas becomes the key," Max replied, "then we both must find a way to help him understand what he must do. To protect him, yes, but also to guide him." She stepped toward him, her hand resting gently on his arm. "Bartholomew, this is not just about legacy anymore. This is about survival. We cannot be weak. We must stand together."

Bartholomew looked at her—this woman who had once seemed so lost in the complexities of their world—and now saw her as a partner. But the dread in his heart remained. He could not help but wonder if she would ever truly choose him over Silas, over her bloodline.

"I will do whatever it takes," he said, his voice tight. "But I am not certain I can protect him as you ask. I'm not sure any of us can."

Max nodded, her eyes full of resolve. "Then we will have to do it together. For Silas. For us all."

As they stood there, the weight of their shared secret pressed on them both. What they had once considered a simple family conflict now seemed a much larger, much darker struggle. And in the distance, Bartholomew could feel the shadow of the vampires drawing closer.

28

ISABELLE (1798)

The carriage rolled smoothly through the streets, the rhythmic sound of the wheels on cobblestone punctuating the silence between the vampires. Larus's thoughts were distant, drifting toward the people he had once known. The ache in his chest, though muted by time and his new existence, never fully went away. His family, his ties to the world of the living—these were the things he had to abandon, and as the years passed, he felt the weight of that separation grow heavier.

Sebastian, ever the observer, caught his mood and gave him a sympathetic glance. "Time dulls the pain, mon ami," he said, his voice laced with a quiet knowing. "But it never completely heals, does it?"

Larus glanced out the carriage window, the darkness outside only interrupted by the occasional flicker of a distant streetlamp. He could feel the pulse of life beyond the glass, but it was a life he no longer belonged to. He had been reborn as something else entirely, something distant from the warmth of his past.

"I suppose," Larus replied softly, "it's a sacrifice that comes with immortality."

Monique's smile softened as she reached over to squeeze his hand.

"You've made your peace with it," she said, her voice reassuring. "We all have, in time. And we do it together. That is what matters."

Haruki, who had been watching the conversation unfold with quiet intensity, spoke up. "The living do not understand us," he said, his words measured and calm, "but that does not mean we must lose ourselves in their world. They forget, as Sebastian says. But we are eternal."

Larus turned his gaze to Haruki, taking in the vampire's ageless features. Haruki's calmness was a source of comfort, and yet, it also reminded Larus of the inevitability of his new reality. It had been five years since he had been turned, five years since Micah had altered the course of his life forever. And still, Larus was haunted by the memories of his family, of the life he had once lived, even as he adjusted to the dark existence he now shared with the coven.

"I don't think they'll ever forget me," Larus murmured, more to himself than to the others. "At least, I hope not."

"You don't need them to remember you," Sebastian chimed in, his voice light but carrying an underlying truth. "Let them live. You are free now, Larus. Free from the ties that once bound you."

Larus nodded, but the conflict still lingered inside him. He had once been part of a family, a world where emotions ran deep and connections meant something. Now, those ties felt like echoes from a distant past, a life he could no longer return to.

"I will watch over them, though," he said, his voice firm. "From a distance, yes, but they won't be forgotten. Not by me."

Monique gave him a knowing smile, her fingers still gently holding his. "Of course, you will. But remember, you are no longer bound to that world. Your heart belongs to the night now. And to us."

The words were both comforting and painful, and Larus felt the weight of them settle in his chest. The night, the darkness, the endless eternity—they were his reality now. But that didn't mean he could simply erase his past. It would always be a part of him, lurking in the shadows of his existence, a reminder of who he had been.

As the carriage continued its journey through the night, Larus settled into the quiet acceptance that came with his new life. He would never fully escape the pull of his past, but he had his coven, his family in the dark. And for now, that was enough.

HER FAMILY HAD MADE THE JOURNEY TO THIS FORGOTTEN SPOT OF GROUND seven days past when they mourned the passing of her brother. Isabelle had ridden out alone to the old cemetery in the late afternoon. It was nearly sunset, and Larus' sister stared at the tombstone with tearful eyes. Larus, before his death, had requested his body to be cremated. The white urn containing his ashes had come from the capital. Isabelle dried her eyes and walked back to her mare, for she found it painful seeing the tombstone bearing Larus's name. She left the cemetery and paused as she pulled the gate shut, for the vision of the old church atop the hill was breathtaking. Her thoughts went to Larus again, for he had always loved visiting the church.

The sun was slowly disappearing beyond the horizon, and it would take nearly an hour to ride back to the manor, yet Isabelle felt the urge to see more of the church. A strange pull rooted her in place, as if something were whispering to her. Somehow, deep in the courts of her mind, she found visions—remnants of memories from her childhood. She was a little girl then; it may have been with their father, for she suddenly remembered sitting on his lap as he spoke of this ancient place. Her three siblings were there with them.

The memories were a blur, but Isabelle found a new interest in this place. Had she gone into the old church before? She gently patted her mare's forehead before ascending the hill.

Once within the massive space, Isabelle drew in a breath, struck by the weight of time within these walls. She found nothing familiar inside the church, and after walking about for some time, she knelt to pray for her family, all those she loved. She prayed for her brother's soul.

Isabelle left the church, shocked to see the darkened skies above. She had not expected to stay so long inside, but she took comfort in that her mare knew their lands well and would have little trouble galloping home beneath the veil of darkness. She made it back to her mare and gently rubbed her forehead again.

"You'll get me home safe, won't you, girl?" she whispered to the beast.

Isabelle was about to mount when something shifted at the edge of her vision. Beyond the cemetery gates.

She shook her head with a smile. No one else would be on Bleddyn lands. And yet, the air felt... different.

Her mare whinnied, its head tossing from side to side as it took several steps backward.

A chill prickled her skin.

"Easy, girl!" She had always been good with horses—Larus was, too. Horses were wise creatures. If hers was afraid, then...

"Did you see someone... hmm?" She patted her mare's muscled neck, and after calming her, Isabelle again tethered it to the gate before stepping toward the cemetery.

She saw no one but found herself walking back to Larus's grave. Now calm, she knelt upon the fresh mound of dirt and placed her hand on the tombstone.

"Oh, Larus... I miss you so..."

Isabelle rose, dusting dirt from her hands, her head bowed in sadness. A breath of wind whispered past her ear.

She looked up—and staggered back.

A figure stood before her.

Pale skin, almost white.

And although darkness was falling, Isabelle could see his eyes—glacial blue, piercing. Unnatural.

A breath hitched in her throat. Her heart slammed against her ribs.

Beyond the gates, her mare screamed, its hooves striking the earth.

The pale stranger tilted his head, watching her. Studying her.

His gaze seized her, pulling her in. Isabelle's limbs refused to obey. The fear inside her screamed Run!, but her body swayed toward him, drawn forward.

His cold, elegant hand cradled her face, and his cherry-red lips parted—fangs, long and sharp, gleamed in the night.

Even as his lips grazed the warm skin of her neck, she did not fight him. She could not.

Then—the bite.

A sharp sting. A fire spreading through her veins.

A wet, sickening sound as he drank from her.

Her body sagged. Her breath shuddered. Her mind frayed, unraveling into darkness.

What was happening to her?

Her limbs were leaden. She struggled to keep her eyes open.

As weak as she was and as much as she wished to fall asleep in this stranger's arms, Isabelle heard a loud hiss before she was released. She fell to the ground upon her brother's grave.

A voice cut through the haze.

"Isabelle!"

The sound of her name was distant. A lifeline slipping through her fingers.

The voice was so familiar.

She was weaker now, barely able to keep her fluttering eyes open.

"Yaro, what have you done?!"

Someone was shaking her, shaking her so hard, so uncontrollably.

With effort, Isabelle forced her eyes open. Everything blurred, fading in and out. But she saw him.

Was she about to die?

Isabelle was too weak. She closed her eyes again.

But she had seen him.

"L...Larus..."

Her voice was a mere whisper.

She needed to sleep, to surrender to the heavy tide pulling her under.

So tired.

SHE LAY IN A PLUSH FEATHER BED, AND AS SHE OPENED HER EYES, ISABELLE wondered whether she lived in a world of dreams. Everything felt surreal.

She had lost all track of time.

The large room was as dark as pitch, yet she saw with perfect clarity.

Micah had explained it—this man, this creature she had met before.

Isabelle pushed away the covers and rose, her movements strange, effortless. The ceiling felt low, the space unfamiliar. Where was she?

She was alone. And yet, she was bound to him.

Her golden hair cascaded beyond her waist in loose waves, and she touched the delicate white lace of her housecoat—Micah's gift. It was beautiful, as were the gowns in the open closet. She traced her fingers over the fabrics, silks and velvets richer than anything she had ever owned. A dressing table stood against one wall, adorned with scented oils, shimmering powders, and glistening jewels. All for her.

She turned at the sound of approaching footsteps, hearing them long before the old wooden door creaked open.

Micah entered, and before she could think, she was in his arms.

"I was afraid you would not come back to me."

He cradled her cheek in his cool hand.

"You must feed," Micah murmured. "A newborn cannot go without blood."

Isabelle held his gaze, drawn to the depth of it, to the quiet power behind his words. She wanted to listen. Needed to.

"You must remember what I have told you, dear Isabelle. This bond only exists because it was I who made you."

She swallowed, feeling the weight of it—the truth she had not yet spoken aloud.

"There is much we need to discuss before you meet the others."

"The others?"

Micah nodded.

"Yes, dear one. We are your family... your coven." He moved gracefully and settled into a chair at the foot of her bed. "With your unexpected addition, we are now ten. One of our kind still sleeps."

Isabelle's fingers tightened around the lace of her robe.

"Where am I?" She looked around the room.

Micah spread his arms wide.

"Welcome to the catacombs," he said. "We are beneath your lands, Isabelle. The Bleddyn lands."

She turned toward the door, confusion clouding her face.

She brought a hand to her lips in thought. Flashes of memory flickered through her mind.

"...I... I was at my brother's grave when..." she whispered.

Her breath hitched.

"That man."

His eyes. Those piercing, unnatural eyes.

"He is as you are."

Her voice trembled. "And I saw Larus."

She turned sharply back to Micah, her heart hammering.

"The grave!" Isabelle's breath caught. "Where is my brother? Where is Larus?"

Micah tilted his head, his smile slow, knowing.

"He lives in death, dear one, as you do."

Isabelle gasped.

Larus. Alive.

Her lips parted in disbelief. Then, joy flooded her veins.

"Oh, Larus."

She pressed a trembling hand to her chest, her emotions a tangled storm.

"I must see him!"

A shuddering breath escaped her. She felt tears sting her eyes, but as she lifted a hand to wipe them away, she froze.

Blood.

Her fingers were stained red.

Micah's voice was calm.

"First, you must feed."

The doors opened again.

A woman entered—tall, elegant, with snow-white hair and hennaed hands.

Isabelle had met her before.

Geraldine.

Geraldine led an old man into the room, his clothing rough, his scent thick with the musk of sheep.

The herdsman.

"Welcome, child."

Geraldine lifted a hand, curling a lock of Isabelle's golden hair around her fingers.

"So beautiful. But you cannot see your brother as you are, pretty one. We must prepare. Larus longs to see you."

Isabelle stared at the old man. Her hunger stirred—deep, insatiable.

She could never return to her family. That truth settled inside her, heavy and unshakable.

And yet—had she not gone to the church for a reason? Had she not stood at Larus's grave for a purpose?

She was meant to be here.

Meant to be this.

Geraldine smiled.

"Come, child. Meet Bernard. He knows what we are and has given himself to you."

Bernard stepped forward, his hands weathered, his shoulders heavy with years.

"For he has just a few days before he meets his maker," Geraldine continued. "You, my dear, must end his pain."

Isabelle hesitated.

She could hear his heartbeat, loud, insistent.

She could feel his fear.

"I… I am sorry," she whispered.

Micah's voice was smooth, unwavering.

"Do not be sorry, my dear."

He leaned back, watching her.

"We have made a pact with Bernard, for he shall help our coven grow."

Isabelle's gaze snapped to his.

"A pact?"

Micah's lips curled slightly.

"I have agreed to take his grandson, Nicolas, into the fold when he is old enough. He will have no one in this world after Bernard is gone."

Bernard said nothing. He only waited.

Geraldine lifted a single sharp nail and dragged it lightly over the old man's skin.

A drop of blood bloomed.

The scent hit Isabelle like a fire igniting in her veins.

Her fangs descended.
A hiss escaped her lips.
And with unnatural speed, she was upon him.
There was no hesitation now.
No regret.
No sorrow.
Her fangs sank deep.

29

NICOLAS

Just three months had passed since his grandfather's death, yet Nicolas was pleased with everything his new guardian had done for him. Bernard had done all he could after his parents died, but they had always been poor, and at eighteen, Nicolas would have had no way to provide for himself.

Then Micah changed his life in a single night.

Vampires. Who would have thought such creatures existed? And yet here he was—proof that they did.

It was nearly sunrise, and Nicolas lay in bed, surrounded by fresh linens that still felt foreign against his skin. He ran a hand over his clean cotton breeches, marvelling again at the transformation of his life. He had spent his childhood in squalor, yet now he lived in a castle, dressed as a gentleman, with more food and comfort than he had ever known. His grandfather, in death, now rested among the rich—buried in the Bleddyn crypts, as if he had belonged there all along. Nicolas smiled at the irony.

Micah had promised him a future. Five years. That was how long he would remain human. Five years to learn the ways of vampires before his turning at twenty-three. Until then, his days were spent under Giles' quiet, watchful eye, learning the refinement of a nobleman, while at night, Ashkan taught him to drive a coach and wield a sword. Nicolas found himself drawn to the Persian's graceful skill, though he admired his humility even more.

The castle was vast, filled with secrets—hidden doors with locks more intricate than anything he had seen. He had explored freely, yet he knew the true heart of his new world lay elsewhere. The vampires dwelled in the catacombs beneath the land. Nicolas had met them all.

Helene, the devoted mortal who never left Babette's side.

Haruki, the samurai, whose kindness had surprised him.

Geraldine, with her snow-white hair and hennaed hands, who had welcomed him as if he were one of their own.

Monique, the dark beauty, who had kissed his cheek with lips as cold as marble.

Then there were the others. The dangerous ones.

Sebastian, whose elegant presence sent chills through him.

Yaro, bold and unruly, whose arrogance made Nicolas uneasy.

But of them all, it was the siblings who fascinated him most.

Larus and Isabelle. Inseparable.

Larus had treated him like a younger brother, kind but fiercely protective. And Isabelle... Nicolas could not stop thinking about her. She was beautiful, but it was more than that. There was something haunting about her presence, something that drew him in.

Nicolas sat up and raked his fingers through his red hair, missing the long locks Giles had clipped away the night he arrived. He had resented it at first, but he could not bring himself to be angry with Giles. The older man had been nothing but patient and attentive, his quiet nature reminding Nicolas of Bernard in a way that both comforted and unsettled him.

For now, the castle was quiet. Ashkan was away. The vampires slumbered beneath the earth.

And Nicolas waited, as he had been taught to do.

Five years.

A lifetime and a moment, all at once.

PART THREE

30

COMING OF AGE (1810)

He was sixteen, and his mother still insisted on treating him like a child. The library was his refuge, a place where he could breathe, yet even here, he felt caged. He stood by the window, staring at the moon—the only thing that ever seemed to calm him. It was well past midnight, and the urge to escape into the night gnawed at him.

Silas had attended one of the best schools, and though he had hated leaving his friends, he was relieved to be home. Here, he could walk the woods he loved, lose himself in their endless silence. But more than anything, he wanted to be close to his cousin, Hannah. She was only twelve, but she understood him better than anyone else.

"Have you heard anything I've said, Silas?" His mother's voice cut through the quiet, sharp as a knife. She was as stern as Grandfather Hearne, and just as relentless.

Silas barely turned his head. "Yes, Mother."

"Then you understand why you cannot go to the taverns."

"Your mother is right," his father added, stepping forward. His grip settled firm on Silas's shoulder. "We have been honest with you about everything. You know what you are."

Silas clenched his jaw.

"The time will come," his father continued, "when—"

"Yes, Father, you've both told me a thousand times... and I am sick of it." He yanked free from his father's grasp and strode toward the fireplace.

Outside, snow had blanketed the grounds for the past two days. He longed to be out there, moving through the cold, losing himself in the stillness. He had always felt at home in the frost, as if his blood recognized the wild. Maybe it was because of what he would become. He wanted to feel it—to know.

Silas grabbed the poker and jabbed at the embers, sending sparks skittering up the chimney.

"It's too risky," his mother pressed. "To be among humans you cannot trust—not in such times. It could happen any day now."

"Any day now?" Silas whirled, his patience fraying. "I have been waiting, Mother! Waiting to turn into this monster, this lycanthrope—and for what? When does this gift of mine decide to reveal itself?"

"Hold your tongue, boy."

His father was in front of him before he could take another breath, hands clamping down on his shoulders. Silas stiffened. His father's grip was firm, his voice a low, controlled warning.

"The servants must not know," he said. "You will do as we say. You will stay within these walls."

Something inside Silas snapped.

His father's hands felt like iron. His own pulse pounded in his ears. And suddenly, he felt it—an unfamiliar surge of rage, something dark and powerful and completely uncontrollable. Before he could stop himself, his hand shot to his father's throat.

For one terrifying second, Silas was ready. Ready to finish him.

"Silas!"

His mother's voice, edged with fear, shattered the moment.

Silas's breath hitched. His father's eyes were on him, steady, unwavering. His grip loosened. He stepped back, as if waking from a dream.

His father coughed, rubbing his throat. Silas stared at his own trembling hands, his pulse slowing, reality sinking in.

What have I done?

The words barely left his lips. His father wasn't angry—just watching him, the sorrow in his gaze far worse than any reprimand.

Shame burned through him.

Without another word, Silas turned and bolted from the room. He needed to run. Needed to get away—from them, from this house, from himself. But leaving would only make things worse. He knew that.

Instead, he took the stairs two at a time, heading for his rooms—the same rooms that had once belonged to the uncle he had never known.

LEAVING THE COMFORT OF HEARNE MANOR TO VENTURE INTO A SNOWSTORM had left Percival vexed. And now, standing in Bleddyn Manor, he was even more displeased. Yet again, they needed him to set things right.

He stood beside Maxwell's desk, watching the old fool sit with the pride of a man who still believed he was in charge. Maxwell Bleddyn had proven to be an even greater fool than Percival had imagined. At least his daughter had more resolve, he thought.

Percival's gaze moved from Maxwell's only son, Bartholomew, to his daughter-in-law. The girl was stronger than her husband—she was the Bleddyn Clan's saving grace.

Max had summoned him, and the moment Percival learned what the boy had done, he left Hearne Manor without hesitation. Silas needed to be reminded of his place. No matter how powerful he was, he was still vulnerable. Even immortals could die.

Percival sneered at Bartholomew and Maxwell. Weaklings.

"Perhaps my grandson would have been better off living with me," he said, letting the weight of his disappointment settle over them. "A parent must keep a child in line." His cold eyes fixed on his son. "Have I not taught you this, boy?"

Bartholomew's jaw tightened. "Silas is different, Father."

"My grandson is a good boy," Maxwell said, too quickly, as if saying it would make it true.

Percival scoffed. "If you coddled him less and disciplined him properly, he would respect you." He was sick of their weakness—sick of their endless complaints. *They forget who I am.*

His voice darkened. "You were wise to send for me, child," he said, nodding at Max before turning back to Maxwell. "At your daughter's suggestion, we have told you everything about the legacy you were so eager to abandon. It was your failure, Maxwell, that pulled this family deeper into its predicament. And once again, I am the one dragging you out of it."

Maxwell had admitted he knew little of Bleddyn history—had chosen to know little. He had tried to leave the past buried, to pretend it had nothing to do with him. Fool. Percival could hardly blame him for his ignorance, but that did not excuse his weakness.

Maxwell sighed. "So, you truly believe Silas will transform?"

Percival saw his daughter stiffen at the question.

Maxwell hesitated before continuing. "My brother... Merrick. That was his name. He knew he was dying and tried to understand why this cursed sickness haunted our family for generations. But I cared little for such things." He exhaled sharply. "I was young. I had accepted my brother's fate. If only I had listened—if I had spent even a moment helping him unravel our history..."

"Merrick's bones are rotting beneath the earth," Percival said coldly. "The past is dead. You must look to the future. To Silas."

He paced toward the fire. "The boy is a wolf. He needs a firm hand. If we do not control him, he will come to rule us all." His tone sharpened. "It is his nature to dominate. Wolves need an alpha—and Silas is a lone wolf." He turned, eyes glinting. "Mark my words. We will rue the day he realizes his true strength."

Maxwell hesitated. "You say my son lives... but I saw his ashes with my own eyes."

He looked toward his daughter, as if hoping she would side with him. Percival smirked. He would find no ally there.

Max's voice was firm. "Think of the night of our wedding, Father."

Bartholomew's hands curled into fists.

"Larus is no family to us. Nor is he our friend. They will kill Silas the moment they have the chance. I will not let them harm my son."

Maxwell looked stricken, glancing between them before bowing his head.

"And what of Isabelle?" Max pressed. "Her death makes no sense."

Maxwell flinched. "No, no! I will hear none of this—not of my Isabelle." His voice cracked with grief.

Percival sighed. "Think, man."

He had already spent hours explaining how careful vampires were—how they ensured humans did not vanish without a trace.

"Your daughter left on horseback that morning and was gone all day. Yet the beast returned without her. Then, she appears days later, well after midnight, saying she had abandoned her privileged life to join a convent? And left that very night?"

Percival scoffed.

"Isabelle had plans, Maxwell," Max said. "She spoke of marriage, of children. And then, a year after she disappeared, you receive news of her death. A few letters in her own hand, and then, nothing."

"I met the abbess myself," Maxwell protested. "I stood by Isabelle's grave."

"But you did not see her body," Bartholomew countered. "Larus's doctor sent you ashes—and Isabelle's supposed burial happened long after her death. Why was she not returned to be buried among her ancestors?"

Silence settled over the room.

Percival's voice was grim. "They had to die to live again."

Maxwell exhaled sharply, running a hand through his greying hair. Percival watched with satisfaction as doubt and dread sank into him.

"They are hiding somewhere," he continued. "And while their numbers grow, all we have is Silas."

He let the words hang between them, his point undeniable.

Maxwell turned away, rubbing his temples. Percival wasted no time—he seated himself in Maxwell's chair. The true seat of power. He pounded the desk, forcing Maxwell to look at him.

"The wolves lost their way, Maxwell," Percival said, voice smooth and deliberate. "Centuries ago, when lycanthrope blood ran strong, some fool decided to break from tradition."

He let the words settle, watching as understanding flickered in their eyes.

"My ancestors kept records. Vampires do not reproduce. And yet, entire families of them exist—some of the elders still keep their children at their side, thousands of years old, possessing powers beyond imagination."

His gaze locked onto Max. "The lycanthropes were once just as strong. But, like the vampires, their power must be preserved."

He let the pause stretch.

"Silas will age... but only until his first transformation. That could happen tonight or five years from now. Until then, he is vulnerable. Larus or Isabelle could tear him apart before he even realizes his strength."

Max's expression was unreadable. "Then what must we do?"

Percival pressed his lips together, hiding his triumph. He had won them over.

"There is one way to strengthen the Bleddyn blood," he said carefully. "A blending of the bloodline. It is the only way."

Silence.

Max understood first.

"You cannot be serious," she murmured. Her arms wrapped around herself. "The poor girl..."

Maxwell's brows knitted. "What do you mean, Percival?"

"You know how close they are," Percival said. "They have always been close."

Finally, Maxwell's face twisted in horror. "She is twelve, you madman! Have you lost your mind?"

Percival's smile did not falter.

"It is the only way to build a strong pack. The only way to survive."

Maxwell recoiled.

"That, Maxwell, was the way of your ancestors. The right way. An alpha does not seek a mate from another pack." His voice dropped to a whisper. "Defy me now... and it will mean your family's destruction."

His gaze shifted to Max. "What say you, girl?"

Max's lips pressed into a thin line. "Father... Percival speaks the truth."

Maxwell sagged in his chair, defeated.

Percival allowed himself a small, satisfied smile.

"Now," he said. "Bring me Silas."

And the lesson would begin.

SILAS ENTERED THE LIBRARY AHEAD OF HIS FATHER, SHOULDERS SQUARED, HIS steps bold and unhurried. He had listened to his parents' worries days earlier, had endured their lectures, but what he wanted—what he needed—was their trust. Sixteen years old, and still they kept him caged, bound to this house like a child. Only Tilley and Hannah understood.

Tilley often spoke of his uncle Larus and how much alike they were. Silas had sifted through his uncle's belongings, wishing he had known the man. His mother had told him that Larus met him once, shortly after he was born, but the memories were lost to time.

Since the fight with his father, the air in the house had changed. Fear clung to the walls, seeped into every glance his parents and Grandfather Bleddyn gave him. And though he loved them, that fear thrilled him.

He strode past his mother and grandfather, eyes fixed on the one man he had not seen in weeks.

"Grandfather," he greeted.

Percival Hearne did not respond. He sat stiff-backed in the chair, a heavy frown settling over his broad features.

Silas hesitated. He turned to his parents, already guessing why they had sent for the one person he feared. His gaze, sharp and unintentional, burned with silent accusation. But when he looked back at his grandfather, something in his chest tightened. He had expected an argument, a scolding. Instead, he was met with a silence so weighted it unsettled him.

"I...didn't know you were here," Silas muttered.

His grandfather did not move, did not even blink. When he finally spoke, his voice was low and rumbling, a slow-moving storm.

"Sit."

Silas obeyed, lowering himself into the chair before the desk, his palms pressing against his knees.

"Is...something wrong, Grandfather?"

His father shifted uneasily behind him, but it was Percival who answered. The man rose from his chair, his cloak shifting like a shadow, his presence seeming larger somehow.

"Is it true," Percival asked, "that you laid hands on your family? That you dared to harm those who love and protect you?"

Heat flared beneath Silas's skin, hotter than the fire crackling in the hearth. A thin sheen of sweat dampened his brow. He pushed himself to his feet, head high, defiant.

"I grow weary, Grandfather. I am tired of being trapped in this place—of being treated like a child!" He threw out his arms, gesturing to the walls that had become his prison. "I am not a boy! I can take care of myself. I will do as I please."

Percival stepped forward. "Strong as you think you are, boy, there is much you do not yet understand."

"You're just like them," Silas snapped, his gaze cutting to his parents and Grandfather Bleddyn. "You cling to your old ways, your old fears. I will not abide by them."

He turned toward the door, refusing to listen to another word.

The sound came first—the sharp crack of a lash slicing through the air—then the bite of leather coiling around his throat.

Silas gasped, choking, hands flying to the braided noose now cutting into his skin. His fingers met sharp silver prongs embedded in the leather, tiny teeth sinking into his flesh. He tore his hands away with a hiss of pain.

His mother screamed.

"What are you doing to my son?"

"You will hold your tongue," Percival snapped.

Silas fell to his knees, vision wavering. The silver burned like fire, weakening him, the pain radiating deep into his bones.

Percival loomed over him, his grip on the whip unwavering.

"You will know your place, boy," he said, voice like iron. "Your survival does not rely on strength alone. I am a Hearne. A hunter. And so are you."

Silas writhed, teeth clenched against the pain, silver-grey eyes pleading as he struggled against the restraint. His breath came in ragged gasps. He could smell the blood dripping from his throat and hands, could hear his mother's quiet sobs.

At last, Percival loosened the grip, letting the noose slip away.

Silas crumpled forward, pulling his knees to his chest. A sharp, ragged sob tore from his throat, shame and fury warring inside him.

"Leave us," Percival commanded. "There are things I must discuss with my grandson."

31

HANNAH

Tilley had always appeared the same in Hannah's eyes; ever since she was a little girl, she'd spent countless hours in the kitchens with the woman responsible for all the meals she'd ever eaten. But on the morning of her seventeenth birthday, as she watched Tilley prepare to bake her cake, Hannah realized just how much she had grown. The signs were obvious. Tilley usually paused to catch her breath, leaning heavily against the table. At times, she seemed to forget where to find things in a place she'd spent so many years working.

Unable to ignore it any longer, Hannah decided to join her at the table. "Oh no, you don't, child," Tilley said with a soft chuckle. "You'll leave this kitchen and let an old woman do her work."

Hannah kissed the top of Tilley's wrinkled cheek. "You'll not get rid of me that easily, Tilley. You know how I love being here with you. Besides, I must learn all I can from you. I intend to be a good wife someday."

Tilley paused, her wrinkled hand brushing a stray wisp of grey hair from her eyes, her gaze steady. "You mustn't speak of such things, my dear... considering..." Her voice trailed off, and Hannah could see the knowing look in her eyes.

Hannah hesitated, lips tight, before turning her gaze downward, feeling suddenly nervous. She dipped a finger into the batter and brought it to her lips, her eyes meeting Tilley's again. She wasn't sure if Tilley had noticed the spark in her eyes, but the older woman seemed to know, anyway.

"Come, child," Tilley said, her voice gentle but firm. "I may be old, but I'm no fool." She shook the messy spoon close to Hannah's face, the tip brushing her nose. "I was young once, you know. I remember what it's like to fall in love."

Hannah's eyes widened in surprise, her mouth turning into a mischievous grin. "Forbidden love, child, can bring pain," Tilley added, her tone shifting slightly. "But you must let it run its course. Soon, Silas will find a woman he wishes to marry."

Hannah froze, her finger still in her mouth, her eyes widening as she looked into Tilley's knowing gaze. "But, Tilley," she said, her voice soft and innocent, "it's not forbidden." She watched Tilley's face shift in surprise. "Father and Mother know about our love. We're to be married someday."

"Good heavens," Tilley muttered under her breath, her face softening, before quickly turning her attention back to the cake batter. She said no more.

"Grandfather says there's no shame in loving your cousin," Hannah added, her voice small.

"I assume you mean Master Hearne?" Tilley replied, her hand reaching up to gently pat Hannah's cheek. "You mustn't fret about it, dear. I only want to see you happy."

Hannah smiled, her heart full. For at that moment, she truly felt like the happiest girl in the world.

32

A HUNTER'S WAY

It was midsummer, a golden afternoon with the sun high in the sky. Birds sang from the trees surrounding the courtyard, their melodies weaving through the fragrant summer air. A carriage stood ready, polished and elegant, waiting to take his grandparents to the capital for their wedding anniversary.

Silas, now twenty-one, felt nothing—not a single sign of the change Grandfather Hearne had warned him about. But the day was beautiful, and he stood beside the one person he adored more than anything. He squeezed Hannah's hand, his smile wide as he watched his grandparents prepare to depart.

Grandfather Bleddyn and Grandmother Igraine waved from the carriage, as joyful as ever.

"Can you imagine?" Silas mused, glancing at Hannah. "Married for so many years."

She leaned in closer, her voice warm. "And still so happy."

"Mother says they take this trip every year on this very day."

Hannah inhaled deeply, as if she, too, dreamed of such a love—one that endured. As the carriage rolled through the gates of Bleddyn Manor, Silas turned to her, already knowing she felt the same as he did. Soon, they would be married.

"Come with me to the woods," he said.

The wind played with Hannah's black hair, sunlight catching in her green eyes like polished gems.

"You mustn't fear, Hannah," he assured her. "I would never let harm come to you. Besides, there's something I need to show you—something you must see."

She nodded. "Shall we take the horses?" She was already leading him toward the stables.

"No, not the horses."

Before she could say another word, Silas swept her into his arms. He ran toward the woods, the world blurring past them. Hannah's delighted laughter rang through the air as she wrapped her arms around his neck, trusting him completely.

Silas had carried her deep into the woods, yet Hannah felt no fear. It seemed as though they had traveled miles—so far from home that she knew she would never find her way back without him. The dense canopy overhead cast shifting patterns of shade, and the birds sang sweetly. She admired the moss-covered tree trunks, giggling as squirrels darted across their path, springing from the ground to the branches as if startled by the two giants invading their domain.

Silas finally stopped at the mouth of a cave, a dark chasm yawning before them. But even as she gazed into its shadowy depths, Hannah felt safe. He gently set her down, his fingers still laced through hers.

"This is my secret place," he murmured. "My lair."

Hannah giggled, amused by the dramatic claim, but as she looked up at him, she sensed the significance of this place. Nestling close, she rested her head against his chest, feeling the deep rumble of his voice as he spoke again.

"I come here at night sometimes... when I need peace."

"But, Silas... Grandfather Hearne has forbidden—"

"Grandfather Hearne lives miles away, Hannah," Silas interrupted. "Mother and Father are not like me... they need sleep. You've seen how fast I run."

"This place is so dark, even in daylight," she whispered, staring into the cave's blackness. "How do you see?"

"I see better in the dark," he said. "And I can smell everything."

He led her deeper inside, sensing her hesitation. Brushing a kiss against her cheek, he whispered, "You must trust me, Hannah. It's safe here."

"I—I cannot see, Silas!" she gasped, clinging to his arm.

"Come."

His arm slipped around her waist, guiding her forward. Slowly, her eyes adjusted, the cavern's contours taking shape—the jagged walls, scattered boulders, the flickering shadows. Then, she heard it: the gentle rush of running water.

Hannah giggled, enchanted by the discovery.

"Yes, my love," Silas said. "My cave has a stream of fresh water."

They climbed upward, moving through another passage, and suddenly, light burst into the darkness.

Hannah gasped in awe. High above, a natural opening pierced the cave's ceiling, allowing a shaft of sunlight to pour into the space. The golden light shimmered upon a crystal-clear pool below, illuminating the cavern like a sacred sanctuary. The opening had to be a hundred feet above them, unreachable, yet magnificent.

"Our secret place," Silas whispered, guiding her down toward the water. "This is ours alone."

He cupped her face in his hands, his lips capturing hers in a slow, searching kiss. Hannah melted into him, her body yielding to the warmth of his embrace. A sudden wave of passion consumed her as his tongue traced the softness of her lips before slipping deeper, claiming her.

But then—something changed.

Silas's body tensed. His grip tightened.

Hannah felt it immediately—the unnatural heat radiating from his skin.

Gently, she pulled back, her breathing uneven as she placed a trembling palm against his cheek. "Silas!" she gasped. "You're burning up!"

His skin was fever-hot, drenched in sweat.

"I feel amazing, Hannah."

"But... your skin—it's like fire." She wiped his brow, worry settling deep in her chest. "Can you not feel it?"

Silas nodded slowly. "Yes..." A flicker of confusion crossed his face. "Hannah... I don't know what's happening."

She took his arm, her urgency mounting. "We have to go, Silas. Now."

MAXWELL HAD TAKEN THIS JOURNEY WITH IGRAINE EVERY YEAR FOR AS LONG as he could remember. The carriage wound its way up the familiar hill, and as he gazed out the window, his eyes lingered on the ravine below. Beside him, Igraine sat quietly, her hand resting in his. He smiled.

Igraine, ever steadfast, had never once broken her vows as a wife, nor wavered in her devotion as a mother. She was a strong woman, and Maxwell loved her all the more for it. He had given her a life many could only dream of, yet in their quietest moments, when he needed a confidante and friend, she had given him far more.

She knew him. She loved him.

Maxwell thought back to the first time he saw her—the beautiful daughter of a thatcher. She had been promised to another, but he had to have her. His grip tightened slightly as he recalled what he had done to make that happen. Regret was a luxury he could not afford. Some things were better left unsaid.

Igraine giggled. He squeezed her hand gently.

"Now, what amuses my angel?"

"You do."

Maxwell raised a brow. "Me? I have said nothing. I have done naught."

"But you think," she teased, laughing as she rested her head against his shoulder.

He chuckled. "I fear you have me at a disadvantage, my love."

"You do this every year," she said with a knowing smile. "Each time we take this road to the capital, you think of it."

Maxwell said nothing, only watching her.

"I know what you did, Maxwell Bleddyn," Igraine continued. "I was young and naive then, but no fool."

"My dear, I have no idea—"

"You do." She laughed again. "Father told me the whole tale. He woke me that very night after you left our home."

Maxwell tensed.

"That was quite the sum you paid to have him break his word to my betrothed's family," she said, watching him closely.

"Igraine, my love, I—"

"Shhh..." She placed a finger to his lips. "I did not love Arthur. Besides, I learned the following evening, after he called off the engagement, that you had also visited his home."

Maxwell's jaw clenched. His youthful arrogance had not considered that loose ends might one day unravel. "They swore silence."

"My father wanted what was best for me," Igraine said, squeezing his hand. "But he would never have accepted your offer without my permission."

"He took my gold."

"He would have returned it if I had wished."

Maxwell studied her, realization dawning. "You knew."

She smiled. "I have always known."

A slow grin spread across his face. He pulled her close, and together, they laughed.

The moment was shattered in an instant.

A sharp whistle cut through the air, followed by the dull thud of an arrow piercing flesh.

Maxwell straightened, his senses on high alert. Above the steady rhythm of hooves and creaking carriage wheels, he heard the sharp neigh of a wounded horse. The carriage lurched.

He tapped the door with his cane, urging the coachman to get the beasts under control. Another arrow struck. A strangled whinny. The snap of leather. The carriage tilted violently.

"Igraine—"

The road beneath them vanished.

Igraine screamed as the horses pitched over the edge, dragging the carriage with them. Maxwell wrapped his arms around her, bracing for impact, but the world spun violently. His grip slipped.

"Igraine!"

And then, the fall.

THE ARCHER DESCENDED THE RAVINE WITH MEASURED CARE, HIS BOW AND quiver secured across his back. He had already retrieved his arrows from the fallen beasts, leaving them to die where they lay. As he slid down the slope, he paused, his gaze settling on the lifeless woman sprawled in the dirt.

Igraine Bleddyn.

Her vacant eyes stared skyward, unseeing. He stood over her for several moments, silent, unmoved. Then he turned away. Time was not his ally. The distant voice calling from behind the wreckage reminded him of that.

"Igraine! Igraine!"

The hoarse cries cut through the stillness.

He moved toward the overturned carriage, ignoring the scattered luggage. The coachman lay crushed beneath one edge of the wreck, his broken body twisted at an unnatural angle. Dead.

The voice persisted.

Rounding the carriage, the archer stopped where Maxwell Bleddyn lay, pinned, bloodied, and weak. His friend's eyes locked onto his, the flicker of recognition followed by something Percival had not seen in years —hope.

"Maxwell, Maxwell," Percival murmured, shaking his head. "You disappoint me."

He crouched low, forcing Maxwell to see him clearly. "You've made everything so easy."

A slow grin spread across Percival's face as he saw anger bloom in Maxwell's eyes—a rage absent in the man for far too long. It almost amused him.

"I'd help, truly," Percival continued, feigning regret. "But you see, I rode out here alone." He shifted, letting Maxwell catch sight of the quiver on his back. "Yes, my friend. It was me. The hunter I am."

He straightened, glancing at the sky. "You'll be dead long before sunset."

Maxwell groaned, his pleas weak, barely formed. Percival ignored him, stepping away. He had no time for the dying.

Yet, he paused one last time, looking back. "You never deserved the power given to you, Maxwell. Your kind could have lived as gods, yet you squandered it. But I shall be the cornerstone of the Bleddyn clan. I will live the life you so foolishly rejected."

Then, without another glance, Percival left him to the vultures.

33

PATRIARCH

They all wore black. It was a hot sunny day, one Hannah had deemed unsuitable for standing among tombstones. She had spent the entire night weeping, as she had several days past when news arrived of her grandparents' deaths. The young girl stood at the foot of their graves, looking at their tombstones. A gentle hand caressed her shoulder, and she knew it was Silas. Hannah leaned into the comforting bulk of his body. "We were the last to see them alive," she whispered. "Silas, they were so happy... and then they died."

"Come, Hannah, we cannot stay in this place. The others are leaving."

Hannah nodded and looked beyond the cemetery gates, where several carriages waited. Her parents beckoned to her. Beyond the carriages, the church atop the hill loomed, casting a shadow over the grounds. Silas began to move toward the gate but stopped suddenly. His nostrils flared, and he paused for a moment, sniffing the air. Hannah noticed it—there was something off about the way he stood, something tense, as though he were picking up on something far beyond the ordinary.

Silas gently scratched the tip of his nose, a slight furrow forming between his brows.

Grandfather Hearne, who stood nearby, ever fatherly and watchful, drew near. "Silas, is something wrong, boy?" He came closer, leaning against his cane, not for support but from habit, his figure as solid and imposing as ever. "Speak up, boy. What is it?"

"Nothing, Grandfather... it's just a scent, over in the cemetery." There was uncertainty in Silas's voice, but his eyes remained fixed on the graveyard. Hannah looked beyond the old fence at the stone mausoleum surrounded by countless graves, the shadows deepening at the edges of the stones. Her gaze lingered on the mausoleum for a moment longer than necessary, an odd unease tightening in her chest.

Grandfather Hearne studied the grounds of the cemetery with a frown, his sharp eyes scanning the stone structures as if seeking something hidden. He shrugged, dismissing it. "Your sense of smell is far stronger than most. What you smell is the stench of death, the dead bones of your kin. Let us leave this place."

Hannah looked at Silas, but he didn't move. He remained rooted in place, a strange stillness overtaking him, like a predator sensing something far off. She reached for his hand, but he didn't take it immediately. She swallowed and followed his gaze once more. The cemetery felt heavier now—something about it seemed to watch them.

Grandfather Hearne's voice broke the tension. "Come now, let's be on our way. The others are waiting." His tone was firm, and all obeyed.

Moments later, Hannah was seated next to Silas in a carriage. The horses began their slow, steady pull as they made their way away from the cemetery. She glanced at Silas again, but his gaze was distant, and his expression unreadable. Tilley had prepared a feast fit for kings, and Grandfather Hearne had decreed there would be no mourning that day. They would celebrate the lives of Grandfather Bleddyn and Grandmother Igraine.

Hannah's gaze shifted out the window as the carriage wheels turned, the weight of their loss lingering, but she knew they were leaving something behind. Something that, despite Grandfather Hearne's insistence, wasn't finished yet.

THINGS COULD NOT HAVE BEEN BETTER. PERCIVAL SAT AT THE HEAD OF THE massive oak table, savouring the moment as all eyes were trained on him. He had just presented what he considered the finest epitaph—a tribute he'd composed himself and had inscribed upon an ivory plaque in memory of Maxwell and Igraine. He studied the faces around him after he finished, finding tear-filled eyes.

Silas sat to his right, with Hannah beside him; Max and Bartholomew were to his left, with Catherine and Morgan by their side. He had graciously offered Tilley a place at the table, but the cook had declined, and Percival had no intention of offering again. Gertrude, his dear Gertrude, sat at the opposite end, her rightful position now that she was the lady of two houses. Percival had crafted this perfect family, and he alone would be their provider. But as he glanced at Silas, he knew that all his carefully laid plans would be for nothing without the boy. Silas had power—power that Percival needed to control, to bend to his will. But Silas was strong. Percival had to tread carefully. He needed to contain the boy, harness that power, and when the time was right, unleash the beast. Percival smiled to himself. His family would come to see the genius of his plan. They would thank him in the end.

Once the servants had cleared the room, Percival shifted his gaze to Bartholomew, then to the others. "You all know the threat we face," he began, his voice steady, yet edged with urgency. "It will not be long before we have vampires at our door."

"But no one has seen one, Sir." Morgan spoke up, glancing at his wife for reassurance, as though uncertain if his words were out of place. Catherine, ever the support, patted his arm gently.

"I cannot believe Isabelle, my dear sister, has chosen such a life," Catherine said softly, disbelief in her voice.

"You forget, sister," Max interjected, "what father-in-law has told us." He glanced at Silas, concern briefly crossing his features. "Our brother and sister are no longer the people we once loved."

"You think only of your son," Catherine retorted bitterly.

"And what of your daughter?" Max countered, his voice rising. "Do you truly believe these blood drinkers would spare any of us?"

"Enough!" Percival's voice cut through the growing tension. The room fell silent immediately, as his commanding presence filled the space. "I will not abide this pointless bickering. The vampires will come. Long after we are all dead, Larus will claim what is yours. Vampires live for centuries. The only thing they desire more than the blood flowing through our veins," Percival continued, his eyes narrowing, "is wealth. They are materialistic, self-centred creatures."

"But father, how can Silas alone defeat an entire coven?" Bartholomew asked, his voice laced with skepticism. The others nodded in agreement, their concern palpable.

Percival smiled, a smile that barely touched his eyes, dismissing the question with ease. "All you need to do is trust me. I am the means to your survival." He turned and placed a hand on Silas's shoulder, his grip firm. "You are of age now, my grandson." His gaze shifted to Hannah, his smile faltering slightly as a fleeting moment of envy washed over him. The bond between Silas and Hannah—unearned, unbroken—pricked at him. He quickly recovered and addressed her. "And so are you, dear girl."

For a moment, Percival held her gaze, the silent challenge between them palpable. He could claim no credit for the love between the two, yet he wondered—did it threaten him? A new age was upon them, and his carefully plotted future was just beginning.

"A new age has begun," Percival declared, his voice booming with authority. "Bleddyn Manor shall host a wedding."

Gertrude rose at the far end of the table, her voice soft yet resolute. "I shall prepare, husband." Percival nodded, a smile tugging at his lips, but his eyes lingered on Catherine and Morgan. Their expressions were tight, the weight of their unspoken doubts hanging in the air. Percival knew he had more convincing to do.

34

WOLF HERO

Morgan could wait no longer. Catherine had begged him not to go to Hannah's rooms until she sent for him, but his heart could not obey. Today, he would lose his daughter, and the weight of that sorrow had broken him. He had spent the night weeping in his wife's arms, pleading with Catherine to run—to take Hannah and leave Bleddyn Manor forever. But Catherine had only shaken her head, whispering that it was too late, that Hannah would never forgive them. She loved Silas too much.

Morgan knew his wife spoke the truth, yet he still wished things had been different. That he had been stronger. That he had been the one making the decisions for his family instead of Percival Hearne.

The night before, he had poured out his soul to Catherine, confessing things that could shake the very foundation of Bleddyn Manor. He had spoken aloud what they both feared: that all of this—the marriage, the deaths, the shift in power—had been Percival's design from the very beginning. But worst of all, Morgan did not believe it had ever been Hannah's destiny to wed her first cousin.

Catherine had thrown herself over him in an instant, pressing a trembling hand over his mouth, her eyes wide with terror. "Never say that again," she had begged, though her silence had already told him she felt the same.

Now, standing outside Hannah's door, Morgan did not knock. He stepped inside, and his breath caught at the sight of his daughter. Catherine was tucking white flowers into Hannah's bound hair, her fingers trembling slightly as she worked.

"Father!" Hannah laughed. "It is not time yet!"

He kissed her rouged cheek. "How could I resist, my pretty flower? You are no longer mine after today."

Tears blurred his vision. "I am sorry, my loves." He looked from Catherine to Hannah.

"Don't be silly, Father," Hannah said, her voice warm. "Silas and I will always live here...with you." But then her expression changed. She looked to her mother, hesitant. "We are staying together, aren't we?"

"Of course, dear." Catherine's smile was soft but practiced. "Where else would we go?"

Morgan thought of his own lands, the Frye family estate that should one day be his. They were not as wealthy as the Bleddyns or the Hearnes, but they had lived comfortably, free of men like Percival. He caught Catherine's gaze and knew she had read his thoughts.

"Your father and I will watch over you...you and Silas."

Hannah smiled, brushing aside their concerns with youthful confidence. "You needn't worry, Mother. Grandfather Hearne has everything in hand."

Morgan swallowed his disgust.

"I am certain he does," he muttered. Catherine shot him a sharp glance.

He hesitated before speaking again. "Hannah, dear...has your grandfather said anything about what would happen if you have children?"

A shadow passed over Catherine's face. They had discussed this—endlessly. The possibility haunted them both.

Morgan winced, closing his eyes briefly. He could not help it. The image of Hannah in a birthing bed, screaming, as she brought forth something monstrous.

Hannah gasped, then burst into laughter. "Mother! Father!" She shook her head. "Oh, you poor dears. Grandfather Hearne says our children will be as normal as I was when I was born. You do remember that lycanthropes—well, shapeshifters—only change when they come of age?"

Morgan exhaled, relieved.

But then Hannah hesitated. Her smile faltered.

"What is it, Hannah?" Morgan's heart pounded. He gripped her shoulders.

"Well...it's nothing, Father." But her voice had changed. "Once, Silas and I were in the woods. We were alone, and...something happened."

Morgan and Catherine exchanged a glance.

"What happened, Hannah?" Catherine's voice was tight. "Is Silas alright?"

"It only happened once." Hannah paused, as if trying to make sense of it. "But Silas...his body became so warm, like he had a fever. No—worse than that. It was like his body was on fire, but he didn't even realize it."

Morgan's blood turned to ice.

"Sweat was dripping from him, but he couldn't feel it," Hannah continued.

Morgan forced his voice to remain steady. "Did he hurt you?"

"No, Father." Hannah's voice was firm. "Silas would never hurt me. But it scared me. I asked him to take me home right away."

Morgan pulled his daughter into a tight embrace, but as he did, his eyes met Catherine's over Hannah's shoulder.

Neither of them spoke.

But the fear in his wife's gaze mirrored his own.

Over two hundred guests had come to celebrate the union of Silas and Hannah. Max sat beside her son, watching him with pride. The wedding ceremony had been the finest she had ever seen, all thanks to Gertrude, her mother-in-law. Though Max recognized only a handful of the guests, the day had gone well, and now, well after sunset, music and laughter filled the great hall.

Silas was radiant with joy, and the sight of it made Max's eyes well with tears. She reached for Bartholomew's hand without thinking.

Her husband stiffened slightly, glancing at her in surprise, but after a moment, his fingers curled around hers, warm and steady. Max felt herself smiling at him. He smiled back.

On the empty dance floor, Silas and Hannah took their first steps together. The crowd hushed, watching as they moved in perfect unison. Max felt her chest tighten. They looked so young. So in love.

A moment later, Bartholomew stood and extended his hand. Max hesitated, then let him lead her onto the floor. Behind them, Bartholomew's parents followed, as did Morgan and Catherine. The four couples danced to the sound of cheers, and by the time the waltz ended, most of the guests had joined in.

Max spun beneath the golden candlelight, laughter ringing in her ears. For the first time in years, she allowed herself to believe—just for a moment—that happiness was possible.

But when the waltz ended and she glanced toward the head of the hall, she caught a glimpse of Percival Hearne watching from his place of honour. He was not smiling.

And just like that, the illusion was gone.

Micah had given him the gift of immortality, and for that, Nicolas was grateful. He loved his maker and coven, for without them, he would have been nothing—a pitiful mortal doomed to the same pointless existence as his parents and grandfather. The plague had taken them all so long ago.

If only I had known Micah then, he thought.

Had he remained human, he would be thirty years old by now, but those days were far behind him. He had not aged a day since his rebirth. Though only seven years into his new life, Nicolas felt as though he had lived a thousand years. He was strong, fast, and could hear the whispers of those within Bleddyn Manor's great hall, even above the resounding music.

Standing alone in the farthest corner of the massive room, he watched as couples swayed in bliss. The joining of Larus's nephew and niece was indeed a grand affair, and Micah had taken a risk by sending him here. But he was not alone. Helene, his sister, was somewhere among the guests, lurking as he was.

His eyes found her easily.

She was radiant, her gown a masterpiece of flowing fabric, her presence impossible to ignore. Every bachelor who passed her paused, drawn to her beauty. She does not belong in the shadows, he thought, and yet, like him, she was a creature of the night.

Before they had left, Larus had shared his blood memories with them, and Nicolas had found the ones he was seeking. He and Helene had orders—avoid Percival Hearne and his son, Bartholomew, for their minds are impenetrable. But Catherine and Morgan...

Their thoughts are open.

Micah's wisdom impressed Nicolas more every day. As he scanned the room, he had already learned much. The humans laughed, feasted, and toasted the union, but their thoughts were darker—full of whispers about how unnatural it was for first cousins to wed.

Nicolas smirked. They would not last a day in our world.

Still, one thing intrigued him. As he watched Catherine and Morgan, he saw something deeper than disapproval.

Sorrow.

Neither wanted the union. Both despised the one who had orchestrated it.

Hannah, however, was radiant, clinging to Silas as though he were the only soul in the room. Nicolas could feel it—their minds were woven together like threads of the same fabric.

He exhaled slowly.

Would he ever know such a bond?

A presence stirred behind him. He had sensed her before she touched his arm.

"Dance with me," Helene whispered.

Nicolas turned, smiling despite himself. "We must do as Micah asked," he said. "We must not be seen together."

Helene tugged at his arm. "Come, dance with me, brother."

Nicolas hesitated. He was cautious, though if discovered, escape would be easy. But Micah's warning echoed in his mind. Beware Percival Hearne.

"Helene," he murmured, glancing at his red hair, his pale skin—distinctive, unnatural. "We mustn't draw attention."

She only smiled. She had no such worries—her complexion was warm, human-like. Micah had sent her for this reason. She could blend in.

Their older brother, Yaro, had no such luxury. With his white skin and ice-blue eyes, he had every visible trait of their kind. So he waited in the woods.

A sudden clap of hands silenced the hall.

"Honoured guests!"

Nicolas and Helene turned to the great table. Percival Hearne stood, his voice commanding immediate attention.

"I am grateful for your presence and well wishes on the day of my grandson's joining with our dear Hannah."

Nicolas tensed. Slowly, he guided Helene deeper into the shadows.

"The time has come," the hunter announced, "for the happy couple to leave us and begin their young lives together." He spread his arms wide. "But you, my friends, are welcome to remain here and enjoy this magnificent feast!"

The hall erupted into cheers, but Nicolas shook his head. Liars. Most of them detest this union.

He glanced at Helene. "What do you suppose this means?" he murmured. "Surely they have no plans to leave the manor."

Helene's brows furrowed.

"The girl..." she whispered. Her voice was distant, her eyes unfocused. "She thinks of a haven... a cave."

Nicolas stiffened. His own mind latched onto the image. Dark stone walls. The scent of earth and damp moss.

He exhaled sharply. "Yes. I see it."

Silas's lair.

And dear Grandfather Hearne knows nothing of it.

He met Helene's gaze. No more words were needed.

"Come," he whispered. "We must find Yaro and wait."

His grandfather alone had accompanied them to the rooms they would share, seeming more excited about their joining than they were. But Silas and Hannah had made other plans.

After Grandfather Hearne left them, Tilley had secretly ushered them down the back staircase to the kitchens, where they slipped out the back door with all the supplies they needed.

More than anything else, Silas wanted to have the first night with his wife all to himself—just the two of them, far from the eyes of their family. Only one place could give them that privacy.

The lair.

He ran with Hannah in his arms, faster than any human could follow. The night air was crisp against his skin, carrying the scent of pine and damp earth. Above them, the full moon watched in silence.

Hannah giggled, tightening her arms around his neck. "You need not hurry, Silas," she said, her voice warm in his ear. "We have the night."

Silas smiled. "And no one knows where we will spend it."

Then, suddenly, he stopped.

His breath stilled. His ears twitched. Something was wrong.

He lifted his head, sniffing the air. A scent, faint but foreign. Something out of place. His fingers flexed against Hannah's waist.

"What is it, my love?" Hannah asked, concern flickering in her voice.

Silas sniffed again. The scent was fading, barely there, like a whisper in the wind. And yet...

"Probably nothing..." he murmured. His gaze lifted to the treetops, watching for movement. "There is a strange scent... something in the trees."

Hannah followed his gaze, but the night remained still. A breeze rippled through the leaves, cool and indifferent.

She laughed softly, pressing a kiss to his cheek. "You're always sniffing the air like a hound, my love."

Silas exhaled, loosening his grip on her.

Perhaps she's right.

Still, as he resumed his run toward the cave, his instincts did not settle.

Something had been there. Watching.

It took far too long to light the fifty candles, but Silas would do it a thousand times if Hannah wanted them. They had placed lights all over the cave and around the small pool of water, and above them, through the opening, glowed the silver moon.

"Silas," his bride whispered, "this is beautiful."

The young wolf smiled as she pressed her head against his bare chest. They had both stripped before setting the cave alight. Now, as he stepped back to admire her, a flutter of nerves twisted deep in his belly.

Grandfather Hearne had explained in detail his husbandly duties, yet Silas felt woefully unprepared. His hands trembled as he placed them around her slender waist, his lips hovering just over hers.

Hannah chuckled. "Oh, Silas, you are a bag of nerves."

He pivoted. "Grandfather said—"

She pressed a finger over his lips. "Forget Grandfather Hearne."

Her voice was soft but firm. "Mother said to trust ourselves...our love."

She led him toward the water, slowly lowering their bodies to the stone floor. "Kiss me, Silas."

Silas obeyed. As their lips met, his nervousness melted into something deeper, something primal. Hannah, sensing his passion, pushed his body against the cold stone. She gripped his wrists, guiding his palms to her breasts, and Silas shuddered beneath her touch.

Hannah bit his tongue.

The sting, the taste of blood—it ignited something inside him.

She grasped his wrists again, lowering her lips to his ear. Silas groaned as her fingers found the stiffness between his thighs. Heat pulsed through his body—a hunger unlike any he had ever known.

"Hannah... my beloved Hannah..."

She pushed his head back against the stone and straddled him. Silas could hear the rapid beat of her heart. He smelled the sweat on her skin, saw the beads of it dripping from her onto his chest.

Then—something changed.

His breath came ragged now, not from passion, but from something else.

Silas' fingers flexed, an ache spreading through his hands. His spine burned. His muscles tensed, stretched—too much, too fast. Something inside him was waking up.

He glanced up at the moon. The silver glow consumed his vision.

Pain tore through him.

A bolt of agony shot down his spine, and Silas screamed—not in pleasure, but horror.

Hannah gasped beneath him. "Silas!"

He tried to move—tried to pull away from her—but his limbs wouldn't obey. His arms locked against the ground, pinning her beneath him.

"Hannah... I... what's happening to me?"

His back expanded, his chest widened—the bones inside him grinding, shifting, twisting. He lifted his hands, watching in terror as short silver bristles sprouted from his skin. His nails blackened, thickened, stretching into long, curved claws.

Hannah screamed.

Silas turned toward the pool of water—toward the reflection staring back at him.

No...

His face was no longer his own.

His chiselled jaw had stretched into a snout, his teeth now sharp, jagged fangs. His silver eyes, once filled with love for Hannah, were now wild, untamed, predatory.

Silas tried to say her name, but his tongue felt too heavy.

The wolf lifted its head and howled.

He knew the woman beneath him.

But he was a wolf now. And as much as he fought it, instinct took over.

"Silas, it is me..." Hannah whispered. She had stopped screaming.

She stared into his silver eyes, willing him to remember.

But the wolf had no choice.

Again, he howled, his head tilted to the moon. His body lowered, teeth bared, and he sank his fangs into her neck.

Her blood filled his mouth.

And then—he sensed something else.

The wolf froze.

Rising, he sniffed the air.

Something was watching.

He turned toward the cave's entrance, his claws tightening into fists. Then, without effort, he leapt across the pool to the opposite side.

The enemy was near.

35

CHANGED

The entire coven gathered within the largest chamber of the catacombs, except for Giles, who remained at White Castle. Since the old caretaker and Ashkan had become vampires, Micah had ensured there were human replacements—he believed every coven needed them. Sebastian disagreed. While Micah saw humans as valuable assets, Sebastian viewed them as liabilities, convinced they would one day betray them.

Larus sat apart at the far end of the great hall. Eleven blood drinkers argued over his family, and he heard the name Bleddyn spoken with bitterness again and again. He gazed at Isabelle, knowing she felt the same unease.

He despised Yaro for attacking Isabelle that night in the graveyard, yet a part of him was grateful for it—because of that, he had her by his side once more.

Micah and Sebastian sat together as equals, though all except Yaro saw Micah as the true leader. Babette and Helene, seldom apart, curled together on a single couch, while Haruki shared another with Geraldine and Monique. Nicolas, the youngest, was practically pressed against Micah's side—he rarely strayed far from his maker. And Yaro, ever loyal to his maker, stood protectively behind Sebastian.

Ashkan lingered near the door, watchful.

"We must decide whether to abandon the catacombs," Micah said. "We all know what Nicolas and Helene have seen."

Larus noticed the way Yaro's pale face twisted in disdain. His long lashes briefly veiled those ice-blue eyes before he took a step forward.

"It was I who tracked them to the cave," he said sharply, his voice thick with disgust.

Micah barely glanced at him. "It appears this war of the two dominant species is set to resume."

"And this war," Babette murmured, "is why Emilio disobeyed the council. He always knew this day would come." She lifted a slender finger. "But we must be careful. Cecil saved us once, but he can just as easily end us."

"I saw the silver wolf," Yaro cut in, unable to contain his rage. "The boy, Silas...he changed right on top of her...right in the middle of fucking her! The Bleddyn wolves are monsters. They must be put down."

Larus winced. Isabelle's hand tightened around his.

"He was large," Nicolas added. "Silas grew twice his size. And he knew we were there."

Nicolas' words seemed to bring an unsettling quiet to the room.

Helene nodded. "If we had engaged him that night, one of us would have died."

"He would have killed you all."

The room shifted toward Larus as he spoke, his tone heavy with warning.

"You speak of my family," he continued, his voice lower now, more dangerous. He pulled Isabelle closer, his expression dark. "We have heard what Micah and Babette have told us—young lycanthropes cannot contain their rage."

Helene sighed. "And that poor girl...killed by the one she loved. The boy had no control. He became mindless."

"It is hard," Babette agreed, her accent thick with regret. "Lycanthropes, they...they are instinctual. The poor garçon—he will never forgive himself."

Micah leaned forward, resting his arm on Sebastian's shoulder. "Brother, do you remember what Emilio once told us?" A small smile ghosted his lips. "We have been fools."

Sebastian tugged absently at a lock of his hair.

"Nicolas," he said, "are you certain the girl was dead?"

Nicolas hesitated. "Well...she wasn't moving." He ran his fingers through his red hair. "He bit her, but then...he sensed us watching. He caught our scent."

Micah's knowing smile widened.

Sebastian let out a low laugh. "Mon chéri...it seems your niece, Hannah, may not be as dead as you think."

Larus stiffened.

"You see," Sebastian continued, clearly enjoying himself, "Micah is right. We have been fools." He let the silence linger before finally delivering the blow. "It is true that lycanthropes—wolves—are born. But wolves are also made. Hannah may have died that night, but she may have lived...made immortal."

Larus' breath caught.

Yaro roared with rage. "I told you we should have killed him!"

"They will multiply," Monique whispered.

"It is not the boy, Silas, who leads them," Helene said. She turned her gaze to Larus and Isabelle. "Your sister, Catherine—she despises the hunter...this Percival. It is he we must fear."

"Morgan, her husband, feels the same." Nicolas nodded. "We saw their thoughts."

Larus looked at Isabelle, his mind racing.

"What must we do?" he asked.

Micah's voice was calm, unwavering. "We cannot be afraid of the hunter. Hunters thrive on fear, and I will not indulge Percival Hearne."

"Your sister's husband distrusts him," Helene added. "Morgan believes this hunter planned everything—from his daughter's marriage to the death of your parents."

Larus' grip on Isabelle's hand tightened.

"He would have kept his plans to himself," Sebastian mused. "Percival Hearne is a wise man."

"He meant to do this all along," Larus muttered, his voice thick with realization. He turned to Micah. "As you said, it is forbidden for a hunter to join with a lycanthrope, yet Percival convinced my father to make the match. Then Silas was born."

"The hunter and the wolf, joined as one," Geraldine whispered.

Haruki, who had remained silent until now, inclined his head. "The hunter and the wolf are alike—both dangerous to our kind. But they were never meant to be joined."

Sebastian's smirk returned.

"But we," he said, pacing now, "have an advantage." His sharp eyes locked onto Larus. "You, chéri, like Silas, shall soon experience your transformation."

Larus stilled.

Babette nodded solemnly. "We do not know when, but you, petit loup, will change—become what we never could. Like Cecil, you are wolf and vampire."

Micah, his face serious now, exhaled. "But we do not know when this change will come. We cannot rely on the unknown—we must use the strength we have now."

Sebastian rubbed his palms together. "And yet...we have Cecil." He scanned the room. "Why not wake our ally from his long sleep?"

Micah's jaw tensed. "We have discussed this, Sebastian."

"Yes," Babette added. "To wake a vampire from long sleep...to wake one as old as Cecil...is not easy."

"How is it done?" Isabelle asked, her voice barely above a whisper.

A shadow crossed Babette's face. She hesitated. Then, finally, she spoke.

"It is...unwise to share this, but I will tell you all." She looked Larus in the eyes. "To wake Cecil, you use his blood...his blood memories."

Micah stiffened. "That would mean—"

Babette cut him off. "We hid his blood with him. It is there, in the chamber." She paused. "It is the only way to make Cecil remember."

Larus' heart pounded.

It was not yet time for Cecil's awakening, but he had to see him.

He needed to know what he would become.

Silas stood over Hannah's bed, weeping. She had not woken since the night he attacked her. Though she still breathed, her skin was pale, her body motionless. He feared her death was near.

His aunt, Catherine, and her husband, Morgan, shot him looks of hatred through their sorrow. His own parents stood by Hannah's bedside, still in shock, torn between love for their son and grief for the girl he had nearly destroyed.

But one person in the room showed no worry at all.

Grandfather Hearne stood closest to Hannah, pressing his palm against her forehead before pulling back the sheet to inspect the wound Silas had inflicted. His expression was unreadable. Silas turned away, loathing himself. *This is my fault.* Hannah lay there helpless because of him.

"You said you would watch over them!" Catherine's voice cracked as she turned on Grandfather Hearne, her face wet with tears. She struck his chest with her fists, sobbing.

"Catherine!" Silas's mother rushed to her side, but Grandfather Hearne raised a hand, stopping her.

"Let her be, Max," he said, his tone calm—too calm. Silas's stomach twisted at the sight of his grandfather's slight, knowing smile.

"You all know nothing."

He turned his sharp gaze on Silas.

"What you bring to us, grandson, is a gift."

Silas stiffened.

"I had my suspicions," Grandfather Hearne continued, "but I had to put them to the test."

He took Catherine by the shoulders now, softening his expression, his voice thick with reassurance.

"Your daughter will not die, child. She will be reborn."

Silas's breath caught as he moved closer to Hannah.

"Reborn?" Morgan's brow furrowed. "What do you mean, reborn?"

Grandfather Hearne leaned over Hannah's still form, exposing the wound on her neck.

"Wolves, like vampires, heal when wounded," he said. "It may not happen as quickly as our enemies, but they heal. You are immortal, Silas."

He pointed to the wound. "Look."

Silas gasped.

The gash he had left on Hannah's neck had shrunk. The dried blood was gone.

"It's... healing." His voice trembled with relief.

Grandfather Hearne nodded.

"Yes, Silas. Wolves are not always born of women." His gaze swept the room, landing on each stunned face. "One bite can make a man a powerful wolf."

He looked at Hannah.

"The Bleddyn blood is all that saved her," he said. "Any other human woman may not have survived a bite from a lycanthrope."

A heavy silence settled over them.

"I know I have kept things from you..." Grandfather Hearne finally admitted. "But it was for the best."

"You risked my daughter's life!" Morgan's fury boiled over as he lunged toward him.

Grandfather Hearne struck him. A swift, brutal backhand that sent Morgan stumbling.

"You will know your place." His voice was sharp as steel.

Catherine rushed to her husband's side, glaring up at the old man, but Grandfather Hearne had already turned his back to them.

"We must stand together now," he said, his voice even once more. "It is vital to our survival."

He gazed down at Hannah, then glanced at the others.

"She will wake a new woman. See that someone watches over her."

Then, without another word, he strode toward the door.

"Silas," he called, not bothering to look back.

"You come with me now."

THE YOUNG WOLF SEEMED LIGHTER NOW—HAPPIER—FOR PERCIVAL HAD given him hope.

After leading Silas into the Bleddyn library, Percival leaned against the desk, watching as the boy paced.

"All I have done, my grandson... everything you are now... I have done for you. Not for myself."

Percival willed tears to his eyes, knowing the boy needed to see them.

"You, Silas... and Hannah." He paused, letting the weight of his words settle. "After long centuries, you are the first of shapeshifters. You shall be the mother and father of immortals."

Slowly, he wiped a tear from his cheek and turned away, gazing out the window.

He waited.

He let the silence stretch.

"And," he finally murmured, with a slight shrug, "years from now, long after I am gone from this world, it will be you, Silas, who must protect them... guide them. But it will not be easy."

Another pause. A sigh.

"There is much I must teach you before..."

He let the words drift into nothing.

"Grandfather..." The boy's voice cracked with worry. Silas had come closer now—Percival could feel his sorrow.

"Grandfather, what you said earlier... about Hannah." His voice had shifted, excitement creeping in. "You said she would become like me. Grandfather, could I not make you—"

Percival turned sharply.

"No, Silas." His voice was firm, yet warm. "My duty is to prepare you for the long life ahead. That is all that matters." He smiled softly. "Then, this poor old man can finally rest."

"No, Grandfather." Silas shook his head, his hands clenching at his sides. "I need you... I beg you to be as I am."

Percival studied him, his eyes narrowing just slightly. Then he stepped closer.

"Are you sure, Silas?" His voice lowered. "You would let me lead?"

Silas met his gaze without hesitation.

"Yes, Grandfather. Only you can lead us."

Percival smiled. Good.

"There is something else," Silas said suddenly. His expression darkened. "I didn't tell you before, but... I sensed something the night of our wedding."

Percival lifted his brows.

"Even as Hannah and I moved through the woods, I knew someone was following us. I caught a scent in the air... something unnatural." Silas frowned. "There was more than one. They were vampires. I could smell them."

Percival straightened, his expression turning grim.

"Then we must act quickly."

His voice was quiet but urgent.

"You are not safe, Silas." He met his grandson's gaze.

"We are all in danger."

She opened her eyes to see just one face gazing down at her.

Grandfather Hearne.

Hannah stretched her arms wide. She felt strong, as if new life coursed through her veins. Yet, she knew what had happened.

Her voice came quickly, urgent—

"Where is Silas? Why hasn't he come?"

Grandfather Hearne stood in silence, watching her with those unreadable eyes. Yet, she could hear the boom of his heart.

His scent filled her nostrils—sharp, spiced, something she'd never noticed before.

I couldn't have sensed this before the bite.

A sudden awareness gripped her. She reached for her neck—

The wound was gone.

“You are healed, my dear,” Grandfather Hearne said smoothly. “You rise this day a new woman… and you are lucky indeed.”

His tone was calm, yet something in his gaze made her shiver.

“I did not believe you would survive the bite of a wolf,” he continued. “But my doubts are no more. For you, like Silas… are a shapeshifter.”

Hannah’s breath caught.

“It was horrible,” she whispered. “Seeing him change. Silas was in so much pain.” The memory of his transformation sent a chill through her. “Where is he?”

“Do not worry, my dear.” Grandfather Hearne’s voice was soft, soothing. But his smile—thin, calculated—sent a pang of unease through her.

“I have sent Silas on an errand.”

Hannah’s stomach twisted.

“But you,” he continued, stepping closer, “must rest. Soon, your change will come.”

Hannah took a shaky breath, willing herself calm.

She knew what she had become.

Yet the thought of enduring what Silas had…

God help me.

She wasn’t ready.

36

PACK OF WOLVES

Bleddyn Manor would never be the same again.

Tilley was certain of that.

She had been with the Bleddyn household for many years. Once, she was a younger woman with a betrothed, a future, a life of her own. But all of that had vanished in an instant.

She had known the previous lady of the manor long before she became a Bleddyn. It was Igraine who brought her here, so many years ago.

Tilley remembered it well.

Igraine had once been betrothed to Tilley's younger brother—until Maxwell Bleddyn walked into their lives and decided he had to have her.

Tilley smiled faintly. Maxwell Bleddyn always got what he wanted, even if it meant paying in gold.

She doubted Igraine ever truly loved Arthur. If she had, she would not have given him up so easily. Not for all the wealth in the world.

Perhaps out of guilt, Igraine took pity on Tilley, whose world had collapsed after the death of her fiancé. She had welcomed her into Bleddyn Manor, given her purpose, and for that, Tilley had been grateful.

On the day she first set foot inside these walls, she had thought little of the life she left behind. And she never spoke of her brother again.

Now, she sat alone in the vast kitchen, surrounded by ghosts of the past.

The Bleddyn children had grown up in this room, under her watchful eye. She had fixed countless plates and baked more pies than she could count for those sweet little loves.

Now, there were only two left.

Maxwell and Igraine were gone.

But it was Larus she missed most. That sweet boy.

Tilley's throat tightened.

And now… now there was talk of beasts and vampires.

She shook her head. Nonsense.

But she had heard the howling the night of the joining.

She had seen the wound with her own eyes—bad as they were.

She had gone to wash Hannah's bandages just days after Silas claimed to have turned into a beast, claimed to have bitten her. But when she pulled back the linens…

There was no wound.

Hannah, pale and trembling, had confessed everything. Silas was something else. A shapeshifter.

Tilley wiped her sweaty palms on her apron.

"What has this world come to?"

But nothing—not the howling, not the impossible healing—had shaken her more than what she witnessed that morning.

She had walked into the kitchen at dawn, expecting to start the day as she always had. Instead, she found Silas—

Gnawing on a slab of raw meat.

Her breath had hitched, her hands flying to her mouth to stifle a scream.

Silas had thrown his head back and laughed.

Since that day, Master Hearne had made it very clear:

No family business must leave Bleddyn Manor.

The servants feared him. Rightfully so.

As for Tilley—she avoided Percival Hearne at all costs.

Because whatever had happened to Silas, whatever was happening to this house—

It had all changed the moment he walked through the gates.

THEY WAITED FOR THE NIGHT OF THE FULL MOON.

The cave was silent, save for the steady drip of water from the jagged ceiling. Shadows flickered along the stone walls, cast by the silver light spilling through the cave mouth.

Percival stood among his family, his heart pounding.

This was it.

Tonight, he would become immortal.

Despite all his planning, all his certainty, a sharp sliver of fear wedged itself into his chest. No turning back now.

He, along with Bartholomew, Morgan, Catherine, and Max, would join the ranks of lycanthropes.

It was late. The moon provided all the light they needed. Silas stood at the centre of the cave, his fingers intertwined with Hannah's. Percival turned to his right, surveying the others.

Silas had done well.

His errand had been a success.

Ten low-born men stood in chains, their eyes flickering with terror. Percival had given them a choice—immortality or death. Seven had agreed. The other three... well.

They could not be allowed to leave.

It was unfortunate, but necessary.

Soon, they would all be thankful.

Percival was their leader now. Their alpha. He would guide them, shape them, command them. And, most importantly, he would wield the greatest power among them—Silas himself.

The boy had no idea how strong he truly was.

That, too, would be Percival's to control.

He looked at his grandson.

"Now, Silas."

Silas stepped forward.

For most of them, it would be the first time witnessing the transformation.

Hannah moved to stand at the mouth of the cave, the only exit. No one would leave until this was done.

All eyes remained on Silas as he stripped away his clothing. He clenched his fists, his muscles rigid with strain.

A low grunt escaped him. His brow furrowed. The pain came swiftly, twisting his body from within.

Percival winced at the sight.

Silas staggered, then let out a shuddering breath.

His bones cracked.

A ripple of change tore through his flesh.

Then, where the boy had stood, a beast remained.

Silas was magnificent.

He was no mindless wolf of the wild—he stood upright, towering, his silver fur rippling under the moon's glow.

More than one man gasped. Some began to pray.

But there was no salvation here.

Silas prowled forward, his piercing gaze sweeping over the ten. The first man trembled, his chains rattling.

Then, in a blur of motion, Silas lunged.

His powerful jaws clamped onto the man's throat.

A scream echoed off the cave walls, sharp and raw.

The others flinched, their eyes wide with terror.

One by one, Silas bit them.

Blood darkened the stone floor. The cave had become a chamber of pain, of terror, of rebirth.

Percival barely heard the cries.

His gaze shifted to his family.

His dear Gertrude was the only one missing. She would live out her days as a human. She would grow old and die as such.

But he would not.

Patience.

He watched as Silas sired his mother.

Max and Catherine lay unconscious nearby, their bodies slick with sweat and blood. They, along with Hannah, would be among the few female lycanthropes.

Percival exhaled, his chest tight.

Then, finally, he stepped forward.

Naked. Vulnerable. Waiting.

Silas turned to him.

The silver wolf loomed over him, his amber eyes gleaming.

A new kind of fear gripped Percival's throat. Damn it, keep steady.

His limbs felt weak. His vision wavered.

Then, pain.

Silas's teeth tore into him, fangs slicing through flesh.

Percival screamed.

The world blurred, tilting—

And then there was nothing.

PART FOUR

37

AWAKENING

They could not agree on whether to wake Cecil.

Larus stepped into the hall beneath the catacombs, hoping Sebastian and Micah would finally reach a decision. For too long, they had clashed over Cecil's fate—whether he should remain entombed in slumber or rise once more.

Nine others waited, their gazes shifting between the two leaders. They needed a resolution.

"We must consider," said Micah, "leaving the Bleddyn lands."

A murmur spread through the gathered vampires.

"The wolves grow in number," he continued, "and they patrol their territory relentlessly. It is only a matter of time before they come for us. We are few, while they are many."

Larus studied his maker. Micah's words made sense, but had he truly thought through the consequences of abandoning the catacombs? They were twelve vampires, surrounded by dozens of wolves. And worse, Percival Hearne, now a lycanthrope himself, commanded them.

Larus hesitated, reluctant to openly challenge his sire. But he had no choice.

"Micah, you say we must leave these lands—and I agree." His voice was measured, careful. "Hunting has become difficult, and Percival is building an army."

"Lycanthropes."

Larus barely got the word out before Yaro scoffed, throwing his hands in the air.

"Who the fuck says lycanthropes?" he barked. "They're wolves. Lycans. Shapeshifters! Call them what they are."

Sebastian chuckled, leaning back in his chair with a lazy grin. "Lycans—yes, much simpler, chéri." He flicked a hand in Larus's direction. "Please, do continue."

Larus glanced between Sebastian and Yaro. He had long suspected there was something more between them, though he could never quite tell where they stood. Of all the coven, Yaro was the one who riled him most. Arrogant, selfish. Dangerous.

He had warned Isabelle to keep her distance from him.

And yet, if Yaro hadn't tried to kill her, she wouldn't be one of them.

Larus smiled faintly at the thought.

"The lycans," he said, giving Yaro a pointed look, "will soon discover we are here. Isabelle and I know these lands, but it is only a matter of time before they find the catacombs."

"I agree with Larus," said Haruki.

The samurai had remained silent all night.

"We should return to the capital. White Castle will offer us safety."

Murmurs of approval rippled through the room. One by one, the others nodded.

Except for Sebastian. And Yaro.

And Geraldine.

"We must build an army of our own," she said.

Her grey hair shimmered in the candlelight, her hands dark with henna. "Vampires protect their homes."

Micah shook his head. "This is but one home," he reminded her. "And it always shall be. But we must be smart. The lycans," he shot Yaro an approving nod, "are everywhere. If we remain, we will be hunted."

Larus seized the moment.

"And what of Cecil?" His voice was calm, but insistent. "What becomes of him?"

"Yes, Micah."

Sebastian rose from his seat, his expression unreadable. Slowly, he moved around the table, trailing his fingers along the surface of the heavy oak slab. Eleven pairs of eyes followed him.

"Shall we abandon the one thing—this gift our maker left us?" He came to a stop behind Yaro, resting both hands on the vampire's broad shoulders. "We cannot entrust Cecil's safety to these walls alone. You know this."

His gaze swept the room, sharp as a blade.

"And what have we accomplished?" he asked. "Hours of talking. Debating. Nothing. Let us end this. Let us vote."

Micah exhaled slowly, then nodded.

The vote was cast.

Only Monique and Ashkan sided with Micah.

Cecil's awakening would take place three nights hence.

Babette would perform the ritual.

HE HAD SAID ALL THE RIGHT WORDS.

And yet, standing beside a massive tombstone, Sebastian rejected his plan.

The night was moonless, the air thick with warmth.

Yaro dropped to his knees, his confidence undiminished.

"Sebastian, listen to me," he pleaded. "I scouted the Bleddyn lands myself. I overheard two guards talking—he will be at the caves tonight. You know I'm strong enough. I can do this."

Again, he explained his plan. Again, Sebastian refused.

"I see a shadow of myself in you, Yaro," said his maker. His voice was low, measured. "Like you, I once believed I could conquer the world. I was naïve."

Yaro clenched his jaw.

"Micah will never allow this," Sebastian continued. "Nor can I. You will stay away from Bleddyn Manor. You will stay away from the wolves' lair. That is an order."

His tone softened, just slightly. "An attack now would be foolish. It would draw attention to us. And we are only twelve."

Yaro's lip curled. "You're both cowards."

He shot a hand toward the mausoleum.

"He sits in there, making plans to run! And you—"

Sebastian was on him in an instant.

One hand closed around Yaro's throat. The next moment, he was airborne, then crashed into a gravestone, shattering it to pieces.

Yaro gasped. Sebastian loomed over him, fangs bared, eyes burning with fury.

"I did not survive centuries to suffer your insolence."

His grip tightened. Nails—razor-sharp—pressed into Yaro's skin, pricking the flesh of his neck.

"I made you," Sebastian growled. "When Larus would have drained you dry and left your rotting corpse beneath the trees. I spared you, Yaro. I chose to give you this life."

He bared his teeth.

"Do not make me regret it."

Yaro gasped out, "Sebastian—"

Sebastian released him with a shove.

"Babette and Micah will perform the awakening tomorrow night," he said coolly. "Think on that. With Cecil on our side, no wolf can stand against us."

And then he was gone.

Yaro lay among the shattered marble, his chest heaving.

Sebastian and Micah were fools.

He rose, dusting the broken stone from his clothes.

He would not obey.

He ran from the cemetery.

He had work to do.

SIX VAMPIRES RACED THROUGH THE TREES, THEIR FORMS MERE SHADOWS IN the moonless night.

Micah. Sebastian. Larus. Babette. Haruki. Nicolas.

They moved as one, bound by a single hope—stop Yaro before he tore down everything they had built.

The fool had gone alone to face the wolves, a suicidal mission. They all knew it.

Larus matched Nicolas's quick strides. Behind them, Babette and Haruki kept pace, while Micah and Sebastian leapt from tree to tree, never touching the ground.

Two bodies lay twisted in the dirt, their throats torn open.

Yaro's work.

The poor bastards had shifted back to human form in death. Yaro was strong, but strength alone wouldn't save him from Percival Hearne. Or worse—Silas.

Sebastian had been the first to notice Yaro's absence. He'd told them of their fight, of Yaro's reckless plan, and swore that if they found him, he would destroy him himself.

"Faster, Larus." Nicolas flashed white teeth in the dark. "Or are you afraid to face the wolves you once knew and loved?"

Larus grinned, though his chest tightened. "Not a chance."

But there was truth in his brother's words. His sisters—Max and Catherine—were among the wolves now. He did not wish to see them harmed. *Micah says I must reject such feelings, he reminded himself. Lycans and vampires are mortal enemies.*

He pushed ahead of Nicolas. "And why are you holding back? Afraid my nephew will break you in two?"

Nicolas chuckled. "Careful, brother. One might think you plan to betray us."

Haruki sprinted past them both. "Enough." His voice was steel. "You waste time."

Another body lay in their path, fresh blood soaking the earth.

By the time they reached the caves, the six vampires melted into the trees.

Micah spoke first. "We take the high ground. The cave's summit."

Nicolas had spoken of this place before—there were two ways in. One through the entrance below, the other from the top. But once inside, there would be no easy escape.

Larus prayed it wouldn't come to that.

A howl tore through the woods.

Micah scaled the rock wall first, Larus and Nicolas right behind him. Below, Sebastian led Babette and Haruki toward the opening.

When Larus reached the summit, he peered down into the cave.

Yaro stood alone.

He wielded a silver whip, its razor-sharp blades gleaming. Two massive wolves circled him, their eyes wary of the weapon. The lash struck, coiling around the smaller wolf's throat. Yaro pulled. The beast choked, gurgling, claws scraping uselessly against stone.

Larus tensed. He and Nicolas moved to leap—

Micah stopped them.

"Always look before you leap, young ones," he murmured.

Nicolas bristled. "But Sebastian—"

"Will be fine," Micah said sharply. "We do not throw our lives away."

Then Larus saw it.

More wolves.

Dozens. Emerging from the darkness, surrounding Yaro.

Larus barely had time to process it before a voice echoed through the cavern, cold and commanding.

"Stop."

The wolves stilled.

From the shadows, Percival Hearne stepped forward.

Yaro hissed, struggling against the hands that restrained him.

Others moved to Percival's side.

Larus's breath caught.

Max.

His sister stood with her son—the silver-eyed wolf.

Hannah.

Catherine.

And Morgan.

Percival stopped before Yaro, still in his human form.

"You dare come to my lands, vampire?" His voice was almost amused. "What did you hope to accomplish?"

Yaro bared his fangs. "From what I've heard, these are Bleddyn lands. You are not one of them."

Percival's lips curled into a smile.

Then he tore away his clothes and shifted.

Larus had seen many wolves. But nothing like this.

The transformation was a horror—bone twisting, flesh stretching, muscle rippling into something monstrous.

When it was done, a beast loomed where a man had stood. Massive. Powerful.

Percival lunged.

One clawed hand locked around Yaro's throat.

The vampire thrashed, spitting curses, but Percival squeezed.

Then bit down.

Yaro's scream tore through the cavern.

The wolf's fangs sank deep into his flesh—then Percival's other hand plunged into Yaro's chest.

A sickening crack.

Larus gasped.

Percival ripped Yaro's heart from his body.

A terrible thing happened then—

Yaro withered.

Even before the wolf withdrew its hand, his body crumbled, flesh turning to dust.

And then—

Nothing remained.

A stunned silence hung over the cavern.

Percival shifted back, standing naked among his pack. He spread his arms wide.

"I know you are here," he called to the shadows. His voice was taunting.

Then—

"This is your future, boy."

Larus was a vampire, but he felt his body go cold.

Percival's gaze was fixed upward.

Larus turned to Micah, terrified.

Yaro was gone.

And neither Micah nor Sebastian seemed willing to fight.

There was no hope.

It was evident Micah saw their sorrow, yet he spoke as though Yaro were still alive.

Larus watched with disgust as his maker and Sebastian moved from one plan to the next, speaking of strategy, survival, and the future—as though one of their own had not just died.

As though Yaro had not been turned to dust before their eyes.

A sick feeling coiled in Larus's stomach. *It could have been me.*

Yaro had withered away like a dry husk, the remnants of his body lost to the wind.

Dawn was approaching. They were safe in the catacombs, but Micah and Sebastian feared the wolves would not let them rest for long.

Monique and Helene had been sent to the docks. By nightfall, they would return to Paris and summon the vampires still loyal to Babette. Ashkan would leave at sunset, spreading word to the capital.

Micah had made his decision. His voice was quiet, heavy with something unreadable.

"Babette has sent word to the council." He did not look at them. "They will likely destroy us all when they come… when they discover Cecil lives. For Babette has betrayed them."

"But." Sebastian's voice was softer than usual. "Cecil's very existence may be our salvation. The elders fear him."

The usual brightness in his gaze was dimmed by something else—sorrow.

"We lost Yaro this night," he murmured. "We failed him."

A pause.

Then he turned to Larus, to Nicolas, to Isabelle.

"He was your brother." A small, wistful smile. "Though impossible at times." His eyes lingered on Larus. "And you, chéri, helped make him."

Larus nodded, his thoughts returning to that night outside the tavern—the night he had brought Yaro into their world.

Micah spoke from where he stood at the far side of the chamber. The others sat upon the velvet couches, their faces drawn in flickering candlelight.

"Sebastian and I have seen many vampire deaths," he said. "Tonight, you have seen your first."

Larus said nothing. But Yaro's final scream still echoed in his ears.

"There are many ways to kill our kind," Micah continued. "And Percival Hearne knows them all."

Silence.

Then his gaze fell upon Larus and Isabelle.

"You must accept this now," he said. "It will be the hardest thing—to fight your family. But they are lycans now. You love them, but they will not hesitate to destroy you."

The words struck deep. Larus clenched his jaw.

Sebastian exhaled, running a hand through his dark curls. "A new day is almost upon us," he said. "It is fortunate we require no rest, for we must keep vigil. The wolves may come by day."

"Sebastian is right." Micah turned, his eyes cold once more. "There is much to do. The sacrifices must be fed and prepared for the awakening."

Larus stiffened.

The humans.

They had been kept below, trembling in the darkness, awaiting their fate.

For when Cecil rose, after centuries of sleep, he would wake hungry.

And there was only one thing that could sate an ancient vampire's thirst.

After they removed the seal and pushed open the heavy stone entrance, Micah, Sebastian, and Babette stepped forward, staring into pitch-blackness.

Larus, his sister Isabelle, Geraldine, Haruki, and Nicolas waited in the torch-lit passage.

It was time for the awakening.

Larus took Isabelle's hand.

He would not have missed this moment for anything in the world—for Cecil Bleddyn was family. He had spent countless hours wondering what Cecil would be like. Now, faced with the abyss of blackness before him, fear coiled in his chest.

Babette had warned them. Cecil could be dangerous.

Babette stepped inside first, Sebastian at her heels. He reached for a torch and lifted it high, illuminating the chamber beyond. As they moved deeper inside, the others followed, their footsteps echoing.

The chamber was ancient.

Cobwebbed crevices. Faded murals, their colours lost to time. Dust-covered shelves crumbling with age.

But all eyes fixed on one thing—the sarcophagus.

It sat upon a raised pedestal in the centre of the chamber, vast and imposing. The granite lid was adorned with carvings of wolves and cloaked vampires, their fangs bared. Four gargoyles crouched at each corner, their wings curled like bats.

Larus turned to Nicolas, and the two shared a glance of awe. Even Geraldine and Haruki, so much older than them, seemed spellbound.

If the carved figure on the lid was truly Cecil Bleddyn's likeness, then the sleeping vampire had once been beautiful.

The eight of them gathered around the sarcophagus. Babette stood at its head. She had been here before. She knew what lay within.

"We lift the cover," she said.

Babette and Sebastian pushed against the heavy stone lid. With a slow, grinding groan, it slid away.

What lay inside sent Larus stumbling back, dragging Isabelle with him.

Spikes.

The inner lid was lined with them, driven deep into the corpse within. And from beneath, even more pierced through the body, save for the heart.

The thing inside was shrivelled, a husk of leathery, parchment-thin skin clinging to brittle bones. The mouth gaped open in an eternal scream, long fangs bared.

Larus stifled a gasp.

"Do not be afraid, petit loup," Babette murmured. "Cecil is alive."

"How can such a thing live?" Isabelle whispered, staring at the grotesque, withered remains.

Larus forced himself to look closer.'

The corpse's black hair had mostly withered away, but remnants of it still clung to the skull. Its decayed clothing had nearly rotted to dust. And yet, on a bony finger, a golden ring gleamed. The Bleddyn sigil. The head of a wolf.

Larus had seen that emblem before—on old diaries, on faded parchments. It had meant nothing to him then. But now...

"Only blood will revive him," Babette said.

She moved toward the wall, pressing a stone panel. A small compartment slid open, revealing a vial no longer than a man's finger. Gold and unmarked.

"Cecil's blood," she said, holding it up.

"And all his memories," added Sebastian.

Micah nodded. "The awakening of a vampire is a delicate task."

Babette returned to the sarcophagus. First, she cut into her wrist with a single sharp nail, holding her hand over Cecil's mouth. Droplets of dark blood fell onto the shrivelled flesh.

Nothing happened.

Larus exchanged a glance with Nicolas. Then—movement.

Cecil's fingers twitched.

A whisper of motion rippled through the corpse. His tongue darted out, lapping at the blood with weak, desperate strokes.

His eyelids fluttered.

Babette unstoppered the vial and poured its contents into his open mouth.

Larus's breath caught in his throat.

Cecil's skeletal hands gripped the edge of the sarcophagus.

Sebastian turned and disappeared into the passageway. When he returned, he was not alone.

Two humans stood beside him.

One was an older man, dark-skinned, his greying woolly hair cropped close. He was tall, beautiful, yet trembling. The other was younger, golden-haired, with grey eyes and a face marked by old pock scars.

Sebastian spoke softly. "We offer you a choice," he said. "Immortality. A new life. But it will not be easy."

The younger man hesitated. Then, as if drawn by some unseen force, he took a step toward Cecil.

Cecil sat upright now, his milky gaze sweeping over them. He turned to Babette. His mouth moved. A rasping breath, barely audible.

"Baaabette."

A name spoken from beyond the grave.

Then, those ghastly eyes found Larus and Isabelle.

And recognized them.

Babette placed a hand on Cecil's shoulder. "You feed now, mon amour."

She beckoned to the pock-faced man. He came forward—bravely, at first.

Then Cecil's lips met his throat.

The moment the fangs sank in, the man screamed.

He convulsed as the blood was ripped from his body. When he finally collapsed, Micah caught him, slicing his wrist and pressing it to the man's lips.

A gift of immortality.

The dark-skinned man had begun to weep. But there was no choice.

Cecil turned to him, his face no longer skeletal, the flesh slowly filling out. His hair darkened, growing thick and lustrous once more.

His hunger was not yet sated.

He seized the man.

And fed.

Larus flinched as he heard the wet sound of flesh tearing, the sickening crack of shifting bones as Cecil moved.

The spikes had impaled him for centuries. Now, they tore free as he staggered upright, weak but whole.

He stood tall, gazing at them all with scrutiny.

Then, at last, he spoke.

His voice was low. Hoarse. Ancient.

"How long," he murmured, "have I slept?"

38

REUNITED

From the privacy of his room, Cecil heard everything.

The murmured conversations. The unspoken fears. Their thoughts.

It had been three days and nights since his awakening. He had asked to be left alone, yet still, he knew them.

The hybrid was older and stronger than all of them—one of a kind. Not even the esteemed council of elders could match him. Their feeble minds were open books to him, their thoughts laid bare long before they had even conceived them.

He could walk in the night. He could walk in the sun.

A vampire like no other.

But Cecil was no fool. Everything created, he knew, could be destroyed.

He had fed on the sick and dying—those who had given themselves willingly. They had come from his lands, his people. He had known their ancestors, had watched over their bloodlines for centuries. When he drank, he tasted not only their blood but the lives they had led. Their joys. Their suffering.

And yet, despite the strength filling his veins once more, Cecil felt... tired.

He glanced at the clothing Micah had brought him. How much the world had changed since he had left it behind to sleep.

A whisper of thought reached him before the soft shuffle of approaching footsteps.

They were coming.

Cecil turned to the door and waited. Five vampires.

He did not move. Did not call them in.

Instead, he willed the door open with his mind—precisely as Micah reached for it.

The heavy wood swung wide.

Five startled faces.

Only Babette was unsurprised. She alone understood the extent of his power.

Micah was the first to step inside, followed by Sebastian and Babette. At the threshold, Nicolas and Larus lingered—newborns, their awe outweighing their fear.

Cecil let his gaze settle on Micah and Sebastian, their expressions unreadable to anyone but him.

"Do not waste your time attempting to shield your minds from me."

His voice was quiet, but the warning carried weight.

Then, his gaze shifted to Larus.

"My powers are boundless."

The newborn stiffened beneath his scrutiny.

"A fact you, blood brother, shall soon discover."

Cecil saw the uncertainty in the young one's eyes, the turmoil clawing at his mind. He felt it.

A disappointment.

Turning to Babette, he then fixed a sharp stare on Micah.

"Why have you not prepared him for what he will become?"

It was Babette who answered. "We waited for you, Cecil."

His chamber was vast and richly furnished—far different from the stone tomb that had held him for centuries.

With a flick of his hand, he gestured for them to sit.

They hesitated.

Worry. Doubt. Cecil saw it in their eyes. Felt it in their thoughts.

He sighed.

"Do not worry, Micah. I have many desires, but taking your coven is not among them." Then, to Sebastian: "And yes. Emilio was everything to me."

Sebastian's expression barely shifted, but the flicker of emotion did not escape Cecil's notice.

"Why did you not take your sleep together?" Sebastian asked.

A bold question.

Cecil's gaze darkened.

"You do not interrogate me."

The words fell like a blade between them.

Sebastian held his ground.

Cecil smirked, but there was no humour in it. "I have no desire to rule these factions you call covens. We may revisit this talk of rulership once I have dealt with those who would see me dead."

His temples throbbed. The relentless hum of thoughts surrounded him, an unceasing tide of voices.

It was exhausting.

Closing his eyes, he lifted a hand to his brow.

A curse. That was what his power had become.

"Are you all right, my lord?"

Sebastian. The clever one.

Cecil exhaled sharply. "Do not think to flatter me with your cunning tongue, Sebastian. I am not Emilio."

Sebastian did not react. But Cecil felt the shift in his mind.

He turned toward the door. "I grow weary."

Then, to Larus:

"There is much we need to discuss, young Bleddyn."

The others understood the command before it was spoken.

Cecil's gaze swept over them once more, cold and unyielding.

"Leave us."

Cecil's wavy black hair fell past his narrow shoulders. His skin—pale, pristine—was nothing like the shrivelled corpse Larus had glimpsed in the sarcophagus.

Larus found himself alone with him.

A family member who should have been dead centuries ago.

And yet, here he stood—majestic in his immortality.

Cecil stared at him without blinking. The weight of his gaze was unnerving.

Then, after a long silence, the ancient vampire closed his eyes briefly and shook his head.

"What relief," he murmured.

When he looked at Larus again, his hands were akimbo, his smirk sharp.

"Unlike you and the others, I find it near impossible to avoid reaching into the minds around me."

He grinned.

"An affliction many of our kind would relish—but not I. I cannot abide the pointless things most beings think of. Especially humans."

He folded his arms, tilting his head as if studying Larus from a new angle.

"They dream of what they wish to do. They worry over things long past. They attempt to change things that have yet to come to pass."

A sigh.

"It is strange looking at you, young Bleddyn. I see my father in you."

Cecil's gaze turned thoughtful, almost distant.

"You have a good heart, but that goodness may one day lead to your doom."

He moved to a chair near a small desk against the wall and sat with effortless grace.

"You must harden your heart, young Bleddyn. It is the key to your survival."

Larus nodded, but words failed him.

What could he say to this ancient creature?

Suddenly, Cecil laughed—a sharp, sudden burst of mirth.

Larus startled.

"You think of Babette's words."

His grin lingered, but there was something knowing in his gaze.

"I have changed, young Bleddyn. I no longer kill what I do not know."

Larus hesitated. "How... how can you read Micah's thoughts so easily?"

"It is my gift."

Cecil leaned forward, his eyes narrowing.

"I hate it. Yet it has saved my life many times."

He paused, as if weighing something unspoken. Then his expression darkened.

"I was a fool to reveal what I was capable of. When the council discovered I could break any defence of the mind—even theirs—they saw me as a threat. They sit at the head of our society, passing judgment, condemning many to death. And yet... they plotted my destruction because they did not understand me."

His voice dropped to something colder.

"They feared me."

Larus said nothing, watching as Cecil absently turned the ring on his finger.

"But I shall kill them," Cecil murmured, more to himself than to Larus. "I shall rid this world of their hypocrisy, for I deal death only to those who deserve it."

Larus swallowed, shifting slightly.

"What am I?" he asked at last.

Cecil's gaze sharpened.

"You are the future."

He leaned back, eyes briefly unfocused—as if seeing something far beyond the room.

"Long ago, in my twenty-fifth year, my father sent me away in a carriage with Rubina and the others. When that carriage went over the cliff and shattered against the trees below, I did not expect to survive."

His voice was quiet now, contemplative.

"At first, I thought it was chance alone that brought Telsiea to my aid. But I soon realized it was not chance—it was destiny."

His gaze found Larus again.

"Destiny alone kept me alive... until a vampire found me."

Cecil's lips curled faintly.

"Telsiea made me. She healed my broken body and gave me new life."

Larus thought of the night he had met Micah, realizing how fragile the line between life and death could be.

"If you had died at the bottom of that cliff," he murmured, "Emilio would never have sent Micah to find me."

Cecil's smile deepened.

"Emilio sent him because of me."

Larus hesitated.

"We are alike, you and I."

Cecil's voice carried something more than certainty. It carried conviction.

"You will change, Larus."

Larus tensed, thinking suddenly of his sisters.

"You would kill your own kind—the lycans?"

Cecil raised his thick brows.

"Lycans," he repeated, rolling the word over his tongue as if tasting it. "A fitting name."

He absently caressed the golden ring on his finger—the Bleddyn sigil gleaming in the dim light.

"Would your sisters spare your life?" he asked softly.

Larus stiffened.

"Do you care to put their love for you to the test?"

Cecil did not wait for an answer.

"Micah spoke of Silas—our kin."

"My sister's son," Larus murmured.

"He is the true leader of the wolves, though he does not yet know it."

"But Percival Hearne is—"

"The boy made him."

Cecil's voice was sharp.

"The maker is always stronger than those he creates."

Larus hesitated before finally asking the question that had been gnawing at him.

"Why not lead us?"

Cecil's expression remained unreadable.

"Do you believe Micah and Sebastian would willingly submit to my rule?"

"That's not what I meant," Larus said quickly. "I just thought—"

"I am strong," Cecil interrupted, "but I am not invincible."
His gaze was dark, unwavering.
"Anything—no matter how powerful—can be destroyed."
Cecil rose from the chair, walking toward Larus with deliberate steps.
"I would not betray those who risked everything to help me."
Then, with a slight lift of his brows, his meaning became clear.
"Besides," he murmured, "I seek a far better prize, Larus."
Larus met Cecil's gaze and felt the weight of the words unspoken.
He understood now.
Cecil would replace the council.
He did not seek to rule a mere coven.
He sought to rule them all.

39

THE INN OF FLOWERS

He stood at the edge of the woods, surrounded by nearly twenty men—all wolves.

They were strong. They were loyal.

But most importantly... they were hungry.

Percival stood boldly, Silas at his side.

The pack was naked, ready to shed their human forms and embrace the beast within.

Max and Hannah had begged to join the hunt, but Percival had denied them. This night belonged to his warriors. He examined the men before him, sharp eyes scanning each eager face.

"Many of you are young," he said. "But you are strong. You are wolves."

Beside him, Silas grinned, his eyes alight with fierce adoration.

He worshipped him.

Percival had not told them where they were going—not even Silas knew their destination.

"This night," Silas said, stepping forward, "you will learn the ways of the hunter. Being a lycanthrope means nothing if you cannot hunt. You must track your prey. You must learn to survive."

The pack listened, their breathing deep and measured.

Silas's grin sharpened.

"This night... we show no mercy. This night... no man gets turned. No prisoners. We destroy."

Percival grinned.

The last light of the sun slipped beneath the horizon. Soon, the full moon would rise.

"Now," Percival commanded, "we run."

His body obeyed.

Heat surged through him, his blood boiling, his bones breaking.

The shift was violent. It always was.

Pain carved through his limbs, his spine curving, stretching.

Sharp claws ripped through his fingers. His skull cracked and reformed, a snout pushing forward. He dropped into a crouch, groaning through clenched teeth as muscle and sinew reshaped beneath his skin.

Then—

A final snap.

The beast took him.

The Alpha rose—taller, stronger.

A monstrous shadow in the moonlight.

He howled, a deep, commanding call that reverberated through the trees.

And the pack followed.

One by one, they surrendered to the change, their cries of agony soon swallowed by snarls and growls.

Then, without hesitation, Percival sprang into the woods.

The hunt had begun.

THE CATACOMBS HAD BEEN LARUS'S HOME FOR YEARS, AND IT SADDENED HIM to leave. Preparations had been made, and the lycans would not easily discover their secret lair. He felt bound to the catacombs, as he was bound to the old church—both were on the Bleddyn lands. And after all this time, Larus had come to believe that Bleddyn Manor, and everything within its borders, was his birthright. But now, it was occupied by wolves, and the vampires had no choice but to abandon the catacombs.

Though Cecil claimed he was no leader of their coven, the aged vampire had taken charge. He shared decision-making with Micah and Sebastian, but it was clear who held the reins. Cecil had insisted they wouldn't leave via the mausoleum; there was, he said, another way.

Larus and Nicolas exchanged a glance and shrugged. Eleven vampires gathered in Cecil's sleep chamber, which had remained undisturbed, just as they'd found it the night of his awakening. Dust settled in the air like the lingering scent of the past.

After Cecil's command, they slid the massive stone slab back in place, sealing them inside the chamber. Larus watched, still amazed. The vampire he'd once seen withered and grotesque, now stood before them—a vision of perfection. Cecil had tied his long black hair with a red silk ribbon, his presence commanding, and Larus could hardly look away.

"I must beg you all," Cecil said, a smirk tugging at the corner of his lips, "to calm your thoughts when in my presence. I am privy to every corridor of your minds." He bared his teeth in a grin. "Would that I were among wolves," he joked, "for I cannot see into the minds of beasts."

Larus and the others chuckled at the quip, the tension easing, if only for a moment.

"Ashkan will meet us at the inn, twenty miles east of here," Micah said, his voice steady. "It's called—"

"The Inn of Flowers." Cecil interrupted, casting a sidelong glance at Sebastian. "I took that from your mind, Emilio's pet."

Sebastian bowed slightly. "The inn is a humble place, but its gardens are beautiful."

"Then we must hurry." Cecil turned away, moving toward a section of the wall. "I alone know of these tunnels... they are my lands, after all."

He pressed his palm against the stone, and with a deep rumble, a portion of the wall shifted, revealing a hidden passage. Larus stared, astonished. No one could have known it was there.

"What is this place?" Larus asked, his voice barely above a whisper. "Where does it lead?"

"To the church on the hill," Cecil replied with a wave of his hand. "Come now."

They followed him into the narrow darkness, the passage twisting and turning as they moved further from the catacombs. "Pull the lever to your right after you pass through," Cecil called back. The sound of stone grinding against stone filled the silence as the wall sealed them in, cutting off any escape from behind.

"It was the intention of our ancestors," Cecil's voice echoed in the dimness, "that these catacombs remain secret. A safe haven for those in need. The records will show the sanctuary beneath the church, but not this passage. It was meant to be hidden."

Larus clung to his belief that his connection to the church was born from this history. All those nights spent beneath its walls, unaware of the refuge lying hidden beneath.

"Magnificent," he whispered.

"Yes," Cecil agreed, his voice rich with pride. "This passage was built so that it could never be found from within the church. My father revealed it to me as a boy." They stopped in front of another stone wall, and Cecil pressed hard against it. The sound of stone shifting filled the air. Moments later, they stood in a chamber with stairs leading up.

At the top of the stairs, the group emerged into a dimly lit chamber beneath the church. Larus's eyes adjusted quickly to the dark, and he could hear the skittering of rodents fleeing at their arrival.

"After you reach the top, push again," Cecil instructed. The stone cover slid away, revealing the sanctuary above.

Stepping into the hidden shelter beneath the church, Larus was in awe. The room was furnished, with several corridors branching off in various directions. Cecil pointed toward another flight of stairs. "The church is just beyond."

As they ascended into the chancel, they passed beneath towering stained-glass windows, the colours shimmering in the low light. Larus had spent many nights in this place, but now it felt different. The weight of history seemed to press down on him. He looked at Micah, his maker, remembering the night they'd first met.

Isabelle moved closer to Larus. He shared the memories of those past visits to the church, and now, as she stood beside him, he found comfort in her presence.

Sebastian joined them. "A strong place, this," he said with a grin. "A church built upon a rock."

Larus nodded, but before he could respond, he noticed the shift in Sebastian's demeanour. His posture became more rigid, and his gaze grew focused.

"We are among wolves," Cecil said, his voice low and urgent. Sebastian and Micah nodded, their expressions grim. "We should not have lingered here this long."

Cecil closed his eyes, taking in the scent of the air, the low growls of the wolves outside. "And they have us outnumbered," he murmured. "We're surrounded... hunted this night."

Larus felt Isabelle draw closer to him. He squeezed her hand, though he could sense the fear creeping in. The older vampires hissed, taking defensive positions, circling, ready for the attack.

"We should return to the catacombs," Haruki suggested, his voice tense.

"No!" Cecil snapped, his eyes flashing. "They know we're here. We cannot simply disappear. We fight!"

Sebastian's voice was calm but firm. "We could retreat to the steeples, or the bell tower."

Cecil's reply was swift and cutting. "Wolves can climb."

The vicious growls grew louder, closer. The sound of paws scraping against stone, the scrape of claws against wood—Larus could feel the fear rising, but he refused to let it overtake him. He glanced at Isabelle, determination hardening his resolve. "Stay by my side," he whispered, his voice steady despite the chaos around them.

Isabelle nodded, a fierce glint in her eyes. "Always."

Cecil turned to face them all, his expression unreadable. "Lycans are strong, but they are not invincible. Sever their spines, and they will never rise again. Do not let fear cloud your judgment tonight. If we protect each other, we all leave these lands alive."

He turned toward the doors, the vampires following in his wake, ready to face the wolves outside. "Come, for if they corner us within these walls, we are doomed."

A MASSIVE WOLF CRASHED THROUGH A STAINED-GLASS WINDOW JUST BEFORE they reached the doors.

For a moment, Nicolas stood frozen, staring at the gigantic beast. It roared, jaws wide with long, sharp teeth, as shards of coloured glass rained down upon it.

Nicolas couldn't move—couldn't—until Larus yanked him out of the way. The two vampires rolled together on the slick floor, and the lycan landed several feet away, skidding across the smoothness of the stone.

As the others readied for the battle, Larus, Nicolas, and Isabelle moved toward the beast.

Larus had spoken of the lycans before, their power, their resilience. They were hard to kill. This one, dark brown and massive, was twice Nicolas's size. Its yellow eyes shifted, locking onto the three of them.

The air crackled with tension.

More lycans had entered the church, their goal clear: to trap them, to destroy them.

Nicolas had seen what Percival had done to Yaro—he had no desire to suffer that same fate. His heart raced.

The three young vampires exchanged glances. Larus led the way. They circled the beast, moving with precision as it watched them, frantic and poised to strike.

Larus was the first to attack, but the lycan swatted him aside with one hard blow. He was sent slamming into the wall, the impact echoing through the church.

Isabelle sprang into the air, a graceful flip over the lycan's head. She punched it hard. The lycan staggered but didn't fall, its roar of pain shaking the air.

Nicolas bolted forward. He kicked into the lycan's hip, using all his strength to push it off-balance. Larus recovered quickly, attacking the lycan from behind, while Nicolas reached for its massive arms. He grabbed its furry wrists—too strong—the beast snarling as its jaws snapped inches from his head.

Then, something changed.

The lycan's strength began to fade. With a mournful roar, it fell to its knees.

Nicolas looked at Larus, whose hands were covered in blood, a portion of the lycan's spine still gripped tightly in his fist.

Before they could react, a loud hiss echoed from across the room.

Randall, the newborn, lay on the floor, a massive lycan atop him, sinking its teeth into his neck.

The three vampires rushed to their brother's aid, but Nicolas's gaze shifted.

Cecil was on the move.

He grabbed a massive lycan by the throat and lifted it off the ground with one hand, as if it weighed nothing. With a brutal twist, he tore into the beast's neck, killing it instantly.

Nicolas's heart raced. Where was Percival? He scanned the room but saw no sign of the Alpha.

Sebastian and Micah fought one lycan. Geraldine, Haruki, and Will faced another. Babette was alone, battling a bulky lycan that seemed to match her speed, yet it managed to slam her body against the wall before she nimbly escaped.

The lycan attacking Randall knocked Isabelle down with a single blow, but before it could deliver another, Cecil struck, finishing the beast off with lethal efficiency.

"These creatures mean to keep us trapped in this place," Cecil growled. "We must leave now. We run now!"

But before they could act, a familiar voice called from outside.

"We have you surrounded, Larus."

It was Percival.

Nicolas's stomach tightened. He knew what was coming next.

"I knew this was the only place you could be, boy," Percival continued. "I took a look in the Bleddyn vaults. I found the sanctuary beneath this church."

The pack of lycans growled, waiting for the command to attack.

Randall lay sprawled on the floor, blood pooling around him. He groaned weakly from his wounds.

Cecil's face twisted with sudden rage. He stepped forward, facing the remaining lycans alone.

Nicolas and Larus moved to join him, but Cecil stopped them. His back was still turned, his voice cold and commanding.

"Larus, Nicolas—stay where you are."

Nicolas froze. His mouth fell open as he watched Cecil change.

His shoulders expanded. His skin darkened. The smooth, pale skin of his hands turned a deep, rich brown, as fine hair sprouted across them.

The lycans prepared for battle.

With a crackling, bone-shaking sound, long black claws sprouted from Cecil's fingers.

In an instant, he slashed through the first lycan's neck, severing its head with a single swipe. The beast crumpled to the floor, lifeless.

The second lycan lunged, but Cecil was faster. He plunged his clawed hand into the creature's chest, pulling out its still-beating heart.

The third lycan struck at Cecil's face.

Nicolas gasped. Cecil's features had transformed. His face was now a deep shade of brown, his brows bushy, his eyes glowing a dark yellow.

He was a hybrid—a force of nature, an ancient being beyond comprehension.

Cecil turned to the vampires, his expression hard.

"This Percival does not know I am here, nor does he know who I am. We must use this to our advantage." His gaze shifted to Randall. "We cannot leave him behind."

"Make your way to the Inn of Flowers. I'll find you there."

"But Cecil," Geraldine protested, "We can't leave you alone."

"Do as I say! Nicolas! Larus! Stay with me."

With a roar, Cecil rushed out the door, and Nicolas was right behind him.

THE CREATURE WAS FEARLESS AS IT CHARGED FROM THE CHURCH, MOVING with terrifying speed. It tore through two strong wolves with barely a thought. Percival gripped Silas's arm as the boy made to approach the creature. "No, Silas," he commanded, his voice low.

The other vampires had already left the church, retreating into the woods with a wounded member in tow. Larus and a young vampire stayed behind, alongside the creature of terrifying power. Silas's eyes burned with an urge to fight, his wolf's instincts roaring inside him. Percival could feel it—his grandson was ready to break free. But even in his human form, Percival knew that this foe was unlike anything they had faced.

As the wolves surrounded the three adversaries, Percival held Silas close, his grip firm. He watched, helpless, as another of his warriors was torn apart by the creature. It was over in an instant. He had never witnessed such effortless destruction.

"Stay back!" Percival shouted. The wolves, loyal to their leader, held their ground, forming a tight circle around the strangers. But Percival could feel the inevitable—they were outmatched.

"What are you?" Percival demanded, his voice carrying both authority and fear. The creature's response was immediate. With a violent shift, it transformed before their eyes. The wolfish form melted away, revealing a tall, pale-skinned vampire.

For a moment, Percival's breath caught in his throat. This was no ordinary vampire. His clothes were torn from the change, but he stood with an effortless elegance, a power that seemed to radiate from him.

"I am all that you are not," the vampire said coldly, his voice smooth, almost mocking. "I am all that you shall never become. That is all you need to know about me."

Percival's eyes flicked to the two others with him. They were not like this creature. He had encountered anything like this before—strange, even for their kind. He had never heard of such creatures, not in all his years of research.

"I am no abomination, Percival Hearne," the vampire added, his tone digging into Percival's mind. It was as if the creature was peeling back his thoughts, reading him like an open book. Percival staggered back, horrified, feeling the weight of the invasion.

"State your name, creature!" Percival demanded, his voice strained.

The vampire's eyes shifted to Silas. "He is the creature," he said, gesturing toward Percival with a grin that made the hairs on the back of Percival's neck stand on end. "You mustn't trust this man, your grandfather." He tilted his head in mock curiosity. "Or is he your father?"

Percival's heart skipped a beat. The vampire's words rattled him to his core. "You will leave these lands!" Percival shouted, his voice laced with a desperation he had never shown before.

The vampire's gaze was fixed on Silas now, his voice a low, cruel whisper. "He is no match for you, Silas. This man has deceived you most terribly."

The command came suddenly, without warning. "Kill them!"

With a primal roar, Percival released his grip on Silas. The boy shifted in an instant, his wolf form emerging, but the pale vampire had other plans. Larus Bleddyn and the other young vampire leapt out of the circle, darting past the wolves with a speed that stunned Percival. Silas charged the vampire, his fury unchecked.

The creature struck him hard, sending Silas crashing to the ground. The wolves hesitated for a split second—uncertainty rippling through their ranks. But Silas was resilient. He recovered swiftly, his rage fuelling his next charge. He struck the vampire with all his might, and the creature staggered back, barely maintaining his footing.

For a moment, Percival saw doubt flash in the eyes of his pack—was their leader's grandson truly capable of defeating this foe?

But Silas, driven by raw determination, charged again, this time landing a blow that knocked the vampire to his knees. With a growl, the pale creature recovered, joining the other two vampires, who had circled back to his side. The three of them fled, vanishing into the night with a speed that left the wolves standing in stunned silence.

Larus scaled the trunk of a tall tree, narrowly evading the swift lunge of a lycan. The beasts were fast, but vampires were faster and far more agile. He moved with precision, trying to keep pace with Nicolas, following closely behind Cecil. They had twenty miles to cover to reach the Inn of Flowers, and Larus hoped they could outrun the lycans hot on their trail.

The church and the Bleddyn lands were now far behind them. The lycans had ventured deep into unfamiliar territory, and Larus hoped they would abandon the chase, wary of being seen by humans in the moonlight.

But Cecil's pace never faltered. "Keep up," he urged, his voice cutting through the rush of wind. "I will not let Randall die."

40

VAMPIRE HEALER

The Inn of Flowers was an old structure with a thatched straw roof. They had taken a large room, and while Ashkan and another coachman waited outside with two carriages, seven vampires gathered around Randall, the newborn, who was near death. Micah had done all he could—he had cut into his own skin, washing the gushing wound with his blood, hoping his child would recover.

"The wound won't heal," Micah said, glancing between Sebastian and Babette.

The door burst open, and Larus, Nicolas, and Cecil entered.

Geraldine met Cecil at the threshold. "His wound won't close!"

"I've never seen this before," Babette added, her voice tight with frustration. "C'est impossible! We've tried everything, Cecil."

Micah watched as Cecil moved past them all, his gaze fixed on Randall, who lay unconscious upon the bed. With a swift motion, Cecil tore away the young vampire's shirt, exposing the deep wound over his heart.

"A crushed breastplate," Cecil murmured. "He will die, Micah. There is only one way to save him."

Micah stared at him, uncertain. He had no idea how to heal a vampire who would not mend. The others watched in silence as Cecil leaned over

Randall and, to their astonishment, sank his fangs into his neck. Randall's body spasmed, his mouth parting in a silent gasp.

Cecil then slit his palm with one sharp nail, letting a few drops of his blood fall into Randall's mouth, then onto the open wound. Rising, he stepped away from the bed with effortless confidence.

"Let him rest," Cecil said. "Soon, Randall shall rise anew."

Without another word, he turned toward the door. "Come, Sebastian. Show me this garden you spoke of—I could use a moment of beauty after such a night."

THEIR WALK THROUGH THE INN'S GARDENS WAS UNEVENTFUL. THE GREAT vampire seemed unimpressed by its beauty, moving through the hedges, dwarfed trees, and blooming flowers with the air of a man trudging through a wasteland. The darkness posed no barrier to their sight, yet Cecil's disinterest made the splendour feel muted. They spoke little, though Sebastian was certain Cecil had sifted through his thoughts.

As they neared the inn once more, Cecil suddenly paused and took Sebastian's arm.

"You have lived recklessly as a vampire and suffered a painful life as a human, yet I see exactly why Emilio cherished you so. Is that not correct, boy?"

Rage flared hot in Sebastian's chest. How could this creature see so deeply into his soul, unearthing secrets he had never spoken aloud?

Cecil smiled knowingly. "Blood memories are messy—useless to one such as myself."

Sebastian exhaled slowly, his anger dissipating. He bowed with reverence, for he admired the hybrid. "You could have ruled us all, yet you chose to sleep." His gaze darkened. "The elders are fools for seeking your destruction."

"They will soon learn of my miraculous survival," Cecil said. "And my existence will be a thorn in their side. They will not come to aid in this war but to finish what they once started."

"Surely," Sebastian countered, "they will understand why Emilio saved you."

Cecil laughed, a dry, knowing sound. "They never change."

"I will stand with you, Cecil."

The hybrid vampire smiled again. "Dear Sebastian, loyal to the end."

Sebastian hesitated before speaking again. "What you did for Randall —it was magnificent."

"Randall will be different," Cecil replied, his dark brows drawing together slightly. "I did the only thing that could save him—a reward for his role in my awakening. I have given him a second bite."

As they resumed their walk toward the inn, Cecil cast a sidelong glance at Sebastian.

"In all my years as a vampire, I have made few fledglings. Not because I hoard the legacy in my blood, but because my maker, Telsiea, was powerful, and she believed my legacy was my power." His voice softened, momentarily lost in thought. "The vampire Telsiea was everything to me."

Sebastian studied him. "You are both wolf and vampire—made of two species."

Cecil smirked. "A magnificent error."

Then his expression changed, his face darkening with an unreadable thought.

"We all suspect that Silas—Larus's nephew—may be Percival's son."

Sebastian stopped just outside the inn. "Yes. What of it?"

Cecil's gaze sharpened. "Though against her will, the boy's mother lay with both her husband and his father. Beware the hunter-wolf, Sebastian. His knowledge alone could cut through our kind like a blade. That Silas exists among us now is by Percival's design. Percival Hearne intended to become a lycan. And Silas adores him."

"You fought Silas—did you reach his mind?"

"Briefly," Cecil admitted. "Silas shifted and charged me the moment Percival set him loose. I cannot read the thoughts of lycans once they shed their human skin." A flicker of concern crossed his face. "I fear Silas may be more powerful than even he knows. But Percival knows everything."

Sebastian hesitated, but he had to ask the question lingering between them. "And Larus? What will he become?"

Cecil's gaze flickered with something unreadable. "I do not know. His maker is a newborn himself. Even you, Sebastian, are young. But I carry the legacy of my maker. I have no doubt Larus will inherit the same. I cannot say when his transformation will come, but like me, Larus will be both wolf and vampire."

He motioned to the garden behind them. "Like these rare plants among the common ones, Larus and I are anomalies—hybrids."

Sebastian regarded him with awe. Cecil had walked through the garden with little care for its beauty, yet now he compared himself to its rarest flowers.

Cecil's expression darkened once more. "He still clings to those he loves—he loves them still. But that, I fear, may be used against him. It is not up to me alone, Sebastian. You and Micah must watch over him."

They entered the inn and climbed the old wooden stairs to their room.

Sebastian stopped short. Randall stood among the others, bare-chested and beaming.

The newborn vampire moved with lightning speed, crossing the room in an instant. "Master!"

Sebastian's brows furrowed. There was no sign of the grievous wound the lycan had inflicted. The damage to his chest was gone.

Randall turned his gleaming gaze to Cecil, his voice reverent. "The lady Telsiea... she was beautiful."

Something had changed. Randall was stronger, more assured, different.

Sebastian looked from the reborn vampire to Cecil, realizing at last just how powerful he truly was.

41

COUNCIL OF VAMPIRES

Paris had been her home, the city she loved more than anything in the world. But her return was not the homecoming she had once dreamed of. She would never again walk its streets beneath the sun's golden glow.

The city was restless. It had not been long since Napoleon's second exile, and France was still reeling. Helene had returned just weeks after the second restoration of King Louis XVIII. But nothing was as she had left it—nothing would ever be the same. She had returned to Paris a vampire.

The carriage rocked to a halt before a grand château, its towering façade gleaming in the moonlight. Helene sat frozen, staring at its looming form, her unease growing. The château was magnificent, a clear symbol of power and wealth, yet something about it unsettled her.

Monique stepped out first, her dark skin catching the light as she turned back. "Come, Helene," she urged.

Helene hesitated. Babette had told her much about the council of twelve, and the thought of standing before them filled her with dread. Still, she stepped down from the carriage, fear tightening in her chest.

Monique took her hand. "We mustn't keep the council waiting."

Helene gripped her fingers tightly. Babette had spoken of the four elders: Nathan, the eldest and most powerful; Athena, the Nubian, once a queen in another life; Lucas, Nathan's son, weak yet fiercely loyal to his father's authority; and Avlon, the enigmatic albino vampire whom Babette had spoken of with unusual fondness.

As they crossed the courtyard, the château doors opened the moment they reached the landing, as if by unseen command. A tall vampire woman with silver hair stood waiting. She was dressed in a sleek black gown, large diamond earrings glittering against her smooth skin. Without a word, she turned and led them down a long, empty corridor.

Helene's breath hitched at the starkness. The walls were bare—no tapestries, no paintings, not even a single sculpture. The emptiness was jarring, unsettling. She glanced at Monique, who merely smiled in return.

Watch your words in the presence of the elders, Babette had warned.

The silver-haired woman led them down another corridor, equally devoid of adornments. At its end, massive double doors loomed. Without pause, she stepped aside as the doors swung inward. Two male vampires, tall and pale, closed them behind Monique and Helene with soundless precision. One of them gestured silently toward a staircase ahead.

Helene's pulse quickened. The descent felt endless, the passage cold. At the bottom, they stopped before yet another door—this one glossy red, the colour of fresh-spilled blood.

A child stood before it.

Helene stiffened. The doorkeeper was a boy of no more than ten, his dark curls falling into his bright eyes as he smiled up at them. She could hear his heartbeat—steady, rhythmic, achingly human.

The boy swept his hair from his face and pulled the heavy door open.

Beyond lay a chamber unlike any Helene had ever seen. The château's bright, pristine walls were gone, replaced by the rough-hewn stone of an ancient fortress. No tables, no chairs, no lavish furnishings—only tiered seating carved directly into the rock, rising high above the chamber floor like the tiers of a vast amphitheater.

Helene and Monique stepped into the centre of the space, the stone seats towering over them. Dozens of vampires peered down in eerie silence.

The boy backed away, shutting the door behind them. The heavy thud of wood against stone echoed through the chamber, sealing them in.

Monique's grip on Helene's arm tightened.

"Bow, girl," she whispered.

Helene dropped into a reverent bow, following Monique's lead.

A voice broke the silence.

"Welcome back to Paris, Monique."

The speaker was tall and lean, his greying hair brushed back from a stern, ancient face. Helene recognized him at once—Nathan, the eldest among them.

Lifting her head, she took in the other elders. Athena, the Nubian queen, regarded them with sharp suspicion. Lucas, the youngest, slouched against the stone, his expression unreadable. His well-groomed red hair gleamed under the chamber's dim light, his freckled face betraying little interest.

But Avlon, the albino vampire, smiled warmly at her.

Helene stared, unable to look away. His skin was even paler than her own, his afro a striking shade of gold. His lips were full, his nose broad, and his green eyes glittered with quiet amusement. He was unlike any vampire she had ever seen.

"Thank you, my lord," Monique said, her voice measured. "It is an honour to stand before the council." She bowed again.

Nathan's expression did not change. "You left me no choice." He gestured toward the other council members. "We wish to know why Babette fled Paris so suddenly and now sends you in her stead."

Lucas tapped his fingers against his knee, eyes narrowing on the letter in Helene's hand. "Babette has always been a friend to the council. But we have heard... troubling news." His gaze flicked toward Helene, sharp and assessing. "Is it true she has killed her own brother?"

Helene's breath caught. She clenched her fists, willing herself to remain still.

"Perhaps," Avlon interjected, "we should allow our guests to answer Nathan's question first." He inclined his head toward Monique.

Lucas grimaced, shifting on the stone bench. Athena merely arched a brow, waiting.

Monique took a breath and raised her chin. "The lady Babette sends her greetings... and her regrets." A pause. "But she also sends dire news. Our lives are in danger."

A ripple of interest passed through the assembled vampires.

"We are on the brink of disaster," Monique continued. "A war has begun between vampires and wolves—" she let the words hang in the chamber, letting their weight settle "—wolves known as lycans."

Silence.

Then, from high above, Nathan leaned forward. "Tell us everything."

MONIQUE BOWED AGAIN BEFORE SPEAKING, GLANCING AT HELENE WITH unease. She did not know how much the council had already pulled from their minds. It reminded her why Cecil Bleddyn was so feared—his mental power was boundless, unmatched. She turned to Nathan, knowing he held absolute power in this room. He was not beloved, only feared.

Their gazes met, and he scowled. "I do not intend to wait for sunrise, Monique," he said impatiently. "The night passes quickly, and I would like to enjoy it."

Babette's letter said nothing of Cecil Bleddyn. Monique chose her words carefully. "My lord," she addressed Nathan alone, "the lady Babette would have you know that—"

Her gaze flickered toward Avlon. Of all the council, he was the only one who might spare them from destruction. Beside her, Helene stood rigid, silent in her fear.

Athena rose abruptly, Babette's letter clenched in her hand. "The lady Babette begs forgiveness for a transgression unknown to us. Yet you speak of wolves—" her tone was sharp with disdain "—wolves you call lycans. Wolves are wolves. And yet you shield your minds, even before us." Her dark eyes narrowed. "What is it you wish to hide?"

"Nothing, my lady," Monique said at once. Babette had warned them: Do not hesitate.

She took a breath and spoke the name that would shake the council. "Cecil Bleddyn lives."

A ripple of shock swept through the chamber. Low murmurs stirred among the council members, but Monique kept her eyes on Nathan. His expression did not change, but she saw fury ignite behind his cold stare. Athena, in contrast, visibly recoiled.

Lucas exhaled, unimpressed. If the news disturbed him, he did not show it. To Monique, it was no surprise. He had never feared Cecil—not truly. Perhaps because he had never understood what Cecil was.

But Avlon... Avlon remained calm, though Monique swore she caught the faintest twitch of a smile at the corners of his lips.

Monique pressed on. "The lady Babette and Emilio—now long dead—spared Cecil's life."

Nathan rose, his voice thunderous. "They defied my command!"

His rage crackled through the room like a violent storm.

"Babette has betrayed us—betrayed me!" He struck the stone seat beside him with a force that sent cracks running through it. "She will return to Paris and answer for her crime!"

Monique's nails dug into her palms, bracing herself. *Babette warned us of his wrath.*

Nathan's gaze burned into them both. "And you!" He thrust a finger toward them. "You bring this treacherous news and expect to walk free? No. You shall share in Babette's fate!"

Lucas grinned. His gaze met Monique's in open triumph. Bastard. He despised her almost as much as she despised him. Once, the son of the most powerful vampire in Paris had loved her. But when she spurned him, that love had curdled into bitter hatred.

She ignored him and turned back to Nathan. "Cecil Bleddyn saved us all from destruction."

Nathan's expression darkened further, but she did not falter. "We fought bravely, but the lycans are strong. They are both wolf and human, able to shift at will. Cecil is the only reason we still live."

Nathan scoffed. "This is what happens when you doubt my word." He turned sharply to Avlon, his fury redirecting. "You convinced the council to entrust Cecil's death to Babette and Emilio. I could have finished him myself."

Helene stepped forward, her voice cutting through the tension like a blade. "The lycans are led by a hunter."

A hush fell over the room.

"Percival Hearne may have sired a lycan even more powerful than Cecil himself, my lord."

The air thickened with unspoken dread.

Athena turned to Nathan, her sharp features tightening. "A blending of the hunter and the wolf?" she murmured. "This is forbidden. It breaks a covenant forged millennia ago."

For the first time, she looked at Helene with something other than disdain. "Tell me of this... lycan."

Helene hesitated only a moment. "He is called Silas, Percival Hearne's grandson." She let the name settle before adding, "Cecil has kept us safe. We knew he could protect us."

Nathan's expression was unreadable. "We know of the Hearnes," he said at last. "A well-respected clan of hunters. Percival Hearne is of the line of Chasen Hearne." His gaze shifted to Avlon. "And what say you of this news?"

Avlon smiled, unhurried. "The lady Babette's transgression may have saved our lives." He spoke not just to Nathan but to the entire council. "We must ask ourselves whether this so-called betrayal"—" he arched a pale brow at Nathan "—was not a blessing."

Nathan bristled. "Cecil Bleddyn was born a wolf, yet now he lives with the legacy of both wolf and vampire. His existence defies what we are. I will never trust him!"

His fury flared once more. "His kind will change us forever! I refuse to see our bloodline polluted by mongrels. We are vampires!"

But Avlon's voice was like a slow, rolling tide, calm and steady. "We fear what we do not understand, Nathan. Perhaps Cecil was meant to survive."

Monique rubbed her hands together, steadying herself. The next words would infuriate Nathan. But the truth had to be known.

"There is another."

Silence.

Then Nathan's voice, quiet but seething. "What?"

Monique held his gaze. "Another like Cecil." She took a measured breath before speaking the name.

"Larus Bleddyn."

The chamber, already tense, seemed to contract with the weight of the revelation.

For the first time that night, Nathan did not immediately speak.

The storm was coming.

It was after sunset. Helene sat with Monique in the hall of Babette's château, surprised when the visitor, Avlon, was announced and escorted in. She was to leave with Monique that night, for they had been in Paris too long. But they would not return alone; many who served Babette had agreed to journey across the sea to fight alongside the lady they loved. The conflict between the wolves and vampires was called the Vampire Wars.

Avlon paused by the door, elegantly dressed in what many saw as the height of Parisian fashion. With an effortless motion, he beckoned someone unseen, yet Helene caught the sound of a heartbeat—familiar, young, steady. She knew it at once.

"Come, Marc," said Avlon. "Meet my friends."

The young human stepped into the room. His dark curls were slightly disheveled, and despite his small frame—barely reaching Avlon's waist—his bright, curious eyes gave him the presence of someone far older. When he saw Helene, he smiled, and she found herself momentarily stunned by the quiet strength in his gaze.

She had seen children orphaned by war before. But never one who carried such weight with such ease.

Avlon rested his pale hands on the boy's narrow shoulders, and Marc reached up to touch them, a silent exchange of trust. The tenderness between them was unmistakable. Whatever Avlon was to the world—council member, politician, schemer—here, he was simply a father.

They took the couch across from Monique and Helene.

"Welcome, Marc," said Monique, leaning forward with a smile.

Helene studied them both, puzzled by what she was seeing. Sensing this, Avlon's lips quirked into an amused grin. "I am all Marc has in this world," he said, stroking the boy's curls. "And he is all I have. My adopted son."

Marc leaned into him. "Father saved me," he said. "After Nathan punished Mama and Papa."

Avlon pressed a kiss to the boy's hair. "You should not speak such things, Marc."

Marc furrowed his brow, confused. "But... Lucas says it all the time, Father."

Avlon's expression darkened, just for a moment, before he turned to Helene and Monique. "Nathan wants Marc to remember that he now lives because of his mercy," he said, his voice tight. "It was I who begged for his life—just a babe, heir to a fortune Nathan coveted. His parents offered everything to satisfy Nathan's demands, but he wanted it all."

Helene's stomach clenched. She knew that life—the burden of inheritance, the expectation that wealth could shield you from cruelty. But Marc had been given no such shield. Only this vampire who had fought for him.

"I watched as Nathan made an example of them," Avlon continued. "His vengeance had no patience for generosity. He saved Marc's parents for last." His crimson gaze settled on Helene. "And now I must beg again."

Helene stiffened.

"I ask that you take Marc on your ship tonight."

For a moment, she hesitated—not in doubt, but in the weight of it. She had made many choices since this war began, but none that would shape a life so young.

Marc, sensing her silence, straightened his shoulders. "I am not afraid."

Helene exhaled and met Avlon's gaze. "Yes."

Relief flickered across his features. "For this, I thank you."

He then turned to Monique. "You know the depths of Lucas's treachery. Nathan has decided his son must leave Paris and join this war. But do not be deceived—this is no punishment. Nathan sends him as his eyes and ears. I beg you both to protect Marc, even after I join you."

Monique nodded solemnly.

Avlon rose. "I must go. I sent Marc's things to your ship." His lips curved into that same mischievous smile. "Yes, I knew you would not deny him." Then, the levity faded. "Nathan does not forgive. He will never forget Babette's betrayal. You must all be careful."

He turned to his son, kneeling to embrace him. Marc buried his face in Avlon's chest, still and silent. If he was afraid, he did not show it.

Helene watched, struck by the boy's resilience. He accepted his fate without protest, without tears—only the quiet, unshaken certainty of someone who had lost everything and learned to survive.

She promised herself she would protect him.

No matter what was to come.

PART FIVE

42

MARC

It had been six months since Monique and Helene returned from Paris. The year was 1816, and Larus stood before his mirror, gazing at the ghostly, faint reflection that had not changed in over two decades. From time to time, he performed this ritual—not out of vanity, nor to bask in the glory of his immortality, but to remember. If he had never been turned, his body would be nothing more than dust and brittle bone beneath the earth.

He raised a hand to his face as if in disbelief, fingertips brushing over smooth, unaged skin. As a human, he would have been in his forty-third year. Instead, time had abandoned him.

Turning away, Larus stepped to the window. Night stretched over the vast estate, the moon casting pale light over the magnificent hedgerow maze below. A smile tugged at his lips. He had met Sebastian inside those twisting green walls. Now, the once-isolated castle teemed with life—nearly two hundred vampires had come, drawn by the presence of their kin and the promise of something greater.

Beneath the castle, hundreds of sarcophagi lay in silent rest, but White Castle's influence extended beyond its walls. Micah owned properties in nearby cities, securing his dominion. And at the heart of it all, the one name whispered with equal reverence and wariness—Cecil Bleddyn.

Larus marvelled at Cecil's sudden popularity. Though they had grown close, he remained devoted to the one who had made him. Micah had given him life. And no matter what bonds he formed with the others, Larus would not forget that.

Cecil had trained them all in the art of killing wolves. Larus's smile faltered as he thought of Yaro—the first vampire to call the shapeshifters lycans. He closed his eyes at the memory of Yaro's gruesome end, but a soft knock pulled him from his thoughts.

He did not need to guess who it was. He had already heard the rhythmic heartbeat, steady and familiar.

"Come in, Marc."

The door creaked open, and the boy entered with his usual bright smile. Larus returned it, shaking a finger playfully.

"No need to remind me, Marc—I know it is your birthday tomorrow."

Marc beamed. "My eleventh birthday," he declared. Then, his smile widened. "Father comes for me."

Larus's expression darkened, though he masked it quickly. Word had come from Paris—Avlon would arrive soon. And though he knew this day would come, Larus found himself dreading Marc's departure.

"And I'm sure you're excited to see Avlon again," Larus said lightly.

"Well… only if he makes me a vampire. Like you."

Larus arched a brow, amused. "Maybe not just yet." He ruffled the boy's dark curls. "And I suspect Avlon would agree. You have many years to enjoy life as a human, Marc. Besides, you may not even want to be like me when you grow older."

"I shall be as you are," Marc insisted.

"You may wish to have a life of your own one day."

The boy's smile faded, his usual joy dimming like a candle in a draft. Larus knelt, sensing the shift in him.

"You're thinking of them, aren't you?" he murmured. "Your mama and papa."

Marc nodded.

Helene had told Larus of the boy's tragedy, but as he brushed against Marc's mind, he saw something strange—memories the boy should not have. Scenes too vivid, too precise. Marc had been only a babe when

Nathan took everything from him. He could not possibly remember. And yet... he did.

Larus tightened his grip on the boy's shoulders, searching his wide, troubled eyes. "Marc... you must tell me how you have such memories of your mama and papa."

The boy shook his head, his breath quickening. Fear flickered across his face, and then, suddenly, tears welled in his eyes. He clutched Larus, burying his face against his chest.

"I don't know," he choked out. "I don't know..."

SIX VAMPIRES GATHERED TO DISCUSS THE BOY, MARC.

Larus sat with Micah and Babette; Sebastian stood beneath the grand portrait of Micah's mother, gazing up at it as though seeing it for the first time. Across the room, Cecil stood with the albino vampire, Avlon. Larus studied the two, surprised to discover they were old friends. Even Babette, who knew much, had looked upon them in awe when they embraced upon Avlon's arrival. The golden-haired vampire had helped save Cecil long ago, and now, as they reunited, Larus saw a different side of Avlon—one that made him all the more intriguing.

Larus had liked Avlon instantly.

But they had not gathered to reminisce. They were here because of Marc. Larus had gone directly to Cecil after seeing the boy's memories, and now Avlon, his father, demanded answers.

"Why have you not brought my son to me?" Avlon's voice was calm, but there was tension beneath it. He turned to Cecil. "Where is Marc?"

Cecil placed a hand on his friend's shoulder. "Ah, my dear Avlon, always so protective of those you love." A knowing smile played on his lips. "Marc will come. But before he does, there is much you must understand." He glanced at Larus. "You are oblivious to what is happening."

"The boy has memories," Larus said simply.

Avlon shrugged. "Don't we all?"

Cecil chuckled. "You know, Avlon, that I have never had much patience for children. But when I met Marc, I found him... different. The boy is intelligent, curious. And yet, the fact that he now carries vivid, firsthand memories of his parents is an impossibility."

Avlon's lips parted slightly, but he said nothing.

Sebastian, who had moved away from the portrait, now paced near the fireplace. The others remained still, watching, waiting—no one had an answer for how a human child could recall things he had never lived.

"Perhaps," Sebastian mused, "the boy overheard things."

"But we have seen them," Cecil countered. "We have all looked into his mind. These are not whispers or secondhand stories. They are true memories, lived memories." His voice dropped, almost reluctant. "Before now, I paid little attention to the boy. But when I looked closer, I saw it for myself. These are not fragments or fantasies—Marc remembers."

"They haunt him," Larus added.

Avlon straightened. "Bring him to me. I will speak with my son."

Sebastian left the room and returned moments later with Marc. The boy hesitated for only a second before running into Avlon's open arms. The albino vampire embraced him tightly, pressing a kiss to his forehead.

"Look how much you have grown, my son."

Marc's large, dark eyes wandered the room, taking in the unfamiliar space. It was his first time in Micah's favourite chamber. As his gaze lifted to the portrait of the negress, Estlyn, something shifted in his expression.

Then, suddenly, Marc clutched his head, covered his ears, and let out a whimpering sob.

"What is it, Marc?" Avlon crouched beside him, concern flickering in his green eyes.

Larus glanced at Cecil, then at Micah—and what he saw on their faces sent ice through him. Micah's pupils were blown wide, his lips parted in shock.

Babette let out a strangled breath. "C'est impossible!"

Larus had seen it too. They all had. An impossible vision, pulled from Marc's mind, had erupted into the room.

Micah's breath shuddered as crimson tears slipped down his cheeks. His voice barely rose above a whisper.

"Mama..."

That was all he could say before he wept.

Larus forced himself to remain still, though he longed to collapse under the weight of what he had seen. His maker's mother—young, heavy with child, her bare back torn open by a whip. The sound of it cracking, the screams—gods, the screams.

How could Marc endure such horrors of the mind?

Babette swept the boy into her arms, murmuring, "Oh, mon pauvre bébé... my little, sweet bébé."

Marc's voice was barely above a whisper. "That woman... she screams... so loud."

Silence hung thick in the room. No one spoke. No one could.

Finally, Cecil knelt before the boy. "Marc," he said gently, "do you know this woman?" He gestured to the canvas.

Marc pointed to Micah. "His mama."

A sharp breath from Micah. No denial. No argument.

Avlon steadied himself. "Tell us, my son. How do you know her? How do you see your parents?"

Marc's brow furrowed. "I don't know, Father."

Moments later, after the boy had been led away, the vampires spoke again, voices quiet but tense.

"None of this makes sense," Micah said at last. He turned back to the portrait. "Not even I could have such memories. I was not yet born. And yet..." He shook his head. "Marc saw her pain. He felt it."

Avlon's expression darkened. "And he knew of her connection to you, Micah."

"Marc is human," Larus said slowly, "yet he sees the past."

Sebastian toyed with a loose lock of his hair. "A wise observation, chéri. But why these memories?"

Avlon exhaled, rubbing a hand across his jaw. "Marc's mother was a descendant of gypsies. It is from her that he gets his dark, curly hair. She believed in the old ways of her people—an ancient faith, long forgotten."

Cecil's voice cut through the room, clear and certain. "The boy is necromantic."

All eyes turned to him.

"It is the only explanation," Cecil continued. "He holds the gift to commune with the dead."

A chill passed through them all.

Avlon's expression shifted from concern to something deeper. "Why has this happened now?"

Cecil met his gaze. "We do not yet know his true purpose. But I believe this boy has a part to play in our war with the wolves."

His eyes darkened.

"We must treasure and protect him."

43

DISCOVERIES

Percival paced back and forth in Bleddyn Manor's great hall, his hands clasped behind his back. Silas and his mother stood nearby, but the weight of the moment pressed heavily on him. Failure gnawed at him, an unfamiliar feeling. The creature at the old church had filled him with an unfamiliar dread, and he couldn't shake the feeling that the rest of the pack had sensed it too.

The creature—half wolf, half vampire—had slaughtered many of their kind that night, but that was just the beginning of Percival's troubles. There was a mutiny brewing among the wolves. They had witnessed Silas's combat skills firsthand, and it was clear the boy was no ordinary wolf. Though Silas had not reached his full potential, Percival knew that he could have defeated the hybrid. The pack had seen it too. The wolves spoke of Silas's strength, his fearlessness, and his growing power. And now, Percival's hold on them was slipping.

He turned sharply toward Silas and Max, his eyes hard.

"The vampires know how to kill us," Percival said. His voice was steady, but beneath it, there was a simmering frustration. "And as we've destroyed many of them, so have they killed ours. Vampires are difficult to hunt. They hide among the humans like vermin."

"Let me hunt them, Grandfather." Silas's voice was filled with resolve. "Send me to the capital; we know that's where they hide."

Percival's lips curled into a faint, almost calculating smile. Sending the boy could put him in danger—perhaps even kill him—but a dead Silas would secure his control over the pack. The wolves would fall in line with one master.

"No," Percival said firmly. "We cannot risk more sightings. Already, there is talk among the humans of large beasts roaming the countryside." He paused, glaring at Silas. "And your last trip to the capital ended in disaster. Ten wolves dead. You cannot chase vampires through the streets of the capital, Silas! To the human eye, a vampire looks no different than any man. We cannot win this war with the humans watching."

"And they're allowed to scout our lands, kill our kind. They're winning, Grandfather!" Silas's voice rose with frustration.

"Silas is right, Percival." Max's voice was soft but firm, her gaze full of quiet determination. She looked at Silas with protective eyes, her brow furrowed. "Many fear running free on our lands now. The vampires strike even when we have guards on the outskirts. We must act."

Percival shot them both a glare, his jaw tightening.

"We know nothing of this vampire, Grandfather. Not even his name." Silas stepped forward, desperation creeping into his voice. "Maybe if—"

"If you think you can do better, then go ahead," Percival snapped, his patience wearing thin. "Do as you will."

Silas stood still, seething with rage. Percival saw it in those silver eyes—eyes that could be so much like his own when angered.

Percival opened his mouth to say more, but he held back. He could have told them of the creature's ability to read minds, to anticipate their every move, but that would only show another weakness, another failure. And he couldn't afford that now.

Without a word, Silas stormed from the great hall. His mother made a quiet sound of exasperation and shrugged.

"Let me speak with him," she said softly.

"You coddle him, Max," Percival growled. "You indulge him far too much. The boy needs to know his place."

"He only wants to do the best for us all, Percival," Max replied gently, though her eyes were sharp.

"And you believe I don't?" Percival snapped, his voice growing cold.

Max paused, then shook her head. "This is not what I meant, and you know it."

She walked toward the door, her expression softening as she passed him. "I'll speak with my son."

Percival turned away, his gaze drifting toward the window. As he stared up at the full moon, a new, deeper resolve took root in him. He couldn't let things slip away from him—not to a boy, no matter how skilled or powerful he was becoming.

He had come this far, and he would not be second to anyone. He had to take control.

Silas found his mother alone in her room. The weight of his burden had pressed down on him for months, a secret he had tried to ignore, even as it festered in his mind. He had spoken of it only once—to his dear Hannah—and she had begged him never to bring it up again, never to voice his suspicions to his parents.

But it was impossible to live with what the hybrid had said to him.

Max sat on a velvet couch, poised and elegant as ever, her dark eyes lifting to meet his. Night had fallen, and he had chosen this moment carefully—while his father hunted beneath the full moon's glow, revelling in the freedom of the forests.

There was no hesitation.

Silas stood before her, his legs firm beneath him as he asked the one thing only she could answer.

"Who is my father?"

She did not answer. Though Silas could send his thoughts to her, he could not see her own, and yet—her eyes deceived her.

His chest tightened. "Grandfather? Is it true, Mother?"

Still, she said nothing. Her gaze drifted to the side, betraying her.

"That night, the hybrid stood with my uncle—Larus. He said things, Mother."

He saw tears gathering in her eyes.

"Silas…"

"He told me not to trust Grandfather," Silas continued, his voice trembling. "And he as much as said Grandfather was…" He stopped, unable to say the words.

Max inhaled sharply. "Your grandfather did what he felt was right, Silas." Her voice was quiet, but steady. "It hurt me then… and I hated him for it. But you would not exist as you are, Silas, were it not for him."

Silas was shaking now. "What did he do, Mother?" The rage was burning inside him, hot and unrelenting.

"What did Grandfather do to you?"

HE TORE OFF HIS CLOTHES AS HE SPRINTED THROUGH THE FOREST, BRANCHES whipping at his face, scratching his skin, but Silas did not stop. He could not stop. He had to get away—leagues away from Bleddyn Manor, away from them all.

His life had been a lie.

They had all lied to him—the ones he had loved most. His mother, his grandfather. The betrayal burned inside him, hotter than the shifting moon's pull. To think his mother had kept his grandfather's atrocities secret for so many years filled him with rage, a fury so overwhelming he saw little hope of ever forgiving her.

It was not that he did not believe her—her words had rung true. But how could he even begin to envision the horror of what she had endured? What Grandfather Hearne had done to her?

Silas ran harder, his breath ragged. Tears blurred his vision, but he did not slow.

The change took him swiftly.

His body surged with the raw, primal power of the shift, stretching and breaking free of human constraints. A single bound sent him airborne, and by the time his feet touched the ground again, he was no longer a man. The last remnants of his shredded clothing drifted to the earth as a great silver beast landed in his place.

The wolf ran.

It was massive—its back broad, its silver coat shining beneath the full moon. Its teeth were long, razored, its claws curved for the kill. Hunger drove it forward. The need to hunt. To kill. To rip something apart.

The wolf barrelled through the forest, slamming into the trunk of a massive tree, splitting it clean in half. The thunderous crash meant nothing to him.

It ran on.

Up a jagged cliffside, the wolf halted, silver eyes scanning the unknown lands beyond. The scent of pine and damp earth filled its nose—then something else.

A scent it recognized.

The scent of the enemy.

A vampire.

The silver beast bared its teeth. Then, with a single, powerful leap, it sprang from the cliff.

The hunt had begun.

Will had ventured far beyond the safety of White Castle to hunt.

The city teemed with vampires, yet Micah and Cecil had long encouraged their kind to feed on livestock rather than humans. Cattle, horses, sheep—blood was blood, and there was plenty of it in the capital and its neighbouring farms.

Tonight, Will had drained three lambs without killing them.

It wasn't the same. Human blood was sweeter, richer—alive in a way that no animal's could ever be. But Will, like many in his coven, found it painful to take an innocent life. He had made his peace with lesser sustenance.

Seated atop a ridge, he wiped his mouth with the back of his hand. The scent of hay and damp earth mingled with the lingering, gamey taste of sheep's blood. From where he sat, he could hear the steady thrum of human hearts sleeping in the farmhouse below. The sound tugged at something deep within him. Hunger. Need.

He exhaled, dragging his fingers over his pock-marked face. The deep scars beneath his touch pulled him back to a time when his life had been nothing but squalor. But now, he would live for ages—because of Micah, because of Cecil Bleddyn.

Because of what his own blood had done.

A faint smile ghosted his lips. The honour of reviving the great Cecil Bleddyn...

Then the wind shifted.

A scent carried with it—sharp, wild.

Will stiffened. He was not alone.

The wolf was upon him before he could flee.

A massive weight slammed him against a tree, knocking the breath from his lungs. A flash of silver fur. Claws dug deep into his shoulder.

Will gasped.

Silas.

Those silver eyes bore into him, piercing, studying him even as the beast's powerful jaws snapped inches from his face. The stench of hot breath filled Will's nostrils—musk and blood, wild and rancid. He turned his face away just as the claws raked down his chest. He groaned, fangs bared.

"You fucking dog!"

Pain spurred him into action. With a snarl, Will wrenched his arms free and drove his fist into the lycan's snarling face.

The beast reeled back, stunned.

Will didn't hesitate. He sprang, scaling the tree in a blur, then launched himself onto the wolf's back. They tumbled down the ridge in a violent tangle of claws and limbs. Dirt and bramble kicked up around them as they struck the ground, rolling.

Will clawed at the lycan's body, his nails raking deep.

But the wolf was stronger.

With a snarl, Silas twisted, pinning Will beneath him, a massive limb crushing his chest. The vampire struggled, but the wolf barely noticed.

Will looked up—into those silver eyes.

He saw the strike coming too late.

A flash of movement. A clawed hand. A sharp sting to his neck.

Then—

Darkness.

44

THE LITTLE DREAMER

Marc jolted upright in bed, his face slick with sweat. His breath came in short, panicked gasps. He had seen death.

Tears blurred his vision as he swung his legs over the edge of the mattress and hurried to the window. The first light of dawn stretched across the sky, its golden hues creeping over the horizon.

The vampires were asleep.

Marc didn't hesitate. He bolted from his room, his bare feet slapping against the cold stone floor. The castle's great hallways stretched around him, empty and silent. He sprinted down the winding staircase to the crypts—but the heavy doors were sealed shut. No human could open them.

Heart pounding, he turned and ran back the way he had come.

If they weren't in the crypts, there was only one other place a vampire might be.

Marc pounded on the double doors of Micah's hall. "Micah! Cecil!" His fists ached, but he kept pounding.

When the doors finally opened, it was not Micah or Cecil who greeted him, but Arturo, the castle's butler. The tall man peered down at him, a rag in hand, brown eyes impassive.

"What is it, lad?"

"I must see Micah. Now! Or Cecil!"

Arturo sighed. "There are rules, young man—"

"The wolf is coming here!" Marc's hands curled into tiny fists. His voice trembled, but his gaze did not waver.

Arturo studied him for a long moment, then nodded. "Come with me."

He led Marc back down to the crypts. As they approached, Arturo shook his head. "Why didn't you simply say we were in grave danger, boy?"

It took him several moments to unlock the first chamber. Inside lay a single stone sarcophagus.

"I only have access to this one," Arturo muttered. He gestured toward the ancient, dust-covered tomb. "You must convince this vampire why the elders must be woken."

Marc swallowed hard. The sarcophagus was covered by a wooden lid, which Arturo pushed aside with ease.

Within it lay Ashkan.

Marc hesitated. The chamber was small, no doors, just stone walls pressing in around them. Slowly, he stepped closer to the sarcophagus, reaching out—

Ashkan's eyes snapped open.

Marc stumbled back, startled.

"Why have you come, dreamer?" The vampire's voice was a whisper, yet it carried through the chamber like a chill on the wind.

Ashkan climbed from the sarcophagus in a single, fluid motion. His gaze locked onto Marc's, sharp as a blade. Then, after a moment of silence, he nodded.

"Return to Micah's hall," Ashkan said. "I will wake him."

Moments later, five vampires gathered in Micah's hall.

Marc sat on the couch, small and trembling, his hands clasped tightly together. He looked up at Cecil.

"He is dead."

Cecil nodded, his face unreadable. "Yes, dreamer."

Marc swallowed. They had seen it, too. The dream Will had sent him—the warning.

"He spoke to me," Marc whispered. "Will told me Silas is coming." His voice cracked. The memory of it—of Will's final moments—was unbearable. His vision blurred with tears. "He was in so much pain... but he wasn't afraid."

He wiped his eyes, but the words kept spilling out. "He was thinking of you, Cecil... and Micah."

A deep sorrow settled over the room. Even Sebastian and Babette, usually composed, seemed shaken.

Micah's eyes were dark with grief.

Marc clenched his jaw, fighting the lump in his throat. "The wolf took his head."

A hush fell over the room.

Larus was the first to move. He knelt before Marc, wrapping him in a cold embrace. "It will be okay, little one," he murmured. "But you must be brave."

Marc sniffled. He turned to Cecil. "Is Silas coming to kill us?"

"Not while I am here," Cecil said. His voice was quiet but firm. Then, after a pause, he added, "The wolf has no idea I can walk beneath the sun."

Marc's breath hitched. A flicker of something—fear, awe—crossed his face.

Then another thought took hold.

Cecil had called him dreamer. But what if he could be more?

"As one of us," Cecil mused, studying him, "his gifts would be boundless."

Micah nodded. "Yet he is too young. He would live inside the body of a boy for eternity."

Marc's eyes widened. "I can be like you?" His sorrow seemed to fade in an instant, replaced by something else.

Hope.

Larus smirked, his long fingers caressing Marc's shoulders. "In a few years, perhaps. For now, you will have to settle with being our little dreamer." He exchanged a glance with Cecil. "You can help us, though. Tell us of your dreams... Be brave."

Marc nodded slowly, tugging at his fingers.

He would be brave.

For now.

45

A WOLF COMES BY DAY

Silas eyed the vampires' home—a great castle of white stone. He had watched the place since dawn, noting the humans moving about the grounds. A grin tugged at his lips. Unlike the blood-drinkers, he could roam night and day. Vampires were weak, vulnerable, dependent on protectors while they slept.

But he had not come here to mock them. He had come for one reason.

The hybrid was inside that castle. Silas would find him.

He lifted his gaze to the bright sky, his silver eyes narrowing. The cobbled road was alive with carriages, their wooden wheels rattling over the stones. The castle stood somewhat isolated, a perfect hiding place among humans. Silas started toward the iron gates, pondering how best to get inside—

"A wolf comes by day."

The voice sent a chill down his spine.

Silas whirled to find a man standing at the edge of the woods. Dressed like a gentleman, he leaned on a cane, at ease beneath the midday sun. Silas was speechless, his thoughts a snarl of confusion. This was no ordinary vampire. The hybrid stood tall, clad in black, a fine top hat resting atop his head. His cane, tipped with a golden wolf's head, gleamed in the light.

Silas suddenly felt like a peasant in the rags he had stolen after emerging naked from the forest.

The vampire stepped onto the road, crossing toward him with slow, deliberate steps. Silas bared his teeth in a low, warning growl.

"To shift now," the vampire mused, "right here, in broad daylight, among humans—that would be unwise."

He drew closer, undeterred. "Besides, what would your dear grandfather think?" He studied Silas with knowing eyes. "You have spoken with your mother, I see."

Silas stiffened. The hybrid smiled slightly, then his expression darkened. "You have taken the life of one dear to me."

"As you have taken many of my kind," Silas shot back. "What are you?"

The vampire's smile returned, slow and knowing. "I am your past, Silas. And I am your future."

A rush of self-loathing flooded Silas's chest. He had been a fool to come here, to think he had the upper hand.

"No, Silas." The hybrid's voice was almost gentle. "Your visit here is welcomed."

Silas's rage flared. "Get out of my head!"

"Seeing into the minds of others is an affliction I cannot escape, Silas Hearne."

He lifted his cane and gestured toward the castle. "Magnificent, isn't it?"

Silas clenched his fists, forcing himself to breathe. He glanced at the passing carriages, then met the vampire's gaze once more. "You were expecting me... how?"

"Vampires have many gifts. We have watchers."

The hybrid turned away from the gates as if the conversation no longer interested him. "You seek answers, Silas. If you are willing, you shall have them."

He reached into his belt, removed a pouch, and tossed it toward Silas. The heavy clink of gold coins met the wolf's ears.

"There is an inn several miles east, in the city." The vampire adjusted his gloves. "Enough coin for food and proper clothing. I will come to you after sunset."

Without another word, the hybrid stepped through the iron gates and strode up the narrow path toward the white castle.

Silas watched him go, every fibre of his being bristling.

Larus walked beside Cecil toward the castle courtyard, where Ashkan waited by their carriage. Micah and Sebastian had both opposed their decision to meet with Silas Hearne, but Cecil had been adamant. Sebastian had insisted on accompanying them; Cecil refused. Micah had suggested at least allowing Ashkan to drive them, though the journey was short.

As they boarded the carriage, Larus saw Micah and Sebastian standing on the castle steps.

"Could we not have brought them along, Cecil?"

"The boy seeks only to talk." Cecil's voice was calm but firm. "And I would use this opportunity to my advantage." He placed his cane across his lap, adjusting it with deliberate precision. "I considered inviting him to the castle, but it would be unwise. Silas is still the enemy."

Larus stared out at the night. His mind wandered, remembering the day he had found his nephew cradled in Max's arms.

"What was it like to walk in the sun again?" Larus turned to Cecil, his voice tinged with longing. He wanted to feel the warmth of sunlight on his skin again more than anything.

Cecil smiled softly, his eyes distant. "Exactly as I remember it, Larus. Those sensations never change."

Larus returned the smile, though it didn't quite reach his eyes. "You know what I mean."

Cecil's expression shifted, growing more serious. "Your change will come, Larus." He ran his hand over the golden wolf's head of his cane, his fingers lingering there. "There's no doubt you will transform. But it's not like the stories you've heard." His voice grew quiet for a moment. "When

Telsiea made me, I was a vampire, just as frightened of the sun as the rest of them. But then, years later, I... transformed." He shook his head slightly. "The horror of it sent me on a killing spree."

Cecil lifted the cane and tapped Larus lightly on the side of his head. "You're fortunate, boy. You'll have a chance to prepare for your first shift. But know this—your body will never know warmth again. It will always be frigid."

Larus shifted uncomfortably but didn't speak. Instead, he turned the conversation back to the matter at hand.

"What are your plans for Silas?"

Cecil's gaze darkened. "I hope to get through to him. He must see Percival Hearne for the impostor he is. That man doesn't belong on Bleddyn land."

Larus' thoughts shifted to Marc. The boy was only eleven, yet Larus could feel there was something special about him—something Marc was yet to fully understand. The albino vampire, Avlon, had visited the boy on occasion, but Larus feared that Marc's gifts would attract the wrong kind of attention. He couldn't afford for Nathan to discover the boy's abilities.

Marc needed their protection, at least for the next seven years. Once he turned eighteen, he would be changed.

AFTER INVITING THEM IN, SILAS STOOD SILENT AS HIS UNCLE AND THE HYBRID entered his room. He looked from one to the other and saw the resemblance immediately. Larus was his mother's twin, and Silas saw his mother's eyes staring back at him. But there was something about this unknown creature, something familiar. Again, he wondered what the hybrid was and why he felt so inexplicably drawn to him. He felt no fear.

The hybrid took note of the clothes Silas wore and smiled. "You've chosen well, young lycan." Silas grimaced at the name.

"A name of honour," the hybrid said, his voice surprisingly warm.

"Given to wolves by the vampire Yaro. Your grandfather killed him in the cave."

Silas looked away, his jaw tightening. "He fought well."

"Yaro was a hothead, but he was brave," said his uncle. Larus took a seat next to the window, while the hybrid remained standing, his cane tapping gently against the floor.

"Too many have died, Silas, in this pointless war." The hybrid paced several feet away, his cane in hand. "Long ago, there was a covenant—a truce between vampires and wolves. This truce lasted for years, maintaining peace between the two species. But they were also hunters, sworn to keep the peace—watchers. They swore neutrality, never favouring one species over the other."

"Your grandfather broke that covenant, Silas." Larus's voice was heavy with regret. "His only purpose was to control our family... and to do so, he committed unspeakable acts."

The hybrid stepped closer, his eyes dark and intense. "You are family, Silas. You and Larus—one a wolf and the other a vampire. Percival Hearne seeks to control the lycans. You act out of rage and sometimes lose control, but I see no evil in you. When I touched your grandfather's mind, all I saw was death and destruction. He will seek to have you destroyed, young lycan. Remember this: you gave Percival Hearne the one thing he wanted —you made him a wolf."

Silas's heart raced, and his thoughts swirled. He had already suspected the truth, but hearing it confirmed shook him. "You're saying... he may be my father?"

The hybrid's gaze softened. "You've seen the truth in your mother's eyes. You need answers, answers your mother or grandfather won't give you. And that's why you came to me."

Silas wiped away a tear that had escaped his eye, his throat tight. "Why should I trust you?" The sorrow in his voice was raw. "I don't even know who you are!"

"I am your kin," the hybrid replied simply. "I am Cecil Bleddyn."

Silas turned his gaze to Larus, seeking reassurance.

"He speaks the truth, Silas," Larus said quietly. "Cecil is the first of his kind—vampire and wolf."

“And Larus is like me,” Cecil added. “He too will one day walk in the sun.”

Silas’s mind struggled to process it all, but the truth felt undeniable. His heart ached with disbelief and a strange sense of understanding. He nodded slowly, trusting their words.

“There’s much you need to know, Silas,” said Cecil, his voice calm yet weighted with experience. “But I will start with this: I have no intention of harming you. I am old, Silas. I’ve fought wolves on Bleddyn lands and killed my own kind. Long ago, I witnessed a war between vampires and wolves that ended in devastation. Yet Percival Hearne has gone to great lengths to reignite this rivalry, one that only brings death. He alone is the bringer of death, Silas.”

Silas’s thoughts raced, and a deep sadness flooded him.

“It was he who murdered my parents.” Said Larus. “Cecil saw it all in his mind.”

Silas looked at his uncle in disbelief.

“My grandfather?” Silas shook his head, as if the idea were too monstrous to accept. “No, he couldn’t have.”

“Percival thinks only of himself,” Cecil’s voice was like ice, yet steady. “And nothing will stop him from using you for his own ends.”

Silas placed both hands on his head, overwhelmed by the weight of it all. His body slumped, and he fell back onto the couch, silent tears streaming down his face as the truth settled in. He wept quietly, feeling the sting of betrayal, confusion, and grief.

He could hear Cecil’s voice softly in the background, soothing yet firm, as if trying to ease the storm within him. “You are not alone, Silas.”

46

GRANDFATHER HEARNE

Silas returned home after spending two days at the inn with Cecil and Larus. While Cecil embraced the daylight, his uncle, Larus, had covered the windows with blankets. But soon, Larus would transform into what Cecil had become.

Upon returning to Bleddyn lands, Silas did not go to his cave, nor did he return to the manor. Instead, he made his way to the old church. It was there, inside its cold, stone walls, that Silas gathered those lycans he trusted—those willing to stand with him against his grandfather.

The sun was beginning its descent, casting long shadows as Silas sat cross-legged on the floor of the church. His clothes, purchased with Cecil's coin, still felt strange to him, but he had no time to dwell on it. He had sent word to the lycans loyal to him, knowing full well that many others stood with Percival Hearne. Still, he had nearly seventy lycans with him tonight—and more would come.

For the first time, Silas truly noticed the beauty of the old church. He marvelled at the intricately painted stained-glass windows, their colours dancing as the last rays of daylight filtered through. He smiled, thinking of his uncle's suggestion to use this place as a refuge. The church was ancient, as old as the Bleddyn family itself, and its gargoyles—both inside and out—gave the building a silent, watchful presence. For a moment,

Silas entertained the thought of restoring the church, not for himself, but for Larus. He had learned how important the church was to his uncle, and a deep sense of respect for the place filled him. It had been here long before even Cecil had been born.

Gavin, his second-in-command and most trusted wolf, approached slowly. Gavin's furrowed brow showed his confusion as he observed Silas's grin.

"We plot to cast your grandfather from these lands, Silas, yet you are smiling?" Gavin's voice held a note of concern.

Silas shrugged. "Grandfather's time here is at its end, Gavin. I'm simply looking to the future." He rose and gave Gavin a friendly slap on the shoulder. "By the way, my friend, we now have a new name—a better name. From this night forward, we are lycans."

A faint smile tugged at the corners of Gavin's lips. Silas grinned back. Gavin was a calm, quiet man, but the respect he commanded from the pack was undeniable. He had a way of keeping them in line and had brought the wolves together when they needed it most.

"I will prepare the men...the lycans, Silas." Gavin's words were steady, his loyalty to Silas clear in every syllable.

Silas's gaze swept across the church, taking in the faces of the lycans gathered around him. The weight of leadership pressed down on him, but it was a burden he was ready to bear. He felt a surge of pride that these wolves stood with him, willing to fight for a future free from his grandfather's tyranny. Yet, a bitter sting accompanied that pride. He knew that some would die in the coming conflict. Percival Hearne would never leave Bleddyn Manor willingly.

War was inevitable.

But Silas had made plans. He would not permit a single wolf to fall that night.

He sat at the table in Bleddyn Hall, surrounded by family, all deeply concerned for Silas. The boy's mother, the last to speak with him before his departure, had not seen or heard from him in days.

"I will not tolerate this foolishness," Percival declared, his voice cold and resolute. "Not even from my own grandson. Silas cannot simply run off whenever things don't go his way." His gaze hardened as he looked at the family around him. Bartholomew was silent, as always; Morgan, indecisive, deferred to Catherine for direction, while Hannah, teary-eyed, seemed lost in her own grief. Max, ever reliable, had been distant, her usual strength diminished. Only Gertrude, his wife, appeared unshaken.

He slammed his fist onto the table. "I will not have every wolf in these lands thinking they can leave on a whim. There must be order here!"

"Silas was angry when he left," his mother spoke up, glancing at Bartholomew with a shared understanding. "We... quarrelled."

Hannah began to sob again, shaking Percival's patience to the breaking point. He wanted nothing more than to have her removed from his presence, but before he could speak, the doors burst open. Everyone turned as Silas entered, his loyal dog Gavin following closely behind.

Hannah rushed to him, throwing her arms around him, but Silas guided her gently away, pushing her into Gavin's protective arms. Something felt wrong—Percival sensed it immediately.

As he took in the scene, the doors opened again, and more wolves entered. Silas and Gavin shifted together, their transformation seamless. The sudden violence of the moment made Percival's pulse quicken. Gertrude screamed, instinctively drawing closer to him. Max, Bartholomew, Catherine, and Morgan remained rooted in shock as Silas's wolves swiftly took down Percival's guards.

Silas returned to his human form, standing naked before them, the tension in the room palpable. He approached the table, his silver eyes burning with rage.

"Your time here is over, Grandfather," Silas declared coldly. "You will leave Bleddyn Manor. I want no more death here." He gestured toward the fallen bodies of Percival's protectors.

"What is this mutiny?" Percival spat, his fury barely contained, but as the words left his mouth, he realized with chilling clarity that he had lost his hold on the boy.

"We have only killed those who opposed us," Silas replied, his voice steady. "Those who choose to stand with you are free to leave. But you are no longer welcome here."

"How dare you plot against me, Silas!" Percival's eyes darted between the corpses and the men who had switched allegiances. He turned to Max and Bartholomew, desperation creeping into his voice. "For heaven's sake, make him see reason!"

"Mother would never betray me, Grandfather," Silas said, his voice almost tender. He turned to Bartholomew. "You have always loved me, whether as a father or a brother. You are welcome here, should you choose to stay."

Percival's gaze flickered from his son to Silas, and the silence between them was thick with unresolved tension. Before he could speak, three figures entered the hall. Percival staggered back as he recognized the three vampires—Larus and Isabelle, and standing between them, Cecil.

"My aunt and uncle belong here, Grandfather," Silas said. "This land is their birthright, not yours."

"You would open these doors to these creatures—vampires?" Percival sneered. His finger pointed accusingly at them. "Have you lost your mind, boy? Have I not taught you enough about your family's history?"

Silas stood firm. "He is kin," he said simply. "Cecil Bleddyn."

Percival's shock was visible. He knew the resemblance now, too clearly. "Yes, Grandfather," Silas added. "Cecil is no different from my uncle. Both have been thought cursed, but they are part of this family."

Cecil Bleddyn, the hybrid, said nothing, his presence almost unnerving. He stood quietly at Silas's side, his hand resting lightly on the boy's shoulder. Larus spoke for them all, his voice calm but heavy with unspoken history.

"You murdered my parents, Percival Hearne," Larus stated, his gaze unwavering. Percival stiffened, but there was no point in denying the truth. He said nothing, but his eyes darted to the shocked faces of the women in the room.

Gertrude, beside him, gripped his arm in fear, but Percival ignored her. His pride would not allow him to show weakness.

"If I had the right, I would take your head, Percival," Larus continued, his voice icy. "But I am not like you."

"It would be better if he were dead," Cecil added, his voice carrying a quiet menace. He moved closer to Silas. "This man will never rest until he sees you all dead."

Percival snarled, his rage bubbling over. "You know nothing about me, creature!"

Cecil's cold eyes met his. "I know your mind," he said. "And I see what you are capable of."

Larus and Silas exchanged a glance, a silent understanding passing between them. For a long moment, the tension hung heavy, and Percival felt as though his fate were balanced on the edge of a blade.

"You must not let him live," Cecil urged again, his voice sharper now.

"You may leave," Larus said, stepping forward. "And if you return to these lands, we will kill you."

Gertrude, trembling, clung to Percival's arm, but he refused to acknowledge her as he turned toward the door. His eyes locked with Silas's one last time. "You have made a mistake, boy. One you will live to regret."

He turned to Bartholomew. "And you? Spineless fool!"

"Goodbye, Grandfather," Silas said, his voice steady and resolute.

Percival strode out of Bleddyn Hall, his thirty-five wolves trailing behind. They moved swiftly through the night, their footsteps heavy as they left the manor behind. It was not yet midnight, and the full moon cast long shadows over the trees. Silas and the vampires had won the battle, but Percival was certain that this war was far from over.

47

FAREWELL TO TILLEY

Larus and Isabelle stood by the carriage as Cecil leaned out the window. He was returning to the capital to meet with Avlon, the albino vampire. Though he had yet to formally accept the title, Cecil was clearly the leader of the new coven of vampires, with Micah, Babette, and Sebastian serving as elders.

"Remember, little ones," Cecil said, his voice light but serious, "say nothing to the lycans of the catacombs. Knowledge is power—and there are certain things we must hold for ourselves." He locked eyes with them, as if peering into their very souls. "Truces can be broken, even when all involved have the best intentions." He smiled, tapping his cane against the side of the carriage. "Keep that in mind."

With a final wave, he nodded at them as the horses began pulling the carriage toward the main gates.

As they waved, Larus chuckled softly. Isabelle gave him a puzzled look.

"Why do you laugh?" she asked.

"Cecil gave us no chance to say a word," Larus replied, his smile widening.

They turned to ascend the stairs toward the manor's main doors, but suddenly, they heard Cecil's voice carrying on the wind.

"I see your thoughts, Larus—even from here!"

Isabelle laughed, shaking her head. Larus took her hand, their fingers entwining as they entered Bleddyn Manor.

"What shall we do with him?" Isabelle teased.

"Come, Larus," she added, "they are waiting."

Inside, they joined the family at the long table in Bleddyn Hall. Larus's appetite for human food had long since dwindled, and tonight, it seemed even more foreign. He smiled, though, seeing Tilley seated with the others. She had cared for him as a child, and he'd loved her his entire life. Yet, even now, he couldn't ignore how much older she had become. Her movements were slower, less sure.

Tilley insisted she was well enough to continue her duties, but Larus wasn't so certain. He noticed the way she looked tired these days, the way she pushed through her aging with a stubborn resolve.

His gaze flicked across the table, landing on his sisters and their husbands. Max looked so happy with her husband, and Silas and Hannah —inseparable—had clearly become close in ways that made Larus uneasy. The fact that they were cousins was a reality he struggled to reconcile.

Silas, always the playful one, leaned over to Larus. "Uncle, Hannah and I were just wondering..." He gestured toward the table, a mischievous glint in his eyes. "Should we have brought...uh...some blood?"

Larus glanced at the empty places at the table where Silas and Hannah should have sat. "Your aunt and I," he replied dryly, "have already dined."

"And we'll say no more about it," Isabelle added with a playful smile, causing a ripple of laughter around the room.

Tilley, seated beside Isabelle, reached up to touch the coolness of Isabelle's cheek. "Oh, dear God, you're as cold as ice!"

"Think about it, Tilley," Silas said with a smirk, "they're not alive."

Max's expression faltered as she placed a hand over her heart. "Silas, you mustn't—"

"It's the truth, Max," Larus said, his voice calm. "We are dead."

Silas tilted his head, a curious look on his face. "What would happen if you ate human food?"

"It would make us sick," Larus replied with a faint smile. "Trust me, I've tried."

Later that night, the family gathered outside beneath the moonlit sky. A sense of unease hung in the air as Larus watched the lycans shift into their wolf forms and run off into the woods. Isabelle sat beside him in a gazebo, her face tense as they observed the transformations. Larus could feel the undercurrent of fear in her. Two vampires surrounded by wolves —her unease mirrored his own.

Silas's authority over nearly eighty lycans was undeniable. The pack obeyed him without question, a clear sign of his dominance. The lycans, natural hunters, killers by instinct, had chosen to follow him alone. That command, that power, was a force to be reckoned with.

A sudden scream shattered the silence. Hannah rushed from the kitchens, throwing herself into Silas's arms, sobbing.

"It's Tilley...in the kitchens!" she cried. "I found her on the floor."

Larus's heart leapt in his chest. He was already moving before anyone could react, his vampiric speed carrying him to Tilley's side. Isabelle was right behind him.

She was still alive.

Isabelle knelt beside them, her gaze full of concern. The others arrived soon after, crowding around the old woman's crumpled form.

"Tilley," Larus whispered, his voice raw as he gathered her frail body into his arms.

"I've been a fool, my dear boy," Tilley murmured, pressing her face into his chest. "My time has come. So cold...you are cold as ice..."

Larus looked at Isabelle, and without a word, they both knew what needed to be done. Tilley couldn't die—not yet.

"I'll carry her," Larus said softly. "Go quickly, Isabelle. I'll meet you in her room."

Isabelle nodded silently, moving to prepare for what they both knew had to happen. Larus lifted Tilley gently, cradling her as though she were the most fragile thing in the world. He headed toward the back stairs, his heart pounding in his chest.

Max's voice stopped him before he could leave.

"What will you do, Larus?" she asked, her eyes wide with concern.

Larus turned to face her, his expression hardening. "Do not try to stop me, Max," he said, his tone firm. "I'm saving Tilley's life."

48

NEW COVENANT

Larus left his chambers and walked down the hall toward Marc's room. The boy had begged to accompany him to the historic meeting of vampires and lycans. The event would take place at White Castle. Marc's door opened as soon as Larus reached it, and he looked down at the boy, surprised. "Have you been waiting by the door, Marc?" The boy grinned, shaking his head from side to side. Larus studied him for several moments, noting how much Marc had grown—nearly twelve years old now. His frame had become leaner, more wiry. His dark curls were becoming more unruly, and there was an almost mischievous light in his eyes.

Larus ruffled Marc's hair affectionately. "Come on." He smiled as the boy's arm slid around his waist, and they began walking down the hall together.

"I will try to keep you with me as long as I can, Marc; Avlon doesn't want you involved in such things," Larus warned gently, his voice softening as he spoke.

Marc, ever perceptive, squeezed Larus's side. "Papa likes you, Larus." He paused, then added in a quiet voice, "He told me."

Larus looked down at the boy, his expression softening. There was something about Marc's unspoken wisdom that always surprised him. Ruffling Marc's curls again, he smiled. "I'm glad he does, Marc."

They descended the staircase, their footsteps echoing faintly. Larus couldn't help but notice how close they had grown recently. The meetings with Cecil, Micah, and others had only intensified his bond with the boy, and he had to admit, there was a subtle unease growing within him—the boy was already so powerful, so perceptive.

As they reached the main level of the castle, the sound of conversation filled the air. The hallways were crowded with vampires, elegantly dressed for the occasion. Larus caught the distinct scent of lycans mixed among the crowd. His eyes scanned the room, watching the interaction between vampires and lycans—friendly and cordial. It was hard to believe any of this peace was possible without Cecil's leadership. Larus took a steadying breath, reminding himself that this was all because of Cecil's vision.

At the door to the great hall, Sebastian greeted them. "I see you bring a guest, chéri." He smiled warmly at Marc, ruffling his hair in a manner far too familiar. "And I see you're dressed for the occasion, young gentleman." Sebastian adjusted Marc's silk ascot with exaggerated care. "The fashions were not quite the same in my time."

He then moved to Larus, gently guiding him away from the door with a hand at his lower back. "Cecil would speak with you before we begin." He turned to Marc. "Come on, little one."

Sebastian's playful laughter filled the air as he walked between them. "I must congratulate you, Larus," he said, clearly amused.

Larus frowned, his brow furrowing. "Congratulate me?"

Sebastian nodded, a knowing glint in his eyes.

Larus shrugged, glancing around. "Sebastian, I have no idea what you mean."

They passed a mirror, and Larus instinctively glanced at his reflection. He had never liked mirrors since becoming a vampire; though visible, his reflection always looked pale and faded, a ghost of himself. But it wasn't his own reflection Sebastian wanted him to notice.

"You, Larus, appear as you should...as all vampires do. Our reflections are mere shadows of what we once were—faded, fading into nothingness." Sebastian's lips brushed against Larus's ear as he spoke. "But look at your twin."

Larus's gaze flicked to Marc. The sight took his breath away.

Marc had dressed exactly as Larus had—every detail, every colour, meticulously mirrored. It was uncanny. Marc, with his youth, his human heartbeat, had somehow managed to channel Larus's own sense of style.

Larus's heart skipped. "Marc... How could you have known I would dress the way I did?"

Marc simply smiled, shrugging nonchalantly. "I... I just knew."

A strange feeling tugged at Larus's chest. Was it pride? Or perhaps unease?

The three of them entered Micah's hall, where Cecil and Micah waited. Larus's eyes immediately fell upon the massive canvas bearing Estlyn's likeness, the artist's strokes capturing her ethereal presence. But the words that followed took precedence.

Micah and Cecil exchanged looks before addressing Larus. "Silas will soon arrive," Micah said, his voice serious. "But Larus, there is something we wish to tell you before we make the covenant."

Larus nodded, his pulse quickening. The air in the room had changed, becoming thicker, more serious.

Cecil steepled his fingers, his long nails touching at the tips. "You are still a newborn, Larus," he began, voice steady. "But we have thought this through very carefully. You have shown potential. You have shown us you can lead."

Larus glanced between Cecil and Micah, bewildered. "Lead? How can this be?"

"You are to join our council of vampires," Cecil declared, his gaze unwavering. "And you will be the last of our five elders."

Larus blinked. "An elder? But I... I've barely had time to understand this world. How could I—?"

"The mere fact that you shall one day become as I am," said Cecil, "has made you worthy. You've shown an ability to lead, to inspire others."

Larus's head spun. How could he be ready for such a responsibility? He was still finding his place in this new world, still learning what it meant to be a vampire.

But before he could speak, Micah turned his gaze to Marc, his expression softening.

"I congratulate you, chéri," Sebastian said, closing the distance between them. He pressed a lingering kiss to Larus's lips, a soft promise of things to come. "Welcome to our council of twelve."

Larus's heart stuttered in his chest as Sebastian's hands moved down his back, pulling him closer. "At the moment, there are but ten members of our council," he said softly, his fingers grazing Larus's skin.

Larus's mind raced, confusion mingling with unease.

"But these seats are being held for Avlon, should he decide to join us," Cecil added, "and for Marc."

"Marc?" Larus's voice cracked slightly as he turned to Cecil. The boy was too young. Too innocent. Larus's stomach tightened. Was Marc ready for this world? He'd only just begun to show the true extent of his abilities. And yet, here they were, talking about his future as one of them.

"Yes," said Cecil. "The boy is to join the council on his eighteenth birthday. I shall turn him myself."

The words landed like stones in Larus's chest. His eyes flicked to Marc, who stood there with quiet confidence, his face still soft, too soft.

Larus felt a shiver of protectiveness surge through him. He hadn't thought about Marc's future this way—hadn't imagined it would come so soon. Would Marc truly be ready for such a burden? Or was this a path that would only lead to destruction for the boy he had come to care for so much?

Larus forced a smile, trying to push down the anxiety gnawing at him. "I see," he said, his voice quieter than he intended. "Marc has a long way to go before he is ready for that."

Cecil met his gaze, steady. "We believe he is capable, Larus."

Larus exhaled slowly. "And so do I," he said, though doubt lingered in the depths of his mind.

Before he could say anything more, Silas entered the room. Cecil motioned to the door. "Silas has arrived."

The ceremony was brief and felt almost pointless. Larus stood with Marc at his side, and together they observed the festivities unfolding around them. Lycans and vampires mingled, laughter and conversation filling the air, and Larus couldn't help but feel a strange discomfort. Many of those present had once fought each other in bloody battles. Now, they were celebrating a new truce, a new covenant. Larus wondered how long this fragile peace would last. He glanced around the room, noting the genuine joy and camaraderie in the air. Perhaps, he thought, Cecil's dream of peace might hold.

Across the room, he spotted Isabelle standing with Catherine and Max. Three sisters, reunited despite the divide between their species—one a vampire, two lycans. Even Tilley stood with them, a part of the circle now, though her journey had been one of pain. Larus had saved her when she was near death, and Isabelle had made her a vampire. The night Tilley was turned, Larus's sister barely made it back with a human in time. After the transformation, Tilley had suffered the brutal hunger that comes with being newly turned. She was no longer the woman she had been. None of them were.

Larus watched them with a distant sadness. They were no longer human. The thought tugged at him, and before he could push it aside, Marc's voice interrupted his contemplation.

"You were never human."

Startled, Larus turned to the boy. His heart skipped, his pulse quickened. "Marc, how... how did you know?"

The boy's face darkened with uncertainty. "I didn't mean to," Marc murmured, his brow furrowing. "I can't always control it... sometimes I just hear your thoughts."

Larus's expression softened. He gently cupped Marc's face. "You must never feel guilt for what you are, Marc," he said firmly, though inside, his heart ached. How much of this boy's future will be shaped by these gifts?

Marc's dark eyes met his, steady and knowing. "Larus, your family... they were never human. You've always been something else."

Larus stared at him, a flash of unease and realization coursing through him. He nodded slowly, his voice a whisper. "Yes. Always something else."

The moment of quiet understanding was broken by the sudden appearance of Avlon. The lycan patriarch's eyes softened when he saw

Marc, and he swept the boy up in his arms, lifting him easily as if he weighed nothing.

"You grow bigger by the day, my boy," Avlon said warmly, planting a kiss on Marc's cheek.

Marc grinned, clearly delighted. "You're late, papa!"

Avlon gave a quiet laugh but quickly grew serious. He glanced at Larus, his expression hardening. "I was lucky to have made it at all," Avlon said, his tone laced with urgency. "I must speak with Cecil and the others immediately."

Larus's stomach tightened. "What's happened?" he asked, his voice low, wary.

Avlon's eyes darkened as he looked toward the door. "I can't explain it fully right now, Larus. But it's urgent."

With a curt nod, Larus led the way from the great hall toward Micah's sanctuary, his mind already racing with questions. What was so pressing that it required immediate attention? As they walked, he could feel the weight of Avlon's presence behind him, his urgency palpable.

Marc's small hand slipped into Larus's, and the boy's voice broke through his thoughts, softer now. "You don't have to do this alone, Larus."

Larus looked down at him, momentarily stunned. Marc's grip tightened, almost protective. "I know," Larus said, his voice rough with a sudden wave of emotion. "I know, Marc."

Together, they stepped into the shadows of the corridor, heading toward whatever waited in the darkness beyond.

Larus listened intently to Avlon, his mind racing as the albino vampire spoke. Avlon stood near the portrait of Estlyn, his piercing green eyes shifting between the gathered group, his posture tense. His words weighed heavily in the air. Cecil sat in the bay window, his gaze distant yet attentive, processing every detail. Larus, sitting on the couch with Marc, felt the boy's warmth beside him, the quiet reassurance of his presence. Marc refused to leave his side, his hand clasped tightly in Larus's.

Silas stood with Micah and Sebastian, while Babette, Bartholomew, and Max occupied the other couch, all equally focused on Avlon.

"What I tell you now," Avlon's voice was steady but edged with urgency, "Cecil already knows. I fear I cannot return to my coven. Lucas watches my every move."

Avlon's green eyes locked with his son's, a silent understanding passing between them. "Lucas has made a covenant," he continued, his voice tight. "And the instructions came directly from his father, Nathan."

The room fell into silence as the weight of his words settled. Babette was the first to speak. "Who did he make a covenant with?" Her voice was sharp, demanding answers.

Avlon raised his blonde eyebrows, as if bracing himself for the inevitable reaction. "Percival Hearne."

Larus could feel the shock ripple through the room. He glanced at his sister and brother-in-law, their expressions frozen in disbelief.

"My father has joined with them?" Bartholomew dragged his hands over his face in frustration, the lines of worry deepening around his eyes. "He said we would regret this, Silas. We've just forged a covenant of peace between lycans and vampires, and now we must face another war."

Avlon's gaze darkened, and he spoke in a low, grim tone. "They will need just a taste of my blood to know everything I've done. I can never return."

Cecil, his voice calm but resolute, broke in. "You are now of our coven," he said, the finality of his words clear. "And you have your seat on our council."

Avlon's lips curled into a wry smile. "You're the reason they make this pact, Cecil. It's you they fear most. And you, Larus." His green stare narrowed, eyes flicking over to Larus as if seeing something deeper. "Nathan plans to be on these shores within a year."

Larus's heart skipped a beat. A year? The urgency of the situation suddenly hit him like a blow.

Silas, who had been standing, joined Larus on the couch, his brow furrowed. "Grandfather will not stop until we are all dead."

Larus turned to Marc, taking the boy's hand in his, needing that small comfort. He looked around the room, studying the faces of those present. Bartholomew had made his choice, yet the thought of facing war with his own father terrified him. Max, on the other hand, was consumed by vengeance; she could never forgive Percival Hearne for murdering their parents. As for the vampires, their expressions were unreadable, and Larus couldn't reach into their minds to gauge their true feelings. Only Cecil remained silent, his expression unreadable, eyes distant as if already weighing the cost of the coming war.

Suddenly, Marc leaned forward, his gaze steady on Silas, breaking the tense silence. "You will have a son." His voice was soft but carried a weight that made everyone pause.

Larus's breath caught in his throat, but Marc wasn't finished. The boy's expression shifted, and a sadness clouded his features. "He will bring much joy to your life," Marc continued, his voice growing somber, "but also sorrow."

The room fell into an eerie silence, as the gravity of Marc's words settled over them all. It was a prophecy, but not one anyone could easily dismiss. Larus watched the others, noting their stilled expressions. No one spoke; it was as if the very air had thickened with the weight of what Marc had foreseen. The prophecy hung between them like an unspoken truth, its implications far-reaching.

Finally, Avlon broke the silence, but the heavy sense of foreboding lingered. "We must act swiftly," he said, his tone dark. "Time is not on our side."

PART SIX

49

ORACLE

Marc had waited seven years for his evolution, yet as he descended the worn stone steps of White Castle with Larus at his side, his stomach twisted in knots. The night air was sharp, carrying the scent of damp earth and the faint, distant trace of burning wood. He should have been ready. He had spent years preparing, but now, standing at the threshold of his own death and rebirth, fear coiled around his ribs like a tightening vice.

Nothing would be the same after tonight.

Marc would become a vampire at Bleddyn Manor, his new existence sealed beneath Cecil's bite. Silas had insisted that Marc's rebirth take place on Bleddyn land, where the old magic still ran deep. Cecil had already gone ahead to prepare.

It was 1823, just a fortnight since Marc had turned eighteen, yet the weight of eternity pressed down on him like an iron chain. It was time to die and live again. The thought left him breathless.

His father, Avlon, was already at Bleddyn Manor, along with the council and the others who would witness his turning. Lycans and vampires would gather in celebration, an acknowledgment of the strange new world they had built. They had even given him a new name—Oracle.

Marc swallowed hard. Was this what he had always been meant to become?

The alliance between Percival Hearne and Nathan had proven a success, just as the truce between Silas's lycans and Cecil's vampires had endured. Their shared war had claimed many lives over the last seven years, and Marc had seen the dead. They whispered to him in dreams, their voices slipping into his mind like echoes from another world. Sometimes they guided him, other times they only tormented him with truths he couldn't fully understand.

He exhaled sharply as Larus nudged him.

"Deep breaths, Marc," Larus said with a grin. "Cecil's bite will be painful... but not for long."

Marc let out a nervous laugh and shoved Larus playfully as he hopped into the carriage. "I only wish this night to be over."

"Just relax," Larus said, settling across from him. "Let Cecil take you. You will feel death claim you, but at the last moment, you will be revived —hungry, but revived."

Marc nodded absently, but his eyes caught on a small black box resting beside Larus, tied shut with a silk red ribbon. Larus, noticing his curiosity, smiled.

"A gift?" Marc asked.

Larus tapped the box lightly. "A gift for my great-nephew, Jude. Silas and Hannah have the most beautiful son."

Marc nodded, but the mention of Jude sent a cold shiver down his spine. Seven years ago, he had seen the boy long before his birth. He had looked into those silver eyes and glimpsed what no one else had—the joy Jude would bring... and the sorrow that would follow.

Jude was only five years old, but the prophecy still haunted Marc. The vision had not faded. And worse, he still feared it would come to pass.

He turned his gaze to the carriage window, watching the trees blur past in the dark. Tonight, his own fate would be sealed. But deep inside, he knew—his visions were not done with him yet.

THE CARRIAGE ROLLED TO A STOP AT THE BOTTOM OF THE HILL. MARC peered out at the church, its towering silhouette outlined beneath the crescent moon. The newly restored stained-glass windows glowed like molten jewels in the darkness, casting hues of crimson, gold, and sapphire against the stone. A bell tolled, its deep chime reverberating in the quiet night. The courtyard was perfectly manicured, bordered by neatly trimmed hedges, the sight so pristine it felt like stepping into a dream.

Beside him, Larus stepped down from the carriage—and staggered back in shock.

His breath caught, his violet eyes wide with wonder as he took in the sight of the church. His gaze lifted, drinking in the gleaming bell tower, the strong, unbroken walls. Then, as if overcome, he fell to his knees in the gravel, his face upturned toward the church on the hill.

Marc had never seen him like this.

From the church's entrance, Silas and Cecil emerged, their forms half-shadowed in the lantern glow. The council of vampires followed in solemn procession.

"You kept this from me." Larus's voice wavered, but he smiled.

"Cecil told me how much this place means to you, Uncle," Silas said, stepping forward. "It shall always be here for you."

Marc watched as uncle and nephew embraced, and for the first time that night, he felt something close to peace.

Then he felt Cecil's hand on his shoulder. Avlon was approaching. The time had come.

Marc's stomach twisted, but he forced himself to breathe.

Moments later, he followed Cecil, Micah, his father, and Larus down the hill. The others remained at the church, their figures fading into the night.

"Where are we going?" Marc asked. He glanced back at the church; he had assumed his transformation would take place inside.

"The process of becoming a vampire is sacred," Cecil said.

They entered the cemetery, their boots crunching over leaves. Shadows stretched long over the ground, cast by rows of timeworn tombstones. They passed a mausoleum, then moved deeper into the burial grounds, where the night grew still.

They stopped beneath an ancient tree.

Its trunk was massive, its roots gnarled and deep, its canopy so broad it seemed to swallow the sky. Marc lifted his gaze, his breath hitching. He felt the weight of its centuries, as if the tree had watched generations rise and fall from this very spot.

Cecil ran a hand over its rough bark. "This great tree was here long before I became a vampire. Tonight, you will be made anew beneath it."

Marc heard footsteps. The crunch of leaves. He turned.

Sebastian approached. A rugged man walked beside him.

Marc studied the stranger's face. There was no fear in his expression, no resistance. Just quiet acceptance.

A lamb to the slaughter.

Marc's stomach knotted. He knew what was about to happen. He locked eyes with his father. Avlon grimaced as they exchanged nods.

Marc had expected a ritual. Some words to be spoken before he died. But before he could think further, he felt cold lips press against his throat.

His heart stammered.

Sharp fangs pierced his skin.

A shock of pain. A rush of heat.

His body froze—paralyzed.

The world around him blurred. Tombstones, trees, faces—everything distorted, swimming in the edges of his vision. He felt the pull of his blood, Cecil drinking deeply, drawing him into darkness.

Then, suddenly, he was drifting.

Floating between worlds.

Marc felt the first whisper of death creeping over him, numbing his fingers, his toes. His mind slipped, unraveling from the present, from the night, from the weight of his body. He was falling, dissolving, vanishing.

Then—something cold touched his lips.

A flood of ice.

It rushed through him like liquid silver, filling the hollow space death had left behind.

His breath stilled.

His body changed.

And when Marc opened his eyes, he was no longer in the cemetery.

He stood upon the lands of Bleddyn Manor.

Alone.

The others had disappeared—Cecil, his father, Larus, Sebastian. Everyone.

It was a dark, mist-laden night. Marc stepped through the iron gates of Bleddyn Manor, alone. The world around him was eerily still, untouched, as if frozen in time. The manor loomed ahead, its towering silhouette bathed in silver light.

The great doors stood ajar.

Marc hesitated, then pushed them open further and stepped inside.

A shrill scream pierced the silence.

Marc's breath caught. He spun toward the sound, his mind racing. He followed the wretched weeping through the dim corridors, out into the rear garden.

There, a woman knelt in the dewy grass, her gown torn, her body trembling. Wounds marred her arms and throat, but she seemed unaware of them, too consumed by grief to acknowledge her own pain.

Marc hurried to her side, stooping to comfort her. "What has happened?"

She did not answer. Her breath came in ragged sobs, her shoulders shaking violently. Then, slowly, she raised a trembling hand and pointed toward the forest.

Marc followed her gaze.

The mist swirled and parted, unveiling the dark expanse of trees. Beyond them, something moved—something massive.

A long, mournful howl split the night.

The woman's body jerked, her voice breaking in terror. "The wolves! The wolves are here!"

Marc's stomach twisted. The beast emerged from the shadows, its eyes gleaming like molten gold.

And clutched between its powerful jaws was something precious—something it had stolen from her.

Marc thrashed against the earth, his body writhing as the others stood around him in silent dread.

Larus had witnessed the making of vampires many times, yet this was different. Something was wrong.

Cecil knelt beside Marc, pressing a hand to his forehead. A deep furrow formed between his brows. "I cannot see his thoughts." His voice was steady, but his expression betrayed unease. "They are shielded from me." He turned to Avlon, his pale eyes questioning. "How can this be?"

Avlon's face darkened with uncertainty. "In all my years, I have never seen this."

"Nor have I," Micah murmured.

Sebastian crouched next to Marc and grasped his hand. His touch should have found warmth, the lingering heat of life still clinging to his skin. Instead, the boy was growing cold. "He will change," Sebastian said grimly.

Larus had already made several attempts to reach Marc's mind, to glimpse whatever storm raged behind his closed lids. But there was nothing—only darkness. And yet, Marc's eyes moved beneath them, trapped in visions unseen.

Then, suddenly, Marc's eyes flew open.

Larus stiffened. He had expected to see the raw, mindless hunger of the newly turned. Instead, he found terror.

Marc was weak, his complexion porcelain-pale, hauntingly beautiful, yet utterly bloodless. Larus cradled his face in his hands, but there was no warmth beneath his touch. Only silence. Only death.

A single blood tear traced down Marc's cheek as he uttered a name.

"Silas!"

Cecil leaned closer. "What is it, child?"

Marc's breath was shallow, his voice breaking. "You must get to Bleddyn Manor at once." He struggled to sit up, his panic infectious. "The lycans—" His wide, glassy eyes met Cecil's. "They have taken the boy. Jude is gone!"

The words struck like a blade.

Cecil's head snapped up. His entire posture shifted from concern to deadly purpose. "Larus, Micah, come with me." Then he turned sharply to the others. "Avlon, Sebastian—see that he feeds."

And with that, he was gone, vanishing into the night as they raced toward the church on the hill.

HANNAH WAS DEAD. SILAS HAD BURIED HER BY THE CAVE—THEIR HAVEN—marking her grave with a massive boulder he had dragged to its resting place. He had wept for days, until grief hollowed him out, leaving nothing behind. Now, there were no more tears. Only rage. Only loss. Jude was gone.

For a week, Silas had refused to hunt, refused to leave the cave. None dared approach him except Cecil and Larus, the only ones who truly understood him. He sat upon the boulder, staring into the dark, unseeing, while they remained nearby, silent. There was no need for words. Cecil saw every thought he wished to hide.

Vampires and lycans had tracked the beasts that took Jude, chasing their scent for miles. They followed it north, past the river, far from Hearne Manor. But Silas had no doubt. This was Percival's doing. His grandfather had orchestrated it all—the death of his only love, the theft of his son. Even vengeance had been stolen from him.

That night, when they lost the trail, Silas had knelt among the trees and screamed his grandfather's name, vowing to destroy him and all he held dear. But Cecil had reminded him—Percival Hearne cared for nothing but himself.

Now, Cecil's voice pulled Silas from his thoughts.

"This alliance between Percival and Nathan has thwarted us," he said. "They are cunning. But I do not believe they would harm the boy."

Silas did not meet his gaze. "A week has passed, Cecil. Jude could be leagues away by now—on a ship bound for some distant land."

"Calm yourself," Cecil urged. He stepped forward, Larus close behind. "Think on what Marc told you before Jude was even born. Think, Silas."

Larus crouched before him, dark eyes filled with sorrow. "Marc did not see Hannah's death," he said. "Only the boy's fate. He spoke of sorrow, yes, but never of Jude's death."

Cecil nodded. "Percival will not harm him."

A joyless smile flickered across Silas's lips. "No. He won't. He will win the boy's affection—poison him against me." His voice darkened with certainty. "By the time Jude is grown, my grandfather's lycans and mine will be at war. And my son… he will be lost to me."

Cecil's expression remained unreadable. "Then we will find him before that happens."

Larus placed a hand on Silas's shoulder. "We will fight by your side."

Silas gave a slow nod, but deep inside, he already knew the truth.

Jude—his little wolf—was gone.

50

NEW WAR (1834)

The moon was full, casting a silvery glow over the quiet grounds. Larus looked down the long, winding pathway lined by trees, his sharp eyes seeing far beyond the iron gates of the castle. His senses were far more acute than any human's, and as he sat upon the stone bench at the mouth of the castle's magnificent maze, he kept watch. Across from him, Silas sat in solitude on the other bench, his expression dark and full of years of pain. They had been silent since sunset, each lost in his own thoughts.

Larus wished there was more he could do for his nephew. Eleven years had passed since Jude's abduction, and in that time, no one had come closer to finding him. Silas had long stopped searching, each failed attempt wearing him down further until, finally, he had given up hope. Jude was lost. And with his son gone, Silas had become a shell of the strong, fierce lycan he once was. It was 1834 now, and Jude would be sixteen years old.

It's been so long, Silas, Larus thought, his eyes softening as they rested on his nephew. *But I know Marc's vision. I know Jude is still out there.*

"Silas, I know—" Larus started, but Silas cut him off with a wave of his hand.

"Uncle, please. I know what you mean to say."

Larus rose from his bench and crossed over to Silas, sitting down beside him. He placed a hand on his nephew's shoulder, firm and steady. "I remember the first time I met you, Silas. Just a babe in Max's arms." He smiled fondly at the memory. "Your mother had been so protective, barely letting me near you. But you didn't want me near you at all. I was a newborn then, yet when I looked into your eyes, I knew what you were."

Larus chuckled softly, remembering the stubbornness of his young nephew. "And you, Silas, knew what I was, too. A blood drinker. You could see it in me, even then. You are more like your mother than you realize, even in this."

Silas, his eyes shadowed with sorrow, looked away, lost in memories of his son, the one he thought he'd lost forever.

Larus's voice softened. "You cannot give up hope. I know Jude lives, and he will know you. He will remember you because you are his father."

"Jude will always be my son," Silas muttered, his voice barely above a whisper, "but in grandfather's care, he will hate me. I cannot expect him to know me... or love me. I fear it is Jude who will end me, Uncle. If the day ever comes when we stand as adversaries, I will not fight him."

Larus's face grew serious as he stared at Silas, holding his gaze. He saw the pain, the deep wound of a father torn away from his child. "That day will never come, Silas."

Larus rose to his feet and placed a hand gently on Silas's head, as though to comfort the child he still saw in him. "Come, Silas. The night is young, and we wear fine clothes with nowhere to go. Let us go out among the humans tonight."

Silas raised an eyebrow in surprise. "You jest, uncle."

"I do not. Come, let us get your good man, Gavin, and go out. I hear there is a ball at the governor's mansion. A night away from all this sorrow might do us good." Larus's tone lifted slightly, attempting to bring some levity to the heavy atmosphere.

Ashkan's horsewhip cracked in the air as the carriage rumbled along the path to the governor's mansion. Larus sat next to Silas, and across from them, Gavin sat beside Isabelle, looking quite the gentleman. Larus had insisted his sister stay behind, but Isabelle, ever willful, had refused.

Larus noticed a strange flicker in Isabelle's eyes as they lingered on Gavin, a glimmer of something that made him frown. His eyes darted back to Silas, his nephew's gaze fixed on the passing landscape. There was an unspoken understanding between them. We have lost so much, Larus thought, but not everything. There is still hope—Jude still lives.

Silas's hands clenched into fists, a silent vow simmering in his chest. He would never give up, no matter the years that passed, no matter how far Jude might be. He would find his son.

The governor's mansion gleamed under the full moon. Hundreds of guests filled the ballroom, their laughter and music drifting through the grand halls and into the night air. Larus led his companions through the clusters of dancers, his sharp eyes scanning the scene, seeking the perfect spot to observe the festivities. Isabelle, as usual, leaned against Gavin with playful seduction, coaxing the lycan to join her on the dance floor. Gavin, though clearly uncomfortable with the pomp and grandeur, could do little to refuse. Larus knew well that Gavin would do anything for Isabelle—he adored her, and it was evident in the way his eyes always followed her, as if drawn by some unspoken tether.

Gavin glanced nervously at Larus, seeking permission. "Dance with my dear aunt, Gavin," Silas chimed in, his voice light, though Larus could sense the sharp edge of sadness beneath it. Silas grinned as he nudged his uncle. "Uncle and I will simply stand here and watch this world sway around us."

Larus nodded, taking in the sight of his nephew, so much like his mother. "Did you see his face, uncle?" Silas asked, his tone amused.

Larus took a long moment before responding, his thoughts turning inward. He had seen it—Gavin's awkwardness, his hesitance, the way his gaze flickered between Isabelle and the dance floor. Larus had always been protective of his sister, and seeing her so easily command Gavin's attention stirred something in him. "I sure did," Larus answered, his tone measured.

"You do know they like each other," Silas continued with a smirk, drawing Larus from his thoughts.

Larus raised an eyebrow, then chuckled softly. "You're hardly the first to notice, Silas."

His nephew's expression grew more serious, and after a long pause, he asked, "Why haven't you found love, Uncle?"

Larus winced at the question. It was one he had asked himself many times over the years, and the answer was always the same. Love had never felt like something he could have. His life, marked by darkness and separation, had never allowed for it. He opened his mouth to answer but found no words to give.

Silas's gaze softened, and for a moment, the years between them seemed to vanish. "Seriously, Uncle... my years with Hannah were the best of my life." His voice broke slightly, and Larus could feel the deep ache of grief that still held Silas in its grip. But before he could speak, two strangers approached them, and Larus's instincts kicked in. He reached out, scanning their minds. They were harmless, but curious, both clearly intrigued by something.

"Hello," said the man. He was tall, handsome, and no older than twenty. Yet there was something odd about him—his face was smooth, but completely devoid of hair, not even a single eyebrow or lash. His eyes, however, were a striking hazel, bright and unnervingly intense. He gestured to the woman beside him, presenting her like a gift. "I'm Dominic," he said with a smile, showing off his perfect teeth. "And this is my sister, Deirdre."

Larus bowed slightly, keeping his smile in place as he observed the two. There was something about them that felt strange, even for humans. Deirdre, with her striking dark hair and full lips, examined them closely, her eyes moving over Larus and then Silas.

"Hello," she said, her voice melodic. "You must be brothers."

Larus exchanged a look with Silas, who gave him a slight, knowing smile. If only they knew the truth. Larus smiled back at them, polite but guarded, and gently lifted Deirdre's hand to kiss it. "A pleasure to meet you, Deirdre," he said, then shook hands with Dominic, who wore gloves. The brief silence between them was palpable, but Larus could feel the tension from Dominic, as though they had just stumbled upon something much bigger than they had expected.

"Uhm, I am Larus," he said, trying to ease the awkwardness. "And this is my younger brother, Silas."

Deirdre's eyes brightened with a mischievous glint. "I win!" she said, grinning at Dominic and elbowing him playfully. "I told you they weren't lovers."

Larus and Silas exchanged surprised glances, then turned back to Dominic, whose face flushed.

"Forgive us," Dominic said, his voice embarrassed. "Deirdre and I simply made a bet."

Before Larus could respond, Isabelle's laughter rang out as she dragged Gavin toward them. Larus swiftly made introductions to prevent any further awkwardness. "Ah, Isabelle!" he greeted warmly, pressing a kiss to his sister's cheek.

As he did so, he noticed a flicker of disappointment in Dominic's eyes, but he refrained from probing further into the human's thoughts. Larus had long ago learned to allow others their secrets. He smiled at Dominic but couldn't help the involuntary nature of it. "Meet my sister, Isabelle."

"And this is... uh, Gavin," he added, nodding toward the lycan. Gavin seemed unusually nervous, but Isabelle's expression was one of quiet amusement.

Deirdre, ever bold, moved closer to Silas, drawing him into conversation. Meanwhile, Isabelle, sensing an opportunity for some quiet time, leaned in toward Gavin, whispering something in his ear.

"Come, Gavin," Isabelle said, taking his arm. "I shall leave my brothers to the festivities."

Silas chuckled softly, his eyes glinting with a mischievous edge. "Good gracious, man!" he said. "You needn't ask to take our sister for a stroll."

Isabelle smiled as she guided Gavin away, and Silas soon followed, leaving Larus and Dominic standing awkwardly together in the shadowed corner of the ballroom. The silence between them was thick, but Larus couldn't shake the feeling that this encounter was far from over.

LARUS HAD DECIDED TO LEAVE THE CROWDED BALLROOM WITH DOMINIC FOR a stroll through the gardens. As they walked side by side, Larus was surprised to find himself enjoying the human's company. He had forgotten what it was like to spend extended time with someone so... mortal. The darkness of the night only deepened the contrast between them, yet Larus's vampiric sight allowed him to see every detail of Dominic's face, even the dilation of his pupils. The sound of Dominic's racing heart reached his ears as their shoulders brushed, sending a strange thrill through him.

Their conversation flowed easily, covering everything from the weather to more personal matters. Dominic seemed eager to share, but Larus was careful not to delve too deeply into his mind, instead relying on the casual exchange of words. He learned that Dominic and his sister came from one of the wealthiest families in the capital, but Larus never shared much about himself. When Dominic inquired about Larus's home, he hesitated—he had no choice but to mention the white castle of Dr. Micah. The lie lingered in the air between them, unspoken but understood.

"I'm glad you decided to attend at the last minute," Dominic said, his voice suddenly nervous. Larus kept his face impassive, doing everything he could to avoid reading Dominic's thoughts.

The two paused as Dominic admired a colourful plant several feet away, its vibrant colours glowing under the moonlight. Larus commented on its beauty, but before he could say more, Dominic moved closer. He hesitated for a heartbeat before pressing his lips to Larus's cheek.

Larus froze. Dominic must have felt the chill of his skin, yet he remained still, caught in the moment. "Forgive me," Dominic stammered, pulling back. "I should not have—"

But before Dominic could finish, something inside Larus stirred. It was as primal and insistent as the hunger he'd felt the night Micah turned him into a vampire. His eyes flickered down to Dominic's neck, where the pulse of blood throbbed just beneath the surface, beckoning him.

Larus's hand shot out, pulling Dominic closer, and before he could stop himself, his lips found Dominic's. The human didn't recoil. Instead, to Larus's surprise, he deepened the kiss, meeting him with a surprising eagerness. Heat and warmth flooded through Larus, and the cold distance between them seemed to vanish. As they kissed, he felt an intoxicating rush—a wave of desire, of life, flowing through Dominic's veins. It was overwhelming. He could feel himself drowning in it, addicted to the vitality, to the warmth that was so foreign to him.

Larus's grip tightened, and in that moment, he realized that he might never want to let go.

LARUS ENTERED THE BALLROOM WITH DOMINIC, HIS EYES QUICKLY SCANNING the crowd. He was pleased to see Silas dancing with Deidre, their steps light amidst the throng of humans. Most of all, he was glad to see the smile on Silas's face. It had been years since his nephew had shown such happiness. Moments later, Gavin and Isabelle passed by, both smiling, their joy infectious. But as they swayed together on the dance floor, Larus's smile faded.

Dominic must have noticed the shift, for he drew near, his presence grounding Larus. Together, they watched Isabelle and Gavin dance. "He loves her," Dominic said softly. "...And she loves him."

Larus thought of peering into Gavin's mind, but Dominic's touch interrupted him—a simple brush of fingers that sent a ripple of warmth through him. Their gloves were off, and the sensation felt more intimate than it should have. "You're as protective of your sister as I am of Deidre," Dominic continued, his voice thoughtful. "Let them find their way... they are stronger than we think."

Larus's gaze remained fixed on Isabelle and Gavin. "I lost Isabelle once," he said, his voice low. "I lost everyone I loved. When Isabelle came back to me, I swore I would never lose her again." His eyes narrowed as he fixed on Gavin. "I fear he will harm her."

"That is for your sister to decide," Dominic replied, his tone gentle but firm. "Look how he holds her... as though she is a precious gem he will cherish forever. See how she invites his touch?"

Larus watched, his doubt slowly receding. He could see it, too. Isabelle's gaze, warm and trusting, as she looked at Gavin. He smiled, though it was tinged with uncertainty.

"It is a privilege, Larus," Dominic added, his voice soft with sincerity. "To share mutual love."

Larus turned away, unease creeping back into his chest. "You seem to know much of love," he replied, their shared glance lingering between them. He remembered the kiss, and for a fleeting moment, wondered if Dominic had been referring to more than just Isabelle and Gavin.

They both turned their attention back to the dance floor. But just as Larus was about to relax, a sudden, unsettling sensation washed over him. He tensed, every instinct on alert. Isabelle, Gavin, and Silas froze mid-step, their bodies stilled in unnatural synchrony. A strange, familiar presence lingered in the air—Larus was certain that he and Isabelle were not the only vampires at the governor's ball, and Gavin and Silas were not the only lycans.

He didn't need to glance at Dominic to know he'd felt it, too. Without a word, Larus took Dominic's arm and guided him into the shadows. His voice was sharp with urgency. "We are not alone."

Deidre, who had sensed the shift, drew closer, her brow furrowed with concern. "Is something wrong?"

Before Larus could answer, the voice of his nephew cut through the tension. Silas stepped from behind a towering pillar, his eyes burning with a fury Larus had rarely seen. Percival Hearne. Larus's stomach clenched at the sight of the man.

Deidre followed Silas's gaze. "Silas, do you know that man?" she asked, but got no reply.

Larus's gaze remained locked on Percival as the lycan boldly made his way toward the high table, his presence an undeniable force in the room. He had not changed.

Silas's rage simmered beneath the surface, and Larus knew they couldn't afford to confront Percival—not in front of so many humans. "We must leave now," Larus insisted, his voice low but insistent. "We cannot stay here."

"He took my son!" Silas's words were filled with grief and fury, but Larus placed a hand on his shoulder, grounding him.

"But we mustn't risk a confrontation, Silas," Larus said, his voice firm. He looked to Gavin for support.

"He speaks true, my lord," Gavin agreed.

But just as they were about to make their exit, another figure moved toward the high table. Larus gasped as he recognized the young man—Jude.

It had been eleven years since Silas had seen his son. The boy was tall, handsome, with black hair and eyes like silver moons. Isabelle and Gavin watched in awe as Jude walked through the crowd, clearly unaware of the emotions his presence stirred in Silas.

Larus turned to Silas, seeing the tears that welled in his eyes. He could feel his nephew's grief as though it were his own, but Silas made no move to approach the boy. Jude sat next to Nathan, the ancient vampire who stood like a shadow, his eyes ever watchful. The bond between the two was unmistakable—Jude leaned toward Nathan with a look of deep affection, as though they shared a father-son connection.

Larus's voice was low, heavy with the weight of their situation. "Come, Silas. We cannot stay here any longer. We must return to White Castle. Cecil will know what to do."

51

CONCERNING JUDE

It was just after midnight when Percival's eyes locked onto Nathan as he strode through the doors of the council hall. The lycan felt a fool as he approached Nathan and his council of vampires, for the leader of this coven sat upon a throne-like chair of mahogany and velvet, his presence exuding the arrogance of a king. But Percival would not treat him as such.

Standing before Nathan and the others, Percival kept his gaze fixed on the vampire. Nathan was ageless, yet Percival could tell he must have been turned at around forty or fifty. His dark hair, streaked with grey, framed a face of sternness, and his dark eyes were as penetrating as ever. Though Nathan had a slender frame, he was no weakling. Fearlessness radiated from him, as strong as the blood running through his ancient veins.

Nathan glared at Percival and his lycans. "Tell us, Percival, why have you come to my coven unannounced and uninvited?"

"I come to discuss the matter of my grandson," Percival answered, his voice rough with frustration. "We agreed, you and I, that Jude would remain here for a few months. Eleven years have passed!"

His gaze swept over the council, and he noticed one vampire was missing. "I see your dark queen, Athena?" Percival's eyes flickered with suspicion. "But where is the pale-skinned vampire, Avlon?"

Percival had struck a nerve; Nathan's expression darkened.

"Avlon is no longer part of this coven," Nathan's voice was clipped, his mouth curling with anger. "Avlon shall be dealt with in due time for his betrayal."

Athena's eyes narrowed, her lips twisted in disdain. "We needn't discuss the troubles of our house with you."

Nathan leaned forward, his voice dropping to a deadly calm. "He betrayed us to join Cecil and the wolves."

Percival sneered. "They... we are lycans." The contempt in his voice was undeniable as he glared at Nathan, disgusted by the way the vampire spat the word "wolves."

Nathan dismissed him with a flick of his hand, turning his head slightly as though Percival were beneath him. "You have no claim to the boy," Nathan said coolly. "Jude will remain here with me... for his protection."

Percival felt his insides clench. Protection? Jude was in far more danger with the likes of Nathan. He had made a grave mistake in handing Silas's son over to this bloodthirsty creature. To Nathan, Jude was nothing more than a pawn.

"Protection from whom?" Percival's voice hardened, but Nathan didn't flinch. His dark eyes never blinked.

"Silas would never harm his son," Percival said, his voice rising with a rare desperation.

"Yet," Athena interrupted, her voice dripping with scorn, "you would." Her eyes scanned him as though he were nothing but an inconvenience. "Jude fears he will suffer the same fate you dealt his father. This has always been his home."

Percival's rage boiled within him. He could feel the animal urge to shift, to tear Athena to pieces, but he knew better than to underestimate Nathan. Nearly forty lycans awaited his command outside, hidden in the forest, but attacking here would be suicide.

"I demand to speak with my grandson now!" Percival growled.

"Careful, wolf!" Nathan's voice was a low hiss, and his long nails dug into the varnished mahogany of his chair. "Are we not friends? You overstep, Percival. Know your place."

Percival felt the surge of transformation rise within him, his body aching to shift. A deep growl rumbled from his chest as his companions also bared their fangs.

"Stop this!" a voice rang out from behind him. Percival turned, and his heart twisted as Jude crossed the threshold into the council hall.

"Grandfather... you cannot do this," the boy said, his voice laced with a mixture of defiance and sorrow.

Jude had grown. At sixteen, he was already tall and well-built, the spitting image of his father. Percival felt a sting of emotion as he looked at him—tears welled in his eyes, but he blinked them away.

"Jude..." His voice faltered, barely a whisper. "Are you alright? You haven't visited."

"I am well, Grandfather," Jude answered, his silver eyes shifting past Percival toward the council. "I have everything I need here."

Percival's heart sank. The boy still hadn't shifted. Jude didn't know the truth of his heritage—how different he was from the blood drinkers. Percival could see it now: the boy had every reason to resent him. The years of silence, of isolation, were written in Jude's eyes.

"You need to be with your own kind, Jude," Percival pleaded, his voice raw with emotion. "There are things you need to understand. Important things."

"No, Grandfather!" Jude's eyes flared with anger, silver burning with fury. "You can teach me nothing—not after what you took from me!"

Percival felt the weight of his past actions crash over him. Hanah's death—his own hand that had killed the boy's mother—had destroyed any chance of healing the wound between them. Jude's hatred was now something he could never undo.

Percival turned his gaze toward Nathan, knowing the vampire had fed Jude the details of his abduction. He felt a dark, cold realization settle in his chest. This was a battle he had already lost.

"This is not over, Nathan!" Percival spat as he turned away, his voice laced with venom. Without another word, he strode toward the door, his lycans following in tow. The conversation was finished. But the battle—this war—was far from over.

Everyone had left the council hall, and Jude stood alone before Nathan. The vampire remained seated upon his chair, graceful and imposing, as though he were still before an audience of thousands. His demeanour had not shifted since Jude's grandfather and the council members departed. Jude had been made Nathan's ward against his will, yet there was a strange bond forming between them. Nathan had been good to him. He had cared for him. But Jude could feel the change within him, something that was slipping past his control.

Jude's senses were growing sharper with each passing day—his sense of smell was the most notable change. He could no longer bear the presence of vampires for long, their scent and coldness suffocating to him. But the strangest realization lingered: even though he hadn't touched his grandfather, he found himself drawn to his scent. Grandfather Hearne's scent reminded him of home, of the warmth and comfort he had lost. Yet, there was more to it.

Jude's body was becoming something else. The wolf inside him was stirring, and it was beginning to overpower him. He could feel it in his bones, gnawing at his mind. But the one thing that haunted him most was the vague, fragmented memory of his father, Silas. Jude longed to know him, to see him again, to understand the man who had left him behind. But Jude knew, deep down, that his desire to find Silas would only bring chaos to his already fractured world.

He was shaken from his thoughts by Nathan's voice—quiet, but sharp. "You are torn," Nathan said. His gaze never wavered from Jude. "You waste hours thinking of a father who has refused to do the right thing... to come to me and beg my forgiveness."

Jude's eyes narrowed as he faced Nathan. "Are you not the one who should beg his forgiveness?" Jude's words were steady, but his heart hammered in his chest. "You've told me about what Grandfather has done, but I know you played your part in my abduction... in my mother's death."

Nathan's eyes flashed with a dangerous glint, his composure cracking for a moment.

"Percival was a fool to think he could use you as leverage to regain control over Silas," Nathan said, his voice dripping with disdain. "I merely went along with his plan. When it failed... when I saw you, dear boy, I made a decision. I decided to take you in... to raise you as my own son." Nathan's eyes softened as his pale hands rose, staring at them as though seeking redemption. "I have never raised a finger against you, Jude," he whispered, his voice low and mournful. "I have only loved you... as a father loves a son."

Jude's gaze hardened as he stepped closer, his voice laced with a quiet resolve. "I know the ways of vampires, Nathan, but I am no vampire." His chest tightened with the weight of the truth he was about to say. "Nathan, I am changing... I need to be with my kind when I transform."

The words hung heavy between them, an unspoken understanding passing between them despite their differences. Nathan did not respond immediately, his eyes shadowed by something deeper, something unreadable.

LATER, JUDE LAY IN HIS BED, UNABLE TO QUIET THE STORM OF THOUGHTS raging within him. Nathan had been kind, and in many ways, he had been the father Jude never had—but at what cost? Jude felt trapped in a gilded cage, watched over by Nathan and his son, Lucas, both of whom seemed to see him as a delicate, precious thing.

Through the darkened window, Jude gazed at the moon, its silver light casting a cold glow upon his face. He felt an odd connection to it, as though it too was in a state of constant change. The longing inside him for his true nature, for the transformation he could feel stirring deep within him, was unbearable. But more than that, he looked forward to the coming dawn—not for the light, but for the quiet escape it promised.

52

BEING A HUMAN

Deidre sat alone inside the carriage sent by Silas, trying to make sense of the strange turn her life had taken. She could hardly understand why he had not come himself; the coachman was aloof, and the late-night journey had unsettled her. Since the first night they met, Silas had always called on her at home, taking her out to dine and showing her kindness. Now, she was being whisked away to his family estate, a place she had heard so much about—Bleddyn Manor. Silas had always loved the night, rarely visiting during the day. And now, after weeks of waiting, she was finally going to meet his family. But something nagged at her. She had many questions, and only Silas could answer them.

When Silas met her in the courtyard, he wasted no time, sweeping her into his arms as she stepped from the carriage. He motioned toward the massive structure behind him with pride. "Welcome to Bleddyn Manor."

Deidre squeezed his hand, her voice trembling slightly. "I thought you would come for me."

Silas must have sensed the unease in her eyes, likely because of the strange coachman. "You need not worry about my men," he reassured her. "They would give their lives to protect what is precious to me."

He led her up the stone steps, and as they entered the grand vestibule, they were greeted by a woman of striking beauty. Silas kissed her cheek warmly. "Mother, this is Deidre."

Deidre's breath caught as she looked at the woman. She was elegant and youthful, and Deidre gasped in surprise. This woman looked far too young to be Silas's mother—she could easily pass for his sister. For a brief moment, mother and son exchanged a knowing glance, as though they shared a secret Deidre wasn't privy to.

"Welcome to Bleddyn Manor," the woman said, her voice smooth and welcoming. "I am Max." She took her time kissing Deidre's cheeks, and Deidre flushed with embarrassment, unsure how to react.

"It's short for Maxine," Silas added with a playful smile in his silver-grey eyes. "Mother hated her full name so much, she insisted no one use it —except for me, of course."

Max's smile was faint but affectionate. "Come, child," she said, her tone kind but with an undercurrent of something unspoken. "My husband is anxious to meet you."

Bartholomew Hearne was as handsome and youthful as Silas but far more reserved. He greeted Deidre with a warm smile, more genuine than his wife's. "I hope the journey was a pleasant one," he said kindly.

As they moved through the manor toward the dining hall, Deidre met Silas's aunt, Catherine, and her husband, Morgan. Catherine was beautiful, but there was an undeniable sadness about her—something empty in her eyes, in her very presence. Morgan, too, seemed weighed down by sorrow, and Deidre couldn't help but feel that her presence at their table was somehow an unwelcome intrusion.

Later, after dinner, Deidre walked with Silas through the moonlit gardens. "It feels strange," she said, wrapping her shawl tighter around her, "that we walk the gardens at night. Couldn't I have come during the day?"

Silas pulled her closer to him, his touch reassuring. "There will be plenty of days for that. Besides, we can walk the gardens again tomorrow."

"And your brother, Larus—he'll be here then?" Deidre asked. Dominic had mentioned Larus would join them the following day.

"Larus will be joining us for supper," Silas confirmed.

Deidre paused, noticing something in the air between them. "Your brother looks more like your mother than you do," she remarked.

At that, Silas stopped near a small tree, his expression changing. The moonlight illuminated his face, and Deidre saw the hesitation in his eyes. "Is something wrong, Silas?"

He grimaced, his expression conflicted. "Deidre, I've been a fool for not being honest with you." Deidre's brow furrowed, puzzled. Before she could speak, he placed a finger gently over her lips, silencing her. "I never thought... never expected I could feel this way again. But I love you, Deidre."

Deidre's heart fluttered, but the tension still lingered. Silas took a slow breath, his voice faltering. "There is something you must know. Larus is not my brother. He's my uncle."

Deidre turned her face away in disbelief. "It makes no sense why you would hide such things from me. You send a stranger in a carriage to bring me here, your mother looks young enough to be your sister—am I to learn she's not your mother at all?"

Silas let out a soft laugh, trying to ease the tension. "No, my love, she is my mother."

"And what of your aunt and her husband?" Deidre pressed. "Why do they seem so sad? Why do they look at me as if I've done something wrong?"

Silas stepped closer and kissed her gently on the lips. "Deidre, you cannot use what I tell you now to judge me. I pray you will not. But I must tell you the truth."

He paused for several long moments, his eyes distant. "I was married once. I had hoped to spend my life with Hannah. But she died. Hannah was the daughter of my aunt, Catherine. After she passed, nothing was ever the same for them."

Deidre's heart clenched. "And that boy at the governor's ball?" she asked quietly.

Silas's voice was barely audible. "My son."

Deidre's eyes widened in shock. "Your son?"

"Yes," Silas sighed deeply. "We had a good life, Hannah and I, before everything changed."

"At the ball... you said someone took your son."

"My grandfather," Silas replied, his voice trembling with emotion. "You saw him. You saw my son." His words were thick with sorrow. Deidre reached for his hand, but he smiled through the pain.

"And his name is Jude," Silas whispered, as if the name was both a blessing and a burden.

"But Silas, why can't you take your son from your grandfather? And why would you marry your cousin?"

Silas's expression became more solemn. "It's complicated," he said softly. "But I will tell you everything. One day."

They resumed their walk, the night pressing in around them, and Deidre could hardly believe that someone so young could have lived such a tumultuous life. Silas seemed far too young to be a father, especially to a boy of sixteen. Yet there were many mysteries in his world—things Deidre was only beginning to understand—and she feared that the more she learned, the more unsettled she would become.

THE CARRIAGE RATTLED ALONG THE NARROW ROAD TOWARD BLEDDYN Manor, its wheels scraping against the uneven stones. As the cool evening air swept in through the small cracks of the window, Dominic felt a sudden chill down his spine when Larus reached for his hand. It was midsummer, just after sunset, but Dominic found himself once again perplexed by Larus's strange habits. They had never met during the day, never shared the warmth of the sun together. It wasn't just the secrecy of their encounters that troubled Dominic—it was Larus's coldness, an unnerving sensation that had haunted him since their first meeting. But he dared not speak of it.

Dominic had never entered White Castle, though he had seen it from a distance, always stopping short at the iron gates. Over the weeks, he had come to care for Larus in ways he could neither explain nor control, but he had grown weary of their clandestine meetings, always shrouded in darkness. They were often spent in the privacy of Larus's carriage, while Ashkan, the silent coachman, walked somewhere in the shadows.

One night, when Deidre and their parents were away on a weekend trip, Larus had arrived at Dominic's doorstep. It was strange to see him standing there, waiting at the threshold, because he would never cross it until invited. It was still early in the evening when Dominic welcomed him inside, hoping to share a peaceful night. But Larus had risen long before dawn, and by the time Dominic awoke, he had already left in a hurry, without explanation.

Now, as they sat together in the carriage, the silence between them felt heavy. Larus squeezed Dominic's hand gently, sensing his unease. "Come back to me," he whispered softly, his voice tinged with concern. "Something troubles you."

If only Larus knew the weight of the thoughts that weighed on Dominic's mind. He stared out of the carriage window, unable to focus on the beauty of the land rushing past them. "I tire of these late-night outings, Larus!" Dominic burst out, his voice sharp with frustration. "Father has started to complain about my late arrivals at his firm. He's always depended on me. And now here we are, off to this other place again —Bleddyn Manor, your other home."

He looked into Larus's eyes, but all he saw was hurt. The sting of his words was undeniable, and yet Dominic could not stop himself. "All my life, I've longed to meet someone like you, someone I could care for... but loving you brings more pain than joy." He tightened his grip on Larus's hand, feeling his pulse quicken as Larus closed his eyes and tilted his head back.

"Larus, I'm sorry," he whispered. "But I can only be honest with you. I must tell you how I feel."

Larus's eyes opened slowly, and Dominic saw the sorrow that lingered there. His flawless skin seemed to glow faintly in the dim light of the carriage, as if there was something otherworldly about him. Larus tapped the roof of the carriage, calling out to the coachman. "Ashkan, stop!"

The carriage came to a halt with a jolt, and Larus stepped out into the dark, his figure barely visible against the night. He extended his hand toward Dominic, his movements calm, almost deliberate.

"We are at the edge of the forest," Larus said, his voice low and serious. "Come, Dominic. It is time you hear my truth. I must be honest with you as well."

Dominic hesitated, his heart pounding in his chest. The last thing he expected was to be led into the forest in the dead of night. The trees loomed ahead, casting long, eerie shadows. "Larus, why have we stopped?" Dominic asked, his voice strained with uncertainty.

Ashkan's steady presence at the side of the carriage was a small comfort, but his eyes betrayed no emotion as he approached. "Wait here," Larus instructed, then walked toward the trees.

Dominic glanced back at Ashkan, who nodded and motioned toward the forest with a single, wordless gesture. Dominic's feet felt heavy as he followed Larus, each step feeling more reluctant than the last. His heart raced with fear as the dark woods seemed to close in around them.

Why had Larus brought him here? What truth was he about to reveal? And why did it have to be in such a desolate place?

Dominic walked alongside Larus, Ashkan following close behind. The revelation still sat heavy in his chest, as inescapable as the night air pressing in around them. He had spent the carriage ride turning the truth over in his mind, testing it, trying to understand how his world had shifted so completely in a single night.

As they neared Bleddyn Manor, Dominic spotted Deidre descending the steps, her gown trailing behind her as she hurried toward him. Before he could brace himself, she rushed into his arms. He knew, without words, that she needed him—perhaps as much as he needed her.

They held each other for some time, longer than usual, before finally parting. As Dominic released her, his gaze flickered to Larus, catching the brief, silent nod exchanged between uncle and nephew. He had always sensed something different about Silas, yet Larus had assured him his nephew was no vampire. And yet, in this moment, the unspoken understanding between them unsettled Dominic.

Deidre's warm hand gripped his own, a stark contrast to the coolness he had grown accustomed to with Larus. As they ascended the stone steps, she tilted her head up to him, eyes searching.

"What troubles you, brother?"

Dominic forced a small, tired smile. "Long journey."

Deidre wasn't fooled. She squeezed his hand, her voice dropping to a whisper. "Brother, I am so happy you have come... I have been so worried. Come to my rooms as soon as you can—there is much I must tell you."

They were far enough from Larus and Silas that no ordinary ears could have overheard. But there was nothing ordinary about Larus. Dominic knew this now. He was a vampire—one who had tasted the horrible sting of death and now lived beyond it.

"There is no need, Deidre," Larus said smoothly, his voice carrying across the courtyard. "We will speak in Bleddyn Hall."

Dominic turned to look at him, at Silas, at Ashkan standing by the carriage. Larus had told him much about his past, yet Dominic still struggled to grasp the full weight of it. He had never imagined such things could be real. How would Deidre ever embrace the horror of what Larus was? And worse—how could she forgive Dominic for loving him still?

Inside Bleddyn Hall, the glow of candlelight flickered across the grand space. Moments later, the old vampire woman, Tilley, arrived with refreshments.

Dominic watched in awe as she entered, carrying a heavy tray as if it weighed nothing at all. She moved with a quiet grace, beaming with pride, her white hair framing a face untouched by time. Her pale skin was pristine, eerily smooth, free of even the faintest wrinkle.

Larus had spoken of her before, of Tilley and of his sister, Isabelle—also a vampire. But Isabelle lived at White Castle, among others of their kind.

Dominic sank onto the beautiful couch across from Deidre and Silas, acutely aware of Larus beside him. Despite everything, despite what he now knew, the love he felt had not changed.

He recalled the woods, the way Larus had pleaded with him not to hate him.

How could I ever?

Even now, Dominic could sense that Larus needed him. That beyond all his power, all his unnatural grace, there was still a vulnerability—a loneliness that Dominic could not ignore.

If Dominic could offer Larus anything, he knew it would not be strength, nor power, nor immortality.

It would be the one thing Larus no longer had.

The gift of being human.

Once again, with Larus and her brother present, Silas had begged her to forgive him.

He begged her to still love him, even after what she was about to see.

They were alone in Bleddyn Hall. The heavy doors were closed. Tilley had left shortly after serving refreshments, and the rest of Silas's family was elsewhere in the manor. The moon hung pale and distant beyond the window, casting cold light upon them.

Deidre barely noticed Larus drawing close to Dominic, their fingers entwining.

Because Silas was unbuttoning his coat.

Then his shirt.

Her breath caught as she saw him undressing, her fingers clenching around the sparkling necklace at her throat. "Silas!" She stumbled backward, averting her gaze. The bodice of her gown felt suddenly too tight, her heartbeat loud in her ears. "Why are you doing this?"

"I show you who I am, Deidre... what I truly am."

He stood naked before them.

"Look at me, Deidre... if you love me, please do not look away. Do not hate me."

She stole a glance at Dominic, who sat frozen beside her, his shock mirroring her own. But Larus—Larus was calm. Too calm.

He knew.

Deidre's skin prickled, though she could not say whether it was fear or something else. Silas had held her hand on their walks. He had kissed her, whispered to her, spoken of their future together. She had never seen him like this. The firelight caught the fine contours of his body, and an unfamiliar heat twisted in her stomach.

But then—

Silas gasped.

His fingers clawed at the air as though grasping for something unseen. His body buckled, spine arching unnaturally. A strangled cry tore from his throat.

And then, before her very eyes, he changed.

His skin darkened, his veins rising like twisted roots beneath the surface. His fingers contorted, bending in ways the human hand never should. His face stretched, bones cracking, reshaping, reforming into something monstrous.

Deidre screamed.

She felt Larus's cold grasp on her arm, the desperate warmth of Dominic's hands on the other. They were trying to hold her, trying to keep her still, but she writhed in their grip, struggling against the horror unfolding before her.

Then Dominic's hands slipped away as he, too, shouted in terror.

The thing before them was no longer Silas.

Deidre could hear Larus pleading with her, his voice firm yet imploring. "Remain calm. Deidre, look at me—"

She could not.

She could not look away from the nightmare standing before her.

"Silas?"

It was the only thing she could say before the world tilted—before the room blurred, the darkness rising to claim her.

And then she collapsed.

53

ALLEGIANCE

Jude waited for the sun to climb high before putting his plan into action. As long as daylight ruled the sky, no vampire could chase him. They relied on human watchers, but Jude knew their habits too well. Vampires never truly rested—they did not tire, did not sleep—but they shuttered their windows against the day. That was all the opportunity he needed.

Nathan had taught him much over the years, especially how to shield his mind. Jude had made a point of learning which vampires could read thoughts, but he was no fool—blood drinkers were masters of deception. He had spent months preparing, watching, waiting for the perfect moment.

After lunch, while the household basked in their midday drowsiness, Jude walked the garden paths, as he often did, moving without suspicion. Then, with one final glance toward the house, he climbed the high fence at the western edge of the estate and dropped into the ravine beyond. He ran without looking back.

Branches tore at his clothes as he pushed deeper into the wilderness, avoiding open roads. He knew better than to slow down. Vampires were swift, and even with hours of daylight left, there would be no second chances if they found him. He had to keep moving.

Jude did not grow weary. He did not stop.

The first place Nathan would search was his grandfather's manor, so that was not an option. He would need to find shelter before sunset—somewhere they wouldn't expect.

For now, all he could do was run.

IT HAD BEEN NEARLY A FORTNIGHT SINCE DOMINIC AND DEIDRE HAD LEARNED the truth of lycans and vampires. Though Larus had expected Dominic to shun him, the revelation had only drawn them closer. Deidre, however, had wept for days and refused to see Silas; only Dominic could console her, especially after discovering Larus was a vampire.

Larus and Dominic departed White Castle just after sunset, the long journey ahead made easier by the comfort of solitude. Seated together in the carriage, Larus held Dominic's hand, knowing without words that they were of the same mind. Dominic had no desire to become a vampire—he had chosen to grow old and die a human death—and Larus had accepted that. He loved Dominic because he was human.

"Your sister will be pleased to see you tonight," Larus said.

"When will she visit White Castle?"

"If she wishes, she can return with us tomorrow. Tonight, we stay with the wolves."

Dominic smirked and gave Larus a playful punch to the shoulder. "That vampire, Sebastian... he is strange."

Larus chuckled. "Sebastian does things his way. But he is good, once you know him." He draped an arm over Dominic's shoulder and kissed his cheek. "He is also troublesome and mischievous. You must be wary—he will invade your mind without permission."

Dominic shook his head. "I like your sister, Isabelle. And the vampire Monique—she is beautiful."

"Marc says you are good for me."

Dominic smirked, as if searching his memory. "Ah, the oracle. I find him pleasant, as is Nicolas." His gaze drifted out the window, thoughtful. "There are so many of you... so many vampires at White Castle."

"It is our home," Larus said simply. "Our refuge."

Silence settled between them, and Larus, still holding Dominic close, closed his eyes and listened to the steady rhythm of his lover's heartbeat, the deep, even breaths of a living man. Outside, he heard the occasional lash of Ashkan's horsewhip and the pounding of hooves against the road. But then—something else. A faint sound in the distance.

Larus's eyes snapped open. He sniffed the night breeze, listening. His body tensed, and Dominic, sensing the change, leaned forward. "What is it, Larus?"

Larus frowned. "Someone is running... in the woods ahead of us."

Dominic's brows lifted. "How can you know that?"

"I am a vampire," Larus murmured. "Our senses are sharper than yours. And this scent... it is a lycan."

Dominic frowned. "A wolf?"

"Indeed." Larus raised a finger to his lips. "Shhh... it cannot be." His expression darkened. "I know that scent."

A moment later, a figure darted across the road ahead of them.

"Jude."

Larus rapped his knuckles against the carriage roof. "Ashkan, stop!"

The carriage skidded to a halt. Before Dominic could speak, Larus was already outside. "Whatever happens, do not leave the carriage," he warned. "Ashkan, make sure no harm comes to him!"

Then he was gone, running into the woods.

He knew where Jude was headed—Bleddyn Manor, only a few miles away. The boy ran fast, fear pressing him forward, but Larus was faster. He reached for Jude's mind and felt the sharp bite of terror. The boy was strong, but his heart raced, his breath came in ragged gasps, and Larus could smell the sweat clinging to his skin.

"Jude," Larus called, his voice low but firm. "I am not your enemy. I am family... your uncle, Larus. Trust me. Remember me."

He felt the hesitation in Jude's mind. Doubt.

"I go to your father tonight, Jude. Let me take you to Silas."

Jude's pace faltered. He glanced over his shoulder, searching Larus's face. His expression changed—recognition. He stumbled to a halt, bent at the waist, gasping for air.

"You... you brought me to the old church," Jude panted. "When I was a boy."

Larus smiled. "Your father wanted to restore it. But he never let you go inside. So, I took you there when he was away."

Jude managed a breathless, weary smile. "You... you look the same."

"I am a vampire," Larus said.

Jude swayed on his feet, and Larus's smile faded. "You look a mess," he said gently. "You cannot see your father like this." He placed a hand on the boy's shoulder. "Come. I know a place where you can clean up before we go to Bleddyn Manor."

They exited the woods. Ashkan had followed on the road, the carriage waiting. Larus gestured toward the open door, but as Jude stepped forward, he staggered, clutching his stomach with a sharp groan.

Dominic leaned out the window. "What's happening?"

Larus's eyes widened in horror.

"No, no, no... he's turning."

His gaze flicked to the full moon, luminous against the black sky. A perfect night for a young lycan's first transformation.

The horses snorted and stomped nervously. The air grew thick with tension. Dominic shrank back, his face pale, and Larus felt a rare wave of helplessness. He knew little about aiding a young lycan's first shift. He had no idea what to do.

Jude let out a strangled cry, falling to his hands and knees. His skin darkened to a shade of red, his black hair thickening into a coarse mane. The seams of his clothing split as his body expanded, muscles stretching, reshaping. Moments later, a towering lycan stood before them, its red fur rippling in the moonlight.

It threw its head back and howled.

Dominic gasped. The horses bucked in terror.

Larus stepped forward carefully, hands open, his voice calm but commanding. "Jude. You know who I am. You will not harm me."

The lycan snarled and slashed at him with claws like blackened knives. Larus ducked, twisting away. The boy was disoriented, overwhelmed by his own power.

Larus moved swiftly, circling behind him. Then, with all his strength, he sprang forward, locking his arms around the beast's massive frame. They crashed to the ground, a tangled blur of limbs and fur.

Dominic cried out. Ashkan drew his blade, ready to intervene.

But Larus held fast, pressing his lips to Jude's furry ear. His voice was soft, steady.

"Remember your mother, Hannah. Remember Silas. The gardens of Bleddyn Manor. The warmth of the sun in the courtyard." His voice became a whisper. "You are in control, Jude. Only you can command the wolf. Send him away. Come back to me."

The lycan's snarls wavered, shifting into low, confused moans.

Then, before their eyes, the transformation reversed.

Fur receded. Claws retracted. Bones shrank and reshaped. And when it was over, Jude lay trembling in the dirt, his body slick with sweat, his breath ragged.

Larus removed his cloak and draped it over the boy's bare shoulders.

Jude shuddered, his face buried against Larus's chest. Then, with a broken sob, he whispered, "I was afraid."

Larus held him close. "You are not alone."

He lifted his nephew to his feet, wiping the tears from his face.

"Come, Jude," he murmured. "Let's take you home."

JUDE SAT INSIDE THE CHURCH WITHOUT SAYING A WORD TO THE STRANGE human. He did not know the man's name, but he knew he was a trusted friend of his uncle's. Larus had left them alone, yet Jude could not imagine where one would find clothing in this remote area of the Bleddyn lands.

Jude had not seen his family's lands for eleven years, and his return calmed him. He gazed about the massive church, amazed by the restorations. Rows of wooden pews stretched before him, and candlelight flickered across the stone walls and high ceilings. Yet, despite its beauty, the place felt abandoned. Did anyone even worship here?

The man beside him looked around with quiet awe, his smooth, sharp features illuminated by the warm glow. Jude pulled his uncle's cloak tighter around his naked body, uneasy. This human had seen what he was, yet he remained—without fear.

Jude's gaze drifted over Dominic's face. He had no eyebrows, no lashes, and yet... there was something strangely striking about him. "You... you have no eyebrows."

The words escaped before he could stop them, and Jude winced at his own thoughtlessness. "I—I'm sorry, I didn't mean—"

Dominic only smiled. "That's the human side of you." He extended a hand. "I'm Dominic. And you—I feel as if I've known you all my life."

Jude hesitated, then took his hand. He found Dominic's bright smile oddly reassuring.

"After my grandfather took me away, I was alone... all those years." Jude looked away, his voice quieter now. "I was only five... living among a coven of vampires."

"There were no other children?"

Jude shook his head. "Never once." He met Dominic's gaze and saw shock mingled with sympathy. Feeling a sudden pang of sorrow, he pushed the memories of Nathan as far back in his mind as he could. "And you? How long have you lived among vampires and wolves?"

"Lycans, you mean?" Dominic grinned, and Jude felt himself relax a little. "Larus has been keeping me well-versed in the ways of your strange world. But to answer your question, I met Larus the night you attended the governor's ball with your grandfather... and that other man I now know is a vampire."

"Nathan."

"I saw you that night." Dominic exhaled, shaking his head. "It all seemed strange then, the way your father reacted. He would have confronted your grandfather and Nathan right there if Larus hadn't stopped him—begged him to wait." He paused for a moment as if reliving it. "I had never seen a man so consumed by grief." Dominic swallowed. "He would have killed everyone in that room to have you back."

Jude's breath caught in his throat. "My father... what is he like?" He felt foolish for asking, but Dominic's expression softened with understanding.

"I never knew him then, Jude, but I could tell he loved you." Dominic's dark pupils reflected the candlelight. "Even after all these years, you are still the one thing in this world he cherishes most. He lost himself that night. He would have done terrible things if not for Larus." Then he smiled. "You have his eyes."

Their conversation was interrupted as Larus entered, a pile of clothing in his arms. He placed a flask of water and the garments on the pew beside Jude before turning to Dominic, cupping his face.

"How are you?"

Dominic gave a small nod. That was all Larus needed before turning back to Jude.

"You must hurry. Your father will arrive soon." He looked around the church, his gaze lingering on the high ceilings, and for the first time, Jude saw something almost reverent in his uncle's expression. "Silas gave this place back to me... now, I give him the one thing he cherishes most." He met Jude's eyes. "Your father does not know you are here. I instructed Ashkan not to tell him. You are his surprise."

Jude later stepped into the sanctuary, dressed, but feeling no less exposed. His heartbeat pounded in his ears, his breath shallow. He was terrified.

Would his father even recognize him? Would he look at him and see only Nathan's influence?

His hands trembled.

He was going to see his father. After eleven years.

Jude closed his eyes, steadying himself.

And then he waited.

The vampire, Ashkan, would not reveal why Larus had sent him to the ancient church on the hill. Silas had questioned him more than once, but the vampire remained frustratingly vague.

Deidre had accepted his life, had accepted what he was. But her love was possessive—unwilling to share him. Unlike her brother, Dominic, who embraced Larus's ways and eagerly learned all he could about Lycans and vampires, Deidre had no such fascination. She loved Silas, but she did not understand. Wolves lived in packs.

Silas had argued with his mother more than once over Deidre. She claimed the woman was all wrong for him, that love had blinded him. But she did not see Deidre as he did.

The carriage slowed near the cemetery, and Silas, with Deidre on his arm, stepped out into the night. Together, they climbed the hill toward the church. Its stained-glass windows glowed from within, candlelight painting colours across the dark grass.

"What a magnificent old building," Deidre murmured, pressing closer to him. "Pity it's out in the wilds... and across from that dreadful cemetery."

Silas smiled at her innocence.

Deidre's gaze lifted toward the towering steeples. "And why would a vampire have such a connection to a church? How can evil be drawn to good?"

"This place is special to him," Silas said. "Larus grew up on these lands."

He leaned down to kiss her cheek. "Why would a smelly wolf fall in love with a beautiful lady?"

She laughed softly, but as they neared the entrance, the doors swung open, revealing Larus. He stepped out, looking almost too pleased.

"Welcome!" He kissed Deidre's cheek before gripping Silas's shoulders with both hands and shaking him slightly.

Silas frowned. "Uncle, why have you invited us here?"

They stepped inside, their footsteps echoing off the stone. Silas spotted Dominic near the altar, and before he could say more, Deidre had already rushed toward her brother.

"We had planned to dine at Bleddyn Manor," Silas reminded Larus.

"A slight change of plans." There was something in his uncle's eyes, something bright and unspoken. "We won't be here long. Just briefly. Then we'll go to the manor."

Silas narrowed his gaze. "You're keeping secrets, Uncle."

They walked further into the nave, toward Deidre and Dominic, but then—Silas froze.

He inhaled sharply.

A scent.

His heart lurched, and he sniffed again, disbelief slamming into him like a physical force. Someone else had been here.

No—someone was here.

The air shifted. A figure emerged from the sanctuary's shadows, stepping forward.

Silas gasped. His knees buckled, and he sank to the ground, trembling.

No.

Jude.

His vision blurred, but the boy—no, the man—was moving toward him.

Somewhere in the distance, he heard Deidre's voice, but the words barely registered.

The first sob tore through him the moment he felt Jude's arms wrap around him. His son smelled the same as he had as a child, yet different—older. Changed. A lycan.

"We should leave them... give them some time alone," Dominic murmured.

Silas barely noticed Deidre hesitate, her reluctance plain on her face as she glanced back. But she went.

Silas turned back to Jude, barely able to breathe. Tears shone in his son's eyes.

"Father..."

Jude's body shook as he wept, and Silas—Silas felt everything. Sorrow. Rage. Joy. Love.

His son collapsed into him, sobbing, and Silas clutched him close, pressing kiss after kiss to his face.

Eleven years. Eleven years lost.

He would never let go again.

54

A WOLF'S BANE

Cecil had been away from White Castle for several weeks, visiting a shrine he had built in memory of Telsiea, his maker. He had crafted it long before his deep slumber. During his absence, the vampires of White Castle seemed unbothered, even at ease. They preferred the calm, pleasant nature of Micah over Cecil's stern ways. The sunrise was near, and as it approached, every vampire retreated to the crypts beneath the castle. Marc, however, loved the maze of the grounds and had spent many nights walking through the labyrinthine hedges. He wished, more than anything, that he had spent more time walking there during the daylight, before his immortality had bound him.

One last glance at the rising dawn, and he turned toward the castle, moving toward the staircase that led to his rooms.

Just as Marc was about to ascend, Nicolas appeared in the grand foyer.

Nicolas was one of the few vampires Marc considered a friend. Since Marc had brought the news of his grandfather Bernard, from the other world, Nicolas had been a steady, grateful presence. The old sheepherder, sickly and nearing death, had sacrificed the remainder of his human life to ensure his grandson's immortality. It had been his blood that nourished Isabelle the night she was turned into a vampire. Marc had seen Bernard's shade, a fleeting vision of the old man's peace. Those words—he is at peace—had brought a tear to Marc's eye. Nicolas had wept, blood tears flowing freely, but had taken solace in knowing that his grandfather's spirit had found rest.

Nicolas's smile, always warm and welcoming, now carried a glimmer of hope in his eyes. "Oracle. Any news from my grandpa?"

Marc grinned back, though there was a sombreness to his reply. "I'm afraid Bernard will no longer trouble my dreams, Nicolas. He is at peace."

They parted ways at the landing, both of them choosing the solace of their rooms during daylight. Like most of the vampires within White Castle, Nicolas preferred the deep, cold crypts below, but Marc found comfort in his own chambers. Every room in the castle came equipped with a coffin hidden within the closet, but Marc favoured his featherbed, with its black satin sheets, soft and luxurious.

Though he never tired, Marc mimicked the human act of sleep, curling beneath the sheets. His body lay still, the stillness of slumber settling over him, as the quiet of the castle enveloped him in its dark embrace.

TWO FIGURES MOVED THROUGH THE THICK FOG BENEATH A MOONLIT SKY, THEIR forms barely visible in the mist. Marc could not see their faces at first, but he sensed the balance between masculine and feminine in their walk. The woman wore a white, silky gown that flowed with the cool night breeze. He followed them in silence, mesmerized as she led him deeper into the fog. Eventually, they came upon a marsh—murky, its stench thick with death. The bride appeared unfazed by the soiled gown that dragged through the muddy silt. She stepped in without hesitation and, with a delicate beckon of her hand, summoned him to follow. Without resistance, he did.

They moved deeper into the marsh, their legs heavy with the thick mud and the wild lilies and vines that crept upward, tangling around them. The fog began to lift with the strength of a sudden wind, and Marc saw Silas, his eyes gleaming in the moonlight, gazing at Deidre with pure devotion. To him, the world outside seemed to vanish. He cared not for his surroundings, for Deidre was his entire world.

But then, just as quickly, the fog and the marsh were gone, replaced by a deep, empty void. Marc blinked, and before him appeared a cave. Seated upon a massive boulder near the entrance was a woman of striking beauty. Yet, the decapitated head resting on her lap, blood dripping from the severed neck, was an image both disturbing and haunting. Her hands gently cradled the head as she spoke, her voice soft but urgent. "Beware Silas's bane," she warned, her eyes filling with tears.

Marc awoke with a jolt, sitting up in bed. The vision had left him shaken. He knew with certainty that he had seen Hannah's shade. The urgency to reach Silas overwhelmed him, a growing dread clawing at his chest. He sprang from his bed with urgency, dressing quickly despite the impending sunset. But Marc knew that delay was not an option. With Larus spending more time at Bleddyn Manor and Cecil absent, Marc could think of only one person who might understand—one person who might help.

Not long after, Marc found himself in Nicolas's chambers, explaining the urgency of his dream. The two vampires donned cloaks of black, their hoods drawn, as a human coachman hurried them toward a screened carriage. The sun still blazed in the sky, and as Marc climbed into the carriage, the rays seared his skin. He gritted his teeth, a sharp cry escaping his lips as he smelled the searing of his flesh. The stench of burning skin filled his senses. Nicolas, ever vigilant, yanked him swiftly into the protection of the carriage's shadowed interior.

"The journey will be long," Nicolas said, his tone thick with concern. "But we are safe within these fragile walls." Marc could feel the weight of his friend's fear and guilt stirred within him.

"Forgive me, Nicolas," Marc muttered, his voice low with regret. "It was wrong of me to ask this of you."

"Nonsense," Nicolas replied, his voice steady but carrying the weight of experience. "Grandpa taught me the value of meaningful sacrifice, Marc." His words held a somber depth that erased the youthful cheer Marc had once known in him. "I can see it—the burden you carry. I can feel it. I will help you ease it."

Marc gave him a grateful nod, though his heart ached with the weight of the task before them.

By the time the carriage arrived at Bleddyn Manor, the sky had turned black, the moon hidden behind thick clouds. Max, Silas's mother, greeted Marc and led him to the great hall. Nicolas, meanwhile, walked the grounds with Larus and Dominic, the human. Marc felt a strange sense of relief when he saw Isabelle, who had spent much of her time at Bleddyn Manor since mating with the lycan, Gavin. He approached Larus's nephew, taking a deep breath before speaking.

"I bring news," Marc said, "from the shade of your wife, Hannah. But I can make no sense of what she has told me."

Silas sat motionless on the couch, his strong hands clutching the velvet cushions as he absorbed Marc's words. He remained silent for several moments, as if lost in thought before he finally spoke, his voice low and uncertain. "I have no clue what this fog means," he said. "Nor the significance of the marsh." He sighed deeply. "But it cannot be good." His gaze drifted distant, and he seemed lost in memories. "Hannah was killed by lycans when they took Jude. They severed her head, and she is buried near the mouth of a cave in the woods, on these lands." Silas closed his eyes briefly, his face shadowed with sorrow. "It was our lair... I remember taking her there. Our son, Jude, was conceived there. Hannah's grave lies beneath that boulder."

Max nodded thoughtfully, her expression sympathetic. "And what of Deidre? Are you to wed?"

Marc frowned, the meaning of his vision becoming more convoluted. "She was dressed as a bride," he murmured, frustration seeping into his voice.

Silas shrugged, his posture weary. "Deidre wishes to marry... but—"

"You feel you are already married, for Hannah was and always will be your heart," Marc said, his smile grim as he watched Silas's reluctant nod.

"I love Deidre," Silas admitted quietly. "She has helped clear my mind —pulled me away from my sorrow." His eyes darkened, guilt flashing across his face. "But when Larus found Jude and brought him back to me... when I look at my son, I see his mother in him."

Marc fell silent, his thoughts tangled with the weight of the vision. "What of Hannah's words?" he asked. He could see her severed head, blood staining her lap, and he whispered the warning she had given him. "Beware Silas's bane."

"I fear someone may harm Deidre," Silas confessed, the weight of his fear evident in his voice. Marc disagreed, the vision's meaning unclear to him, but he kept his thoughts to himself. After a long pause, Silas's voice grew urgent. "Tell no one this—not even Deidre."

The door to the hall swung open, and Jude entered, looking every bit the man he had grown into. Marc hadn't seen Silas's son since he was a boy, and now, standing before him, Jude resembled Silas so closely, save for the features of his mother. The scent of lycan filled the air as Jude's gaze landed on Marc.

"Father, forgive me... I thought you were alone." Jude looked at Marc with curiosity. They would have been close in age if not for the curse of immortality, and Marc caught the telltale flare of his nostrils. Jude sniffed the air, and Marc did the same, sensing the wolf within him.

"This is Marc, Jude... friend and ally of our pack. He comes from White Castle." Silas pulled his son close with a loving embrace.

"I knew you briefly," Marc said, his voice filled with nostalgia. "When you were a boy... but I fear you may not remember me."

Jude's brow furrowed as he thought for a moment, then grinned as recognition bloomed. "Mother spoke of you," he said. "Said you saw me before I arrived." He pulled Marc into an embrace, then moved back to his father. "Dreamer... that's what she called you."

Silas laughed, the sound filled with warmth. "Marc has earned many names."

As the father and son shared a heartfelt moment, the doors swung open once more, and Deidre entered. Marc's gaze shifted toward her. The woman was beautiful, but there was something uneasy in her presence. When her eyes landed on father and son, her smile faltered. She looked displeased, though she quickly masked it behind a smile.

Marc's gift was not reading minds, and no vampire could read his thoughts, not even Cecil Bleddyn. Whether this was a blessing or curse, Marc couldn't tell, but at that moment, he wished he could glimpse into Deidre's mind. Something within her stirred suspicion in him, though he could not quite place what it was.

———

———

———

———

DEIDRE HAD LEFT BLEDDYN MANOR IN FRUSTRATION, HAVING TO FEIGN illness, for she could no longer endure being third to Silas's son and mother. Silas's mother was the lady of the manor, a fact Deidre accepted, though it still stung. But ever since Jude's return, she had spent many weeks alone within that den of wolves. The other she-wolf, Catherine, was tolerable, for she seemed to care little for Silas and the boy, though Jude was her grandson. But the mother was a problem; together, mother and son doted on the boy as though he were an infant. Each passing day, Deidre could feel her place in Silas's life eroding, the space between them growing wider as his attention shifted to his son. Deidre's attempts to win Jude's affection had been met with coolness, and her gestures of kindness went unreturned.

It was nearly noon, and as soon as the carriage left Bleddyn Manor, Deidre had given the coachman instructions to detour from her route home. Her hands clenched in her lap, but it wasn't from the roughness of the ride; the tension had been building inside her for weeks. She didn't dare show it, but Silas's devotion to his son left her feeling unseen, insignificant. No one, not even Dominic, could ever discover what she was about to do.

Deidre sat alone within the carriage, her thoughts spiralling. Silas spent most of his time with his son, as though Jude had always been a part of his life. Deidre tried, oh, how she tried, to make the boy like her. She tried to be understanding, to be a figure he could trust, but nothing ever seemed to break through the wall Jude had built around himself. She loved Silas with all her heart, but as strong as that love was, she could not accept his son. The boy's return had brought only pain, neglect, and a gnawing feeling of being cast aside.

Each time she saw them together, father and son, it felt like a reminder of everything she couldn't have—a family that was whole, a place where she no longer fit. The jealousy that gnawed at her insides was not something she was proud of, but it was real. It was becoming harder and harder to hide. Silas's love had once been her anchor, but now it felt like the tide was pulling her out to sea, leaving her drowning in a sea of doubt and resentment.

But it was more than that, wasn't it? It wasn't just the boy; it was Silas's past. Deidre had always known he had a history, but now that history had returned with such force that it left her wondering if she was merely a shadow in the corners of his life. She had been patient. She had tried to stand by him, but as the days passed, she couldn't help but feel like she was being asked to share something she was never meant to.

Her eyes stared out the carriage window, but she wasn't looking at the passing landscape. Her mind was far away, lost in a storm of emotions. Silas and Jude had become inseparable, and there was a part of Deidre that wondered if she had ever truly been needed. The thought stung, but she couldn't deny it. She was starting to wonder whether Silas would ever see her for who she was, rather than just a placeholder in a life that had already been defined by the boy he had once lost.

She reached for the edge of the seat, her nails digging into the leather. It wasn't that she didn't love Silas—it was the opposite, in fact. Her love for him had always been fierce, unyielding, and she was willing to sacrifice everything for him. But what if that wasn't enough? What if the space she had in his heart had already been taken by someone else, someone he couldn't let go of?

Her jaw clenched as the carriage rattled on, but she couldn't escape the thought. No matter how she tried to rationalize it, the jealousy lingered, heavy in her chest. And it made her question just how far she was willing to go to hold onto the man she loved.

55

PROPHECY

With Cecil still on his travels abroad, it was left to Micah and Sebastian to preside over the council. The two vampires sat side by side, their presence commanding attention as they faced the other council members. Marc stood before them, a figure of somber gravity as he relayed his vision. Larus had already known what was coming, for Marc had come to his chambers with Nicolas, and they had listened together as Marc spoke of terrible things. The dreamer had seen death, and now it was their shared burden to face the truth of what Marc had foreseen.

Marc had seen the aftermath of battle—a grim vision of carnage. Silas, Jude, Gavin, and even the lycan, Bartholomew, had been summoned to hear the warning. Marc had seen countless corpses of wolves piled in great mounds, and woven among them, the ashen remains of vampires scorched by the unforgiving midday sun.

Marc stood firm, flanked by Nicolas and Dominic, as he recounted the chilling prophecy. "This is a warning," he declared, his voice heavy with the weight of what he had seen. "A prophecy."

Micah, ever superstitious, cast a lingering glance around the room at the assembled vampires and lycans, now united by an unspoken bond. "We, the vampires, do not face this danger alone," he said, his tone carrying the gravity of ancient truths. "We must stand together to face our enemy."

Larus's eyes moved over the faces in the room, pausing momentarily on Helene and Isabelle. Neither of them were council members, but Larus had extended the invitation. He studied them, as he did all the members of the council, sensing the currents of tension that ran beneath their composed exteriors. His thoughts drifted briefly to Deidre—his sister—and the distance growing between her and Silas. It had been months since she had been seen among the council, and now, as he glanced at Dominic, he could sense the unspoken conflict. When he had asked Dominic about Deidre, he simply said that she had been avoiding him. Larus's lips quirked into a faint, knowing smile.

Silas, however, had changed. His gaze softened as he looked at Jude, his son, standing proudly at his side. Jude was an eager pupil, ever ready to prove himself. As Larus watched, his thoughts were momentarily distracted by the sight of Silas's transformation. The man had become a new father, and in his son's presence, he seemed whole again.

Jude, sensing the shift in the room, stepped forward to speak. His voice was steady and filled with conviction. "You are right, Micah," he said, his sharp gaze sweeping over the council. "But who else could cause such carnage, if not one of our own, whether vampire or lycan?" His words were laced with the same urgency he had carried for years—a need to protect, to act before the danger arrived at their doorstep.

Sebastian nodded, his face grim with concern. "We must be vigilant. With Cecil gone, I fear we are left vulnerable. We must protect each other." He turned his gaze to Micah, who met it with a solemn nod in agreement. There was no room for hesitation—not when the prophecy loomed so heavily over them all.

When word came that Deidre had arrived at the manor, Silas hurried to Bleddyn Hall. He hadn't seen his love since the day she had abruptly left, and his heart ached to be near her again. As he neared the entrance, he met his mother by the doors. Though he was eager to reunite with Deidre, she stopped him with a hand on his arm.

"You are not to see her," his mother commanded, her voice firm.

Silas blinked in surprise, his frustration mounting. "Mother, why? What has Deidre ever done to you?"

"A devoted woman does not leave the man she loves for a fortnight without good reason, Silas," his mother replied, her eyes scanning the hall as if searching for unseen threats. "I am a woman, Silas, and I trust my instincts. In my heart, I sense that this girl is trouble."

Silas crossed his arms, his muscles tensing. "Mother, that's nonsense. Deidre loves me. I am happy." He raised his hands in exasperation. "Jude is home again, and—"

His mother's gaze hardened. "She left for one reason alone—because of Jude. Because of your love for your son."

Silas shook his head, the words not settling. "That's not true!"

"She pretends to like me," his mother continued, her eyes narrowing with disdain. "I have never liked her, Silas, and I see no need to pretend."

Silas sighed deeply, his frustration turning to pity for his mother's inability to see what he felt for Deidre. He kissed her cheek gently, offering a small smile. "You worry too much, Mother. Deidre admires you."

But his mother wasn't finished. "You must have Larus look into her mind."

Silas recoiled, astonished. "Uncle Larus has chosen to refrain from violating the privacy of others. You know this, Mother. I would never ask him to do such a thing." His mind drifted briefly to Marc's disturbing vision of Hannah at the cave. If Deidre were in danger, he would protect her, but the idea of intruding on her thoughts was beyond him.

With a final glance at his mother, Silas entered Bleddyn Hall. The moment he crossed the threshold, Deidre ran into his arms, her eyes brimming with unshed tears. She wept against his chest, her voice trembling as she begged for his forgiveness.

"I was confused, Silas. When you called, I was there—but I refused to see you." Her words were heartfelt, and Silas held her tightly, letting her emotions wash over him. Marc's prophecy had warned him to keep Deidre close and protect her, but the weight of his love for her was all-consuming.

Deidre pulled back slightly, looking up at him with a question in her eyes. "Where is Dominic?"

Silas's voice was gentle, soothing. "Larus took him to one of Micah's estates... somewhere in the country. They left days ago." He smiled down at her. "Your brother has been worried about you, Deidre. But he is happy in his new life with Larus; he's happy with a vampire."

Silas kissed her lips softly, his heart swelling with the joy of her return. "I want you to be happy, Deidre, always happy. Forgive my absent-mindedness, my love."

Deidre smiled up at him, her hands tracing the contours of his chest, sending waves of passion through him. Silas kissed her again, hard and fervently, the hunger rising in him. His hands moved eagerly over her, finding the buttons of her gown, pulling them open. Deidre didn't protest as her gown began to fall away. She welcomed his desire, her hands exploring his bare skin with gentle caresses that only stoked the fire within him.

With a final tug, the last of her gown slipped to the floor, and they were left in each other's arms, their bodies entwined. As they fell together, their passion was relentless, each movement a desperate need for connection. The world outside ceased to exist; there was only the warmth of their bodies, the softness of her skin, and the raw, consuming love they shared.

When their passion finally subsided, they lay together on the floor, Silas staring up at the ceiling, his chest rising and falling slowly as Deidre rested her head on it. The room was silent, save for the faint sound of their breathing.

"I am glad you came back to me, Deidre," Silas murmured, his hand resting lightly in her hair.

Deidre stirred after a long pause, sitting up suddenly with a smile that lit up her face. "The governor holds a lunch at his mansion in two days," she said brightly. "Please, Silas, come with me. I usually attend these events with Dominic." She paused, her expression turning sad. "Good heavens, I've been terrible to my brother."

Her eyes became wistful as she continued, "Dominic and Larus are away somewhere, Silas. Let's have some fun together."

Silas grimaced. "We could even bring Jude with us."

Deidre's eyes sparkled with excitement. "That would be wonderful! You, me, and Jude."

Silas hesitated for a moment, then nodded. "Gavin and Isabelle are with Larus as well," he said, thinking of the arrangements. "I'll ask Father if he would attend. I believe he knows the governor."

Deidre kissed his face with joy, and Silas grinned, feeling the tension of the past days slip away in her arms.

THE GOVERNOR'S ANNUAL LUNCHEON OF FLOWERS WAS A GRAND AFFAIR, hosted by the lady of the manor herself. Deidre arrived with six lycans in tow, feeling a sense of satisfaction. She had only hoped to attend with Silas and Jude, but the presence of the pack filled her with satisfaction. Stepping from the carriage, Deidre inhaled deeply, the fragrance of rare flowers greeting her with a sweet, almost intoxicating embrace. The entire manor was draped in blooms, a tradition that had become legendary. As they entered, the air was thick with the scent of blossoms from every corner of the globe. Guests mingled, admiring the flowers, and taking home bouquets and potted plants, but Deidre cared little for the spectacle. She was more focused on the bright blue skies above and the blinding sun.

As the Bleddyns were honoured guests of the governor, the lady of the manor invited them all to the library. Deidre never left Silas's side, but her gaze wandered as his mother and aunt, Catherine, engaged in conversation with the governor's wife, discussing the magnificent bouquets adorning the room. Jude, ever the loyal son, remained close to his father, while Bartholomew and Morgan trailed behind their wives, talking softly among themselves.

The governor's wife was a delicate woman, her elegance barely concealing the sharpness of her mind. Deidre suspected the governor had married her for her dowry rather than her beauty, but she held her tongue. "My love for flowers goes beyond admiration," the governor's wife said, addressing Silas's mother. "As a woman—and a scientist, I've had to improvise. In these times, it is not always polite to pursue what we believe in or love."

Lady Max nodded, clearly intrigued, her nose twitching as she sniffed the air again. Deidre's heart skipped a beat. "What is it you do with flowers?" she asked, her curiosity piqued.

The governor's wife smiled mysteriously, bringing her wrist to Lady Max's nose. "Breathe, my dear."

Catherine and Silas's mother inhaled deeply, their eyes wide with wonder. Lady Max turned to Bartholomew and then back to the governor's wife. "Perfume!" she exclaimed, realization dawning.

"Yes, my dear," the woman replied, a gleam in her eye. "My lab is just below, if you wish to see it." She leaned closer, her voice dropping to a whisper. "...My husband has no idea I do any of this." With a sly smile, she pressed a finger to her lips, signalling secrecy. "Come." She pulled a sconce beside a bookcase, revealing a secret passage. She led them down a winding flight of stairs, speaking softly about the manor's history. "These lands belonged to my father... the most valuable part of my dowry. And I know all of its secrets."

Deidre followed last, Silas and Jude just ahead of her. As they descended, the space below opened up before them—a cavernous room filled with flowers arranged on counters, alongside bottles and vials. But as the bookcase slid shut behind them, a sudden chill ran down Deidre's spine. The door had locked.

Silas's mother's gaze sharpened, her eyes narrowing with suspicion. "Why have we been locked in?" she asked, her voice calm but filled with an edge of warning. Deidre smiled faintly, sensing that it was already too late to turn back now.

Silas and Jude, now realizing the danger, exchanged wary looks. Deidre moved quietly to stand next to the lady of the manor, who seemed to be watching the unfolding scene with a knowing glint in her eyes. And then, the air shifted. Strange, sharp sounds filled the room, followed by the unmistakable sound of needles piercing flesh. The lycans staggered, one by one, as they fell to the floor, immobilized by the poison coursing through their veins.

Deidre gasped as she watched Silas's eyes widen in shock, the moment of realization hitting him just as he collapsed to his knees. Her heart raced as she moved closer to him, but it was too late. The entrance above them opened again, and a familiar figure descended the stairs.

Percival Hearne stood before them, his eyes cold and triumphant. He glanced at Deidre and spoke in a low, smooth voice. "You have done well, girl... You have kept your word."

NIGHT HAD FALLEN, AND THE GOVERNOR'S GUESTS HAD LONG SINCE departed. Nathan cared little for the human girl, Deidre. She had betrayed the one she claimed to love. To him, such humans could never be trusted. Nathan stood with Lucas, the only member of his coven he could rely on. Together, they observed the family of lycans in chains before them. The wolves dared not transform in his presence, for they were vulnerable. With Lucas at his side, they could end the wolves swiftly.

He saw fear in Jude's eyes, but Nathan knew he could do the boy no harm. "You've changed, Jude," he said, his voice cold but oddly understanding. "I forgive you. I understand why you ran away."

Silas's spit landed near his feet, but Nathan ignored it. He glanced at Percival, noting the sorrow in the old wolf's eyes. His son and grandson were chained before him, helpless. The she-wolves were terrified, but Silas's mother seemed more concerned for the lives of her son and grandson than for her own. She was ready to die for them.

The sister clung to her husband, and Percival's son glared at Nathan with hatred.

"There's no turning back, Percival. Not now," Nathan said, his voice final. "We must push forward."

"Only Silas and Jude were supposed to be taken!" Percival protested. "Not my son!"

Nathan turned to face the elder wolf. "And what would you have me do, release them? They stay here. I will decide their fates." His gaze shifted to Silas, then to Deidre. "It wasn't I who planned this, Silas. I played no part in this plot between your grandfather and the woman you love." He saw the vicious way Silas's mother glared at Deidre.

"Why, Deidre? Why have you done this?" Silas's voice cracked with frustration.

Deidre pursed her lips into a hard line before answering. "Because of him," she pointed a finger at Jude. "He belongs with them. Not you. Not us."

"He is my son!" Silas shouted, but Deidre remained unfazed.

"Silence!" Nathan ordered, stepping toward the girl. "I will know the real truth, girl… and that truth flows through your veins." He saw her fear before he sank his fangs into her neck. She tried to scream, but his venom quickly subdued her. As he drank, Nathan's gaze never left the wolves. He saw the satisfaction in Silas's mother's eyes, as Deidre's blood memories revealed her true nature.

THE CARRIAGE ARRIVED AT ITS DESTINATION, AND DEIDRE SAT WITHIN, WAITING for a moment as the coachman held the door open. "Wait here," she instructed him, stepping out. "I won't be long."

Moments later, she entered a cluttered study where Percival sat. "Grandfather Hearne," she greeted, taking the wingback chair closest to his desk as he invited her to sit.

Percival studied her carefully, licking his lips. Though he was Silas's grandfather, Deidre found him oddly charming—yet still a wolf. His gaze never wavered from her.

"I didn't know who you were until you spoke, young girl," Percival said with

a mischievous smile. "I have two grandsons, and they both address me as Grandfather Hearne. Why has Silas sent you here?"

"I came of my own volition," Deidre replied, her tone firm. "Silas can never know I was here."

Percival leaned forward, intrigued. "Your grandson, Jude... belongs here with you."

Percival tilted his head as he studied her. "My grandsons have shared a bond since Jude came into this world," he said thoughtfully. "It's unlikely they would be at odds."

"I am at odds," Deidre replied, her voice cold with conviction.

Percival laughed scornfully. "You stink of jealousy and envy," he said, his eyes narrowing.

Deidre sprang from the wingback, heading toward the door. "Wait," Percival called, his voice softer now. She turned to find him standing, closer than before. He reached out, taking her hand gently, and kissed it. "Envy and jealousy lead to baneful consequences, Deidre. Why have you come here?"

Deidre withdrew her hand, returning to the wingback chair. "I love Silas, and I know you care for the boy... for them both," she said, watching as Percival leaned against his desk, eyes fixed on her.

Deidre shifted uneasily in her seat, wondering what would come of her presence in the home of the man Silas hated most.

The old wolf smiled again. "Then we shall find a solution, my dear Deidre."

NATHAN RELEASED THE NOW LIFELESS CORPSE, ALLOWING IT TO CRUMBLE TO the floor. She was nothing now. His gaze flicked to Jude. "She hated you more than your grandmother," Nathan remarked coldly, before looking to the she-wolf. "Like you, I believe this wretched human deserved to die. She was worse than poison."

Nathan saw the mixture of rage and sorrow in Silas's eyes. "The girl's love for you would have caused far more death, Silas... far more than you'll witness this night." His grin widened. "Yes, some of you will die tonight."

Percival rushed to his side, fury evident in his movements. "Nathan, no one was supposed to die!"

Nathan turned, striking Percival so hard that the old wolf slid across the floor and crashed into the wall. "Your precious friend, the governor, has chosen wisely, Percival. He rejected your offer to make him a wolf, and I've given him an offer he can't refuse."

"I'll kill you!" Percival screamed, but Nathan only looked at Lucas. His son was already upon the old wolf.

"Father grows tired of your feeble ways, wolf," Lucas said, a smile stretching across his face. "I begged him to let me kill you myself."

Nathan saw the satisfaction in his son's eyes. "But not before you witness your family's destruction."

Nathan took Bartholomew's head first, savouring the sound of Percival's mournful cries. The she-wolf, Catherine, and her husband screamed for mercy, but they, too, fell. Silas's mother, Max, stood strong. She looked Nathan in the eye, not begging, not showing fear. "Your end will come," she said quietly.

Nathan broke her neck with a swift motion.

He looked at Jude and his father, seeing only hatred in their eyes. The boy tried to shift, but his father quelled his rage with a few soothing words. Nathan knew he could never harm Jude, but Silas—Silas would die. Yet, he wouldn't strip the boy of everything. Someday, Jude would thank him for this mercy.

Father and son wept in silence, their eyes locked on the headless corpses.

Nathan turned to Percival, disgust apparent on his face. The old fool was in such shock from losing his son that he had forgotten to fight for his own life. He wept like a child.

"All these years, I worked and plotted with you," Nathan said, his voice dripping with disdain. "I knew you were beneath me. You're just a hunter. You should have stayed where nature intended you."

He turned to Lucas. "End it."

Lucas stepped forward, and in a swift motion, separated Percival's spine from his body, granting the hunter a lycan's death.

56

RETRIBUTION

Cecil returned that night to discover that several members of the Bleddyn family were dead. Silas and Jude were gone. Two lycans remained alive, but Nathan had taken them. Cecil's fury was all-consuming as he glared at the council, blaming Larus for the loss. "Those lycans were our allies!" His rage was directed solely at Larus, though he noticed the sorrow and guilt in his eyes. "You forget what you are, Larus. You are a vampire—more even!" The erratic thoughts of the lone human in the room were noticeable. Cecil turned to Larus's mate. "Why are you here?" Dominic met his gaze before looking at Larus, but his lover remained silent. "It's because of you that my family is dead, human!"

Larus defended Dominic. "Cecil, Deidre was—"

"A treacherous human, Larus!" Cecil's voice cut through the room. None of the other council members dared speak. Micah and Sebastian stood side by side, their support unspoken but palpable. Babette stood in silence with Avlon; Nicolas, though not a council member, sought refuge behind Geraldine and Monique. Haruki's hands rested on the hilts of his swords, ready for a fight. Giles and Ashkan lingered near the door. But Marc—Cecil's greatest challenge—sat alone across the hall, troubled. Cecil's rage turned back to Larus. "This senseless belief that reading minds is a violation, Larus, has cost us dearly! Had you only read the girl's thoughts, my family would still be alive!"

Cecil had learned much since his return. Silas's coachman, a wolf, survived the massacre at the governor's mansion. He had witnessed Nathan's arrival and hidden himself. Later, after seeing the vampire leave in darkness with Silas and Jude in chains, the coachman had watched as five lycans and one human were burned on the governor's lands. "They will pay for what they've done, but Percival Hearne and your sister, Deidre, got what they deserved." He glared at Dominic, wanting the human to feel the weight of his displeasure.

Silas's second-in-command, Gavin, seemed eager to turn sorrow into vengeance. "Nathan has kept Silas and Jude alive for a purpose." He approached Cecil with a determined stride. "We must act quickly. If we don't strike back, we will appear weak."

Cecil nodded, pleased with Gavin's words.

Micah stepped forward, his voice calm but filled with urgency. "Percival's second now controls the Hearne lands...given to him by Nathan."

"Bought for a price," Cecil murmured. "Nathan is clever. I shall take pleasure in destroying him. But we must fight against vampires and lycans alike."

Sebastian spoke next, his tone cautious. "He surrounds his coven with lycans by day. It stays our hand."

Cecil's gaze hardened. "We, too, do the same." He pounded his fist upon the arm of his chair. "We fight this war to win, and we do it quickly. We will spare only those who join us. Nathan and his council must die. Prepare yourselves; we take the fight to them." He then beckoned Avlon forward. "You know Nathan's lands well, former council member. Share everything with Micah and Sebastian."

He turned to Babette. "Gather the strongest among us, but leave the newborns here."

"As you command, Cecil," Babette said before departing with Geraldine and Monique, leaving Nicolas exposed.

Cecil's gaze shifted to the sheepherder's grandson. "And you, Nicolas, will prove your worth to me. At sunset tomorrow, you will lead an attack with Gavin upon the governor's mansion. Leave none alive."

Avlon interrupted. “Nathan has left his son, Lucas, there. He may have already turned the governor and his wife.”

“Foolish,” Cecil muttered. “How can one rule a city if he must hide from the sun by day? He should have become a wolf.”

As most of the council members departed, Cecil leaned forward, his eyes fixed on the remaining two individuals. Larus was in visible distress, yet Cecil said nothing to ease his suffering. “Why have you not turned this human?” He pointed at Dominic.

“We… Dominic would like to remain human, Cecil.” Larus spoke with hesitation.

Cecil probed their minds, understanding their decision, though he saw Larus’s silent concession—he needed Dominic by his side forever. “Dominic must stay here. Tomorrow, we go to war.” He paused and looked between the two, then added, his voice colder, “In battle, Larus, you cannot think of those you love. Let the human remain here. Let him live in torment and worry. But he must stay far from you.”

Cecil dismissed them with a wave of his hand and turned his attention to Marc, still seated across the room. He knew his attempts to probe Marc’s mind would be futile, but he tried anyway—finding only darkness. However, Marc’s eyes spoke volumes. The young vampire appeared weak, not from fear, but from the weight of his gift. Cecil had experienced this before, the struggle to close one’s mind from others, but unlike Marc, he had embraced his vampire nature.

Cecil rose from his chair and walked toward Marc, placing a hand upon his head. “It will eat you up from inside, Marc, until you embrace what you are. You must welcome it—the doom, the shadows of death. Only then will the shades of the dead spare you the torture they bring. It is your resistance that calls them.”

Marc opened his mouth to speak, but Cecil silenced him with a touch to his chin. Lifting his face to look into his eyes, Cecil continued, “I cannot see your thoughts, Marc, but I know you have no desire for this battle.”

“How can I kill, Cecil?” Marc’s voice trembled, “When the shades of those slain by my hand would return to me?”

Marc stepped closer, his face just inches from Cecil’s. “I compel humans before I feed upon them, and they wake where I leave them, with no memory of what I’ve taken. Only the wound remains.”

Cecil placed his hands on Marc's face, his touch lingering as he met the young vampire's gaze. "Shhh... You will remain here, Marc. I would not have you harmed. But remember what I've told you. You will find peace only if you embrace what you truly are. You are a vampire, Marc. Would you spend your years tormented by your gift? It is the essence of who you are. Love yourself."

As Marc moved toward the door, he paused and without turning back, said the strangest thing. "You will have your vengeance, Cecil. You will bathe in its glory. Nathan will die by your hand, but his destruction will not be in vain."

THEY HAD BEEN HELD CAPTIVE BY NATHAN FOR WEEKS. SILAS FOUND IT NEAR impossible to calm his son. Jude, unable to contain his rage, was eager to escape.

Their prison was an iron cage—large enough for two fully grown men, but cramped beyond reason for a pair of lycans. Over time, Silas had grown a full beard, his skin thick with grime. He had not been afforded the courtesy of a bath. The stench of filth clung to the damp stone walls, and in the corner of their cage sat a wooden pail filled with waste. Silas grimaced at the sight.

"He keeps us like dogs!" Jude snarled, slamming his fist against the iron bars for what must have been the thousandth time.

Silas gripped his son's shoulder. "Patience, Jude," he murmured. "We will have our moment."

He motioned toward the door, their only link to the outside. Their cage stood within a large chamber beneath Nathan's mansion, the walls thick stone. "The crypts are across the hall," Silas said. "The vampires rest in a chamber much like this one, but larger. And I suspect there are more crypts. Nathan has many in his coven."

Jude, newly engaged, set aside his rage. "I don't remember ever coming here as a boy... after they took me." His gaze drifted over the room. "I was with Grandfather for only a short time before Nathan came for me." His voice hardened. "Did you know he considered turning me when I was just eleven?"

Silas turned sharply, his eyes narrowing.

"I think he wanted to create something magnificent," Jude explained. "Like Cecil."

Silas inhaled sharply, realization striking him like a blow. "That's why Nathan has kept us alive." His grip on Jude's shoulders tightened. "Do you see? Larus spoke of Cecil's past. Nathan's greatest aim is Cecil's destruction. And what better way to do it than to create someone just as powerful?"

Jude's expression darkened. "Or more powerful." He hesitated, brows furrowing. "Nathan... he cares for me like a father would." His voice was quiet, uncertain. "Father, that must be why he hasn't killed us."

Silas felt his stomach coil in rage at all the years stolen from him. "Jude, don't be deceived," he said. "Our blood is the only thing of value to him. Nathan is cunning. Once he creates the warrior he wants, he will take our heads."

Jude held his gaze.

"If he was certain turning you would create a being as powerful as Cecil or Larus, he would have done it already," Silas continued. "But you were born of wolves. Your mother and I made you what you are. Cecil and Larus suffered from an affliction caused by generations neglecting the ways of the Bleddyn wolves. Nathan must know this—Grandfather Hearne may have told him."

Silas clenched his fists, the thought of his grandfather bringing a bitter taste to his mouth. The possibility that Percival Hearne was his true sire made his stomach churn. He pushed it aside.

"We must be ready, Jude. Larus and Cecil will not let us rot in this place. They will come."

Jude searched his father's face. "Do you really believe that?"

Silas nodded. "I am certain of it."

Nicolas followed Gavin's lead, for the lycan was an experienced warrior. They had watched the governor's mansion for some time and found it heavily guarded by both vampires and lycans. Gavin and Nicolas had each brought twenty warriors, knowing stealth would only carry them so far. The enemy had fifteen watchers, a number that would make a prolonged battle inevitable.

The decision was made: they would rush the mansion, eliminating as many as possible before the alarm spread.

Nicolas had killed before, but never like this. Never in a full-fledged battle where every movement was a gamble between life and death. The scent of blood filled his lungs as they attacked, the air thick with the primal energy of lycan and vampire alike. Nicolas led a team of ten lycans and ten vampires while Gavin fought his way into the mansion with the others, tearing through the enemy in a wave of violence. The fight was brutal. By the time Nicolas and his team had finished the battle outside, only nine remained standing with him—five lycans and four vampires.

Their victory was hollow. Nicolas had watched his own cut down, heard their screams. The shock of it threatened to paralyze him, but he swallowed his fear. This was war. He had chosen this path.

With blood-drenched hands, he bolted toward the main doors, the sounds of combat raging from within. The moment he entered the foyer, he was overwhelmed by the chaos. Dozens of lycans and vampires clashed, turning the governor's home into a slaughterhouse. It was difficult to tell friend from foe in the madness, but there was no time for hesitation.

A lycan at his side fell. Nicolas moved instinctively, stepping into his fallen ally's place to face the attacker. The enemy was another lycan, larger and more seasoned, but it didn't matter. Nicolas fought with lethal precision, using speed to evade and counter. His lycan teammate struck the enemy to the ground, and without a thought, Nicolas severed its spine from the body.

There was no time to breathe, no time to grieve.

His gaze swept the battlefield and landed on the corpse of the lady of the manor, her headless body sprawled across the floor. There was no humanity left here. The governor—his target—fought desperately against one of Nicolas's own.

Nicolas didn't hesitate. He lunged, striking like a viper, and in one swift motion, he severed the governor's head from his body. The head hit the floor with a dull thud, rolling to a stop in a pool of blood.

A roar caught his attention—Gavin.

Nicolas turned to see the massive lycan locked in a deadly struggle with Lucas. Nathan's son had Gavin in a headlock, his grip iron-tight as he fought to pry the lycan's jaws apart. It was clear what Lucas intended—to rip Gavin's face from his body.

A surge of rage flooded Nicolas's veins. He would not let Gavin die.

He moved before thought, launching himself at the pair. His impact sent them tumbling to the ground, and in that brief moment of chaos, Gavin broke free. They rose instantly, resuming the battle. This time, Nicolas was at Gavin's side. Lucas was trapped.

Nicolas grabbed a broken chair leg, its splintered end jagged and sharp—the perfect stake. He levelled his gaze at Lucas, unshaken. "This night, we end you. And it will also be your father's end."

Lucas laughed, though blood dripped from his lips. "Father will not be defeated—not this night." His arrogance was infuriating. Even as he stood on the brink of death, he remained defiant.

But something flickered in his eyes—something Nicolas recognized. Fear.

The moment Lucas glanced past them toward the wall, Nicolas knew.

Lucas pressed his back against the paneling, and before either could react, his hand shot out, pulling the wall sconce. A panel revolved, and in an instant, the wall swallowed him up.

Gavin roared, slamming his fists into the hidden door, his claws tearing at the paneling. But it was too late. Lucas was gone.

The mansion was silent except for Gavin's heaving breaths. Then, with a furious snarl, the lycan turned and slammed his fist into a nearby pillar, cracking the stone. "Coward!" His voice was thick with rage. "We had him! We had him!"

Nicolas felt his own fury simmering beneath his skin, but he forced himself to stay calm. Lucas's escape would haunt him, but they had still won. They had wiped out Nathan's forces here, left his grip on the city weaker than before.

Placing a hand on Gavin's shoulder, Nicolas spoke with quiet resolve. "He'll run straight to Nathan. Let him. Next time, there won't be a door to save him."

Gavin exhaled sharply, trying to rein in his fury. He nodded. "Next time, we rip him apart."

And with that, they turned their backs on the ruined mansion, the stench of blood and fire thick in the night air.

The battle had ended—but the war was far from over.

LARUS HAD TRAVELED BY DAY IN CARRIAGES WITH SCREENED WINDOWS. CECIL had initially thought this too risky, but Nicolas and Marc had convinced him otherwise. Nicolas had suggested the plan after he and Marc had once made such a journey to Bleddyn Manor. The lycans traveled on foot, their endurance rivalling that of vampires, forming a protective force around the many carriages moving along the road.

Cecil rode beside the coachman, the only vampire able to walk beneath the sun. He had left White Castle with eleven carriages, each carrying eight vampires. Nearly one hundred lycans had traveled alongside them in their human forms, moving through the forests and along the road. Now, several miles from Nathan's manor, they waited. At sunset, they would strike.

Within the carriage, Larus sat with Sebastian, his thoughts on the other battlefield. His fingers rested against his knee, tapping absently, betraying his unease. "How do you think Nicolas and Gavin fared?"

Sebastian exhaled, tilting his head slightly, his gaze heavy with knowing. "I have seen many wars, chéri, fought many battles. Think not on Nicolas or the others with him, for many will not return." There was sadness in his voice, though he never once admitted he feared for Nicolas's life as much as Larus did. Instead, he reached for Larus's hand, gripping it firmly. "You must think only of the adversary before you, chéri. Let us survive this night." He cast a glance at the others in the carriage. "We shall pick up the pieces after the battle."

CECIL HAD ORDERED LARUS TO STAY CLOSE TO HIM DURING THE BATTLE, AND as they stormed through the gates of Nathan's manor, Larus matched his mentor step for step. The air filled with deafening roars and hisses as vampires sprang at their enemies and lycans shifted mid-charge. To his right, Larus met Micah's gaze and exchanged a nod; to his left, Sebastian moved quickly, a grin flashing across his face. Ahead, Haruki severed a lycan's head with a single, fluid strike of his sword.

As they breached the mansion, many of Nathan's vampires surrendered at the sight of Cecil. But those who chose to fight met swift deaths. Cecil was magnificent—untouchable. The power of his mind warned him of every attack before it struck.

Larus barely had time to react before a massive lycan slammed into him, knocking him flat onto his back. The beast loomed over him, its jaws snapping mere inches from his face. He shoved against its chest with all his might, but the creature was too strong. A swipe of its massive paw tore into his face, claws raking deep into his skin. The searing pain barely registered before the creature suddenly jerked, a sickening crack echoing in Larus's ears. The beast slumped onto him, dead weight pinning him to the ground.

Larus shoved it off, looking up to see Sebastian towering above him, smiling.

"Careful, chéri." Sebastian's voice was light, but there was an edge to it. "Remember my warning—we pick up the pieces after we win the battle."

Larus said nothing, only offering a sharp nod before Cecil's call rang out.

"To me, Larus!"

Fighting raged all around him, but Larus followed, his boots slipping in pools of lycan blood. He cast one last glance back at Sebastian and Micah.

"We're right behind you," Micah assured him. "Go."

Sebastian called to another. "Avlon, you're with us! Babette and Haruki will hold things here."

Larus took the stairs two at a time, knowing what lay ahead. The crypt.

But when they reached the massive chamber beneath the mansion, Larus felt a cold dread coil in his chest. The sarcophagi were empty.

"They've moved," he said, glancing to Sebastian, Micah, and Avlon. But Cecil was already gone.

"There's another door," Larus muttered. They ran across the hall, through a second entrance—straight into a fight. Cecil stood in the centre of the chamber, surrounded by Nathan's council. All but one.

Lucas was not there.

Larus barely had time to register the thought before the battle engulfed them. He dodged a vampire's attack, but a familiar voice made him hesitate.

"Uncle!"

His heart clenched. Silas.

Larus's gaze snapped to a steel cage across the room—Silas and Jude, imprisoned.

"Get us out of this thing!" Jude shouted.

But Larus had no chance. A vampire crashed into him, knocking him back against the cage. His ribs rattled from the impact, but he recovered swiftly, slamming his attacker to the ground. He drove his knee into the vampire's back, gripped his head, and tore it clean from his shoulders. Larus rose, hissing as he lifted the severed head in a silent, primal victory.

But the fight was not over.

He turned toward Cecil, ready to aid his mentor, but Cecil shoved him back. "Help the others!"

Larus hesitated. Cecil was still in his weaker form, battling Nathan and four others. But before he could protest, a cry ripped through the chamber.

"Micah!"

Sebastian's voice.

Larus whipped around just in time to see his maker—held fast by two vampires.

No.

Sebastian fought desperately, but he was too far. And Larus—Larus was too late.

The vampires wrenched Micah's arm from his body.

Then, they took his head.

Larus's world tilted. His heart slammed against his ribs. A roar—deep, guttural, inhuman—tore from his throat as rage consumed him.

Heat exploded through his veins, his vision narrowing into a red haze. He charged, his movements different—faster, heavier, something more. He struck one vampire down, then the other, severing both their heads with effortless, brutal precision.

The chamber spun.

Silence fell.

Eyes turned toward him.

Larus froze, panting. His hands—his hands were covered in thick black fur, his fingers tipped with razor-sharp claws. He glanced wildly around—Silas and Jude stared at him in awe, admiration flickering in their eyes. But something else—awe of what?

Then, he heard it. The growl was not in his head. It was his own.

But there was no time to dwell on the change. Athena stood above Avlon's lifeless body. Only three adversaries remained—Nathan, Athena, and one other.

Cecil smiled.

And then he struck Nathan's chest.

Nathan countered, his hand plunging just as deep into Cecil's body.

Larus saw the moment the battle shifted. Athena and the last vampire lunged to aid their master. But before they could reach him, Larus and Sebastian cut them down.

Now, only Nathan and Cecil remained, their hands buried in each other's chests.

They were locked in place, neither willing to release their hold.

A moment passed. Then another.

They stood like statues, frozen.

Then, suddenly—impossibly—Cecil smiled.

And in the next instant, both he and Nathan withered into dust.

Many members of his coven had perished, including the great Cecil Bleddyn. But Sebastian knew what had to be done. Emerging from Nathan's crypt, the grim reality of the aftermath set in. Babette, Haruki, Geraldine, and Randall were dead. Isabelle, Monique, Helene, and Ashkan were among the living, though visibly shaken, their battle-weary eyes reflecting the weight of the night. With a long, exhausted sigh, Sebastian's gaze lingered on the headless corpse of Giles. His mind drifted for a moment, a silent prayer for those lost, before he turned his attention to the survivors.

Larus and his sister embraced tightly, a brief moment of solace amidst the devastation. But their peace was fleeting, as Gavin and Nicolas burst through the doors, their faces grim, accompanied by seven lycans and five vampires. As soon as Isabelle saw Gavin, she broke from her brother's arms and rushed into his embrace, a bittersweet reunion in the midst of chaos. Silas's lycans surrounded him and his son, their expressions unreadable, and Sebastian could feel the shift in the air—the loss of Micah and Cecil had left an unmistakable gap. He had no choice but to lead now.

"All are dead at the governor's mansion," Gavin announced, kneeling before Silas, the weight of his words sinking heavily into the room. "But Lucas has escaped."

Silas gave a sharp, dismissive shrug. His reaction spoke volumes; whether from exhaustion or his endless pragmatism, he seemed unmoved by Lucas's escape.

Nicolas approached Larus and Sebastian, his eyes searching the carnage for answers. He glanced over the bodies of their fallen comrades with sadness. "Where are Cecil and Micah?" His voice was hoarse, the sorrow in it palpable.

Sebastian shook his head slowly, the loss settling in his chest. "They're gone." His voice cracked, though he quickly regained his composure. Nicolas and Larus looked to him, the heavy expectation clear. What now?

"We pick up the pieces," Sebastian said with quiet authority. His tone left no room for doubt. "There must be no trace of this battle after tonight. Burn the bodies. Burn the dead." His words cut through the tension, and though they were soaked in grief, they were resolute.

Silas nodded in agreement, his usually stoic face reflecting the weight of the decision. Without another word, the vampires and lycans moved together to dispose of the dead. The night would be long, but there was no other choice—survival, and the promise of what would come next, was all that mattered now.

57

EVOLUTION OF A VAMPIRE

White Castle would never be the same again. It had been a month since the second deaths of Cecil and Micah, but the losses didn't stop there. So many others had perished.

It was early morning, and Larus slowly rose from his bed, the weight of his sorrow still heavy in his chest. He moved toward the window, the cool morning air brushing against his pale skin. Turning to glance at Dominic, asleep beside him, Larus felt a twinge of something—something that pulled him from the darkness of his grief, if only for a moment.

He had never known such loss, nor had he ever witnessed so much death. His family, once vast and strong, was now reduced to so few. He had only his sister Isabelle and his nephews, Silas and Jude, left. That thought alone was enough to hollow him out. But they had Tilley. The old matron had taken charge at Bleddyn Manor, her strength holding things together in ways Larus hadn't been able to.

For weeks, he had retreated to his old rooms at Bleddyn Manor, unwilling to face the truth. He'd stayed there, lost in the darkness, until Tilley had forced him to leave. "You're drowning in it, Larus," she had told him, her voice gentle but firm. "Your grief is suffocating them. Go." And Tilley had been right. Larus had spent so many days locked away, refusing to feed, barely caring for himself. His reflection had been a stranger—

pale, gaunt, and distant, a mere shadow of the man he had been. The sunlight had become his only comfort, but even that felt hollow.

Cecil, Micah, so many others—they were gone. And Larus? He had no joy left in what he had become. The world felt empty, and nothing seemed worth the effort anymore.

As the first rays of the sun crept over the horizon, Larus stood by the window, allowing the warmth to wash over him. His senses, honed over centuries, picked up the sound of Dominic stirring beside him, the soft sound of his breathing filling the room. Larus closed his eyes, letting the moment stretch on as he tried to steady his racing thoughts.

He felt Dominic's arms slip around him, a comforting presence behind him. Dominic's lips brushed gently against the curve of his neck, and for a moment, Larus leaned into the touch, seeking solace in the warmth. "I've wanted this for so long, Dominic—to feel the sun against my skin," Larus whispered. "But now... now that I have it, Dominic, it means nothing..."

Larus swallowed hard, the weight of his words pressing down on him. "I still grieve," he replied softly, his voice heavy with exhaustion.

Dominic's arms tightened around him as if trying to pull him from the abyss that had claimed him. "Sebastian worries for you, Larus." His voice trembled with the unspoken pain beneath it. "He grieves as you do. I grieve for my sister, too."

Larus could hear the pain in his words, and it struck a chord deep within him. Dominic, ever the constant, had lost so much as well. Larus glanced back at him, his thoughts muddled.

"Seven of your council members are dead, Larus," Dominic continued, his voice soft but urgent. "Sebastian needs you. We all do."

The truth hit Larus with the force of a crashing wave. Of the council, only Sebastian, Monique, Marc, Ashkan, and Larus remained.

The world had changed. His world had changed. But still, there was a part of him that refused to let go of the darkness. He had lost too much—too many—but perhaps it was time to return, to pick up the pieces, and help those who were still here.

Larus entered the room known to all as Micah's Hall. Marc walked beside him, but Larus felt the weight of sorrow drag him down, the very air around him heavy with grief. The first thing his eyes landed on was the portrait of the beautiful Estlyn, Micah's mother, her serene expression a sharp contrast to the storm raging within him.

Sebastian stood by the window, his silhouette framed by the flashes of lightning. It was a dark, oppressive night, as if the heavens themselves shared Larus's sorrow. The thunder rumbled, and raindrops pelted the window with a force that mirrored the turmoil inside him. He longed for his maker, clinging to the desperate hope that this was all some horrible dream. But Larus knew, deep down, that Micah was gone. So many others whom he had loved and cherished no longer walked the earth.

He saw it in his mind again—the flames that night at Nathan's mansion, lycans and vampires alike piled together and burned. The vampire corpses, easily ignited, consumed by the flames and reduced to ash within moments. But the lycans, they burned through the night. Their bodies slowly returning to human form as death claimed them.

Sebastian broke the silence, though he still didn't turn from the window. "Isabelle, Helene, and Nicolas have been appointed to the council," he said. His voice, usually filled with mirth, now carried a solemn edge. "You, chéri, are second. We are a council of eight... more will come."

Larus heard the words, but they felt distant, almost hollow. He was pleased, yes, but it was a fleeting emotion, one he could barely hold onto in the wake of so much loss.

Marc moved closer, placing a gentle hand on Larus's shoulder. Even the warmth of his friend's touch did little to soften the numbness inside him. Larus's voice trembled as he spoke, barely above a whisper. "If only I'd listened to Cecil. If only I'd helped Micah, as he asked me to. None of them would have died."

Sebastian turned sharply, his eyes burning with a mix of anger and pain. "You don't know that, Larus." His voice was harsh, raw. "You blame yourself, just as I blamed Micah for Emilio's destruction!"

Marc stepped forward, his hands grasping Larus by the shoulders with a tenderness that contrasted the fury in the room. "I knew Cecil would die," Marc said softly, his voice steady despite the weight of his words. "I told him he would have his vengeance, but what I saw—it was unclear. I didn't understand it, not at the time. But I told Cecil Nathan would die by his hand. I told him Nathan's death would not be in vain..."

Sebastian's voice dropped to a near whisper, his words heavy with realization. "You saw his death..."

Marc's gaze flicked from Sebastian to Larus, his eyes intense, almost compelling. "I believe Cecil alone understood my prophecy, when even I failed to see what it meant. He knew his time was coming. He was no fool. But I live by his words now. Before the battle, he told me I would be tormented if I didn't accept what I am." Marc shook Larus by the shoulders, his grip firm, forcing Larus to meet his eyes. "Do you see, Larus? I ran from my visions, instead of embracing them. Cecil was right. Accept what you are! Be what Cecil knew you would become. I know now, he had no love for this world. Cecil was old, Larus—he traveled to Paris to visit his maker's shrine. He wanted to die, but only after he had his vengeance. And do you think, for one moment, Nathan could have defeated Cecil if he had transformed into the hybrid he once was?"

Larus stood frozen, the weight of Marc's words hanging heavy in the air. The pieces of the prophecy began to fall into place, but it didn't make the pain any easier to bear.

Sebastian's voice broke the silence, soft but urgent. "The coven needs you more than you know, chéri. I need you, for I cannot rule this coven alone." His gaze softened as he stepped closer to Larus. "Much of Nathan's vampires have pledged allegiance to us—to me. Some have fled, searching for the one they believe is their true master. Lucas still lives, Larus, and I fear we have not heard the last of him."

Sebastian's eyes darkened, and his voice grew firmer. "We've seized his father's lands, and all lycans now serve Silas as master. It is time to build, Larus. It is time to live. Do what none of our kind can—because you can. You are the only living vampire who can walk in the sun. You are evolved!"

PART SEVEN

58

NYC (2014)

Larus's office occupied the entire fifty-fourth floor of the skyscraper that bore his name. It was a bright, sunny day, and for a moment, Larus relished the view of the clear sky. There had been a time, long ago, when he had shunned the warm rays from above. Now, they felt like a reminder of the life he had fought so hard to carve out for himself. He gazed at the world below, his eyes scanning the city that never ceased to amaze him. The Empire State Building stood majestic in the distance, and he smiled faintly. He had stood at its pinnacle countless times, and he was there the day construction had begun in 1930.

Larus was born human in 1773, 241 years ago, and the transformation to vampire had changed his life in ways he could never fully explain. As the founder and CEO of Bleddyn Media, he lived a life of fortune and privilege. The world knew him as Maxwell Bleddyn, though his true identity remained a well-guarded secret. His father had long since passed, but Larus had continued to build the organization around his father's name. Over the years, he had mastered the art of altering his appearance, living multiple lives as various ancestors of Bleddyn's founder. But it was all his work, his vision.

In a world driven by technology and awareness, Larus had learned to thrive. His coven, too, had adapted, using their wits to survive in an ever-watchful world. But despite the wealth and influence he had amassed, Larus could never forget the loss of those he had loved. Cecil, Micah, and so many others had perished on that fateful night at Nathan's mansion, and the wounds still lingered in the deepest corners of his heart.

Beatrice entered the room, her tablet in hand. She was a rare find, efficient and proactive in a way that Larus both admired and relied upon.

"Mr. Bleddyn," she said, her voice calm and businesslike, "they're here."

Larus turned and nodded. "Show them in, Beatrice."

He sank back into the white leather sofa, letting the sun's warmth settle on his neck. He closed his eyes for a moment, savouring the rare pleasure that only a few vampires could experience. When Silas and Jude walked into his office, Larus's lips curved into a grin. "The gentlemen of Bleddyn Manor! Come on in."

Silas, the immortal lycan, had not aged since his transformation, yet there was a maturity about him now that hadn't been present in years past. His son, Jude, still looked as youthful as the day Larus had first met him.

"You look well, Uncle," Silas said, stepping forward and embracing his uncle with a firm hug.

Larus rose to return the gesture, his heart swelling with affection for his family. "I've missed you both."

"Marc tells us you hardly leave this place," Jude added. "Do you not miss the country, Uncle Larus?"

"I've missed you," Larus said, kissing the young man's cheek. "How is Bleddyn Manor? How is Isabelle?"

Silas laughed softly. "The old church still stands." He gave his uncle a knowing look. "But we've discovered something beneath the building—something deep in the catacombs. Chambers... fit for vampires."

"You weren't meant to discover that place," Larus said, his voice laced with concern.

Jude shifted uncomfortably. "How is Isabelle?" he asked, clearly eager to move past the subject.

"She's happy," Silas replied. "And so is Gavin. They've never been happier."

"Tilley sends her love," Silas added, walking toward the window and gazing out at the Empire State Building. "Beautiful, isn't it?"

Larus joined him at the window, his eyes tracing the outline of the city. "It is. How have you been, Silas?"

Silas's tone shifted. "Sebastian asked us to come here. He worries about you. We all do. After Dominic... you left us. Now you're here with this life." He gestured at the office around them. "You're hiding away in this tower, Uncle."

Larus stiffened at the mention of Dominic, the love of his life. The pain of losing him was still raw. "I've enjoyed a life of solitude," he said softly. "Since Dominic..." His voice trailed off as he lost himself in the memories of the past. Dominic had been his everything—his companion, his world. Watching his mate grow old and die had been the greatest torment of his existence. And even as Dominic lay on his deathbed, Larus had considered turning him, desperate to hold on to him. But it was too late.

"My life is good here," Larus finally said, his voice steady once more. "The lycans live in peace. Sebastian rules the coven, and we have learned to coexist with humans. The world may not be what it once was, but we adapt. We thrive."

Silas's eyes darkened. "Uncle, Monique is dead."

Larus froze, his gaze snapping to Silas, the words slowly sinking in. "What happened?"

"Hostile vampires," Silas said grimly. "They were all taken to a property owned by someone of great wealth, a vampire who had built a death chamber specifically designed to destroy vampires."

Larus's blood ran cold. "A death chamber?"

Silas nodded. "These chambers are constructed with one door. They're designed to expose vampires to the sun at its zenith. No vampire can survive the sunlight in these chambers."

Larus felt the weight of the situation settle on him. "And you think Lucas is behind this?"

"Yes," Silas replied. "It was Lucas—Nathan's son. We're certain of it. The two vampires who escaped are certain of it."

Larus turned away, staring out at the city as the enormity of what Silas had just revealed washed over him. The peace and solitude he had come to enjoy had just been shattered.

"All our investigations and the information we've gathered point here, to this city," Jude added, his voice quiet but filled with determination.

Larus clenched his fists. The past was coming back to haunt him, and the battle was far from over.

It was after midnight when Larus walked through the main doors of his New York City residence. The doorman nodded politely, and Larus greeted him with a warm smile. Quickly, the vampire probed the man's thoughts, curious as to why humans so often feared those with wealth and power. Larus owned the building, and his penthouse occupied the top floor of the fifty-one-story glass tower. His private elevator whisked him upward to the penthouse, and as he exited, he was greeted by the distinct scent of death—another vampire. Someone was waiting inside.

Larus entered his massive suite without hesitation, knowing the vampire within was a friend. Marc, now known widely as *Oracle*, stood by the window, his back to the door. Larus smiled, a surge of affection coursing through him as he realized just how much he loved the young vampire. "By human standards," he said as he moved toward Marc, "we haven't seen each other in a lifetime."

The two embraced, and Larus felt a rush of nostalgia as he held Marc in his arms. How had he stayed away from Bleddyn Manor for so long?

Marc, slightly shorter than Larus, tilted his head back to meet his eyes, then softly kissed his lips. Larus felt his body shudder, his gaze momentarily drifting to the dark expanse of the night beyond the glass windows. Marc moved toward the pristine beige sofa and, only after sitting, spoke again. "I would have risked the journey to your offices by day with Silas and Jude, but alas, I have yet to achieve the ability to walk beneath the sun. And I fear I'll never be that lucky."

Larus couldn't help but smile at Marc's rare, wry grin.

Taking the wingback chair across from Marc, Larus shrugged. "You've always been wary of the long, dreary days spent within the shadows of stone walls, while the sun shines brightly beyond them. I, too, remember that life." His thoughts briefly turned to his nephews, the wolves. "What of Silas and Jude?" he asked.

"Hunting." Marc replied. "They crave city blood, but I've warned them not to make any new lycans in this city."

"Marc, our kind are everywhere, and so are the wolves."

"A newly turned lycan in New York would cause much trouble," Marc said. "Besides, they can hunt other beasts." His eyes locked with Larus's. "When I heard Silas and Jude were coming to find you, I had to make the journey. There is much I must tell you."

Larus arched an eyebrow.

"You have no desire to return to Bleddyn Manor or White Castle, but you will have no choice, Larus. All paths will eventually lead you back to your ancestral lands. I've come to warn you." Marc rested his chin upon pale steepled fingers, his voice growing softer. "I was hunting far from White Castle, deep in the thickets. Where have the days of carriages and steeds gone, Larus? Life was so simple then." Marc laughed, a sound tinged with nostalgia. "I sound like an old fool."

Larus remained silent, the weight of Marc's words pulling him back to a time when the nights were calm, and all he could hear with his keen senses were the hoots of owls and the rustle of rodents beneath dry grass and leaves. The world had changed.

Marc's voice broke through his thoughts. "It was after I found a doe and fed that I saw the future—puzzling as it may be." He ran a hand through his hair, clearly unsettled. "You will meet someone from your past," Marc said.

Larus leaned forward, his heart quickening. "...Though," Marc added, "it's someone you've never met."

Larus dragged a hand down his face in disbelief. "Seriously? That's puzzling enough. How can I meet someone from my past if we've never met?"

"I can only tell it as I see it." Marc sighed deeply. "It was the strangest of visions—nothing I've ever experienced before. Nothing was clear, and yet..." He shook his head, as if struggling to piece the fragments together. "Come, I shall show you."

Larus frowned, confused. Marc knew it was impossible for any other vampire to read his mind—not even Cecil had been able to do so.

"You cannot read my thoughts, Larus," Marc said, as though reading his mind. "But you can taste them."

Without another word, Marc sank his fangs into his lips, and a rich flow of dark blood spilled from his flesh. "Quickly, before I heal," he urged.

The young vampire's movements were swift, and within an instant, he was atop Larus's thick thighs, his lips pressed against Larus's mouth. The scent of Marc's blood filled the air, and Larus closed his eyes as he lapped at it with his tongue. His fangs found their mark as he sank them into Marc's tongue, momentarily losing control.

Suddenly, a rush of visions flooded his mind—sharp, vivid flashes. Larus remembered long ago when Micah first shared his blood memories; he knew what to do. Patiently, he sifted through the chaotic flow, searching for the answers he sought. And then, he found it.

He had seen so much in mere seconds from tasting Marc's blood, and the experience left him drained. Larus had never imagined that Marc endured such pain, such sorrow. But he'd found what he sought.

Marc lay on his back, still as death, yet he lived. Around him, mounds of lifeless, headless bodies—humans, lycans, and vampires—piled up like discarded remnants of a forgotten war. Marc wept, his grief raw and unending, until his wailing ceased, and an indistinguishable figure approached.

"Why do you weep, vampire?" The voice was neither man nor woman—only a raspy, hoarse whisper.

Marc turned his head, his breath ragged. *"What are you?"*

The figure chuckled softly, its voice playful and cryptic. *"I am the messenger, and you, vampire, are the oracle."* The figure gestured toward the dead mounds around them. *"This shall come to pass if he does not return. You know of whom I speak. He will meet one from his past—someone he has never met. They are bound together."*

The words hung in the air like a thick fog, lingering long after the figure faded into the shadows. *"Larus Bleddyn must return."*

"But who are you?" Marc asked, still staring at the fading figure. *"I can see nothing of what you are."*

The figure laughed again, its voice distant but somehow mocking. *"I am of a line long forgotten, long dead. Yet, remnants of my existence linger in your world. Larus Bleddyn and the last of me are bound together. Fate or chance shall unite them."* Another eerie chuckle rippled through the air.

Marc continued to gaze at the blurred figure, unable to tear his eyes away. *"This person... who—"*

"They are of each other's pasts," the messenger replied, its voice cracking with a hoarse laugh. *"Though they have never met..."*

LARUS COULD HARDLY AVOID LOOKING AT MARC'S LIPS, EVEN AS THE thoughts from the young vampire's blood memories—still fresh in his mind—left him confused and perplexed. "How do you withstand such torment, Marc?" he asked, shaking his head to dispel the rush of images that now haunted him. He couldn't forget the softness of the oracle's lips against his. He remembered the human boy he once knew over a century ago—Marc, the son of Avlon, the beautiful Afro albino with piercing green eyes. Avlon had died in battle with Cecil, along with so many others Larus had loved. A sudden wave of sorrow washed over him, pulling his thoughts to rest. "It must be...difficult, what you endure."

The young vampire nodded. "I embrace what I am. Only then can I master the torment." Marc's eyes sparkled with a fleeting smile. "It was Cecil who told me that. He made me accept who I am. Remember what they taught you, Larus. Cecil and Micah wanted you to lead."

Larus turned away, a frown tugging at his lips. "Did I not leave Sebastian in charge? It was his desire to lead a coven." He faced Marc again. "Sebastian now rules over a coven of vampires and a pack of lycans."

"Sebastian and Silas are usually at odds." Marc's voice was soft but firm. "The wolves and our kind lead separate lives, and rightly so. We are separate species, after all."

"Silas and Jude are family," Larus said. "And I am—"

"Unique." Marc's pale hand reached out to touch Larus's face. "You are a rare breed, Larus. It is your destiny to lead us. You're a hybrid. Isabelle's marriage to Gavin, the wolf, will not be enough to bridge the natural divide between lycans and vampires. We are enemies by nature. Eventually, the bond between us will weaken."

Larus frowned. "Is there trouble at Bleddyn Manor?"

"Nothing Silas and Tilley can't handle." A faint smile tugged at Marc's lips. "That old woman runs Bleddyn Manor with a firm hand."

Larus grinned, pride swelling in his chest.

"Several lycans have defected over the years," Marc continued, his expression darkening. "Many have left the safety of Bleddyn lands to fend for themselves. Small packs of lycans will grow over time, and that can only spell trouble for the vampires. You must protect us, Larus." Marc rose from the sofa and walked toward the door. "I must go. The others will be waiting before daylight."

He paused, glancing out into the city's sea of lights. "This city... I can't say I like it much."

Larus smiled at the sound of Marc's voice. "You must stay tonight. I have the entire floor to myself, and besides, I built this place to keep out the sun. Pick any room you like."

"Vampires were never meant to live in the skies," Marc replied.

Larus patted his friend's shoulder. "Don't be silly. It's 2014, Marc—the middle of July! New York is the best place to be!" The two walked down a pristine hallway, and Larus suddenly felt a wave of happiness at having Marc with him. It had been far too long. "You've missed the most exciting occasion—the 4th of July!" He saw the confusion in Marc's eyes and laughed. "Marc, don't tell me you've let all these years pass without living. That's the beauty of immortality."

"The world has changed," Marc said softly.

"No, Marc. It's changing." Larus smiled, his voice warm with optimism.

Marc chose the first room on the right, and Larus followed him inside. "I must get Silas and Jude here tomorrow night," Larus said. "Hector, my VP, and his wife, Yvette, are throwing a charity ball in my honour. I think you should come."

59

CHARITY BALL

Hector Drake's wife, Yvette, had orchestrated the lavish fundraiser in Larus's honour. As the vampire's limo glided to a stop before the Chrysler Building, Larus took a moment to admire the towering Art Deco masterpiece. He had seen it before, of course, but had never thought to visit.

Stepping out of the vehicle, he slid his hands deep into his pockets and tilted his head back, his keen vampire eyes tracing the intricate details of the great gargoyle above. "Magnificent," he murmured. He knew his companions had heard him.

He glanced at Silas, Jude, and Marc, wondering if they, too, felt the weight of history pressing upon them. "Less than a century old," he mused, "yet a lifetime for many in this new, strange world."

"Lycans were never meant to live among the clouds," Silas remarked.

Larus smirked. "Wolves prefer to keep their feet on the ground, I know." He turned his gaze back to the shimmering skyline. "But times have changed. We can cling to our ways, but we must move forward with the world."

Marc stood apart, his expression unreadable, his pale eyes reflecting the golden city lights. Larus recognized that look—disinterest, perhaps even detachment. He sighed and placed a casual arm around Marc's shoulder.

"This is just one night," he assured him. "Yvette Drake is a good woman. She has done this not only for charity but to impress the wives of wealthy men. A social game, yes, but her intentions are not without merit. Unlike most in these circles, she was not born into wealth."

Larus gestured toward the grand entrance. "We have lived for centuries, Marc. Just this once—enjoy yourself."

YVETTE STOOD BY HER HUSBAND'S SIDE, HER PALM DAMP AGAINST HIS AS THEY held hands. Again, she searched his eyes for reassurance, for they had always drawn strength from one another—especially now. This was her biggest, most expensive event yet, the pinnacle of her efforts since Hector's appointment as Vice President.

Bleddyn Media wielded power in New York—perhaps even the entire country—and her husband stood near its helm. A Black man who had come from nothing.

"Just think of all the money we'll raise tonight, baby." She kept her voice low, measured. "Think of all the people we can help—all the charities we'll support."

Hector chuckled, brushing a kiss against her cheek. "And I suppose raising millions has nothing to do with throwing it in the faces of your enemies?"

Yvette squeezed his hand and gritted her teeth. "Those bitches." She smiled as her gaze flicked toward a cluster of women—the wives of the city's elite. Her rivals. They had come tonight not to celebrate her success, but to watch her fail.

"Honey, I grew up poor. I scraped by my entire life, and it kills me to see them look down on me for it."

Hector kissed her cheek again, lingering this time. "Darling, I've told you a thousand times... all this"—he gestured toward the glittering hall, the sea of rich and powerful guests—"means nothing if you're miserable. These women? They're nothing."

"You rub shoulders with their husbands every day. Men are different." Her voice tightened, but she forced another smile. "But at the end of the day, Hector, you're the Black guy who got the job because Bleddyn likes you, and I'm just the daughter of a maid."

"Be happy, Yvette." His fingers tightened around hers, warm and steady. "That's all that matters."

But before she could respond, he straightened his shoulders, smile widening as his boss approached—flanked by three striking young men.

60

LOLA

Lola yanked the bowtie from her neck and unbuttoned the stiff white shirt, exhaling sharply as if shedding a noose. She stuffed the tie into her pocket with a muttered, "Fucking noose!" before reaching for the tray of champagne glasses.

She hated this gig—playing servant to a swarm of cackling moneybags—but five hundred dollars in cash for a single night? She wasn't about to turn that down. At least half would go straight into Basil's college fund. If only her little brother knew how hard she worked to keep a roof over their heads.

Moving through the glittering crowd, she fought the urge to sneer. The room was filled with the rich, all here to donate a fraction of their wealth—none of which would ever find its way to people like her and Basil. Hypocrites. Lola bit down on her irritation, but it was hard. Every time a bejewelled hand plucked a glass from her tray, its owner barely acknowledged her existence. As if the drinks simply appeared in midair. As if she didn't exist.

The rich never gave thanks.

"Spoiled, ungrateful fucks." The words slipped out under her breath as she counted down the hours until she could grab her cash and get the hell out.

Still, despite everything, she couldn't deny the Chrysler Building's beauty. She'd lived in Manhattan all twenty-five years of her life but had never set foot inside. And now, her first visit was to serve drinks. The thought made her stomach twist, but she forced it aside. The money was what mattered.

Basil was seventeen now. She'd raised him alone since their mother died when he was twelve. Losing their mom had shattered him, and Lola had done everything she could to hold their world together.

She wove back across the room with her empty tray, brushing a long plait of hair from her face—and that's when she noticed him.

The pale man stood motionless, staring at her, mouth slightly agape.

Lola's stomach clenched. Her lip curled in disgust.

What the fuck is he looking at?

He found the courage to move toward her. Larus left Silas, Jude, and Marc behind, knowing they had seen what he had—the undeniable likeness. The resemblance was impossible to ignore, and yet, how could this be? She clutched a serving tray against her chest, her skin dark and flawless, her long plaits cascading over her shoulders, framing sharp, striking features. Just like the woman in the painting he had kept for over a century.

Larus forced himself to resist the temptation to read her thoughts. It felt like a violation. And yet, as he approached, a strange fear coiled within him—fear of speaking, of naming what he saw. He had faced centuries of bloodshed, ruled over empires in the shadows, but the scornful look on this woman's face made him hesitate.

She was sneering at him, but it didn't diminish her beauty.

"If you weren't so damn young, I'd say you're a perverted old man." Her voice was sharp, unimpressed. She eyed him up and down, assessing him without a hint of restraint. "And you're so damned white, it's a shame. You need to get your ass out in the sun, dude." She rolled her eyes, unimpressed, and Larus felt something tighten in his chest.

He did everything in his power to hold back his vampire tears.

"Look, fool, if you ain't got nothin' to say, step aside and let me get on with my business, which is serving this jewelled piss to all these spoiled brats." She smirked. "Sorry—these rich asses." She tapped the back of her tray with her fingers. "So if you're thinking of making a pass at me, you can forget it, sucker."

She studied him again, more carefully this time. Something flickered in her expression. "I mean, you cute and all that...but you ain't my type. Boys ain't my thing." A pause, her head tilting slightly as she pursed her full lips. "At least not at the moment." Then she scoffed. "And definitely not dudes like you."

"I...am Larus Bleddyn."

She narrowed her eyes. "Wait, hold up." She exhaled sharply and clenched her jaw. "Shit, shit, shit." Her gaze darted around, as if suddenly aware of something bigger at play. She shook her head. "You're the top dog these snobs have been fussing about?"

She didn't wait for his response.

"Boy, these idiots would kiss your ass if you asked them to. Your name's been rolling off every one of their tongues." Then, a wary look crossed her face. Suspicion.

"I assumed this Larus Bleddyn was some old dude."

Larus smiled, but the weight of the moment pressed down on him. He had to move quickly.

"This may seem strange, Lola James," he said, his voice quieter now, "but it is imperative that we speak in private. You and I."

Lola's breath hitched. Her brows drew together.

"And just how the hell do you know my name?"

By then, Silas, Jude, and Marc had joined them, standing just behind Larus. He could feel their silent stares, the unspoken questions hanging in the air. But all he could focus on was the fire in Lola's eyes—the fierce, defiant glare that challenged him.

LARUS HAD NO IDEA HOW HE WOULD DO IT, BUT ONE THING WAS CERTAIN—Lola had to come with him. She needed to see Micah's portrait of Estlyn.

Surprisingly, she had agreed to follow Larus and his companions to a private room on the same floor as the event. Once inside, Larus shut the door behind them, but when he turned to face her, the words failed him.

How was he to tell this young woman that she was the near-perfect likeness of her ancestor?

His thoughts drifted to Estlyn's portrait, and suddenly, memories of his maker surged to the forefront of his mind. The old church on the Bleddyn lands. The night he was sired. The catacombs. Micah's cold hand pressed against his cheek—

"Well, are we all just gonna stand here?"

Lola's sharp voice snapped Larus back to the present. She folded her arms, her piercing gaze bouncing between him and his companions. "Y'all know I'll scream like hell if you get any crazy ideas, right?"

She studied them, her expression shifting from irritation to curiosity. Her head tilted slightly as she pointed toward Silas and Jude.

"You two must be brothers or something."

Then she turned to Marc. "And you, the gangly one—you seem a bit sketchy, but there ain't nothing about you that looks like them." She motioned toward the lycans again. "But you? You and them got something in the eyes. I think you're related."

Larus smiled, impressed. "You are observant, Lola."

He glanced at his nephew and great-nephew. If only she knew the truth.

"These are my nephews—Silas and Jude." He gestured to the lycans. "And Marc is a distant relative."

Lola studied them for a long moment before smirking. "Y'all look like porcelain dolls."

Marc took a step forward. His voice was smooth, deliberate. "This may seem strange, my dear, but our meeting was long foretold."

Larus watched as Marc reached for her hand. Lola didn't resist, but the moment their skin touched, she yanked away.

"Dude, you're fucking cold!"

Marc simply smiled.

Larus knew he had to convince her to come with them willingly. He had no intention of compelling her, but she needed to see the portrait.

"Lola, there is much we need to discuss," Larus said, his voice calm but firm. "You must trust me—trust us all. But before anything else, there is something you need to see."

"Everything will be explained," Silas added.

"We just need you to come back to our place tonight," Jude said.

Lola narrowed her eyes. "If y'all are looking for some one-night family gang bang," she said flatly, "Lola James don't roll that way."

Larus stifled a chuckle. "Nothing of the sort," he assured her. "We simply need to discuss your family."

"My family?" Her tone hardened. "What the hell do you know about my family? Did Basil get himself into some shit I don't know about?"

Larus caught the name in her thoughts. Basil—her brother.

"No, Lola. Not him. I'm talking about before... long before."

Her expression flickered with uncertainty.

"I promise you," Larus said, stepping closer, his voice quiet, sincere, "we mean you no harm. I just have some questions, and I need you to see something. After that, my driver will take you wherever you need to go."

Lola stared at him, arms still crossed, her expression unreadable.

Larus could feel the weight of the moment hanging between them.

Would she come?

61

ESTLYN

Lola was impressed by the wealth of this strange man, though she'd heard of Bleddyn Media before. Who would've thought she'd be standing in the penthouse of one of the richest men in New York City?

From the moment they left the Chrysler Building, she'd known this group was strange. The way they had all looked at her—as if shocked by her very existence—had set her on edge. Now, they were seated in a massive room, and Lola found herself momentarily distracted by the glittering skyline beyond the glass wall. The city stretched out before her, a sea of lights against the dark of night.

She grabbed a glass from a tray but hesitated before taking a sip. She was thirsty, but something about this whole situation made her uneasy.

"So," she said, finally breaking the silence, "here I am. What's so important that you couldn't tell me at the party?"

Larus stood by the window with his back to them, staring into the night.

Lola's gaze shifted to Marc first. She trusted him the most out of the bunch. The other two seemed okay, but there was something about them—aloof, hesitant. And the younger one, Jude... Why was he watching her like that?

It was clear they all deferred to Larus. Everything began and ended with him.

Finally, he turned, raising a single dark brow before motioning toward a door.

"Come."

Lola followed, the others trailing behind as the pocket doors slid open at Larus's touch.

The room was just as elegant, sparsely furnished. But it wasn't the decor that stole Lola's breath—it was the painting.

She gasped. "What the fuck!"

She stared at the massive canvas, her pulse spiking. Because staring back at her—fixed in paint and time—was herself.

"Dude, do you need my permission to have a big-ass painting of me on your wall?"

The woman in the portrait looked older, wiser. Her dark eyes held a quiet strength that Lola wasn't sure she possessed. And yet...something about her felt familiar.

"She...she looks like me," Lola murmured, stepping closer. "Even like my mama, kinda..."

"She is Estlyn," Larus said.

He approached the painting with a kind of reverence, as if introducing her to a queen.

Lola's fingers tingled as she reached toward the canvas, drawn to the woman's gaze. "Estlyn? Who...who is she?"

Larus smiled. "She is the reason you are here now, Lola."

He let the words settle before continuing. "Estlyn was born in 1612. She had a son named Micah in 1628—after she was forced to lie with her owner. Later, out of spite, Micah's father, Massa Duncan, sold Estlyn. They never saw each other again. Micah spent the rest of his life believing his mother had died."

Larus turned to her, his hands settling gently on her shoulders. His gaze was filled with something raw. "But you are proof, Lola, that Estlyn lived." His voice softened. "I only wish Micah were here to see you with his own eyes."

Lola blinked. Then frowned.

"Hellooo! Dude! How in the hell could he be here right now to see me if she had him way back in 1628?" She folded her arms. "For a rich guy, you suck at math."

Larus simply smiled. "What do you know of your family's history, Lola?"

She shrugged. "Not much. My mom said most of the women in our family never made it past fifty." A shadow crossed her face. "Cancer."

She rarely talked about her mother. It only ever brought pain. But now, standing in front of Larus Bleddyn, that pain was tearing at her insides.

She took a breath. "Look, I never heard of no Estlyn before. But the women in our family don't usually have sons, so I guess that's rare, but they live long lives. That's why I worry about my little brother. Basil's all I got. I get regular checkups and all, but if something happens to me... that kid is on his own."

She caught the quick glances exchanged between Larus and the others.

"I'm sorry about your mother, Lola," Larus said, his voice quiet. "I lost mine, too. A long time ago."

"It happens." She blinked back the burn of tears. Then, forcing herself to focus, she nodded at the portrait. "So how did you get it?"

"It was given to me."

Again, he looked at his companions. Something unspoken passed between them. A silent agreement.

"Micah painted it," Larus said at last. "Many years ago. And he gave it to me."

Lola let out a short laugh, waiting for one of them to crack a grin, to admit they were messing with her.

But none of them did.

Their eyes—solemn, unwavering—left Lola James utterly confused.

His staff knew when he wished to be alone, and although he did little work that day, Larus still lingered in his office. Three days earlier, he'd told Lola to find him at Bleddyn Tower. He'd shared only what he felt was necessary, and though it took some time for Lola to believe he truly knew Micah, she eventually accepted his word. What choice did she have? He'd shown her exactly what he was—a vampire.

Lola had left his penthouse just before dawn, escorted by a concierge in a company car. Reclining behind his desk, Larus questioned his decision to reveal the existence of his kind to her. Despite his doubts, he still believed it had been the right choice. Marc agreed.

He shook his head briefly, unsure whether he should laugh, recalling the terror in Lola's eyes when he'd revealed his fangs. But it was the sight of the wolves' transformations that had sent the girl fleeing toward the door. It took several minutes, a glass of whiskey, and Larus's reassurance to calm her nerves.

Marc had explained afterward that only the truth would help Lola understand the past. "Whether for good or ill," Marc had said, "I cannot tell, but this human's existence holds some importance. We must keep her close."

Lola had left still in shock, but she'd promised to consider Larus's offer—an offer of a job at Bleddyn Media. She said she needed time to think. A few days, perhaps.

62

BASIL

It had been nearly three weeks since Lola started working at Bleddyn Media, and Basil had spent the last two days begging her to take him on the tour she'd promised him days after she began the job. A swipe of her badge and a stern look from the security guard were all it took for them to get in.

"Is your new boss in the building?" Basil couldn't help asking. Everyone knew the name Bleddyn, and the slightest chance of meeting the man made him both nervous and excited.

Lola shrugged dismissively.

"Come on, Lo. You know how it is. All my friends will freak when they hear I met the guy."

"I ain't telling you again, Basil. I show you the place, then you get your ass to class. And you'd better be home when I get back."

He waved his hand as if to brush her words away. "Any chance you can hook me up with a part-time job? I mean, you've got connections now."

"Worry about school and keeping your grades up."

"Gosh, Lo, just lay off for a bit. You know I get straight A's. I swear! You sound just like Mom. My grades are always up."

Lola swiped her badge again as they entered the elevator. "Do your part, Basil, and I'll lay off a bit." She slapped the back of his head. "And cut the 'Mom' stuff."

He met his sister's gaze, seeing it again—the hurt. It pained him that Lola had hardly spoken of their mother since her death. Suddenly, Basil felt like he'd been hit by a block of ice. The anxiety hit him in an instant—the rapid beating of his heart, the shortness of breath, and that overwhelming feeling that something deep within him wanted to break free. He hadn't mentioned it to his sister—God knew she had enough to worry about. But Basil had been struggling with these panic attacks since the day he received news of their mother's death.

HE'D LIVED FOR CENTURIES, BUT FOR THE FIRST TIME IN ALL HIS LONG LIFE, Larus was in utter shock. He sat behind his desk, staring at Lola and her younger brother, Basil, for what seemed like an eternity. Larus was speechless. What he saw before him was a young man who resembled his maker, Micah.

There were, however, several differences. Micah had been mulatto, the product of a slave owner and a negress, while Basil had cool, dark skin. The boy's complexion was flawless. He was tall, with full brown lips and wide eyes. Still young, yet already possessing the physique of a grown man.

It suddenly occurred to him that he'd been silent since Lola entered his office with her brother. "You must forgive me," Larus said, his voice regaining its composure. "I've been... preoccupied." He gestured toward the wingbacks facing him. "Do sit down."

He studied Basil's eyes, feeling the urge to peer into his mind, but something stopped him.

"Welcome, Basil," Larus said. "Lola has spoken very highly of you. It's a pleasure to finally meet you."

"Uh... thank you... uh... Mister Bleddyn." Basil glanced at his sister as he nervously rubbed his palms together. Larus could smell the sweat, see the goosebumps appearing over the boy's long arms. The sound of his heartbeat was clear to Larus, racing in his chest. Basil moved toward the chair, nudged by Lola's impatient roll of her eyes. Once seated, he wiped his sweaty palms against his knees.

"It's... kinda nice of you to take time out of your busy day to meet me, Mister Bleddyn... Sir."

"Larus," the vampire corrected with a smile. "Call me Larus."

Lola cleared her throat gently, standing beside her brother. "Kid, you gotta get going now." She crossed her arms. "School time, remember?"

"Lola, come on." Basil seemed to forget for a moment that he was in the presence of his sister's boss. "There ain't much going on at school today."

"Lots more will go on if you don't get your butt out of that chair." Her tone was firm, and Larus couldn't help but marvel at how much she resembled Micah's mother. "You'd better get moving before you miss the bus. It's a long walk across town."

Larus smiled, the hint of amusement in his expression. "My driver will take you wherever you need to go, Basil."

"He needs to get his ass to school," Lola said, not softening her tone. "As far as I'm concerned, that's the only place he's going."

Larus buzzed his assistant's desk. "Beatrice, have Brian prepare my car. His passenger will be Mr. James."

Larus watched as Lola ushered her brother out of the office, noting Basil's reluctant farewell.

HE'D SPENT THE LAST TEN MINUTES ENDURING ANOTHER OF HIS SISTER'S endless lectures. Though he was disappointed about leaving so early, he was relieved to escape Lola's wagging tongue. With a nod to the guy at the front desk, Basil made his way toward the main exit—only to freeze at the sight of the black Aston Martin Lagonda Taraf idling at the curb. The windows were tinted as dark as night.

No way. The words barely made it past his lips.

As he stepped outside, the chauffeur greeted him with a grin.

"Fuck no! This can't be happening."

Suddenly, school felt like a trivial concern. If he was lucky, his friends would see him stepping out of this car later.

The chauffeur opened the rear door. "Mr. James, I'm Brian, your driver for the morning."

Basil nodded, mouth agape. He took his time sliding into the plush interior, drinking in the luxury—then froze again when he realized he wasn't alone.

"Mr. Bleddyn!" He whipped his head toward the building, then back to the pale-skinned man beside him. How the hell did he get in here? "How... how'd you—?" He gestured toward the tower.

"Private elevator." Larus Bleddyn smiled.

Something about that smile made the hairs on Basil's arms rise. Not in fear, exactly—but there was something too smooth about the man, the way he seemed to glide through the world without effort. Like nothing could touch him.

"Where to, my friend?"

Basil hesitated, still trying to wrap his head around this. "Oh... uh, A. Philip Randolph. It's at 433 West 135th."

Larus reclined as the Lagonda Taraf eased onto FDR Drive. "I wanted a chance to talk alone," he said smoothly. "In private. I had the sense there was something you wanted to say to me. But your—"

"Lola is driving me crazy, Mr. Bleddyn."

"Call me Larus."

"I told her I wanted to find a part-time job, earn some cash, you know? But she's just like Mom was—always making rules, always forgetting I'm seventeen now."

"Your sister loves you, Basil. It may not seem like it, but she would do anything for you."

Basil huffed. "Then why won't she let me chip in? Why does she keep pushing college like we've got the money for that?"

"I'll speak with her," Larus said. "Perhaps I can convince her to reconsider."

Basil's head snapped up. "You'd do that?"

Larus shrugged modestly, but Basil could see the amusement in his eyes.

"I get out at noon on Thursdays and Fridays!" Basil blurted, already extending a hopeful hand.

Larus took it gently, his grip firm—but the second their skin touched, a shiver ran through Basil's body. Cold. Too cold.

He fought the urge to pull away. Maybe Larus had poor circulation or something, but it wasn't just the temperature that unsettled him. It was the effortless way the man took control of everything, the way he always seemed one step ahead.

Still, he had to admit—it would be pretty damn cool to have a job working for him.

Basil felt a chill rush over his body, his hand still trapped in Mr. Bleddyn's firm, cold grip. But the icy touch, the almost unsettling composure of the man, the impossible agelessness of his face—these thoughts drifted to the back of Basil's mind.

Larus Bleddyn was a rich man. A powerful man. He had already given Lola a job, and somehow, Basil knew his own luck was about to change.

His mind became a labyrinth of tangled thoughts, but one leapt to the forefront: Mr. Bleddyn owed him nothing. Why had he just assumed this man would give him anything? Lola was different. Lola was a woman. Lola knew her way around men—though Basil had always known she was more into girls. It wasn't something they ever needed to discuss. Lola was Lola. And though he'd never say it to her face, he was damned proud of her.

"Beatrice will look into a position for you, Basil," Mr. Bleddyn said.

Basil blinked, realizing he'd gone quiet. "Beatrice?"

"My assistant." Larus placed a hand on his shoulder. "Yes, the tall girl."

For a moment, Basil stared at him in shock. He had been thinking about the girl outside Mr. Bleddyn's office—the tall one. But how had Larus known that? Was he that easy to read? He chose not to say anything, yet a strange sensation coiled in his stomach. The awe he'd felt toward Lola's boss began to shift. Not to distrust exactly, but something closer to fear.

The car slowed to a stop outside his school, and again, Basil found himself lost for words. He reached for the door instead of offering his hand.

"Thanks for the ride, Mister... I mean, Larus."

For a moment, he hesitated. His mother had always told him to show respect to his elders. But Larus Bleddyn didn't seem old at all. And yet... there was something ancient about him. It was in the way he carried himself, the way he tilted his head as he said goodbye—like a figure pulled from another century.

Basil let out a nervous laugh, shaking his head as the words tumbled out. "There's something different about you... like you're one of those gentlemen from an old English movie. Or, I don't know, a historical novel."

Mr. Bleddyn's brows lifted ever so slightly.

"Uhm... sorry. Just thinking out loud."

"You're quite perceptive," Larus said smoothly. "Maybe I'm the one that is easy to read, Basil James."

Basil's breath caught.

For a moment, they held each other's gaze, and he knew then—this man was something else. There was more to Larus Bleddyn than he could understand.

And Basil wasn't sure he wanted to know what it was.

63

WITHOUT A TRACE

Lola was going to make him pay for being late—Basil was sure of it. It was well after sunset, and even though he was seventeen, living under his older sister's roof came with rules. He'd agreed to be home right after class on school nights unless she knew ahead of time. But he'd lost track of time, first hanging out, then shooting hoops with his friends.

He'd tried telling Lola before—boys played ball, they hung out—but all she ever said was, *do it closer to home.* His friends had stayed behind, but Basil had to come up with some excuse, some reason he couldn't stay. The truth? He was broke. He'd spent his last cent on food and didn't want to bum bus fare off anyone. So, he walked home, picking his usual shortcuts through the city.

Earlier that day, Larus Bleddyn had freaked him out a little, but that didn't stop him from using the man's name to boost his popularity. His friends thought it was badass that he was going to work at Bleddyn Media. Hell, they even asked if he could get them jobs. Basil had promised to see what he could do, though he had no idea if that was even possible.

The last streaks of red in the sky vanished behind the darkening skyline as he turned down an alley. Lola's lecture was inevitable, but he could handle it. She'd been even more on edge lately, digging through their mother's old things, searching for something—documents, history, answers. What was the point? Basil didn't care. What was there to find except more death? The women in their family never made it past a certain age.

The alley was quiet. Too quiet.

Basil's stomach tightened.

Something felt off.

He kept his pace steady, eyes scanning for any sign of life—a beggar, a passerby, anyone. He heard it then. Footsteps? No—something else. A faint rustling, a whisper of movement. His pulse picked up. Up ahead, a lone figure stood motionless about fifty paces away.

Basil hesitated.

He couldn't tell if he should be relieved or afraid.

The figure didn't move. It just stood there. Waiting.

"Fuck this shit," Basil muttered, turning sharply—

And ran straight into a man.

Pale. Deathly pale.

Even in the alley's darkness, Basil could see every detail of his face. Worse, he could see his eyes.

He barely had time to react before a hand—ice-cold, impossibly strong—clamped around his throat and lifted him clean off the ground.

His feet kicked uselessly in the air.

The fingers tightened.

And then there was nothing but panic.

It was well after midnight. Larus, Marc, Silas, and Jude stood out on the terrace, where the night breeze carried the city's distant hum. Larus had been telling them about the boy, Basil. Silas and his son listened with keen interest, but Marc had already made his stance clear.

"This is dangerous," Marc warned.

Larus met his gaze, unwavering. "It is the only way. Why else would Lola come to us if not for this? She is a descendant of Estlyn—Micah's mother." His voice held steady, but beneath it was something else. He wanted Marc's approval. "Besides, you saw her in your vision, did you not?"

Marc exhaled. "Yet we still do not know her true purpose, Larus." His fingers tapped the stone railing. "My visions, at times, are as clear as cut glass—other times, they are as murky as the foggiest night."

Then Marc went still. He lifted his head, nostrils flaring.

Silas and Jude caught the scent as well.

Larus smiled. "Surely, this is a sign."

Jude was already moving. "I shall let your guest in."

Moments later, the young wolf returned, and with him came Lola James.

Her eyes burned with fury.

She strode onto the terrace, her gaze sweeping the space. "Where the fuck is my brother?"

Larus studied her—the sharp set of her jaw, the way her chest rose and fell with barely contained rage. The likeness to Estlyn was unmistakable. He took a measured step forward.

"Basil?"

"Dude, why the hell you think I'm here?" she snapped. "You think I'd step foot in your house if Basil was home? It's nearly one in the morning—he ain't back."

Larus glanced toward the others, though he already knew the answer. He had looked into Lola's mind. *She believes her brother is with me.*

"Why do you think he would be here?"

Lola folded her arms. "Because the guy at the front desk told me he left with you this morning." Her voice sharpened. "What the hell do you want with my little brother?"

"He asked for a job," Larus said evenly. "Something after school. I told him I would have Beatrice find him a position. My driver dropped him at his school."

Lola's frown deepened. Her breath hitched ever so slightly.

"You're doing that fucking shit right now, aren't you?" she said. "Picking through my head." She shook her head, her voice tight. "Dude, I thought you said you—"

"Your brother is veiled within a shroud of darkness."

All heads turned to Marc.

His eyes were closed, but Larus knew his sight was sharper than ever.

Lola moved toward him, but Larus caught her arm. Her pulse thundered against his fingertips. He could feel the fear rolling off her, taste it in the air.

Marc's voice came soft, distant.

"The boy is taken."

A shudder ran through Lola's frame.

"Basil is terrified."

Basil's eyes flickered open to darkness.

For a moment, confusion clouded his thoughts. Then it all came rushing back—the alley, the cold grip around his throat, and those blue eyes. A pale, translucent face, red hair, a scatter of freckles, and the thin, unsmiling mouth of his captor. He didn't know this man. Had never seen him before.

And yet, one thing stood out.

Basil didn't know why, but he felt it in his gut—something about this man didn't make sense. His hands had been cold. As cold as Larus Bleddyn's.

And that meant something.

He turned the thought over in his head until a metallic groan filled the air. The heavy steel door creaked open, spilling dim light into the room. Then, as his captor stepped over the threshold, Basil caught a glimpse of the walls—thick, rusted steel.

A ship.

An old one.

The realization sent a jolt through him. He knew exactly where he was. Somewhere near 12th Avenue. There was only one abandoned ship docked at the cruise port, and as far as he knew, no one was allowed on board.

"You are a clever one."

The voice sent a chill down Basil's spine.

The pale redhead stepped closer, but he wasn't alone. Three others flanked him, their expressions unreadable.

"You thought right, Basil" his captor continued. "You are at the docks." A grin curled his lips. "But not for long."

Basil's jaw tightened. "Who the hell are you?" he demanded. "And how the fuck do you know my name?"

The man loomed over him, smile widening.

"I am Lucas. Your executioner…" He let the word linger, tasting it. Then, softer, "Or your friend. The decision is yours."

Basil wasn't small—he was tall, well-built for his age—but this man had lifted him like he weighed nothing.

Lucas chuckled. "Yes, I am strong. Very strong."

Basil's pulse quickened. How the hell—

Lucas tilted his head. "It's simple. I can read your thoughts."

Basil stiffened. "Gimme a fucking break, dude."

Lucas shrugged. "Very well."

He began pacing, his eyes on the floor as if lost in thought.

You were with Larus Bleddyn earlier today," he said. "What was that about?"

Basil scowled. "You're the mind reader—you tell me."

For a split second, he wondered if Lucas really could read his mind. And if he could—had Larus done the same?

Lucas smirked. "Oh, he can, Basil. But Larus follows rules—he won't enter a mind without permission." He stopped pacing, gaze locking onto Basil's. "So tell me, why would he break those rules for you?"

Basil swallowed. The weight of Lucas' words pressed down on him.

This can't be real.

Lucas grinned. "Oh, but it is." His voice dropped, turning cold. "Because we are vampires, boy. Superior to your kind."

Basil let out a harsh breath, shaking his head. “This is some kind of joke.”

But then Lucas moved.

Faster than thought.

Before Basil could react, Lucas was there, inches away, his lips peeling back to reveal sharp, gleaming fangs.

Basil’s breath hitched.

His heart pounded.

And in that moment—when his instincts screamed run but his body refused to move—he believed.

64

TWICE BITTEN

Lola had wept before Larus and the others left.

She'd begged to go with them, but Marc had forbidden it. He warned that if she went with Larus and his lycan nephews, she wouldn't like what they found.

Now, she stood alone on the terrace of Larus's penthouse, hugging herself against the cold. The night was fading, the city stretching toward dawn, but she barely noticed. She could feel Marc's eyes on her, even though she kept her back to him, staring out at the skyline.

She'd questioned the vampire known as the Oracle. Pushed him for details. Demanded answers.

But Marc had told her nothing new.

He had only spoken of Basil's fear—his racing thoughts, the scent of sweat and steel. His body had twitched when he described the howling, a deafening sound in a darkened place. It had been Lola who said the words cruise docks first.

Marc had only nodded.

"My visions may appear unclear at times," he had murmured. "But they always make sense after—"

"After?"

Lola turned sharply, eyes blazing.

"After what?" she demanded, stalking toward him. "Look, I know you could sink those fangs into my neck and suck the life outta me." Her voice was raw. Dangerous. "But I swear to God, I'd fight like hell in my last few seconds. Maybe, just maybe, I'd take your pale ass to hell with me."

Marc's expression didn't change. His skin, luminous in the moonlight, betrayed no fear.

Lola clenched her fists. "I can't read your mind," she said, "so tell me what the fuck you mean."

The vampire studied her in silence. Then, in his measured, eerie calm, he spoke.

"My visions come from the dead," Marc said. "From those long gone... or those recently deceased."

Lola's breath hitched. No.

Her heart pounded as she forced herself to say it. "Go on."

Marc tilted his head slightly, watching her with those fathomless eyes.

"I warned Larus of your existence, though I had no knowledge of it," he said. "That vision was linked to Estlyn, a woman long dead." His voice dropped lower. "I usually see the dead. They appear to me. Speak to me."

Lola felt herself swaying.

"But in my vision of Basil," Marc continued, "I did not see him."

The words hit like a blow.

"I only felt him," Marc murmured. "I saw the darkness. Smelled the rancid sweat and iron. Heard the echoes of his fear." He paused, letting the weight of it settle. "But I cannot say he is dead."

Lola swallowed hard.

"Because I did not see him," Marc said. "He did not speak to me."

THE WOUND TO HIS NECK WAS EXCRUCIATING. BASIL'S VISION SWAM IN AND out of focus, but there was no mistaking what had happened. He'd seen Lucas—the vampire—his eyes cold and full of menace. Basil had witnessed the transformation of the two men, their bodies contorting into beasts with black claws and razor-sharp teeth. He had no strength left to struggle, his body fading into dizziness. But even as weakness overwhelmed him, he could hear the beasts' heavy breaths, the scent of their fur and the bitter tang of blood.

Basil could feel his own blood dripping from the first wolf's dark fur, and though his body felt as if it had been hit by a tranquilizer, his mind fought to stay awake. It had been nearly an hour since the wolf had bitten him, yet his captors remained silent, watching with an unnerving stillness.

Finally, Lucas looked at the other beast. "It's time."

A strange sensation spread through Basil's body—something that felt like it was about to tear him apart. His joints screamed with pain. His heart pounded furiously, as if it wanted to break free from his chest.

And then the beast approached.

Fear washed over Basil, amplifying the pain. He couldn't fight back. The wolf's teeth sank into the same wound, and the pain was so intense he couldn't help but cry out. The beast pulled away, and Basil collapsed to the floor, gasping for air.

"My youngest recruit yet," Lucas observed, his voice oddly detached.

Basil looked up, his vision blurry, his eyes swimming with tears. "What've you done?"

"I've given you a gift, boy." Lucas's lips curled into a wicked smile. "I've given you power."

Basil shook his head weakly, his voice a hoarse whisper. "I'm dying?"

Lucas's smile grew. "In a way, yes..." His fingers brushed a lock of his red hair back from his face. "But not like the death I had centuries ago. You'll simply change. The boy you were before this night? He's dead."

"Why... why did you do this?" Basil whispered, the pain coursing through him in waves.

"Because I can." Lucas's tone was casual, as if the life of a human was little more than a game. "Because I felt I needed to."

"What the fuck is happening to me?" Basil's voice trembled with fear.

"You're evolving," Lucas said, motioning to the two wolves. "Becoming something new. You're like these creatures, but different." His eyes darkened. "Larus Bleddyn showed interest in you, so I took it upon myself to take you from him. And though he may have considered making you a vampire, I've robbed him of that. You'll be a lycan—a wolf."

Lucas's laugh was low, mocking. "But there's a catch, you see. Killing you would have been too easy..."

Suddenly, Lucas's eyes flicked to the door. Basil felt his body shake with fear, but he couldn't move.

The steel door flew off its hinges with a deafening crash. Standing in the doorway were three figures. Larus Bleddyn entered, exuding an aura of triumph that filled the room.

"Lucas, we meet again after so many years."

Larus didn't even glance at the two roaring wolves, so Basil quickly learned why. Two more figures followed Larus into the cabin. They were wolves too, their forms already shifting, their clothes tearing as they transformed. The battle was over in an instant. The two beasts fell, their bodies slumping lifeless to the floor. Larus's companions stood behind him, their claws dripping with blood.

"There is no place to run now, Lucas. Nowhere to hide. You slipped away over a century ago—not this time."

Basil felt Lucas's grip tighten around his neck, but he could barely register it as he focused on the scene unfolding before him. How could these creatures speak of centuries as if they were mere days?

"I could kill him," Lucas sneered. "If I'm to die, so must he."

Basil felt Lucas's laughter as he pressed a taunting kiss to his face. "Yes, Larus, I've made the boy a wolf—half of what you are, hybrid. You are like Cecil Bleddyn, maybe even stronger. But I'm smarter."

He turned, his grip still unyielding on Basil's neck. "The boy," Lucas continued, "he's been turned. But he's nothing like them." He motioned toward the two fallen wolves. "He's diminished."

Larus's gaze darkened, and Basil saw the confusion in his eyes. "Lucas, what have you done?"

Lucas laughed again, cold and mocking. "You are unique, Larus. You may even be the strongest of us all. But even with all your years, you are still a young vampire. I am much older. I know more. Does that not make me stronger?"

Larus's fangs flashed as his rage surged. "Tell me what you've done, or I shall end you now."

Lucas's grip tightened on Basil, but Basil's gaze was fixed on Larus. Long, black claws sprouted from the tips of Larus's fingers. Dark hairs covered his face.

"Ah, there he is!" Lucas's voice dripped with glee. "The hybrid. Half vampire, half lycan."

"Like I said, Larus," Lucas sneered, "if you end me, I end him."

He patted Basil's face mockingly. "The boy's been twice bitten."

Before Larus could react, Lucas provided the chilling explanation. "If you turn a human with one bite, then wait—just at the moment that first bite begins to take effect—and bite a second time, from a different lycan... the human experiences two turnings."

Lucas backed away, a sinister smile curling on his lips. "Now you begin to understand, Larus. Knowledge is power."

Basil felt the shifting inside him, his body rebelling against the transformation. Something was happening.

"The boy's first turning will be permanent," Lucas taunted. "He'll be more beast than man. The second will be... more unpredictable. He'll shift back to his human self once a month. But the wolf will be dominant. The human will be weak."

Basil was dragged near the door. Lucas shoved him to the ground, his laughter echoing through the cabin as he slipped into the shadows. "I must bid you adieu."

Larus's voice was a low growl, full of menace. "Lucas, you will burn for this."

But Lucas was already gone.

JUDE AND HIS FATHER STOOD STARK NAKED OVER THE BOY AS HE THRASHED AT their feet. Basil was changing. Like his father, Jude looked to Larus for a solution, but their leader appeared as shocked as they were. What were they to do with a newly turned lycan who could never return to his human form at will? Dawn was breaking, casting a pale light across the scene. Jude looked to Larus, seeing the tears in his eyes. "What must we do?" he asked, desperation rising in his voice.

There was no answer from his father or from Larus. "Father! Uncle! What now?" His father stared at Basil, dumbfounded.

Finally, it seemed Larus came to his senses. "Daylight is upon us. We cannot stay here." He said, his voice low and urgent. "Soon, this place will be swarmed by the homeless and tourists. The police will be doing their rounds." He glanced at the two dead lycans, now returned to their human forms. "We will have to leave them behind."

Jude shook his head. "But he's changing! Did you hear what Lucas said? After he changes, he'll remain like this for weeks."

His father sighed heavily. "He's a large fellow and will be much larger after he changes. It will be difficult to subdue him."

"You are an alpha, Silas." Larus said, his tone firm. "He must heed your commands."

"Why is his transformation taking so long?" Jude asked, his voice trembling slightly.

"It's as Lucas said," Larus replied, pinching his chin in thought. "The boy was twice bitten." He glanced at Basil, his eyes filled with a mix of pity and strategy. "We lock him in the trunk of the car and drive as quickly as we can to my place. It's the only way."

The vision of dragging a shrieking beast up the elevator, two naked men with Larus at the lead, was terrifying. Jude knew his uncle's plan would never work. A newly turned lycan needed a remote place.

He gazed down at Basil, feeling his agony. He couldn't shake the thought of the boy's curse. Basil was condemned to a life of imprisonment, trapped in a body that would forever fight against him. Jude pitied him deeply. For the first time in his life, Jude felt the weight of his immortality. He had never hated himself for what he was... until now.

Suddenly, his only thought was to ensure Basil's safety. "He needs a remote place, uncle..." The words flowed from deep within him. "He's a lycan, not a vampire."

Larus nodded, a flicker of hope in his eyes. "Oyster Bay. I own property there." He turned toward the door, urgency in his every step. "I'll get the car. The place is empty, but we should get there in forty minutes if we move quickly."

"Come, Jude." His father's voice was heavy with decision. "Help me move him."

They managed to put Basil into the trunk. His body was covered in patches of silver hair, his dark skin struggling against the change. He fought, but Jude could only hope he could hold on for a little longer.

65

VOW OF VENGEANCE

Lola took exit 41N, both hands gripping the steering wheel so tightly that her fingers ached. Jude sat next to her in the passenger seat of Larus's company car. She had spent the first twenty minutes of the long drive to Oyster Bay firing questions at him, but the wolf remained silent, offering nothing in return. It was nearly sunset, and Lola couldn't shake the absurdity of the situation. The night before, she'd spent it alone in Larus's high-rise mansion with a vampire. She almost laughed at the thought. Here she was, driving a lycan to an estate in the middle of nowhere.

She glanced at Jude; he seemed terrified, his body tense and stiff. "What's the matter? You mean to tell me you've lived all these years and you're scared of a bit of speeding?"

"I am of a different time, Lola," Jude replied, his voice distant. "Things back then were... different." He grimaced, not meeting her eyes. From the moment he returned, Lola had noticed something in his expression—something sorrowful, something heavy.

"Oh, carriages and shit like that..." Lola muttered, trying to lighten the mood.

"Yes. Like that." He didn't look at her. The silence in the car was oppressive.

"Look, dude, I know something's happened to my brother." She slapped the steering wheel in frustration. "Just fucking tell me what happened to Basil. I'm not sitting in this car just for Larus to tell me my brother's dead."

"He lives," Jude said, his voice low.

Lola exhaled, the relief washing over her. "And?"

"My uncle will explain."

"God damn it! He's my brother!" Lola pressed her foot down on the gas, the engine roaring as the car sped up. More than anything, she wanted to see Basil, to take him home.

"For centuries, there has been a war between vampires and wolves. They are mortal enemies," Jude began, his tone serious.

"But you're a..." Lola snapped her fingers. "...A lycan, and Larus is a vampire. What gives?"

She glanced at him, catching the frown on his face. "Gives?" Jude seemed confused.

"I mean, why the hell are you his nephew if you're a wolf and he's a vampire?"

"The Bleddyn clan has always been wolves," Jude replied, his voice steady. "It's in our blood. But Cecil Bleddyn was the first of our kind to be turned by a vampire—the first hybrid."

"A halfbreed."

"Yes, but stronger. My uncle is a hybrid."

Lola's mind raced as she processed this. "But what's any of this got to do with my brother? Why are we driving all this way for him to tell me Basil is okay?"

Jude sighed, dragging his hands down his face in frustration. "Lola, there's something you must know..."

A massive country house stood upon an estate, acres of land stretching far into the distance. Lola stared at it from behind the wheel, her palms sweating profusely. She had no idea such a peaceful place existed so close to the city. But now, as she took in the sight, the calm surroundings felt like a facade. She knew what awaited her inside that house.

"Dude, I know he's my brother... but after what you've told me, I'm terrified."

Jude's expression darkened, the weight of the situation settling over him. "I watched it happen, Lola. We had to restrain him. You must remember that the cage is for his protection... as well as our own."

"You put my little brother in a fucking cage?" Lola's voice wavered with disbelief, her eyes widening. A wave of red-hot anger coursed through her veins.

"He nearly killed my father after we got him inside," Jude continued, his voice steady but grave. "Your brother is strong... and he's yet to feed."

"Feed?" Lola dug her fingers into her hair, trying to clear her thoughts. "What the hell does that mean?"

"A lycan must feed shortly after turning. It's their primary goal... to kill."

Lola shook her head in disbelief, her hands trembling. "I can't believe any of this shit."

Jude's eyes softened, but the gravity of the situation still lingered. "Come. We must go inside."

As he reached for her hand, Lola recoiled instinctively, her eyes flashing with a sudden intensity. "You keep your fucking hands off me!" she snapped, pointing a finger at him.

Lola walked into the room, her presence felt the moment she crossed the threshold. Larus reached into her mind, realizing she already knew what awaited her. The weight of Basil's fate pressed down on her like a physical force. Jude had eased the burden of telling Lola what Lucas had done to her brother, but the hybrid seemed to think it was all his doing.

Larus stood beside a disheveled desk littered with papers and books, his eyes locked on Lola as she approached. He studied her carefully, sensing the fury burning in her dark eyes and the sorrow that weighed heavily in her heart. His own heart ached with guilt, and he found himself at a loss for words.

From the cellar, the haunting sounds of Basil's growls echoed through the house. The thundering crash of his body slamming against the iron bars reverberated like a warning. Lola froze. Tears welled in her eyes as she stopped before Larus, her chest heaving with anger. For a moment, the room was still—silent, even.

Finally, Larus spoke, though his voice was strained. "I should have taken care of him. I should have known my enemies—"

Before he could finish, Lola snatched a letter opener from the desk and slashed it across Larus's face. The sharp blade cut deeply, but the wound healed almost instantly, leaving only the faintest trace.

Lola stumbled back, her breath quickening, but her voice, fierce and raw, filled the room. "You take my brother from me, and now you take my vengeance!"

Larus said nothing. Part of him wanted her to keep going, to keep slashing at his skin, but he knew it would heal. What he truly needed was for her to release the rage she held inside. But even that was not enough to erase the sorrow he could feel radiating from her.

Lola's breath came in ragged gasps as she spat out, "You go off with my little brother, and now he's some damned beast? A freak like them?" She pointed toward Silas and Jude, her finger trembling with emotion.

Larus caught the scent of another approaching vampire, one whose presence seemed to fill the room. The oracle. Marc had found them. Within moments, the door opened, and Marc stepped inside.

His eyes locked onto Lola, and he moved directly toward her. With a gentle touch on her shoulder, the storm of emotions inside Lola seemed to settle for a moment, her features softening as she turned to face him.

"Your brother's journey has begun, child," Marc said, his voice calm, almost soothing. "It is up to you to decide whether you will aid him or end him."

Gently, he lifted her chin, his thumb brushing her skin. "It is clear to me now. I told you I could not see him. Basil did not speak to me. He is dead as you knew him... yet he is very much alive. But it will be difficult," Marc continued, his gaze thoughtful. "For you both."

Lola's voice was steady, resolute. "Take me to my little brother."

Without a word, Larus moved toward the door leading to the cellar. Lola followed, the others trailing behind them. Larus knew there was no need to explain further. Lola would see for herself. She would have to witness the creature her brother had become.

As they reached the foot of the stairs, Larus saw the yellow eyes again. The silver-black fur. The massive form of the lycan, his long teeth gleaming in the dim light.

"Careful, Lola," Larus warned, his voice low. "He won't know you."

But Lola's gaze was unyielding. Marc stepped forward, standing between Larus and Lola, shaking his head. Larus exchanged a confused look with Silas and Jude. What did Marc know that they didn't?

"Open it," Lola's voice was unwavering, her fury palpable.

Silas stepped forward to open the cage, but the moment he did, Basil's beastly rage erupted. He lunged, a deafening roar echoing through the room.

"Lola, he will rip you apart..." Silas's voice was filled with panic. "He's mindless now."

"Open the fucking cage!" Lola barked, her voice cutting through the tension.

Jude, without hesitation, obeyed her command. The heavy iron door creaked open. Lola hesitated for only a second before stepping toward her brother.

The lycan, towering over her, lifted its massive arm, its black claws gleaming in the dim light, ready to strike. But Lola didn't flinch. She moved closer, stepping forward with determination. The lycan let out another guttural growl, his rage barely contained.

Larus noticed that the creature had not fed—it was wild, frantic. But then Lola did something unexpected. With the letter opener still clutched in her hand, she threw herself against her brother, pressing her body to his. The blade fell to the floor with a sharp clang, forgotten in the heat of the moment.

For a moment, Basil's rage subsided. The lycan, still towering over her, stepped back, his massive arms instinctively protecting her.

Larus watched in stunned silence, his eyes wide. Basil, though newly turned, was unlike anything he had seen before. Larger, more powerful. But what struck him the most was the way Lola was not afraid.

Basil had been twice bitten.

Silas stood with his son, Jude, observing the massive lycan within the cage. He felt confident that Lola was in no immediate danger, but there was something unsettling in the air. Marc, the oracle, appeared calm, as though he had foreseen everything. His piercing eyes held secrets that Silas had learned to respect over the years. Marc smiled softly, his gaze shifting between the girl and the lycan, but he said nothing.

The alpha of the Bleddyn Lycans stood silently, watching Lola as she gently stroked Basil's furry cheek. For a brief moment, Silas found himself contemplating what it would be like to exist trapped inside a beast's body after living for so many years as a human. Basil was only seventeen, but now he was trapped in a form he couldn't escape from—except for a few short days each month when he could revert to human form. Silas glanced at his son, knowing Jude was likely thinking the same. For them, changing at will was natural. But what Basil had become was a curse. And yet, Lola had done what no one else could—she calmed the beast inside him.

As she left the cage, Basil's mournful roar echoed through the room, but he was subdued by his sister's presence. She pushed the gate shut, her voice carrying an unshakable calm as she spoke. "Settle down, Basil!" The lycan, twice bitten, tilted his head, staring at her in silence.

"I won't leave you. Not ever," Lola said softly, her words a promise. She then turned to Silas, her eyes locking with his. Her gaze was steady, resolute. Without hesitation, she pointed toward the cage. Her words came not as a question, but a command. "Make me like him."

Silas's brows shot up in surprise. He stood there speechless, processing her words. The room seemed to hold its breath as the others waited for a response.

Larus, who had remained silent until now, stepped forward. "No."

Lola's eyes narrowed as she shot back, her voice fierce. "And who the hell are you to decide that? My little brother wouldn't be locked up in that cage if it weren't for you!"

Larus's expression softened, but his stance remained firm. "You would make a better vampire."

"You think you're better than us?" Jude, standing between his great uncle and Lola, spoke boldly, his voice full of defiance. "It's Lola's choice to decide what she wants to become."

Larus sighed and placed a hand gently on Jude's shoulder. "Forgive me, Jude. That's not what I meant. It's just that... Micah—"

"It is how it must be," Marc interjected, his voice calm and steady as always. He moved to Lola's side, his presence a quiet reassurance. "Only she can tame him. Better she be like him."

Marc turned to Larus with understanding in his gaze. "Remember, lycans and vampires are natural enemies. Basil will trust who she trusts." His eyes softened as he looked to Silas. "It was never destined for Micah's kin to be as he was. The girl is strong. Together, she and her brother will be a force to be reckoned with. They will be as one."

Silas nodded, acknowledging Marc's insight, but still unsure of the weight of what was being proposed. Marc's gaze shifted to the stairs as he began to leave. "Come. Let us leave Silas to his work."

Silas found himself alone with Lola, standing in silence as they both watched Basil, caged and wild. The room felt colder now, the weight of the decision before them palpable in the air.

Finally, Silas turned to Lola. "It will be painful at first. There's a chance you may not survive the change. The choice is yours."

Lola didn't hesitate. "My mind's made up. Do what you gotta do."

Her resolve was clear, and Silas knew there was no turning back. The girl had made her decision, and now, he had to prepare her for the unimaginable pain that would come with the transformation.

66

SHE WOLF

Lola stood on the rear terrace of Larus's Oyster Bay estate, staring out into the vast expanse of trees and sky, lost in thought. It still astonished her how drastically her life had changed since that fateful night at the Chrysler Building. Above her, sparrows darted through the air in swift, coordinated flocks, and she marvelled that she could hear the delicate flap of their wings. The scent of unseen creatures drifted from the woods, mingling with the crisp night air, while far in the ravine, water trickled over smooth stones.

She felt powerful. Majestic, even. And yet, deep in her gut, she knew the truth—this wasn't a gift. It was a curse, one she had brought upon herself.

No human was meant to live forever.

But then, she wasn't human anymore.

The realization still rattled her. Vampires, lycans—monsters once confined to whispers and folklore—were real. And she was one of them now.

Lola let out a slow breath and dragged her palms down her face, closing her eyes against the ache in her chest. "Oh, Mama," she murmured, her voice barely above a whisper. "If only you'd held on a little longer—long enough to meet Larus..."

She knew it was unfair to torment herself with thoughts of what could never be, but she couldn't help it.

She sensed her brother before he even stepped onto the terrace, his heartbeat steady but tinged with something deeper—resignation, maybe. Basil lowered himself onto the steps near her feet, resting his head against a wooden post. He said nothing.

Lola understood his silence.

For the past three and a half days, Basil had been human again. And soon, that would be over.

After his transformation, she had spent hours with him, asking questions, trying to understand. She had told him how she had nearly died after Silas's bite, how excruciating it had been to endure the change. And Basil had shared what little he remembered of his own experience.

"It was your scent," he had told her. "That's how I knew it was you, Lola. Everything—everyone else—was the enemy."

Now, she studied him carefully. As if sensing his thoughts, she reached out, trying to offer whatever comfort she could.

"You know I'll always have your back, baby brother, right?"

Basil exhaled sharply and slammed his fist against the wooden deck. "Why'd this have to happen to me?" His voice was thick with frustration. "This life, Lola... it's a goddamn prison sentence. Who the fuck wants to live caged up for almost a whole month? Why me?"

Lola sighed, shaking her head. "What did Mama always say to us when things got hard? When she could barely afford to put food on the table?"

Basil didn't answer at first, but she waited, unwavering. Finally, his shoulders slumped, and he muttered, "You work with what you got."

The words hung between them, and Lola knew the moment he understood—there was no changing their fate. This was their reality now.

She moved beside him, nudging his shoulder with her own. "We're family, Basil. I chose this because of you. Mama begged me, with her dying breath, to look after you. And this... this was the only way I knew how."

Basil pressed his head against her shoulder, the weight of his grief, his frustration, settling between them.

And for now, she let it.

LARUS STUDIED THE BOY CAREFULLY AS HE SAT ACROSS THE ROOM WITH HIS sister. Basil and Lola—inseparable. It was something Larus had noticed from the start, but it was also something he had discussed at length with Silas and Jude. If Basil ever became a threat, they had vowed to exhaust every option before resorting to the one thing they all feared—the one thing Lola would never forgive.

Larus sat with one leg crossed over the other, observing the siblings in silence. He could sense their bond, their unspoken understanding that they were stronger together. Still, he knew they had to face the reality of what Basil had become.

"Every lycan needs a pack, just as every vampire needs a coven," Larus said at last. His gaze locked onto Basil. "I didn't make you, but I am your alpha. I am not just a vampire. I am a hybrid."

Basil watched him warily.

"Lucas believes he's struck a blow against us by turning you, but we will not sit idly by and do nothing. You are one of us. And we take care of our own." Larus leaned forward slightly. "Twice bitten you may be, but you are still human. You are young, Basil, but you must learn to discern friend from foe."

The boy clenched his jaw, his hands curling into fists. "You have no idea what it's like, Larus." He closed his eyes for a brief moment, as if trying to push something away. But Larus had already caught the violent images swirling in his mind—chaos, hunger, and an insatiable thirst to kill.

"I just want to rip everything apart," Basil muttered. "That's all I know. That's all I can remember."

Larus nodded, unfazed. "I've spoken with Sebastian." He held up his mobile. "Gone are the days when messages took weeks to cross leagues and oceans. Now there's this." He tapped the device, then returned to the matter at hand. "Sebastian is much older than I am. Silas and I explained your situation, and he has given us some hope of changing it."

"More like altering it," Silas interjected from where he leaned against the wall near the window, arms crossed.

Lola frowned. "What does this Sebastian know that you two don't?"

"In our world, age is knowledge," Larus replied. "And knowledge is invaluable—sometimes it's the key to survival. It was knowledge that allowed Lucas to put us all in this predicament."

Basil let out a sharp breath. "Alright, then, what the fuck did he say?" His chest heaved as he braced his elbows on his knees, burying his face in his hands. Lola placed a reassuring hand on his shoulder but said nothing.

Silas spoke next. "It may not work. But the solution Sebastian suggested is worth a try." His tone was grave. "However, it comes with its own risk, Basil." He hesitated. "You may not survive it."

Basil looked up, his eyes hard with determination. "Go on."

Larus exhaled. The boy needed to know everything before making his choice. "Had we known this before, I would have done it the night you were bitten. But now, we have a decision to make." His voice was steady, unwavering. "I am a hybrid—vampire and lycan. Sebastian believes that a bite from me could disrupt the cycle between human and lycan. It may even grant you the ability to transform at will. But there's a risk. We may have waited too long. The bite should have been given before your first transformation."

"But there's still a chance," Silas added. "If you're bitten now, while you're in your human form, it could change the cycle."

Larus saw the flicker of hope in Lola's eyes. "Change things how?" she asked.

"You've been human for nearly five days," Larus said. "You could transform at any moment. If we're going to do this, I must bite you before you turn."

Basil nodded.

Lola remained silent, but Larus could see the conflict in her expression. She knew the choice wasn't hers to make. It was Basil's.

And he had made his decision.

THE HYBRID HAD TASTED HIS BLOOD.

Basil could feel the excruciating pain spreading through his limbs, his joints locking and twisting as the transformation began. It was faster this time—brutal, but mercifully brief. He was losing control, and the fear of it gripped him.

Larus had insisted he not be locked in the cage again. Basil had agreed—on one condition. If he became a danger to his sister, to Larus, or to Silas, they had to kill him. He had begged Lola to accept this, but in the end, it was Larus who had sworn to carry out his wish.

"Remember, Basil," Silas warned. "We have no idea what will happen now..."

Basil barely heard him. His body was already tearing itself apart.

"Keep hold of yourself, little brother," Lola urged, but her voice drifted away, distant, as if she were slipping out of reach.

His shirt split at the seams as the transformation took hold. It happened so quickly. Bones cracked, muscle swelled, flesh stretched. In mere moments, the lycan stood where Basil had been—a towering, broad-shouldered beast.

The creature lifted its massive head, nostrils flaring. A familiar scent—a she-wolf. It turned toward her, eyes flashing with something primal. A deep, guttural roar filled the space as it took slow, deliberate steps forward.

The other two figures remained still. Their scents were different. The beast hesitated, claws flexing as it lowered into a predatory stance. One scent belonged to another wolf. But the other... something else entirely.

The young lycan growled, baring its razor-sharp teeth. Another roar ripped from its throat as it stepped closer, its movements laced with aggression.

Then it stopped—mere inches from Larus's face.

The beast inhaled sharply, drawing in that strange scent again. There was something there. Something... familiar.

Larus did not move. Slowly, he extended a hand, palm up. The lycan hesitated, breath heavy and uneven. Then, as Larus's cold fingers brushed against its snout, something in its posture shifted. Its lips curled, but the growl softened.

Basil—somewhere within the beast—recognized him.

The lycan let out a low whimper and pressed its massive head into Larus's hand, trembling like a pup.

LARUS HAD NEVER EXPECTED TO SEE THE BOY HAPPY. NOT AFTER WHAT LUCAS had done to him.

It was just after sundown, and Larus sat alone on the terrace, watching Basil, Lola, Silas, and Jude tossing a football in the open field. They were laughing, joyful, and for the first time in a long while, Basil seemed free—at least in this moment. Larus observed them with a faint smile, though a quiet heaviness lingered beneath it.

A movement at his side drew his attention. Marc stepped onto the terrace, the last traces of sunlight long gone.

Larus arched a brow. "Ah, you come as the sun has veiled itself. How was your sleep, my oracle?"

"Rejuvenating." Marc settled beside him, his gaze fixed on Basil. "twenty days each month—that is all the time he shall have as a man."

Larus nodded. "I had hoped my efforts would grant him more time. Yet he does show promise. Basil is happy again."

"And he knows us as friends, even in his lycan form." Marc's voice was steady, assured. "Larus, your efforts were fruitful. The boy will adjust to his new fate. Give him time."

Larus grunted, neither fully agreeing nor disagreeing. Two months had passed since he'd bitten Basil, and while Sebastian's instructions had worked, the outcome was bittersweet. Basil was no longer lost in blind fury when he transformed, but he was still bound to the cycle of the moon, caged in his lycan form for too many days.

Still, Marc was right—Basil would adapt. And at least Silas and Jude had taken him and Lola as their own. A pack. A family.

"I am certain you have noticed the affection that has kindled between Jude and our new she-wolf," Marc remarked.

Larus nodded. "They have said nothing to me, yet I have seen the way they feel about each other in their minds." A frown tugged at his lips. "Leave them to their secrets."

"Secrets?" Marc raised an amused brow. "Do you think their affections require your blessing? Larus, they know full well you can see into their minds."

"I did not say that, Marc."

Marc studied him for a moment before speaking again. "Lola will forever keep you at a distance unless you abandon this notion that you own her."

Larus turned to him sharply, fury flashing in his pale eyes. "Own her? You think—"

"Your love for Micah is eternal, but Larus," Marc interrupted, his voice calm, deliberate, "you seem to claim everything connected to your maker. He gave you his lands, his wealth, and now you have found his kin." A pause, then, "The girl is fire. You cannot tame her. But you must remember—it was Micah and his mother, Estlyn, who were slaves long ago. Not Lola. If you treat her as such, she will resent you for it."

Marc rose to his feet, the conversation settled in his mind even if it wasn't in Larus's. Without another word, he turned and ran toward the woods.

It was a good night for hunting.

PART EIGHT

67

RECKONING

Daniel was one of the last to leave the Pyramid Club. Soon, the sun would rise. At twenty-one, he had spent the last seven months revelling in his newfound freedom, but as he walked toward E 7th St., he wondered why he had longed so desperately for adulthood. Nothing had changed. He could come and go as he pleased, yet he was still filled with rage.

His mother—the only person who had ever understood him—had been gone for two years, leaving him in the care of his namesake, Daniel Turner. The very thought of his father's name made him cringe. They were nothing alike. Though he had just left the only place that made him feel alive, Daniel dreaded returning to that house, to the man waiting inside, ready to tear him down as always. Freak. Unnatural. Fag. His father's voice echoed in his head. What was the point of those fleeting hours of joy among kindred spirits if he was always bound to return to such cruelty?

He bummed a Marlboro from a friend before leaving and now lit it up, smiling slightly. The streets were strangely barren for this hour, a silence stretching over the city like something had swallowed the usual sounds of early morning.

Then—footsteps.

Daniel tensed, his grip tightening around the cigarette as he turned abruptly. A lone figure stood in the distance: a woman in a dark hooded cloak. Pale skin. Red lips. Her bangs were cut neatly across her forehead, just above her brows.

"Katarina desires you, my friend, but I say no. Not tonight."

The male voice seemed to come from everywhere. Daniel whipped around, his cigarette slipping from his fingers.

"You mustn't scare him, Lucas," the woman murmured.

Daniel exhaled sharply. "Look...uhm...Katarina, you're barking up the wrong tree."

The voice was behind him now. He turned slowly and found himself staring into deeply set eyes, red hair, and skin so pale it looked powdered under the moonlight.

"Such limited minds, you humans," the man—Lucas—said. "He hates you more than you know, Daniel."

Daniel's pulse quickened. "What?"

"Your father," Lucas clarified. "He knew your dear mother's secret."

Daniel's unease sharpened into something colder. "Who the hell are you?"

Katarina moved fast. Before he could react, she had him in a vice-like grip, her palm pressing against his throat. A chill rushed through his body at her touch.

"You poor thing," she whispered in his ear before laughing, turning her gaze to Lucas. "He wonders if his father's loan sharks have finally come to collect."

Daniel stiffened. "How the hell did you know what I was thinking?"

Lucas moved closer, peering deep into his eyes. "Because your mind is an open book. And frankly, your thoughts give me a headache." A slow smirk curled on his lips. "Your father despises that you carry his name, you know. After all, your mother betrayed him. She wanted a child, but he had long decided he'd be childless."

Daniel's breath came quicker now, confusion clouding his thoughts.

Lucas continued. "He knew he could never father a child, yet she came home one evening, joyful as ever, announcing he was to be a father. When all she'd done was visit a sperm bank."

Daniel felt his stomach drop. Images of his father flashed through his mind. They looked nothing alike.

"I don't know who you are," he muttered. "And I don't care. My father hates me, and I hate him. So if you don't mind, I'd like to go home now."

Lucas nodded. "Release him, Katarina."

Her grip loosened, and Daniel stumbled back, his heart pounding. He turned, putting distance between them, but as he reached the end of the block, Lucas's voice drifted to him—calm, almost amused.

"He killed your mother, you know."

Daniel froze.

Lucas continued, his voice like silk. "He took the only thing you ever loved. And I can give you vengeance."

Dan Senior heard the boy walk in just as he drained the last of his beer. He grimaced, the usual disgust curling in his gut. He'd tolerated Olivia's betrayal, but what still burned was the audacity of her giving the kid his name.

He crushed the empty can in his fist. Beer spurted over his knuckles, cold against his hot skin. His thoughts drifted back to when the little freak was younger. Olivia had protected him, shielding him most of the time, but behind closed doors, she had been the one to take the blows. The memory stoked his rage, a fire he never quite put out. Maybe it was time to remind the boy who was boss.

Daniel usually slipped down the hall without a word, acting like he owned the place, like he paid the damn bills. But this morning was different. Instead of disappearing, the boy walked right up to him, standing there, staring down with those goddamn scrutinizing eyes.

Dan sneered. "What the fuck you looking at?" His voice slurred, thick with alcohol. He stared back, challenging the boy to look away.

He didn't.

Dan's lip curled as he studied the narrow face, the sharp lines, the high cheekbones—Olivia. Every year, the resemblance grew stronger. He gave a rough shrug, trying to shake the image from his head. But when he blinked, the boy was still there, still watching.

Rage surged. "What the fuck, you little bitch! What the hell you looking at? Don't you goddamn stare at me like she did!"

A sudden movement to his right.

Dan's head snapped toward the motion, and his gut twisted. The boy wasn't alone.

Two strangers stood in the dim light. The redhead spoke first, stepping closer.

"Dan, Dan, Dan," he murmured, his tone mocking. "I think it's time we have a little chat about Olivia."

A jolt of fear shot through Dan's chest. His pulse pounded in his skull. "Who the fuck are you freaks?"

The redhead smiled. "No need to play dumb, Dan. I've never met Olivia, but I've seen what you did. And I know how you did it."

Dan lurched to his feet. "Get the fuck outta my house!"

The stranger ignored him, turning lazily to his female companion. "Katarina, darling, seal the windows, will you?"

Dan barely registered what that meant before he saw it—the glint of sharp, curved fangs behind the

stranger's grin.The beer can slipped from his fingers, hitting the floor with a hollow thud.

Night had fallen again, and Dan had watched it all—seen the boy change right before his eyes.

His first instinct had been to run, but there was nowhere to go. He was trapped inside his own house, caught in a nightmare made real. The creature—no, the boy—had made him confess everything. Every last detail of what he'd done to Olivia. And only when the words had left his mouth, raw and damning, did he truly understand what the pale man and his lady friend were.

If he had only heard it, he never would have believed. But he had seen.

Vampires.

They had spent the day barricading the house, shuttering the windows to keep out the sunlight. Now, as the darkness stretched over the sky, Dan sat with his heart hammering, watching his three captors with the growing, gut-deep certainty that his time had run out.

Dawn had been the beginning of the end. Just hours after the boy had brought these monsters into his home, Dan had watched in silent horror as the one called Lucas sank his fangs into Daniel's throat.

At first, Dan thought the kid was dead. He had collapsed to the floor, his body shaking, convulsing. But then—after long, torturous minutes—the boy rose again.

A new man.

Pale. Flawless. All the boyhood scars Dan had inflicted over the years —gone.

But it wasn't just his body that had changed. It was his eyes.

Daniel looked at Lucas with something Dan had never seen in him before—devotion. He called the vampire Master.

Then, he turned his gaze to Dan.

For the first time in his life, Dan understood what it meant to be hunted.

"What the fuck's wrong with you, boy?" His voice cracked as he backed away. "Daniel! Get the fuck away!"

The young vampire stepped forward, red tears streaking down his pale face. "You will die now," he said. "Just as you made my mother die."

Dan slammed against the wall. His legs shook. His stomach twisted. "Oh, shit—oh, fuck—" He dragged his trembling hands down his face, the room tilting as the terror took hold. "I was goddamn drunk... I—I didn't mean to hurt her!"

Daniel didn't speak. He didn't need to.

I see her death in your mind.

Dan choked on a sob. His bladder gave out. Warm piss soaked his legs, but he barely noticed. All he saw was the fangs.

Then—pain.

Daniel's cold hand pressed against his chest, pinning him in place. Sharp teeth pierced his flesh.

Dan gasped, but the scream never came. His body sagged. A dizzy, sinking sensation took hold, like a rat paralyzed by a serpent's venom.

His heartbeat slowed. His vision blurred.

The room dimmed...

Then darkened...

And at last—there was nothing.

LUCAS'S COVEN WAS HOUSED IN A GREAT MANSION NEARLY TWO HOURS FROM Manhattan. The city of Hudson was beautiful, and Daniel could hardly believe how drastically his life had changed in mere days. He was immortal now. And the fact that he'd drained the blood of the one man he had hated his entire life filled him with no remorse. His mother's murderer was dead. His first taste of blood—Dan's blood—had been the sweetest.

Vengeance is sweet indeed...

Daniel stood on the rear terrace, gazing at the full moon.

"A vampire's first lesson," Lucas's voice drifted from behind him, smooth and commanding, "is to guard his mind."

Daniel turned abruptly. He hadn't even heard his maker approach.

"You must always be watchful," Lucas continued, stepping up beside him. "Comfort is a dangerous illusion—not when the enemy still hunts us."

"You said I can't die," Daniel reminded him.

"We are immortal, yes, but not invincible." Lucas placed a firm hand on his shoulder. "A vampire perishes if his head is severed. And that is not the only way we can be destroyed." His voice lowered, almost conspiratorial. "Immortality means something only if we are clever enough to keep it. I have outlived even my own father, Nathan. That was no accident."

Intrigued, Daniel followed Lucas from the terrace, past the mansion's rear gardens, to an old cemetery surrounded by rusted iron gates. The air smelled of damp earth and aged stone. At the centre of the grounds stood a lone sepulchre, its entrance sealed by an immense slab of stone.

"This place is ancient," Daniel murmured.

Lucas smiled. "Yes, it is," he agreed. "And yet, I am much older than this place."

With effortless strength, Lucas pushed aside the heavy stone, revealing the darkness within. He gestured for Daniel to follow.

"Many of the others envy you," Lucas said as they descended into the sepulchre's depths. "A vampire coven provides a sense of family. A place to belong. But do not be deceived—most are here for protection, not kinship. True immortality comes with loneliness, Daniel. Everything has a price."

Daniel studied him. "Why are you telling me this?"

Lucas smiled faintly, but there was no warmth in it. "Already, they whisper that you are my favourite." He gestured toward a stone vault at the centre of the room. "Open it."

Daniel hesitated, then placed his hands against the heavy lid. With shocking ease, he lifted it. Inside, a body lay draped in an extravagant, dust-covered gown. The flesh, dried and brittle, had receded from her bones, leaving a skull-like face framed by cobwebs. Her long, yellowed fingernails curled around a massive golden ring that gleamed even in the dim torchlight.

Daniel swallowed. "Who… who was she?"

"She is my dear grandmother, Odelia," Lucas said, gazing down at the corpse with something close to reverence. "She sleeps."

Daniel stiffened. "What?"

"She is the oldest of our kind," Lucas continued, unbothered by Daniel's reaction. "She sired my father—but not until after I was born. Long ago, covens were built upon family bloodlines. Grandmother was condemned to death by my father."

Daniel's mind reeled. "Your father... wanted his own mother dead?"

Lucas's laugh echoed through the tomb. "The lust for power corrupts even the best of men—and vampires." His expression darkened. "My father feared dear Grandmother. Just as he feared the hybrid, Cecil Bleddyn. So he ordered them both destroyed."

Daniel clenched his jaw. Thoughts of his own mother, stolen from him by Dan Turner, crashed through his mind like a storm. His voice was tight. "And how could you allow that?"

"I was foolish," Lucas admitted. "I believed I was the only one trying to save someone I loved. But Emilio and Babette... they had plans of their own."

Blood memories surged through Daniel's mind—the sheer power of knowing a vampire's history simply by drinking from them was intoxicating. It was the essence of all life. And yet, despite all the knowledge now flooding him, he couldn't shake the memory of Dan Turner's terrified eyes, the way his father had screamed when Daniel had finally avenged his mother's death.

"You must not let such memories weaken you," Lucas warned, watching him closely. "They will make you vulnerable. Your mother is gone. You avenged her. Be thankful I have given you such a gift."

Daniel exhaled sharply. "Then tell me this—why are you and Larus Bleddyn enemies? I thought vampires never killed their own kind."

Lucas's lip curled. "That rule does not apply in this case," he said simply. "But should any vampire in my coven commit such a crime, they will be destroyed."

Daniel frowned. "Larus Bleddyn is a hybrid, as powerful as Cecil Bleddyn once was—"

"Almost as powerful," Lucas corrected. "And yes, he has the Lycans on his side." His smile returned. "But so do I. Though I doubt Grandmother will approve."

He turned back to the stone vault, brushing his fingers over the golden ring on the corpse's withered hand. "Father wanted this ring. By all rights, it belonged to her, not him. I made certain it would take the long sleep with her." His grin sharpened. "But now, she is back with us."

Daniel watched in silence as Lucas slid the lid shut.

"Come," Lucas said smoothly. "We must prepare for Grandmother's awakening. She will know how to deal with Larus Bleddyn and his Lycans."

His voice softened into something almost intimate as he traced a final, lingering touch over the stone.

"I brought you all the way from Paris, Grandmother. I will need you by my side."

68

ODELIA

It was twilight, and all the members of Lucas's coven had gathered in the great hall to witness Odelia's awakening. Daniel stood by the massive bay window of Lucas's estate, gazing out at the vanishing sun beyond the horizon. His eyes lingered on the reddish sky, but his mind wandered to the strange new world he had been thrust into. He turned to observe the many vampires at the gathering, noting the subtle tension in the air. The older vampires—those who remembered Odelia—loathed the fact that Lucas was about to resurrect an ancient vampire, one who would become their leader. There were few who knew Odelia personally, but all knew the power she wielded, and many resented the threat she posed to the established order.

As the last glow of sunlight disappeared, Daniel couldn't help but feel the loss—his days of walking freely beneath the sun were over. He would never again enjoy long walks through Manhattan or bask in the daylight. And yet, there was something that pulled at him deeper. Why was he expected to fight against vampires like himself, those who had never wronged him?

His thoughts were interrupted when he sensed someone nearby. He turned sharply, and there stood Katerina, her eyes unreadable as they locked with his. The silence between them thickened before she spoke.

"I gave Lucas my honest advice about you the night we found you," she said coolly, her voice laced with disdain. "And I stand by it even now. He should have killed you. The gift of immortality is a privilege."

Daniel's brows furrowed. "What did I ever do to you?" he asked, his voice edged with confusion.

Katerina sneered, her lip curling with contempt. "It's not what you've done, boy," she spat, her words sharp as daggers. "It's what you will do. You're weak. You stand here, your mind swarming with irrelevant memories, questioning the war we're fighting. You refuse to guard your mind as Lucas has taught you. You don't belong here."

"What the hell do you expect me to do?" Daniel's frustration flared. "It hasn't been a month since you turned me, for God's sake. What the hell do you want from me?"

"Lucas turned you," Katerina reminded him, her voice a quiet venom. "Remember that. I would have drowned you in the Hudson if it had been up to me, for I would not have even wanted your weak blood." She looked him up and down as if she were appraising an insect. "Heaven knows why he's chosen you. A newborn to drink from Odelia."

"Drink from... What the hell are you talking about?" Daniel's voice was thick with confusion, but Katerina had already turned and walked away, her words hanging ominously in the air.

Daniel barely had time to consider what she meant before Lucas's voice echoed through the great hall, carrying over the murmurs of the gathered vampires. "Bring the humans!" he commanded.

The room went silent as vampires turned their attention to the entrance, awaiting the arrival of their prey. Daniel's heart beat faster, though he wasn't sure if it was from excitement or dread. He looked once more to the moonlit sky, then back at the coven. The air had thickened, filled with anticipation and something darker—a hunger that made the room seem colder.

But what was truly troubling was the feeling that Lucas was not the only one plotting in this ancient game. A part of Daniel wondered if he was nothing more than a pawn in a war that had already been fought long before he ever stepped into this world.

Ana, her brother, and their parents had come to Manhattan on vacation—a trip long-awaited and carefully planned. Her father, always her closest confidante, had even arranged it during the week of her sixteenth birthday. It was supposed to be a celebration, a memory to cherish for a lifetime. But now, standing in the vast, ominous hall filled with hundreds of strangers, Ana felt the weight of that day turn to something darker. It was no longer her birthday—it was the worst night of her life.

The family had been taken from their private villa the previous day, and now, Ana walked reluctantly in line behind her parents and brother, her body trembling with each step. Her eyes were brimming with tears as she whispered to her brother, her voice barely audible in the heavy silence.

"What do they want with us, Alex?" she asked, her words full of fear.

"Ana, be quiet," Alex snapped, his voice tight with anxiety. "They said we shouldn't speak."

Ana bit her lip, her fingers clutching the sides of her white chiffon dress until the fabric wrinkled in her grasp. Her mother, too, wore the same delicate chiffon, and her father and brother were dressed in long, linen nightshirts. No one wore shoes. They had been well fed, she realized, but why? Why had they been brought to this strange place, dressed like this? Was it some sort of cult? Were they going to be held for ransom?

Her father was the first to step forward, approaching a massive table draped in blue velvet. The room was eerily silent as they were led to stand before it.

"Welcome, my friends," a pale man with striking red hair said, his voice smooth but chilling. Ana's gaze flickered over him, her heart hammering in her chest. She still couldn't understand what this was, who these people were, or why they were here.

"What do you want with us?" her father demanded, his voice laced with panic. "Who are you people?"

The pale man said nothing, and her father's question hung unanswered in the air. Ana's mother clung to her father's arm, trembling, her face pale and stricken with terror.

Ana's eyes wandered past the pale man's shoulder, and her breath caught. There, standing in the crowd, was a boy—her age, maybe a little older. His skin, too, was as pale as all the others in the room, but it was his eyes that locked with hers that held her attention. There was fear in his gaze, the same fear she felt bubbling up inside her. And for a fleeting moment, her gaze pleaded with him for help, her desperation reaching out to him across the sea of strangers.

But he didn't move. He didn't speak. He was one of them. Whatever they were.

THE VELVET SHEET WAS PULLED AWAY, REVEALING THE STIFFENED, DECAYED corpse of a woman dressed in a beautiful black gown. Ana screamed in terror, the sound sharp and unrestrained, but the room responded with cruel laughter. She clung to Alex, her hands shaking, and she could feel his body trembling in response.

The dead woman had striking red hair, but her face—what was left of it—was like that of a mummified corpse, eyes sunken, mouth barely ajar. Ana's gaze fixated on a golden ring on the right hand of the corpse. The man standing before them, the one with red hair just like hers, looked down at the body with an expression of adoration.

"Grandmother," he said softly, almost reverently.

He approached the body and slowly raised his hand to his lips. Ana gasped when she saw his sharp white fangs gleaming, and before she could react, he sank them into his own pale wrist. The blood flowed dark and thick, dripping into the air as he held it over the corpse's lips.

Ana leaned against Alex, her heart hammering in her chest as she felt his arm tighten around her. The blood dripped down, splattering against the dry, cracked skin of the corpse's lips, staining the teeth a deep red. Ana couldn't look away, frozen in shock. Vampires. Could they be real? She'd read comics, seen them in novels and movies. But vampires—real ones—couldn't exist, could they?

"We are real, dear Ana," the pale man said, his voice smooth, almost cruel. "You shall see."

Ana could hear her mother weeping softly behind them, but her attention was fixed on the corpse as it began to twitch. The fingers moved first, followed by the slow, jerky movement of the neck. The jaw shifted, and a blood-stained tongue licked at the lips. The horrific transformation was unfolding before her eyes.

Her father stumbled backward from the table, his face a mixture of disbelief and terror. "What in God's name?" he shouted, panic in his voice. He looked around, but there was nowhere to run. "What is it you want from us?"

The pale man laughed darkly, tilting his head. "Just a little bit of blood, Oscar."

Ana's breath caught in her throat. How did he know their names?

The old woman's limbs began to move with unnatural speed. Her skin, once dry and decrepit, seemed to revive with each passing second. Still, she was a grotesque sight—her form rejuvenating but never quite beautiful. Ana's brother, Alex, dropped to his knees in horror as a vampire with long, jagged nails sliced through their father's throat. Blood poured from the wound, and Ana could only watch, paralyzed by shock, as her father's life drained away.

The old woman seemed to sense her own revival. With one swift motion, her left arm reached out and dragged their father's limp body down toward her face. Then she bit into him. Ana heard the sickening slurping of her father's blood being consumed, and her body shook with silent sobs.

When the feeding stopped, their father lay lifeless, discarded like an empty vessel. The woman's transformation was complete. Her skin, though still slightly wrinkled, no longer appeared dry and dead. Her hair, once dull, gleamed under the candlelight, vibrant red like fire. Without a second glance, she tossed the corpse aside, and Ana's mother was next. Her death was swift, the woman ravenous and famished.

With her parents now lying lifeless on the stone floor, Ana clung to

Alex, her heart pounding in her chest, bracing for her own turn. But just as she thought she'd succumb to the same fate, something strange happened.

The vampire boy—the one who had looked just as terrified as she had—moved. Fast. He was suddenly between Ana, Alex, and the old woman, blocking her path.

"Odelia, that's enough!" he commanded, his voice strained but firm.

A collective gasp echoed through the hall. The vampire woman—Odelia—looked at the boy with eyes full of fury, and in an instant, she swatted him aside with a force that sent him crashing into the far wall. He was little more than a rag doll in her hands.

But it wasn't just the boy who intervened. The man with the red hair, the one who had called the corpse "Grandmother," knelt before Odelia. His voice was low, coaxing.

"Grandmother," he said softly. "I've kept my promise. I've done as you asked. We are together again."

For a long moment, Odelia stared down at him, her blue eyes cold but calculating. "You have slept for centuries... You need time to gather your thoughts. To see my blood memories."

The boy—Daniel, the pale man had called him—gently took Odelia's hand in his, pressing a kiss to her ringed fingers. For the first time since her awakening, Odelia seemed to recognize him.

Her blue eyes softened, and her lips whispered his name: "Lu... cassss."

A wide grin spread across his face. "Yes, Grandmother. It is I."

69

A MASTER'S GIFT

He waited alone in Lucas's private rooms, an extravagant space decorated in the style of Louis XV. The gilded furniture, the silk-draped walls—it all felt like a world out of time. Living among vampires centuries older than him was still disorienting. They longed for the past, clinging to it like a lifeline.

As he awaited his maker's arrival, Daniel's mind churned. Lucas was a Frenchman, and most of his coven seemed to be as well—except for the ones sired in America. But had vampires existed in his own country centuries ago? He knew Lucas had fled to New York City long ago, but how had Odelia crossed the ocean from France?

The door clicked open. Daniel turned to find his maker watching him, a slow grin spreading across his face.

"One can easily comb through your thoughts, young one, and take their pick of your mental bombardment." Lucas strode forward and pressed his lips gently against Daniel's. "I've had many complaints," he murmured. "Many demand your destruction after your stunt with my dear grandmother. Pity she didn't kill you."

Lucas moved toward the window, hands clasped behind his back. "Never interfere in a vampire's awakening. Their minds are in turmoil, their memories tangled. It takes time for them to settle. I carried all of my grandmother's memories within my blood. I was the only one who could have woken her properly." He paused. "Not that someone else couldn't have—but it would have taken days, perhaps weeks, for her to become herself again."

Daniel hesitated. "I haven't seen her... since I—"

"Forget about grandmother for now. She forgives you." Lucas waved a hand dismissively. "She longs for her old home in France. She dislikes this new world—she slept through our vampire war and woke to an unfamiliar age. When I fled here, I had her moved from France. Only I knew where she was hidden. But those days were different, Daniel. I needed only a ship, men I could trust, and gold."

Daniel considered this. "And the vampires of this side of the world—were they here back then?"

"They were." Lucas's eyes darkened. "Their leader wanted nothing to do with my war with Larus."

"They're in Manhattan?"

Lucas shot him a warning look before his expression softened. "Forget them. We have more important matters." He turned toward the door.

"Ah... grandmother comes."

A slow dread settled in Daniel's stomach.

Odelia studied the newborn and instantly understood why Lucas was drawn to him.

"You see yourself in him," she said.

It was impossible to forget little Lucas as a boy—fearless even then, unshaken by the knowledge of what his grandmother truly was. She wore a black gown of silk and lace, and the ring bearing her family crest gleamed, freshly polished to a golden lustre. As her gaze shifted from her grandson to the newborn, realization dawned.

Ah. That was it.

"And you," she said, motioning toward the fledgling. "You are as defiant as he was... lifetimes ago."

Daniel hesitated. "Odelia, I... I'm sorry for—"

She dismissed his apology with a flick of her ringed hand. "Ah, save it, my dear."

Gracefully, she moved to the long chaise by the window, where moonlight spilled in silver ribbons across the floor. She had always loved the full moon.

"Come, sit with me, young one."

ODELIA'S BLUE EYES WERE PENETRATING. LOCKED IN THE ANCIENT VAMPIRE'S gaze, Daniel felt powerless, though he knew she meant him no harm. She was nothing like the decrepit corpse he had seen in the old sepulchre. Now, the coven's so-called queen was ageless, her skin smooth, unmarked by time. She must have been a woman in her early forties when she was turned.

Odelia was beautiful.

Lucas, swept up in sudden joy, paced before them, his adoring gaze fixed on his grandmother. "Will you grant my wish?" he asked eagerly. "Will you let him drink from you?"

Daniel's eyes flicked between them, puzzled. He remained silent. He would not make the mistake of interrupting Odelia again.

She studied her grandson before exhaling softly. "I would not have unleashed a twice-bitten lycan so recklessly," she said. "Always, you act before you think." Yet there was amusement in her tone, as if she were indulging a beloved child.

Daniel watched their exchange with quiet fascination. It seemed Lucas could do no wrong.

"I was desperate, grandmother," Lucas argued. "You have not met Larus Bleddyn. He thinks himself better than us—better than you."

Odelia chuckled. "This hybrid does not know me," she murmured. Her expression darkened slightly. "But I know the Bleddyns well enough. I knew Cecil Bleddyn." Her gaze sharpened. "This Larus must be strong if he is what you claim." A flicker of anger passed over her features. "I remember too well that your father—my own son—plotted to destroy me out of greed, to take my coven for himself."

Lucas's smile was slow, triumphant. "Which is exactly why I acted, grandmother. I unleashed Basil upon them, gambling that the feral lycan would rip Larus and his kind to shreds. But the fool has thwarted my plans."

"He has tamed him," Odelia said, nodding thoughtfully. "This Bleddyn is no fool, young as he may be."

"The Bleddyns are of a wolf's lineage," Lucas continued, his voice thick with disdain. "And like Cecil before him, Larus has not forsaken his family. He has joined with his nephew, Silas Hearne."

Odelia's lips curled slightly. "Hmm… the hunter's bloodline mingling with the wolf. Percival Hearne was no idiot." Her gaze shifted back to Daniel, pinning him in place. He immediately lowered his eyes in reverence.

"Newborns are meant to be left to mature over long, long years," she mused aloud. "But you, young vampire… you shall surpass most within my coven with my legacy running through your veins."

Daniel's brow furrowed as he glanced at Lucas, still uncertain.

"To drink from an old vampire is a privilege," Lucas said smoothly. "You will be the envy of the entire coven."

"They already hate me."

Odelia laughed. "Yes. But they will also fear you. Almost as much as they fear me."

Daniel hesitated before asking, "And the humans? What will happen to the girl… and her brother, Alex?"

Odelia's smile turned knowing. "It was the boy you wished to save, not his sister."

Daniel pressed his lips together, embarrassed. But then Odelia did something unexpected. She cupped his face, her fingers cool against his skin, and as he met her gaze, he felt certain the human boy would not be harmed.

"They watched us murder their parents," Lucas said flatly. "They think us monsters. Releasing them is out of the question. Most unwise."

"Then make them like me."

Lucas's expression twisted in disbelief. "Have you lost your mind, boy?" He flung his arms up. "You expect me to make vampires of those who would seek vengeance? They are nothing but food!"

Odelia rose, placing a calming hand on her grandson's shoulder. "We must leave this in his hands, Lucas. Let Daniel decide."

Then she turned to Daniel, bringing her wrist to her lips. She bit down, opening her veins.

"Drink," she commanded. "And accept the legacy I give."

70

LOYALTY

Alex had stopped keeping track of the days, but he was certain it had been well over three months since his parents were murdered. He and Ana had been confined to the depths of the old mansion, denied fresh air or even a glimpse of daylight. Yet, their prison was nothing like a dungeon. The rooms they were given were as extravagant as a five-star suite in Manhattan.

Ana, though she despised their captivity, had a room of her own. But every waking hour, the siblings clung to each other, mourning their parents and cursing the monsters who had taken everything from them.

The heavy clank of locks turning made Alex tense. Nighttime. It was always nighttime when the doors opened. A moment later, the young vampire entered—the one who had spared their lives.

Ana stiffened, her fingers digging into Alex's shoulder. Alex, though gripped with terror, stood his ground. He would not show fear.

"No need to be afraid," the vampire said.

His voice was calm, but that only made it worse. He looked no older than twenty, his pale skin almost luminous in the dim light. He shut the door behind him with an ease that told Alex he had no fear of them.

"Why hasn't she killed us?" Alex asked.

"You murdered our parents!" Ana spat.

The vampire exhaled, looking almost... tired. "You saw what I did," he said. "Odelia nearly killed me for it. But I begged her to spare you." His gaze flicked to Alex. "We can't let you go."

He stepped closer, so close that Alex could see the faint pores on his face, the near-perfect symmetry of his features. Something about him made Alex's pulse quicken. The vampire extended a hand.

"I'm Daniel."

Alex's heart fluttered. He had wanted to know his name. Slowly, he reached out, but the moment their palms met, he recoiled at the icy touch.

"Yeah, we get kinda chilly," Daniel said with a wry smile, revealing slightly crooked white teeth.

"Alex," he replied. "But I'm sure you knew that."

Ana turned away, hugging herself, unwilling to acknowledge the vampire at all. If Daniel was offended, he didn't show it.

"Alex and Ana," he mused. "You've been the talk of the coven ever since... well." He hesitated, clearly thinking of their parents. "Look, I'm sorry about what happened. I'm new here too. Like you, I was taken. But unlike you... I chose this."

Alex's stomach twisted. "What will they do to us?"

Daniel hesitated before answering. "Odelia is leaving that decision to me." He glanced toward Ana. "You have two choices—join us, or... join your folks."

Ana spun toward him, eyes blazing. "You'd let us choose to die?"

Before she could lunge at him, Alex grabbed her by the shoulders, holding her back. "Ana, please!"

Daniel remained eerily calm. "They'll never let you go, not knowing what you might do. Vampires survive on secrecy. You either become like us and live forever, or it ends here."

The locks turned again, sealing the door from the outside. Alex flinched.

"What are they doing?" His voice came out unsteady.

Daniel met his gaze, and for the first time, Alex saw something unexpected in those dark brown eyes. Fear.

"Our queen has spoken," Daniel murmured. "By her command, I haven't fed in days. I am a young vampire, and I cannot endure the hunger for long."

A chill ran through Alex.

Ana trembled in his arms, but he had already made his choice.

"Ana," he whispered. "I know how you feel about them. About what they are. But I don't want to die. And I don't want to lose you." He swallowed hard. "Whatever you decide, I'm taking their offer."

Ana buried her face against him and sobbed.

THE NOVEMBER NIGHT WAS COLD, THE AIR SHARP AGAINST THEIR SKIN AS they ran from Lucas's estate to Greenport Conservation Area. Daniel came to an abrupt halt beneath a massive oak tree, turning to Alex with a triumphant grin.

"Told you I'd beat you, slowpoke."

He hadn't felt this alive in years. The loneliness that had defined his existence since becoming a vampire now seemed like a distant memory. Two months had passed since Lucas turned Alex, and though they both struggled with the weight of their pasts, Daniel knew things had never been better. Like him, Alex was a newborn, and they shared a bond forged in tragedy—though Daniel had been the one to take vengeance upon his own father.

At times, he had glimpsed into Alex's mind, seen the torment still lingering in the wake of his parents' deaths. Yet, Daniel's own suffering had dulled beneath the intoxicating power of Odelia's blood. He had been weak before, but now? Now he could slip into the minds of others, shield his own thoughts, and feel the undercurrent of fear from those within the coven.

"That's unfair," Alex said, breathless but smiling. "You have Odelia's blood coursing through you. I still remember the way she struck you down... when—"

His smile faded. The weight of memory settled on his face. "How can I think of that without remembering what she did to my parents?"

Daniel stepped closer, drawing him into his arms. His fingers traced the side of Alex's face, a tender contrast to the violence that had shaped them.

"You shouldn't hate her for it," he murmured. "Odelia won't like the idea of you holding her responsible."

"But she is."

"We both know that." Daniel's voice was quiet but firm. "But to think it—especially in her presence—is dangerous." He leaned in, pressing a kiss to Alex's lips. "Lucas favours me, but even now, he grows jealous of us. I've shown you how to shield your mind around Odelia, but she's old, Alex. Old and powerful. I think she already knows you still hold a grudge."

Alex looked away. "I can't stand being in the same room with her sometimes."

"And I can't bear the thought of losing you."

Daniel tensed, suddenly alert. His hand shot up, a single finger pressing against Alex's lips. "Hush. We're not alone." His gaze shifted past Alex's shoulder, his voice turning playful yet firm. "Come on out. I know you're there, silly."

Ana stepped from the shadows, dressed in black, her hair pulled away from her face. She smirked. "Are you two sneaking off to be alone again?"

With effortless grace, she sprang up onto a thick branch, perching six feet above them.

Daniel grinned. "You're frisky."

"Lucas knew you'd disappear again." Her gaze lingered on Alex, playful but knowing.

Daniel had never imagined Ana—the same girl who had once despised the idea of becoming a vampire—would take to her new life so effortlessly. Unlike Alex, who remained distant and withdrawn, Ana had embraced the coven, made friends among their kind, and grown especially close to Lucas. That bond had not gone unnoticed, least of all by Katerina, whose jealousy was plain for all to see. The tension between the two women had become a source of quiet amusement within the coven.

"We're here to hunt, Ana," Alex said. "You know how Daniel and I feel about pointless killing."

Ana rolled her eyes. "So, you've both decided to feed on wild animals. Why settle for the blood of beasts when we sit atop the food chain?"

She was still a ravenous newborn, and unlike Alex, she had no qualms about killing, even when the victim was innocent. It was a rift that had grown between them.

Alex turned away. "Blood is blood."

Ana scoffed. "Fine. Enjoy your deer." With that, she leapt from the branch and disappeared into the darkness.

Left alone once more, Daniel pulled Alex close, kissing him deeply.

"You shouldn't be too pissed at her, you know," he murmured against his lips. "Ana's alright."

"It's as if she's forgotten them."

"That's just her way of dealing with things. Let her be who she is." Daniel brushed his fingers over Alex's cheek before smirking. "Come. I hear our dinner."

THEY RETURNED TO THE ESTATE JUST BEFORE DAWN.

The great hall was filled with every vampire in the coven. Something had happened.

Daniel entered with Alex at his side, their footsteps soft against the stone floor. At the head of the room, seated in a throne-like chair, was Odelia—the vampire most regarded as their queen. Lucas sat to her right, their positions radiating authority, a silent proclamation of power.

Kneeling before Odelia was a disheveled vampire, his head bowed low in fear.

"I beg your forgiveness, Odelia," he pleaded, his voice trembling. "We were outnumbered—Jerome and I—we couldn't hold them off." His hands raked through his dark, tangled hair. "I managed to escape, but I'm certain they only needed one of us. Once they had a strong hold on Jerome, I was as good as dead." He swallowed hard, his gaze darting upward before he looked away. "Larus Bleddyn and his lycan nephew—the one called Silas—they have a new pet. The one twice bitten."

Murmurs rippled through the gathered vampires.

"I assure you, Odelia," he continued, voice raw with fear, "the feral beast is ruthless. It will go to great lengths to protect those with him."

Odelia's piercing gaze shifted to Lucas. "If you were not family, dear grandson, you would be dealt with."

Then, with terrifying speed, she was upon the kneeling vampire. Fangs sank deep into his throat, and a sharp gasp of pain escaped his lips. Odelia drank swiftly, then released him, her eyes closing for a moment as she sifted through the blood memories. When she looked at him again, her expression was one of cold disappointment.

"They have a she-wolf," she announced.

"Yes, Odelia," the vampire rasped. "But—"

"Silence."

Odelia turned to Lucas, nostrils flaring slightly as if she could still taste the scent of truth on the air. Her golden eyes darkened.

"The she-wolf and the one twice bitten are kin."

A flicker of shock passed over Lucas's freckled face. "Grandmother, I never expected the girl would choose that path."

"You would be surprised, grandson, what family will do for each other." Odelia's gaze swept across the hall, her voice cold and commanding. "Our coven has been compromised. By the next sunset, I have no doubt this place will be crawling with the enemy. Larus Bleddyn will strike soon—he has only a few days before the pet my grandson so graciously gifted him becomes human again. We must prepare for battle."

She rose, her presence filling the vast chamber. "Ready yourselves to defend your coven."

The hall stirred as vampires moved swiftly to obey. But as the messenger turned to leave, Odelia's gaze snapped back to him, her expression shifting as if something had just dawned on her.

"And where do you think you're going?"

The vampire froze.

"Jerome would have held out as long as he could," she said, her voice now a whisper of lethal intent. "But you... you made it so easy for the enemy by returning here."

Before he could react, Odelia flicked her wrist.

In one swift motion, his head was severed from his body. The silence that followed was thick with terror.

The hall emptied quickly, the gathered vampires eager to escape the queen's wrath. Daniel took Alex's hand and ushered him through the doors, blending into the retreating crowd.

But just before he crossed the threshold, he glanced over his shoulder.

Only two remained standing beside Odelia—Lucas and Ana.

JUDE CROUCHED AT THE BASE OF THE RIDGE, LOLA BESIDE HIM. THE MASSIVE estate housing Lucas's coven stood still, eerily peaceful. Not even a groundskeeper moved across the grounds.

"Not a guard in sight," he whispered.

They had stayed well back, careful to avoid detection. Larus had warned them to be cautious. Jude pressed a kiss to the side of Lola's neck. "I'm glad you're with me, lover."

She pushed him aside gently, barely sparing him a glance. "Simmer down. We've got a job to do—this ain't the time for frolicking."

"Lola—"

"You don't think it's strange?" she cut in, motioning toward the estate. "A whole coven of vampires, and not a single one standing guard?"

Jude hesitated, following her gaze.

"They know we're coming," she continued. "We never should've let that vampire escape."

"And how, dear Lola, would we have tracked him here?" He ran a hand along the curve of her hip.

Lola swatted him off. "Larus got the same information from the other one in seconds—all it took was a taste of his blood." She narrowed her eyes at the darkened windows of the estate. "I'm telling you, they're waiting for us."

Jude's head snapped up. "Look there! To the left."

A figure emerged from the thicket behind the estate. Then another. And another.

"Lycans," Lola murmured. She lowered into a crouch. "There's more of them now."

Jude exhaled sharply. "We've seen what Larus suspected. The lycans guard the coven by day."

"What's Larus gonna do about it?" Lola asked as they turned to leave.

Jude kept his voice low. "Our numbers are few. We are but six, and they are many—four lycans, two vampires, and an entire coven waiting for nightfall." He glanced at her. "Even with our strength, we can't stand against them."

Lola nodded. "And that's not even counting how many more could be inside." She glanced over her shoulder once more at the stone estate. "No way in hell we're getting in there."

They broke into a slow jog toward the tree line, using the cover of the forest.

"Where the hell did Larus go last night?" Lola muttered. "He was still gone this morning."

Jude shrugged. "You know Larus... always with his secrets."

71

THE BATTLE

The old sugar refinery, built in 1882, long before Basil was born, stood imposing before them. As they approached the brown brick structure, the young lycan glanced around, sniffing the night air. It felt strange to find this area of Brooklyn so deserted. Larus walked ahead, ever watchful, while Marc stayed by Basil's side.

The building had many windows, its architecture stunning in the moonlight, especially the massive chimney that towered far beyond the eighth story. Basil's mind drifted back to his childhood. He had vague memories of a visit to the city long before his mother's death.

He studied the building ahead, wondering how such an old structure —one built so long ago—could house an entire coven of vampires. Larus had made all his plans with Basil in mind, knowing that there were only two days left in his cycle as a human. The plan was to strike at Lucas's coven while Basil was at his strongest. The thought of being in his first battle within forty-eight hours made Basil's heart race, but there was still much to do before then.

"You seem troubled tonight," Marc said, breaking his thoughts.

"It's all so crazy, you know." Basil kept his eyes fixed on the old refinery. "To think my mama brought me to Brooklyn all those years ago to visit some friend of hers... and there were vampires right here. I can't believe it."

Marc regarded him with what seemed like a frown. "Well, you do know that vampires and lycans are mortal enemies. Many of these vampires have probably never seen a lycan before, but they'll definitely smell you."

"Even as I am now?" Basil asked, surprised.

The vampire nodded. "It's the scent of an unwashed dog—only much stronger." Marc glanced at him without so much as a smile.

"Damn, dude, I can never tell if you're joking."

Marc glared at him, puzzled.

"Humour is one thing you'll never get from our dreamer, Basil." Larus's voice carried from ahead as he stopped just before they were about to cross the street. Two figures were watching them approach. "Remember, Basil," Larus said, his tone serious, "these vampires will see you as the enemy, and they have every right to. But I will never allow them to harm you." He gestured toward the refinery. "Come."

SAMUEL, THE VAMPIRE, WAS WELL KNOWN AMONG HIS KIND ACROSS MANY states, though Larus had never met him. Since moving to Manhattan, the hybrid had kept to himself, but he was certain his presence was known to them all. Samuel, he'd learned, was a fair and benevolent leader—respected, yet feared. He had begun his immortal life as his maker's favourite, his loyalty and duty earning him the position of second elder. However, a pointless war between the Manhattan and Brooklyn covens left Samuel's coven leaderless. Samuel had stepped in, sealing the breach—not just between the two covens, but uniting all five boroughs of New York City into one stronger, more unified coven.

Larus had moved to the territory over a century ago, shortly after the war where Micah, Cecil, and many others had been destroyed. He wondered if his presence now would bring about yet more unnecessary deaths among his kind.

Four vampires met them in the middle of the street, two of whom were identical twins. Larus bowed his head in peaceful greeting, quickly attempting to read their thoughts, but they were strong. Samuel kept an impeccable house; Larus could glean nothing from them. The twins, of African descent, appeared to have been turned in their thirties. Their dark skin gleamed beautifully beneath the moonlight, and their eyes—full and suspicious—revealed nothing. Both wore their hair in neatly braided rows going backward, with long plaits resting on their shoulders. Both had silver hair.

The other two vampires also shielded their minds to perfection. Larus couldn't gain anything from them. One had cropped black hair and piercing blue eyes, while the other was much older, with a full silver beard. The bearded one wore a balmoral atop his head and spoke first, pointing a cane at Basil.

"Ah kin reek th' dug," said the Scotsman.

Larus bowed again to acknowledge the vampire's objection. "I made him bathe twice," he said, attempting to lighten the situation. "I am Larus. We've come about the vampire Lucas."

"Speak o' th' de'il." The Scotsman kept his eyes fixed on Basil. "Lucas haes bin a thorn in oor sides, he has."

The first of the twins moved to the Scotsman's side. "Welcome to our coven, Larus Bleddyn." He bowed his head. Larus smiled.

"I see your coven is well informed," Larus said. "It seems Samuel and I will have much to discuss."

The other twin grinned, while the Scotsman, still glaring at Basil, showed no sign of backing down. "Samuel watches o'er all," said the second twin proudly. His identical half threw an arm around his shoulder, and they smiled wide.

"I am Oraine," said the first twin. "My brother is Oran," he added.

Oran pointed a finger at the Scotsman. "And this here," he said in a playful Scottish twang, "is Mr. Brùn."

"Mynd yer geggy, laddie." Mr. Brùn gave a faint grin. His eyes then turned back to Basil, and the grin vanished. "Ye kin come in, but th' dug bides ootdoors."

Larus shook his head. "Basil goes where I go," he said firmly. "I'll have it no other way."

SAMUEL, KNOWN AS THE VAMPIRE WITH ONE GOOD EYE, WAS RESPECTED FOR his leadership, yet many feared him. Never had anyone tried to take his place as ruler of his coven. As the visitors were brought before him, he sat confidently on his simple leather sofa. Larus Bleddyn, a rich vampire, might have owned an old sugar refinery, but within these walls, One-eyed Samuel was king. Nearly sixty percent of his coven were of African descent, yet Samuel had made a point of welcoming any vampire, so long as they abided by his coven's oaths and rules.

Samuel passed his palm over the smoothness of his bald head as Larus Bleddyn and his companions were ushered into his hall. Despite only having one eye, Samuel could tell the hybrid had been turned while still young. But in their world, the young were never underestimated. It was the passage of years that made vampires truly strong. Larus carried himself with the aura of a seventeenth-century gentleman, his every movement deliberate and graceful, as though he had stepped from the pages of a forgotten history. Samuel had been there, though as a slave. The other vampire with Larus was young, but not newly made. His calm eyes, dressed in the old French style, betrayed no fear, yet Samuel sensed something else beneath the surface.

He shifted his gaze from Larus to the Frenchman, noting that while the hybrid had shielded his mind, the other vampire—the calm one—offered nothing. Puzzled, Samuel made another attempt to pry into the vampire's thoughts. Nothing. Samuel's brows furrowed as he passed his palm over his shiny head again. One of his greatest gifts was the ability to peer into the hearts and minds of others, yet this vampire offered no resistance.

"Marc's mind will give nothing, try as you may," said the hybrid. "He is an oracle."

Samuel nodded, understanding. "A dreamer." His eyes gleamed with intrigue, his mind drifting back to a time before his turning. "I knew humans with this gift, long before they took me from those I loved."

Samuel quivered at Marc's first words. "You were one of the first to land at Point Comfort."

Samuel closed his one good eye, suddenly overwhelmed by memories of that long voyage across the sea aboard a Spanish ship. Just days later, many others like him arrived aboard the ship Treasurer. Samuel relived it as if it were yesterday.

"You were defiant indeed," Marc continued. "The Dutch traders took your eye while at sea."

Samuel nodded, still unsure why he had been allowed to live. "Hardly anyone remembers the birth of slavery in this land. But I was there, nearly four hundred years ago. The vampire who turned me, the second year after I was sold, took pity on me. Saved my life, miserable as it was."

Marc nodded. "At the time of your arrival at Point Comfort in 1619, nearly two hundred years before I was born, France would have been under the rule of King Louis XIII."

"Yes, but as an African slave who couldn't even write my own name," Samuel replied, "I had no knowledge of such things or of other lands across the seas." Samuel found himself liking the oracle more than he cared to admit, but a more pressing matter demanded his attention. He turned his gaze to the boy. "Why have you brought this wolf into my coven?" His voice was sharp, laced with warning. "Does this dog have a death wish?"

The words had barely left his mouth when a rush of memories surged through him, unbidden and unwelcome. For a fleeting moment, the past threatened to drag him under. But that was then. This was now. And Samuel was not the man he had been. The boy was tall and strong, though not yet twenty. His youthful appearance would hardly change in the centuries to come...if he lived that long.

The boy stepped forward, anger flashing in his eyes. "I'm standing right here, asshole! Try talking to me, not him." He glanced at Larus.

"Have you no control over your underlings?" Samuel ignored the lycan, instead fixing his gaze on Larus.

"Forgive him," Larus said, placing a calming hand on the boy's shoulder. "Basil is…different. He's a newborn. And twice bitten."

Samuel grinned. "That explains his insubordination. But that's an ancient practice—and a dangerous one."

Larus shrugged. "Not my doing. But I'm sure you've heard of the vampire, Lucas."

Samuel dismissed six members of his coven with a wave of his hand. "Leave us." Once the massive doors closed, Samuel rose from the sofa, tugging at his goatee. "I've met Lucas. He came to me with promises, but all he kept saying was 'Larus Bleddyn.'"

"You are a wise man, Samuel," said Larus, "but mark my words: Lucas is cunning."

"And he spoke as highly of you as you speak of him now," Samuel replied, his gaze shifting between Larus and Marc. "There's something in your eyes that makes me trust you, but trust doesn't come easy. It's about outliving each other." Samuel's eye narrowed. "Lucas wants you dead. He came to me for a pact, one that would ensure your destruction."

Larus grimaced. "Rejection doesn't sit well with Lucas."

Samuel laughed. "He didn't ask. He demanded. I told him I don't roll like that."

Larus spoke with resolve. "We're not here to command you, Samuel. We need your help. There's a war brewing. We're fighting to protect our kind, and we're asking you to stand with us."

Samuel stroked his goatee thoughtfully. "Involved in a war that doesn't concern me will only get my people killed."

Marc, ever graceful, stepped forward, his gaze piercing Samuel's single eye. "You became involved the moment Lucas walked through your doors. I knew him before I was turned. His father, Nathan, murdered my parents for their wealth. I was his captive, a mere doorkeeper." Marc's voice softened. "Larus's maker gave me a home. When I fled France, Avlon, my surrogate father, died fighting at Larus's side."

Samuel regarded Marc with new understanding. "I know it's a lot to ask, Samuel. I can't promise no casualties, but I will fight to protect all who join us."

Samuel nodded slowly. "And what about your little lycan?" He grinned at Basil. "Why'd you bring him into my den of vampires?" He hoped for a sign of humour.

It took Basil a moment, but a faint smile crept onto his face. "This fucking guy..." He turned to Larus, then back to Samuel. "Den of vampires? Dude, are you for real?"

"Basil's cycle as a human is nearing its end," Larus explained. "The cycle gives him only fourteen days each month. We plan to attack Lucas's coven two nights from now."

Samuel raised an eyebrow. "Your first battle?" Basil nodded with a grimace. Samuel's voice grew serious. "You should be proud of what you are, kid. No matter what anyone thinks of you. A lycan, twice bitten? You're stronger than you know."

Larus nodded. "I bit him a third time to tame him."

Samuel tugged his goatee again. "Hmm... and how did you gain that knowledge, being nearly two hundred years my junior?"

Larus grinned. "I take no credit. It was Sebastian, my second. He came to my aid."

"Ah, the pretty one with the golden tongue," Samuel said with a chuckle. "I thought that bastard died centuries ago."

"You know Sebastian?" Larus asked, surprised. "I don't think he's ever been this far."

"And because I'm a one-eyed piece of shit who was sold off a slave ship back in 1619, I've been nowhere else but here?" Samuel chuckled. "Sebastian and I met on a ship bound for Spain."

He closed his one eye for a brief moment, the memory pulling him into the past. Pleasant memories, ones he'd promised himself never to forget, flooded his mind. Samuel's lips curved slightly as the recollections took shape. "He was with his maker... Emilio."

Larus's eyes widened in shock. "My maker, Micah, was turned by Emilio in 1649. Was Micah on that ship?"

Samuel jogged his memory. "I took that ship in 1652. I remember a young mulatto boy—quiet, but with a strong presence. He would've been about three years old at the time."

Samuel turned to Basil. "Come to think of it, that vampire—he looked similar to your little wolf here, Larus."

"They are kin." Samuel saw blood tears forming at the corners of

Larus's eyes. "Micah's mother, Estlyn, was a slave. Basil and his sister, Lola, are descendants of her."

"You mean there's a female version of you, kid?" Samuel chuckled. "You're not bad-looking, lycan, but a girl version of you? Jackpot!"

"She's a wolf," Basil said darkly. "And she'll rip you apart."

Samuel raised an eyebrow. "A feisty one, I take it?"

"She nearly ripped me to pieces even before she was turned," Larus said, grinning.

"I'm loving this challenge already," Samuel said with a chuckle. He looked to Marc, sensing his unease. "So, what's the plan for dealing with Lucas? How are you going to take that bastard's head?"

Opting not to accompany the others to his Oyster Bay estate, Larus returned to his Manhattan home, craving nothing but solitude. He sat facing the lone piece of art on his wall, his gaze locked onto the enigmatic eyes of Estlyn, the mother of his maker. Each time he looked upon her dark face, he saw something new. Sadness lingered in her brown eyes, yet beneath it, there was hope.

He closed his own eyes, unwilling to banish the melancholy settling over him. The moment he returned to his towering suite above the city, he had shut out the Manhattan skyline, shuttering every window.

Now, as he stared into Estlyn's painted eyes, he wished—foolishly—that he could ask for her advice. But she only gazed back at him from her perfect, painted world, making him ache for her son even more. Learning that Samuel had crossed paths with Micah so many years ago had been a shock. And now, Larus found himself longing for Dominic, regretting the choice he had made—the choice not to grant him eternal life.

But how could he have condemned the man he loved to such a fate against his will? Dominic would have hated him for it. Yet, a cruel thought lingered: *Would he have forgiven me, in time?*

Dragging his hands down his face, Larus wondered how different his long existence might have been had he made other choices. Would he have lost so many of those he loved? Micah. Dominic. His sisters. His parents. Even Cecil. One by one, they had all fallen—just names now, ghosts in his memory.

And soon, more would join them. War was coming, and Larus knew there was little he could do to stop it. Lucas would never relent. There was only one way to save countless lives—human, vampire, and lycan alike.

One death could end it all.

Lucas had to die.

THE MOONLIT SKY WAS BEAUTIFUL. NEARLY MIDNIGHT, AND MARC WALKED beside the taller vampire at the edge of the forest behind the Oyster Bay estate. The cool night air felt good against his skin, crisp and still, a fleeting comfort in the midst of so much uncertainty.

"You knew I'd be coming, didn't you?"

Samuel's single eye gleamed in the moonlight. His full lips were dark, almost purple, and his black goatee was perfectly pointed at the tip. Before Marc could answer, he felt an arm drape around his shoulders, firm yet unhurried. He stiffened at the sudden touch, a quiet gasp slipping from his lips.

Samuel's voice was a murmur, low and teasing. "I'd like to say I'm trying to keep you warm, but... we're vampires."

Marc exhaled, forcing his body to relax. The weight of Samuel's arm was a welcome one, though he wasn't sure he should admit it. "I hoped you would come... but I wasn't certain. I didn't think you felt—"

"No, you're tripping."

Marc glanced at him, puzzled.

Samuel smirked. "Forgot you're not from these parts. 'Tripping' means you're kidding. Not serious."

Marc shook his head with a faint smile. "I thought you came only to meet the she-wolf, Lola."

Samuel tilted his head, flashing a knowing grin. "Boy, you know I wasn't serious. I mean, don't get me wrong..." His gaze flickered toward the trees as if picturing her. "The girl's fine."

Marc shifted, suddenly uneasy. "You should speak with Larus. Basil will turn in just a day."

"You're right, Larus and I need to talk." Samuel's expression darkened. "My coven knows nothing about this war they'll be fighting in. They'll fight because I tell them to."

"Many will die."

Marc didn't mean for the words to sound so final, but they hung in the air like an unspoken sentence. He knew war was inevitable, but that didn't mean he had to accept it. If there was a way to stop it, to prevent more loss, wasn't it worth seeking out?

He caught the flicker of pain in Samuel's eye before the taller vampire masked it with a smile.

"Will I die?"

Marc hesitated. He wanted to say no, wanted to offer some reassurance, but visions didn't work that way. "I can never decide what I see," he admitted. "They just come."

Samuel stopped beneath the canopy of a massive tree, his grip on Marc shifting, his fingers barely grazing his arm. "Then do me a favour. If you see my death, don't tell me." His voice softened, turning almost wistful. "Just promise me you'll fight by my side—give me something to live for."

Marc's breath hitched.

Samuel was always bold, always flirting at the edge of seriousness, but this? This felt different. His presence was intoxicating, the closeness of him overwhelming, and Marc was suddenly aware of how easy it would be to step back, to sever whatever was forming between them before it could root itself too deeply.

But he didn't step back.

Samuel lifted his chin with a single finger, his touch light yet certain. The kiss that followed was slow, deliberate, full of promise and something deeper—something Marc didn't yet have words for.

And this time, he didn't resist. He let himself fall.

THE NIGHT OF BATTLE HAD ARRIVED, AND LARUS'S OYSTER BAY ESTATE swarmed with vampires—many of whom he didn't know. Yet, they had all gathered for the same purpose. A single accord.

It was his hope that Lucas's coven would be caught off guard, but deep down, Larus doubted it. The enemy had to know. The silence felt too calculated.

Samuel had arrived with nearly three hundred vampires, while Silas, Jude, and fifty others had already gone ahead to the rendezvous point several miles from Lucas's territory. Samuel suspected things had gone too smoothly. No messengers had returned. No signs of trouble. And that, more than anything, unsettled him.

Larus had listened to the concerns, weighing them carefully before making his decision. The original plan—to strike on the night of Basil's transformation—had been postponed. A week had passed. Now, there would be no more waiting. Whether Lucas anticipated their attack or not, they would move.

Reluctantly, Lola had gone ahead with Jude and his father, but Larus had made one thing clear—Basil would remain with him. There was no room for error.

An hour later, Larus stood at the edge of the forest, the ferocious Basil at his side. The estate emptied as their army of vampires moved out, leaving only a handful behind to guard the grounds.

Larus glanced back at the towering stone structure, exhaling slowly.

The ones left behind—they were the lucky ones.

They would not fight tonight.

DANIEL CHARGED FROM LUCAS'S STONE MANSION WITH ALEX AT HIS SIDE. Their eyes met—just for a moment—and Daniel saw the fear in Alex's gaze. He understood.

A single nod passed between them, silent confirmation of what they had already discussed in secret. They would not kill unless they had to. But looking ahead, Daniel saw the sheer scale of the battle waiting for them. Hundreds of vampires. Lycans storming the estate, their snarls rising over the night air. Their home was being destroyed before their eyes.

They had made their choice. They would leave. If they could make it out alive.

Daniel had begged Alex to keep their plans from his sister. Ana idolized Lucas, clung to Odelia like a loyal pet—she couldn't be trusted.

"I think I should go back for Ana," Alex said suddenly.

Daniel clenched his jaw. "I'm telling you, if you do that, we'll both die." He grabbed Alex's arm, leading him away from the thick of the fighting. "Come on. We have to avoid getting caught up in—"

Before the words even left his mouth, something massive slammed into him. A shirtless vampire, fast and brutal, sent Daniel flying. He collided with Alex, both of them crashing hard against the trunk of an oak tree.

Daniel gasped, trying to shake the impact from his mind, but the vampire was already on them. Old. Strong. Deadly. His one good eye studied them with unsettling patience.

Daniel struggled beneath his grip. "Please." It was all he could say.

The vampire exhaled sharply, then released them. His voice was calm but firm. "Leave these two."

He turned his attention to Daniel and Alex, his gaze settling on Alex with measured intensity. "Take the woods. Head north. If you need a coven, find me in Brooklyn."

Before releasing them fully, he leaned closer to Alex. "You mustn't doubt this one. Now go—both of you—before I change my mind."

Another vampire stood beside him—a beautiful one. He placed a hand lightly on Daniel's arm, his expression unreadable. "Your mother watches over you." His attention shifted to Alex. "Your sister will find her own way. She will not die this night." He offered a faint, reassuring smile. "But if you want to survive, you must leave. Now."

The battle raged on around them, the air thick with death. Headless bodies littered the ground.

Daniel grabbed Alex's hand, ready to run, but hesitated. He turned back to the two vampires who had spared them. "Who are you?"

"I'm Samuel. This is Marc." The answer was curt, direct. Then Samuel's voice hardened. "Now get the fuck out of here."

Daniel barely had time to process it before Alex came to a sudden halt. He turned back toward them, urgency in his voice. "Lucas knew you were coming. But that's not all."

Daniel tensed. He knew exactly what Alex was about to do. Their eyes met, another silent exchange.

"There's an old vampire here," Daniel said, his voice low. "Lucas's grandmother. Odelia is a strong bitch… I don't think even you can kill her."

Samuel's jaw tightened.

Alex added, "…They know you've tamed your lycan. The one twice bitten."

A flicker of something passed over Marc's face.

Daniel had no time to linger. He took off through the trees, dragging Alex with him.

Behind them, the battle raged on. The hissing of vampires, the snarls of lycans, the scent of blood thick in the night air.

Daniel didn't know if he'd ever see Samuel and Marc again.

But he hoped he would.

Within the Hudson estate, Odelia stood before her grandson, fury crackling in her ancient eyes. "They have outnumbered us!" she snapped, pointing an accusing finger at Lucas. "You assured me he would be here—with that pet lycan you so foolishly gifted him."

Lucas lowered his gaze, the same way he had when he was just a human boy centuries ago.

Odelia's voice sharpened. "The entire coven will be destroyed by dawn, and we have yet to see this Bleddyn. Why has he not come to face you?"

"I don't know, Grandmother!" Lucas shrugged, exasperated.

Odelia peered into his mind and saw only desperation, thoughts of escape swirling chaotically. No strategy, no counterattack—just the realization that he had miscalculated. And now they were trapped within their own walls.

"The coven is surrounded," she said, her tone like a blade. "We began this night with over a hundred vampires, and now I fear most of them are dead." Her lips curled with disgust. "Did you wake me from my long sleep just to see me destroyed in one of your pointless battles, boy?"

Lucas stiffened.

Odelia exhaled, steadying herself. She was strong, but she was no fool. Even the most ancient could be killed. "I am old, but my years will not save me from destruction. We must fight."

"We have seven lycans, Grandmother," Lucas said quickly. "Surely they will—"

"What you fail to understand, grandson, is that most creatures will do anything to survive." She gestured toward the great hall's massive doors. "How many of your seven lycans will remain loyal once they realize you are not out there fighting alongside them? Loyalty is earned, Lucas. It is not forced."

Her gaze flicked to the newborn. "Prepare yourself to fight for your life. Do as I say, and you will walk away from this night with your head."

Ana nodded, clearly afraid, but she stepped toward the doors with surprising resolve.

"Where is your brother?" Odelia asked.

"I haven't seen him or Daniel since sunset." Ana's brows converged in sudden rage.

Odelia chuckled darkly. "Then most likely, the two have fled together, and Daniel has taken my legacy with him. Clever boy..."

Lucas scoffed. "Why would Daniel leave this coven? I gave him everything."

Odelia sighed as though speaking to a child. "If we survive this night, grandson, you must take a lover. Only then will you understand why they abandoned us. They may have even betrayed us."

Ana's expression hardened. "Alex would never do that to me. He would never leave me behind."

Odelia laughed. "Come. We must go. Our aim is to leave this place alive and destroy anyone or anything in our way."

She stretched her mind beyond the great hall's doors, sifting through the chaos. There were too many minds—too much blood, too much death. Dawn was fast approaching, and she had no doubt that Larus Bleddyn had planned for the coming day.

She turned to Lucas and Ana, her voice calm, decisive.

"Open the doors."

LUCAS MADE SURE ODELIA WAS THE FIRST TO PASS THROUGH THE DOUBLE doors, and Ana didn't hesitate to follow. Deep inside, she loathed her maker for sending her before a group of savage lycans and vampires like a lamb to slaughter.

As she stepped forward, her gaze fell upon the severed head of Katerina at her feet, and Ana stumbled back with a gasp. Several feet away, the headless body of a vampire she barely knew lay sprawled on the stone floor.

A low growl made her freeze. Two lycans stood with two vampires nearby, but Ana knew there were many more lurking in the shadows beyond the walls of the stone estate—waiting, watching.

The shrieks of death echoed outside. Lucas's coven was being torn apart. Ana couldn't move forward. With every glance, she saw the faces of the fallen—vampires she once knew, their lifeless forms scattered across the ground.

She looked back at Odelia, but the ancient vampire was indifferent, too absorbed in shielding Lucas to concern herself with Ana's fate. The sudden, horrifying thought of Alex's headless corpse among the fallen flooded her mind.

"Your brother is safe," came a voice—gruff, steady. It was the one-eyed vampire. "Now, if you're smart, you'll get out of here and leave these two to us."

"Alex betrayed you, Ana. Don't be a fool." Said Lucas.

The one-eyed vampire's words were sharp. Ana's gaze flickered between Lucas and the towering figure before her. "Listen to me, girl, not him," the vampire barked, his finger pointing toward the massive foyer behind him. "The front door's just down the hall. Get to Brooklyn, and find your kin."

It was the dark-haired vampire standing next to the one-eyed figure who gave Ana the courage she so desperately needed. He stepped forward, his voice calm but firm.

"I am Marc," he said. "You must go now. Take the shades of your parents from this place. They will never leave you."

Ana's breath hitched, and with a hesitant step, she began to move forward. But just as she did, Lucas made his move.

"You stupid bitch!" Lucas lunged at her, rage contorting his features. But before Ana could react, Marc intercepted, shoving her aside.

The impact sent Marc flying across the room, crashing into a massive marble pillar with a sickening thud before crumbling to the floor.

Ana didn't look back. She bolted down the hall, her heart pounding in her chest. The deafening sounds of battle—clashing swords, growls, and screams—filled her ears, mixing with the cries of the dying.

She had to escape. But the cost of her survival would haunt her forever.

Samuel kept his eye fixed on Marc, still shaken from Lucas's brutal blow. Behind him, Lucas and his grandmother stood back-to-back, hissing, poised for the next move. The lycans, Jude and Lola, charged first, their intentions clear: tear the old vampire apart.

But Odelia was no ordinary vampire. With the precision of a predator, she seized Jude's thick neck, swinging the massive beast into his mate. They collided and tumbled across the floor, a mess of snarls and fury. Lola, however, was more agile. The she-wolf sprang upward with a snarl, her limbs propelling her up the stone wall. With a roar of rage, she leapt over Odelia's head, swatting the ancient vampire from behind as she soared. Odelia staggered but quickly regained her balance, crouching low, ready to strike.

Samuel wasn't distracted by the chaos surrounding them. He focused solely on Lucas. The young vampire, known for his cunning and occasional cowardice in the midst of battle, would not escape today—not if Samuel had anything to say about it.

"I gave you a chance, One-eye Samuel," Lucas sneered, eyes narrowing.

From where Samuel stood, he grinned back. "Dude, you're the one who just lost your entire coven." His grin widened. "And by the way, I gave your vampires a chance to live. Only the stupid ones are dead. Can you hear their screams out there?"

Lucas clicked his tongue dismissively. "They mean nothing to me." But then, something shifted in his expression. He suddenly seemed to realize something—and his eyes darkened. "Where is Larus Bleddyn?"

Samuel's smile never faltered. "Can't you hear the squeals outside?"

Lucas attacked then, moving to the left in a blur of motion. Samuel blocked the blow with ease, laughing at his foe's strength. Lucas's long claws raked across Samuel's face, digging deep. The pain was sharp, but Samuel barely flinched, feeling the old wounds begin to heal instantly. Samuel realized Lucas had snatched his leather eye patch in the process.

"How ugly you are," Lucas taunted. "Your eye was taken before you were turned."

"Don't worry about my eye," Samuel replied coldly, his voice gruff. "The bastard who took it was my first kill."

The two vampires surged forward with lightning speed. They collided midair, both of them clutching onto the other's arms in a fierce test of strength. They landed with a crash, each struggling to pin the other down. Through the roar of battle, Samuel could still hear Odelia clashing with the lycans, but his focus remained locked on Lucas.

His coven had been ordered to stand down, to hold the grounds while Larus's team handled the fight. Samuel had already lost nearly fifty vampires; he would sacrifice no more. It would end here—with Lucas and Odelia.

One of Samuel's newborns entered the fray, knocking both Samuel and Lucas to the ground, Lucas was swift. He grabbed the newborn by the neck, ripping through the bone with a single, brutal yank. Samuel roared in fury.

"No!"

"I will kill them all," Lucas growled, his voice low and menacing. "One by one. None will survive."

With a feral growl, Samuel slammed into him, driving Lucas's back against the wall with bone-crushing force. They were inches from a massive stained-glass window, its colourful angels and saints now nothing but a backdrop to their vicious clash.

Lucas was strong, though. With a powerful shove, he pushed Samuel off and swept his legs out from under him. Before Samuel could react, Lucas pinned him to the floor. The victor's grin spread across Lucas's face as he looked down, smug and triumphant.

"Like I said," Lucas sneered, "I will kill all of them—but you won't be alive to see any of it."

Meanwhile, Odelia had swatted Jude aside and now had Lola—the fierce she-wolf—in her grasp. The battle seemed to come to a sudden, eerie standstill. Samuel, struggling beneath Lucas, spotted Marc slowly rising to his feet, still disoriented.

Samuel's gaze softened for a moment, and he offered Marc one last smile. This was it. His end had come.

Odelia could smell victory in the air. She knew she needed to kill the she-wolf first, then deal with the other—Lucas's one-eyed adversary who was already in her grandson's grasp, moments from meeting his end. But as Odelia scanned the battlefield, she saw they were surrounded by countless vampires. Most of them were young—easy prey.

The she-wolf, though fierce, clawed desperately at Odelia's face. It wasn't just strength that kept the beast alive; it was her will to survive. Odelia could feel the wolf's struggle, but the animal's fate was sealed. She would die before the male lycan could recover from the brutal strike she had delivered earlier. Together, the two wolves were a formidable pair, but Odelia knew she could only deal with them one at a time.

Suddenly, a massive crash of glass shattered the tense silence. Everyone, even the dazed one-eyed vampire, froze. Through the stained-glass window, a gargantuan lycan—twice the size of the others—burst into the room, sending jagged shards of colourful glass scattering across the floor. The creature's mere presence gave the remaining lycans a surge of hope, a glimmer of strength.

Odelia's instincts flared. She had to kill the she-wolf now, or the entire tide of battle would change. The she-wolf was the sister of this new beast, and Odelia knew it would be the key to tipping the scales. But before she could react, the appearance of the Bleddyn hybrid and the other lycan turned the tables. The one twice-bitten charged Lucas, its massive jaws clamping down on his shoulder and neck. The beast tore through Lucas's flesh with ease, severing his head in a brutal, single strike.

"Grandson!" Odelia hissed in fury. She tightened her grip on the she-wolf, swinging her with all her strength. The beast's heavy form slammed into her brother, sending him reeling back.

"You will not leave this place alive," the Bleddyn hybrid growled, stepping forward with a menacing calm. He shifted, his form transforming into something Odelia had seen before. It was a shape she knew all too well—Cecil Bleddyn's hybrid form.

"A Bleddyn," Odelia spat, her eyes narrowing. "I knew the other one well. Cecil was not strong enough for me centuries ago. Do you think you can kill me now?" She crouched low, her fangs flashing as she hissed, scanning the battlefield for the weakness she needed. "Did Cecil tell you I nearly killed him once?"

The hybrid said nothing, his focus unreadable. Even the one twice-bitten was poised to strike, but Odelia saw they were all waiting for the hybrid's command. Fools. They were all fools.

Her gaze locked onto her target—the vampire with the veiled mind. Beautiful, yes, but to Odelia, he was nothing more than an obstacle. She would take his head.

She moved swiftly toward him, her senses tuned to every movement, every breath. But as she closed the distance, the hybrid's voice rang out, sharp and commanding.

"Protect Marc!"

But it was too late.

Samuel halted, his one good eye widening in shock. Odelia was almost upon Marc.

A rush of air. Coarse, prickly fur grazed his face as Basil lunged over him, a massive blur of muscle and claws. The lycan slammed into Odelia midair. They hit the marble floor hard, skidding across its smooth surface before crashing into a towering pillar.

Odelia rose first.

Her fist struck Basil's skull with a sickening crack, sending the massive lycan hurtling backward. He crashed against the ground, groaning.

Samuel and Larus attacked in unison, their strikes swift and unrelenting. But Odelia was a wall of steel. A monster of impossible skill. She caught Larus's wrist mid-strike and twisted, forcing him to stumble back. Samuel landed a punch to her ribs—her only reaction was a sharp exhale before she sent him staggering with a counterblow. The plan had been to give her no rest, yet Samuel was the one feeling worn.

Jude, Silas, and Lola closed in. Marc knelt beside Basil, pressing a hand to the lycan's massive shoulder. He was still dazed, crouched on all fours, shaking his head.

Odelia was surrounded. Trapped. Yet her golden eyes gleamed with certainty.

"Our quarrel was with Lucas," Larus said, his voice cold. "And he now lies dead." He gestured toward the headless corpse of her grandson. "Let us end this now and go our separate ways."

Odelia scoffed. "You would let me leave, knowing I will hunt you down and kill you all?"

Larus's expression darkened. "Surely," he said, "you realize your grandson was more trouble than he was worth."

"Do not presume to think you knew him better than I did, hybrid. You are an abomination. Impure."

"Yet I hold your life in my hands."

Odelia smiled.

Something was wrong.

Samuel sensed it a second too late. A whisper of steel sliced the air.

His body tensed—he turned—

Ana.

She was crouched low, eyes burning with purpose, both hands gripping the hilt of an ancient blade. A two-handed swing. A blur of silver.

A faint sting bloomed at his neck.

72

HOME

They were thousands of feet above the sea. Night cloaked the sky, and though the Bleddyn private jet carried him home, Marc felt lost. Disconnected. Even the lands he was returning to—the place he called home—felt distant.

Three long weeks had passed since the battle. They'd waited to travel, unable to transport Basil in his Lycan form. It would have been impossible to move a lycan of his size unnoticed, let alone arrive at the hangar without exposing themselves. Now, in the dimly lit cabin, Marc sat beside Lola, while Jude and his father conversed near the rear. Across from him, Larus watched in silence, his gaze unyielding.

"You pine for him," the hybrid said at last.

Marc tensed. For a fleeting moment, he considered turning the words back on Larus, asking if he had not done the same for Dominic. But he swallowed the thought.

He still saw it—Ana springing forward, blade flashing. There had been no time. No way to stop it. Samuel had stood there, whole one moment, severed the next. His head sliding from his shoulders in a clean, ancient cut.

Odelia had known. She had counted on Ana. The girl could have struck any of them, but her true purpose had been diversion. And the moment Samuel fell, Odelia had fled, wasting no time.

Marc wiped the blood tears from his face, suddenly aware that Larus was still watching him. "I hadn't seen his death," he murmured. "Not for a moment. How could I not have seen it?"

"You mustn't blame yourself, Marc. You've said many times—your visions come in their own time."

"But I haven't seen his shade." Marc's voice was quiet, troubled. "Why won't he come to me?"

Larus said nothing, letting Marc's words linger.

"He smiled at me," Marc went on, his voice almost hollow. "As the blade struck. He looked into my eyes."

"I know you loved him," Larus said. "And I know what you feel, Marc. Not a day has passed that I haven't thought of Dominic."

Pain flickered in Larus's eyes. Marc saw it and, deciding to shift the conversation, he asked, "You're the leader of Samuel's coven now. How do you think the old Scotsman, Brùn, will fare?"

"They respect him," Larus said. "And I trust him most."

"We all thought you'd offer Daniel and Alex a place with us."

A faint smile touched Larus's lips. "They must prove themselves."

Marc leaned back, considering this. "And Bleddyn Media?"

"Hector Drake is at the helm," Larus replied. "I'm sure I've left a few executives furious, but it was the right move. He'll dispense funds to the numbered account each month without asking questions. The coven will be well taken care of—so long as Brùn remains alive."

Marc arched a brow. "You think they'd kill their own?"

"The need for power changes everyone, Marc. Even vampires."

Marc fell silent, remembering his own childhood. Remembering what Nathan had done to his family for the sake of wealth.

"You haven't changed," he said at last.

Larus shrugged. "Let's just say I changed for the better. I was born into wealth, and Micah's estate only added to it."

Marc studied him, admiration flickering in his gaze. Over centuries, Larus had built an empire.

After a pause, he asked, "Do you think Odelia will seek vengeance?"

Larus's brows drew together. "I doubt it. But if she does, we'll be ready."

He exhaled, shaking his head with a half-smile. "Though I find it strange you'd ask about Odelia."

A shadow crossed his expression.

"It isn't Odelia I fear," he murmured. "It's the girl. Ana."

Marc stiffened. A realization struck him, sharp as a blade.

"Larus." His voice was barely above a whisper. "I have been a fool."

Larus narrowed his gaze.

Marc exhaled sharply, shaking his head. "I saw the girl's part in all of this—though I hadn't yet met her. When we stormed the building, I told her brother she would live. That she would find her own way." He clenched his jaw. "I did see Samuel's death. However faint the warning was..."

A weight settled in his chest. The truth had been there all along. He simply hadn't seen it in time.

ALL OF BLEDDYN MANOR BUZZED WITH JOYOUS ANTICIPATION. IN THE GREAT hall, Nicolas stood tall, his chest swelling with pride. He could hardly wait for Larus and the others to arrive.

Tilley's voice rang through the corridors, sharp and efficient, as she directed lycans and vampires alike. Everything had to be perfect for the return of the manor's master. And from what Nicolas could see, it was.

Preparations extended beyond the manor itself. Sebastian, Silas's second, had gone with Gavin and Isabelle—Larus's sister—to ready the ancient church atop the hill. The old structure had been well maintained over the centuries, a sacred place preserved through time. In fact, much of Bleddyn Manor remained as it had been in ages past, save for necessary upgrades and maintenance. Even the cave where Silas and Hannah had once stolen nights together, back when Percival Hearne ruled these lands, still remained untouched—a silent witness to history.

Tilley had put Ashkan to work, though the quiet vampire clearly preferred solitude. Over the years, he had seemed lost without his master. His loyalty to Larus had been as unwavering as it had once been to Micah.

Gavin, now settled into a pleasant life with Isabelle, had been entrusted with the manor's lycans in Silas's absence. But it was clear he was more than ready to relinquish command back to their rightful alpha.

"Where do you want these?"

Nicolas turned to see Helene, breathtaking as always, standing before him with an armful of flowers. She had once been an heiress in Paris, her elegance untouched by time.

He took the massive bouquet from her, exchanging a knowing smile. It never ceased to amaze him how lycans and vampires from all walks of life coexisted within these walls—many of them centuries old. He could hardly forget his own humble beginnings: the grandson of a poor shepherd, born into a mortal fate. But fate had other plans. His grandfather had given what remained of his own life to ensure Nicolas's immortality.

He glanced upward, tracing the high ceilings with his gaze, remembering the days he had lived in a crumbling shack—until he was left in the care of vampires.

"Tilley says the flowers go in the foyer," Nicolas said with mock authority. "Not here in the great hall, dear Helene."

She laughed, the sound bright and unrestrained, as he exaggerated his imitation of Tilley's commanding tone.

"Did I get that right?" he teased.

"Don't think I can't hear you from where I'm standing, young man," Tilley's voice carried from a corridor.

Nicolas clapped a hand over his mouth, his eyes twinkling with mischief.

"I think they've arrived!" Helene gasped.

Without hesitation, the two rushed from the great hall together.

Larus was the first to step out of the limo, and before he could take another breath, Nicolas was in his arms.

"I've waited so long for you to return!" Nicolas clung to him, the embrace fierce, a reunion of father and son in all but blood.

Larus held him tightly before pulling back, hands on his shoulders, studying him. "Nicolas, you've not changed one bit. Is Tilley not feeding you enough?"

Nicolas laughed as Larus kissed the side of his face, but before he could respond, a familiar voice rang out.

"There's my little young master!"

Tilley bustled down the stone steps, dabbing at the blood tears streaking her cheeks. She shoved Nicolas aside without hesitation and wrapped Larus in her arms.

"To think I raised you from the day you were born, young man. I pulled you from your mother's womb, you know—"

"Tilley, please," Nicolas groaned, cringing.

Larus chuckled. "Don't worry, Nicolas. She used to say that to me when I was a boy."

The manor's entrance teemed with vampires and lycans, all gathered for the homecoming. Silas and Jude exchanged embraces with their pack. Helene practically launched herself into Larus's arms, while Ashkan, ever the reserved one, greeted him with a respectful bow before taking his place at his master's side.

But then, the focus shifted.

Two unfamiliar figures stood apart from the rest. They were in human form, yet there was no mistaking what they were—lycans. And they were kin.

Nicolas's gaze darted between Larus and the she-wolf in confusion.

"The woman by the tree," he murmured. His mind reeled back to the countless hours he had spent studying Micah's work, the brushstrokes that had brought history to life. And now, as if stepping out of one of those paintings, she was here.

He took a tentative step forward. "I am Nicolas."

The woman rested a hand on her stomach, absently stroking the small swell of her belly. Before she could speak, Jude appeared at her side, beaming.

"This is Lola," he announced proudly, patting her belly. "And this is my son."

Lola shot him a look before shoving him aside. "Boy, get your ass away and give me some space so I can meet these nice people on my own."

Jude laughed, pressing a quick kiss to her cheek before stepping back.

"I was about to say I'm Lola," she said, shaking her head, "but that idiot beat me to it."

Beside her, the male lycan extended a hand. "I'm Basil."

Nicolas grasped it but hesitated, staring at the man's face. The resemblance to Micah was startling.

Larus clapped his hands together, breaking the moment. "Where are Sebastian and Gavin? And where is my dear sister?"

Nicolas recovered and smiled. "They're waiting for us at the old church. Bleddyn Manor has been prepared for your return."

"Even the old catacombs beneath the graveyard," Tilley added, with a satisfied nod. "I've added my own touch to it."

Larus cringed. Micah had always kept that place sacred, known only to vampires. "You restrained yourself from throwing anything away, I trust?"

Tilley met his gaze with nothing but love. "Come on, petal. What are you waiting for? Let's go and see it."

And so, together, every creature set off into the darkness, making their way toward the church on the hill.

73

AFTER

The halls of Bleddyn Manor were quiet, but Marc could not sleep. He stood before a mirror in his chamber, staring at his own faded reflection as though it held the answers he sought. His fingers curled at his sides.

"Come to me, Samuel," he whispered, his voice barely audible. The candlelight flickered. He closed his eyes, his gift seeking something, anything.

For weeks, he had tried to summon Samuel's shade, but the dead refused him. It made no sense—he had seen countless spirits before. Why not Samuel?

Then, suddenly—visions.

He was crossing a river. The water stilled, then darkened. A face swam into view—not Samuel, but Ana. Her eyes gleamed like a cat's in the dark. Behind her, shadows moved, whispering voices just beyond his reach. Then, a flicker of a blade. Blood sprayed. A hand reached for him—Samuel's hand?—before the vision shattered.

Marc gasped, stumbling back, the river vanished.

"Still no peace?"

Marc turned sharply to find Larus leaning against the doorframe, arms crossed. His piercing gaze softened as he took in Marc's shaken state.

"I saw her," Marc murmured. "Ana."

Larus stepped inside, silent for a moment. "Then it isn't over."

Marc exhaled, pressing a palm to his temple. "I should have seen it before. Samuel's death... it was always there, buried beneath my doubts. And now, I don't know what I've missed. What comes next?"

Larus placed a hand on Marc's shoulder. "Then we stay vigilant."

Marc looked up, catching his reflection once more. His own eyes seemed unfamiliar.

"We will have to be."

THE CAVERNOUS HIDEOUT WAS COLD, ITS STONE WALLS DAMP WITH THE breath of the earth. A single lantern cast a dim glow, its flame barely illuminating the two figures seated in silence.

Ana knelt before a whetstone, dragging her blade against its surface in slow, measured strokes. The rhythmic scrape of metal on stone filled the space, steady as a heartbeat.

Odelia watched her with an unreadable expression.

"You hesitate less now," Odelia finally said, tilting her head.

Ana did not look up. "I've learned."

Odelia's lips curved faintly, but there was no mirth in it. "Did you?" She stepped forward, crouching beside the girl. "When you killed Samuel, did you feel regret?"

Ana's fingers tightened around the hilt of her knife. The blade paused mid-stroke.

"Regret?" she echoed, testing the word on her tongue. She lifted her gaze at last, and in her eyes, there was no hesitation. No doubt. Only certainty.

"No."

Odelia studied her for a moment before a slow smile spread across her face.

"Good," she said. "Then we begin."

The lantern flickered, casting their shadows long against the wall—two figures entwined in darkness.

And the blade in Ana's hand gleamed, hungry for what was to come.

EXCLUSIVE PREVIEW FROM THE VAMPIRE MICAH

BLEDDYN LEGACY

Bleddyn Manor sat on vast lands, a sprawling estate that had been home to the Bleddyn line for generations. The vampire Emilio walked uphill toward the old church, his keen eyes fixed on the steeple. He had lived for centuries, and in those long years, he had watched over these lands—lands that had once been inhospitable to a lone vampire, especially at night, when wolves roamed. The Bleddyns had been strong, and these lands belonged to the wolves.

The church atop the hill had stood for ages, its weathered stone still sturdy despite the ravages of time. The full moon bathed it in cold light, casting shadows across the stained-glass windows that shimmered faintly in the darkness. Emilio paused for a moment, admiring the ancient structure, before turning his gaze toward the Bleddyn cemetery below. His eyes lingered on the crypt behind the iron gates, his mind already drifting downward toward the catacombs hidden beneath the church and cemetery—catacombs that held secrets not even the living Bleddyns knew of.

Emilio had kept these secrets for centuries. His thoughts turned briefly to his maker, the hybrid Cecil Bleddyn, and a smile tugged at his lips. He had watched the Bleddyn family through the ages, always waiting for the return of something more than just their bloodline. Yet, despite his watchful eye, there was no sign of the lycanthrope, the wolf legacy that ran deep within the Bleddyn blood.

But Emilio knew the truth: the legacy of the "beast" was not lost. It lay dormant, waiting for the right moment to stir. It would only be a matter of time before the wolves roamed free upon these lands again.

As he turned to leave the Bleddyn lands, Emilio's thoughts drifted to the elder, Nathan Von Ruden, and the dire ramifications that awaited him should the vampire council ever discover the truth. He had broken the most sacred of laws—the command to destroy his maker, the one he loved.

Cecil had been his mate. How could one carry out such a command, especially against the one who had given him life and purpose? The thought alone twisted Emilio's insides. He shook the memories from his mind, pushing the regret back into the dark corners of his mind where it had remained for centuries.

His secret was safe—for now. Babette and her twin, Benoît, had kept it hidden, and Emilio knew they would continue to do so. He allowed himself a brief moment of longing for Paris, for the fleeting memories of their time together. But that would have to wait.

With one last glance at the Bleddyn cemetery, he moved quickly, his mind focused on the present, the future, and the safe rest of Cecil in the catacombs below. Emilio felt a small flicker of satisfaction as he disappeared into the night, knowing his maker slept undisturbed.

He made it back to White Castle before sunrise. The castle, with its maze on the grounds, was just one of Emilio's homes, though White Castle was his alone. Despite having a coven and siring several children, this place remained his sanctuary. He had done what was needed—the vampire, Cecil, still slept in peace. Now, it was time to return to his children before embarking on another long journey across the sea.

The carriage came for him at sunset; the journey to the ship was long.

Emilio had packed several trunks with important belongings for the voyage and secured a cabin and a cell aboard the vessel. The night was dark, but his vampire eyes pierced the shadows as he gazed out the window.

Emilio's thoughts turned to the Bleddyn line and its future. The shapeshifting wolves had been dormant for centuries, their true nature fading from memory. But Emilio knew the wolves still lived deep within the forests. They were mere beasts, not lycanthropes. Lycanthropes were something different—creatures that could shift from human to wolf, becoming massive and terrifying. The wolves, by contrast, were vicious but had long been the enemy of vampires.

A smile crept onto Emilio's lips as he gazed into the night. Thoughts of Cecil filled him with joy. "Someday, my wolf hero, I shall awaken you," he whispered to the darkness.

There were risks if Cecil were to awaken from his long sleep. Nathan would have them destroyed. The council feared Cecil, unable to comprehend what he was. Cecil was a Bleddyn, destined to become a wolf, yet when the vampire Telsiea turned him, he became a hybrid. A wolf and a vampire. This made him a threat to the council. Nathan feared that Cecil had the power to destroy him. The oldest of them all wanted the creature eliminated. But Emilio could not obey such a command.

SAMUEL (1619)

The White Lion rocked from side to side in the storm, its hull groaning as crashing waves pounded the vessel. On that July night, the winds howled, sending shudders through the ship. Samuel clung to the iron chains that bound him. The one thing that held him captive had become his only comfort. From above, he could hear the captain's terrified shouts, his voice swallowed by the fury of the sea, as he barked frantic orders to the crew. The crew, too, were frantic—everyone aboard knew they would not survive the night. The storm would devour the White Lion, and its remains would be scattered on some distant shore.

Samuel had lived freely his entire life—until the raiders came to his village and sold him to this ship of men with eyes the colour of the sea.

He had lost track of the days spent upon the water, and though it was clear he held some value to his captors, Samuel could not fathom why they had kept him alive after his countless attempts to escape. Death seemed a far better fate than the life that awaited him. No life could ever compare to the one he had known.

The ship keeled to the right, and Samuel's heart sank. But he was not alone below deck. Nearly thirty-two others were locked in the dark belly of the ship—men and women taken from the land they had once known and loved. As Samuel glanced at their dark faces in the dimness, he saw they eyed him with a hostility that made his skin crawl. It was as though they blamed him for the very storm that raged against them, and in their eyes —set in dark skin like his own—he sensed they would rejoice if the sea took him.

He held their gazes, one by one, refusing to break. They had forgotten they, too, were in chains. It had been several days since Samuel struck one of his captors while being whipped, and now the storm had come, just as the captain had been about to punish him. A smile tugged at Samuel's lips. Something had spared him.

Looking around at the other captives, he saw disdain in their eyes. They had resigned themselves to their fate. Samuel frowned, refusing to forget the lessons his father had taught him—that he was born a free man. But grief and sorrow washed over him as memories of his father's death surfaced. Samuel was nearly thirty now. He had even found a woman to love, but the thought that he would never again see her smile filled him with despair. In that moment, he understood how the others must feel. Like them, he had lost everything.

He heard the familiar jingle of chains as he raked his fingers through his thick, tangled black hair. The shackles had bruised his wrists, but he had no time to focus on the pain. A loud crash echoed from above, followed by gasps of fear from his companions. Something terrible was happening up there.

THE CAPTAIN BARKED ORDERS AGAINST THE HOWLING WINDS AND DRIVING rain. He grimaced as the raindrops lashed his face, stinging his skin and blurring his vision. Though the wind carried the shouts of his crew away, the crash of splintering wood rang through the storm. A massive chunk of the mast came down hard against the deck, and the captain threw up his arms with a furious curse.

"Ah, fuck!"

He had seen storms before—but none like this. For a fleeting moment, a thought slithered through his mind: Had his cargo brought this upon them? He was a superstitious man, and dark omens whispered at the edges of his thoughts. But there was no time for doubt. Gritting his teeth, he filled his lungs and let the fury of his voice cut through the tempest.

"This storm won't take me! Not tonight!"

He turned to a nearby crewman, his gaze locking onto him like a striking blade. "Martin! Get that mast mended—now!"

Martin hesitated for only a second, eyes wide with unspoken protest, but he knew better than to defy his captain. He shouted back through the wind, "I'll use three from the hold—the negroes!"

The captain gave a curt nod. "Do it. And don't waste time."

FOUR OF THEIR CAPTORS STUMBLED DOWN THE STAIRS INTO THE DARKNESS, their boots heavy against the damp wood. As they removed Samuel's shackles, his heart pounded like a drum against his ribs. He was a strong, broad-shouldered man, and as he saw two others—men of similar size—being unshackled as well, realization settled in. They needed strength.

A rough hand shoved him toward the steps. "You try anything this time, and I'll gut you right here in the rain and toss your black ass to the sharks, you hear me?"

Samuel turned his gaze on the man, though the words meant nothing to him. His captor bared his teeth in a grin, mistaking silence for submission.

"Yeah, go on! Try it!"

Another crewman spat to the side. "Lay off, Tom! Cap'n wants that mast mended. Better they die doing it than us."

Samuel was shirtless, barefoot, his thighs exposed. The rain lashed his skin, cold as iron, as he lifted a hammer and drove nails into the wood. The other two captives worked beside him, their muscles straining with each swing. One was an older man, his breath already laboured. The other —just a boy, no more than twenty—trembled as he worked.

Shouts broke through the storm.

"Wave!"

A crewman pointed toward the sea, his face pale in the lightning's glow. Samuel didn't need to understand their words—he saw the horror in the young boy's eyes.

He turned.

The wave loomed, black and monstrous, swallowing the sky.

"Brace yourselves, fellas!" Someone's voice—rough, desperate—cut through the chaos.

The ocean crashed over them.

Samuel lurched forward, wrapping an arm around the boy just as the world vanished in a roar of water. He clung to a post with the other hand, muscles burning, the ship rocking like a leaf in a hurricane. Then, just as suddenly as it came, the storm passed.

The White Lion drifted, silent and still.

Their captors wrenched them back below deck, shackles clamping around their wrists once more. The boy sagged against the wall, shivering. Their older companion was gone, lost to the sea.

THE NEXT SEVERAL WEEKS ABOARD THE WHITE LION PASSED IN UNEVENTFUL drudgery. No storms came to test them, only the relentless march of days under the August sun. The captain had released the captives from the ship's belly, putting them to work. Their labor was gruelling—back-breaking toil from dawn to dusk, with only the barest sustenance to keep them from collapse.

Davu, the young captive Samuel had saved from the storm, clung to him now like kin. Samuel understood. He had given Davu his life, and in return, the boy gave him unwavering trust.

Of the remaining captives, only thirty remained—another had succumbed to sickness days after the storm. Death had become familiar company.

At night, when the crew lingered on deck and the other captives lay in restless slumber below, Samuel and Davu walked together. The captain no longer shackled them—where could they go, after all, with nothing but the endless black sea stretching in all directions?

The night air cooled Samuel's skin as he leaned against the ship's rail, breathing in the scent of salt and brine. The White Lion rocked gently with the wind, its sails creaking above them. Davu stood beside him, staring at the distant horizon. They spoke in their shared tongue, though they were of different tribes. Samuel listened with quiet pride—Davu had learned much of the captors' speech.

"Where do you think they take us, Samuel?"

Samuel shrugged, still struggling to grasp Davu's words. The boy had been teaching him what little he knew. "I... do not know, Davu."

Davu had tried to teach him their captors' tongue, but Samuel resisted. It felt like surrender.

"They show you how to read their words," Samuel continued, hesitant. "These... these... b-b-books?"

Davu moved closer, their shoulders brushing. For a long moment, Samuel gazed into Davu's dark eyes and saw the moon's reflection within them. His heartbeat quickened.

The cool air curled around them, but Samuel felt nothing but warmth. The silver light of the moon touched Davu's lips, and a shiver ran down Samuel's arms. Something inside him ached, unfamiliar and insistent. What was this power Davu had over him?

He longed to close the space between them. To feel the softness of Davu's lips against his own.

"Hey!"

They turned abruptly.

Martin stood about thirty paces away, watching them with narrowed eyes. He sneered, jerking his chin toward the hold below. "Seems you two been enjoying your freedom a little too much." His voice dripped with suspicion. "Cap'n was fuckin' crazy to let you roam free." He spat onto the deck. "But you ain't gonna be free for long now, are you?"

The darkness below deck was thick, pressing in like damp cloth.

Samuel and Davu found their usual corner, lying side by side on the rough wooden planks. Around them, the others slept, their breath rising and falling in the rhythm of exhaustion. But Samuel knew Davu was awake, just as he was.

In the quiet, Samuel studied Davu's silhouette. After several moments, he shifted closer, slipping beneath their thin, moth-eaten blanket.

His arm went around Davu from behind. A sigh of relief escaped his lips as Davu nestled into him, seeking the warmth and safety of his embrace.

Samuel pressed a kiss to the back of Davu's neck. His lips tasted the salt of sweat, the heat of living flesh. Davu turned to face him in the darkness, and Samuel saw the faint glint of his eyes.

A smile touched his lips as Davu's mouth met his, soft and sure.

Their tongues brushed—hesitant at first, then eager, discovering one another in the hush of the sleeping ship.

www.ingramcontent.com/pod-product-compliance
Lightning Source LLC
Chambersburg PA
CBHW070551310726
48982CB00011B/1547/J
* 9 7 8 1 0 6 9 6 7 0 6 6 3 *